Starstruck

a BALEY NOAL *novel*

Copyright © Baley Noal, 2024

All rights reserved. No part of this publication may be reproduced, distributed, or transmitted in any form or by any means, electronic or mechanical methods, including photocopying, recording, or any other information storage or retrieval system without the prior written permission from the publisher, except as permitted by U.S. copyright law. For permission requests, contact the publisher.

The story, all names, characters, and incidents portrayed in this production are fictitious. No identification with actual persons (living or deceased), places, buildings, and products is intended or should be inferred. This work contains adult content and potentially sensitive themes.

Cover by Baley Noal & ElfElm Publishing
Interior and ebook formatting by ElfElm Publishing

ISBN (KDP hardcover): 9798339587583

10 9 8 7 6 5 4 3 2 1

First Edition 2024, Hardcover Edition

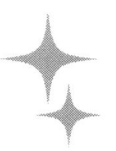

I'd like to dedicate this book to some very special individuals:

To the best Mom and Dad a girl could ever ask for—thank you for always being so supportive in everything I do. If you're planning on reading this book, please put it down until I can glue a few of the pages together or I will have to consider putting you in a home much earlier than planned.

All of my amazingly supportive friends and family who are forever encouraging me to follow through on my whack-job ideas for expressing my creativity. Y'all are the real MVPs!!

All of my 'Barons' who have been model four-legged besties and have ensured my books will always include a lovable fur baby.

And finally to anyone kind/curious/brave enough to take a chance on this book. I adore these characters and their world, I hope you do too.

One

"Holy shit." It was the first day on set and Trent was checking out the house where they would be filming for the next few months. "The production designer didn't give this place the justice it deserves with the sketches I saw," he walked through the custom doors carved out of mahogany and into an immaculate mini mansion. The country luxury style was chic, and he noted all of the rustic cottage touches and overall darker aesthetic that made the enormous home feel somehow cozy. As he toured his jobsite, he noticed the pre-production crew had completed many of their changes for the movie; there were already pictures of the cast placed strategically around the home as if they were in fact the ones who lived there. He made the assumption that the family who lived here full-time was likely an older couple who often had adult children visiting, given the size of the house and the six bedrooms he had seen so far. Trent made his way through the main foyer from the grand staircase and headed towards the kitchen. The kitchen, dining and living rooms were all open to one another, with twenty-foot vaulted ceilings and the entire back wall of the house was almost completely covered in windows.

"Damn." Trent's jaw dropped.

The director was already in the kitchen. "I told you guys, there's nothing like the beauty of the Pacific Northwest, Hollywood can't fabricate this majestic scene." Phil walked around the second island in the kitchen and spread his arms before pushing the folding glass doors that seemed to just keep opening wider, with no end in sight. He finally stopped them when there was about twelve feet of passageway for everyone to walk through. The group walked out onto the porch that was partially covered and spanned along the length of the house. They all looked out into the enormous backyard which was covered in lush green grass and transitioned straight into a serene lake with the Olympic mountains as its background.

"Come on," Phil urged the small group to follow him out to explore the rest of the grounds. Besides the mansion, there was a large garage that looked more like a modern barn tucked to the left of the house with four large, black doors on the front of it. Down towards the bank of the lake, there was one smaller, almost cottage-like house. The style mimicked the main house to include the stack stone and black shutters. The crew was bustling around every room in the main house to finalize all preparations for shooting so the group of directors and cast members made their way down the porch stairs and onto the expansive lawn.

Trent took a deep breath of fresh mountain air to welcome what he hoped would be several weeks of a carefree and relaxing shoot. Phil was talking in the background, but Trent was too busy soaking up the scenery to notice what he was saying. Trent had been among the leading 'Hollywood Hunks' as arguably the most highly sought-after action star for the last few years. Several blockbuster scripts had made their way to him, and this was going to be his first horror film. He was just over six feet tall and maintained a muscular build, which was often put on display in his movies. His olive skin was so smooth it looked like glass, and he had overall dark features besides his electric blue eyes. His outward personality matched his appearance as he was constantly walking a fine line between confidence and cockiness, according to most.

Lately, he felt like he was in a whirlwind; he hadn't been able to settle down in any one place because it seemed like all he was doing was working. Going from set to set for a solid four years, which he was grateful for, was taking its toll. He had decided to sell his house a couple years prior because he couldn't remember the last time he had the luxury of even spending an entire weekend there. These days home seemed to be wherever he was working. He could get used to the slower pace he'd noticed in this small town so far, even the quaint motel the cast decided to stay at was the vibe he was looking for. He had only been in town for a few hours, but it was as if everything was in slow motion here. The population was minimal compared to any place he'd ever been, which would allow him to truly relax with no distractions. The fresh air and the sound of the country was exactly what he needed. His only regret was the shoot would only last a couple of months before he was sharing his time between promoting the last film he had wrapped and reporting to the next set for a sequel he had signed on for.

"Oh my God!" Michelle, the leading female co-star, started, "Look, at that hawk up in the tree!"

The group turned to see an American Bald Eagle sitting proudly atop a tree branch just off the porch. Its focus was set on the lake in front of them. They continued to watch as the eagle spread its colossal wings and took off towards the lake, they continued to watch as the eagle plunged into the water with flawless precision to grab a meal.

"That was pretty fucking amazing," Pete, another co-star commented. "Can you fucking imagine?! I can barely see the colors of the cushions on the dock furniture down there and that bird just plucked a fish out of the damn water!"

Trent smiled and took another deep breath, filling his lungs with the clean rural air and exhaling the stress of the city. This was the perfect place to recharge.

"Well, let's go take a closer look at that dock down there then so you can see better, Winters," Michelle aimed towards the water. The young actress was pretty seasoned in Hollywood and never had a problem speaking her mind. She was a very slender 5'10" blonde, usually; for this movie, however, she was given a dye job to a deep autumn color that flashed hints of plum when it hit the sun just right.

The wooden dock they were all headed to was narrow from the shore but then widened towards the end to accommodate a gazebo and the perfect lounging set-up for taking in the lake.

While the group was observing all of the nature around them, they had to pause about halfway down the lawn as an unusually large, tri-colored pit bull was trotting towards them. The dog was pure muscle, with clipped ears and no defined neck, his head went straight into his body. No one noticed a collar and as he got closer he picked up speed. Suddenly, a woman's voice called out, "Bare!" The dog stopped immediately and sat, keeping his focus on the flock of strangers on his property. Trent and his group froze as well, thinking that any movement would initiate a reaction from the dog. The woman jogged towards them, accompanied by what looked to be some kind of law enforcement officer, his approach was much slower than hers. As the woman reached her dog, she caught Trent's eyes.

"Sorry." The woman rubbed the dog's head affectionately. He didn't move, he simply looked up at her. "This is Baron. He's actually really harmless, he just has to meet everyone." She leaned down and firmly patted his sturdy chest. "Is everyone okay with dogs?" She smiled up at the group who mostly nodded their heads.

The woman snapped her fingers, allowing Baron to stand up, carefully watching her dog approach the group before she directed her attention to Phil. "Good morning, Phil, it's really good to see you again." Her tone was friendly, and she opened her arms to lean in and hug him. As they continued to greet each other Trent couldn't help but stare. She looked like she just walked off the set of a fitness video. She paired her multi-colored Nike's with black ankle length yoga pants; her conservative sports bra was a luminous blue that complemented her shoes, and she had a very sheer and loose white tank top that was cropped short enough to just barely show her toned and tanned midsection. While her smile was dazzling, Trent was disappointed he wasn't able to see the rest of her face behind the oversized sunglasses she was wearing. He guessed she had long hair by the size of the brunette messy bun on top of her head. He was lost in his thoughts about how attractive she was when Phil reached out to him. "Trent," he bumped his arm.

"Oh." Trent shook his head. "I'm sorry."

"Trent," Phil started again. "This is the owner of the house and the property here." He gestured to the woman. "Presley Williams."

Trent reached out to shake her hand, but when they touched, he fumbled for words. "Beautiful." He swallowed and started over. "It's beautiful out here." He smiled and tried to regain his voice. "I'm looking forward to filming here."

"It's so nice to meet you." She smiled warmly back at him and finally lifted her sunglasses so Trent was able to see the rest of her face. She was gorgeous, seeing her full face now he was exposed to her captivating green eyes and lush lashes. Her smile was infectious and Trent continued to hold her hand, not wanting to let go.

"Wow, Trent Hayes." She giggled. "I would've never guessed I'd have the opportunity to meet you."

"Ms. Williams…," Trent started before she quickly cut him off.

She put a hand to her chest. "Presley, please." She corrected him, laughing, also not pulling her hand out of his.

Trent put his second hand on top of their already engaged hands. "Okay, Presley," he agreed with a smile.

The officer finally jumped in to introduce himself. "I'm Officer Bando." He held his hand out to Trent first. "You guys are all welcome to call me Mike though."

Trent reluctantly let go of Presley's hand and turned to offer his hand to Officer Bando. He furrowed his brows for the slightest second as he could swear the officer gave him an overly rigid handshake in return.

"I work with the Mason County Sheriff's Department." Mike held on to his duty belt and puffed his chest. "I spend a lot of time on the property here and so you'll be seeing a lot of me over the next couple of months."

Trent wondered if Mike spent his time there as Presley's other half. From what he could tell they were around the same age, probably late 20's and neither of them had wedding rings. Mike could be a compliment to Presley's already seemingly perfect appearance. He was an inch or two shorter than Trent and kept himself in better than average health. Trent noticed a military tattoo peeping on his light skin from beneath Mike's short sleeved uniform top. He couldn't make out Mike's hair cut as he had it hidden under a ball cap, but his hair was short and a very dark brown color. Trent let out a small laugh through his nose as he examined Mike's mustache, *total cop stash*, he smirked—*could Presley really be into that?*

"While I'm here to offer protection and assistance for your production, I also want to remind you that my town and its citizens are my top priorities." Mike adjusted his duty belt. "So, please keep that in mind and conduct yourselves accordingly."

"Great," Phil started. "Officer Bando, this is my head of security detail, Marco. I'd like the two of you to go over the production schedule, logistics of where we'll be around town and such. Get those things taken care of, will you please?" He waited for nodding before he turned to Presley again. "And I was hoping maybe you could give us all a quick tour of your home and property here, please Presley?"

She looked up from stroking her dog's mammoth sized head and smiled. "Oh sure, I'd love to," she agreed. "I mean, I'm a professional tour guide now since the crew already had theirs a week ago and since then, they seem to be settling right in." She smiled and gestured to the main house.

"Yeah, they're making themselves at home," Phil assured her. "Not sure if you've been in there since they got here, but they're just about ready for filming."

"Oh good." She nodded her head along. "I've been trying to stay out of the way, but I'm really anxious to see what they've done." She smiled at the group. "Let's start the tour outside though since you guys just came from the house." She began walking them down to the dock. It didn't take long for her to start talking again. "So, sometimes Mike comes off as a little much, I'm sorry if he offended anyone." She looked at Phil. "He sometimes pretends he's like personal security here or something," she laughed. "He just gets slightly overprotective from time to time."

"Is he, uh, does he live here too?" Phil asked.

Ah, Phil for the win, Trent smiled to himself as he was wondering the same thing.

"No," she said very quickly and definitively. "I've just known Mike since forever." She smiled and then bopped her head from side to side. "We went to school together, his mom worked for my dad for a longtime, ya know, small town so ya kinda just know everyone," she shrugged. Presley took a couple more steps and then put her sunglasses back down and looked at Phil. "He's also running for Sheriff in the upcoming election so I'm sure that's why he's being so puffy chest around here today," she chuckled. "Heaven forbid he be nice to anyone who can't cast a vote for him."

Trent was already attracted to her glowing personality; he had only known her for about ten minutes but she was all smiles and chatting with them as if they were all just old friends. He had become accustomed to meeting only two types of women around his age, either the starstruck, barely getting an audible word out type or the women who literally threw themselves at him as an offering. Not Presley, she had a level of confidence that he admired as she was holding her own among a group of Hollywood professionals. In fact, she was going along as if she personally knew each of them; she was so friendly and welcoming in the humblest way.

"Oh." Phil scrambled through the papers he had in a folder he was carrying. "Before I forget, there were some updates to the schedule, last minute things, but since you're planning to be on site I was hoping you could make the adjustment to avoid disruption during these dates and times." Phil shook his head. "Shit, I hope I gave these updated copies to Officer Bando just now."

Presley looked at the stack he handed her and just nodded her head. "I know, sorry, I'm sure it'd be much easier for you guys if I actually moved out for a couple months, I can totally work around this though."

"Oh my gosh!" Michelle began. "Here we are invading your home and you're apologizing," she laughed. "I would've had a hard time agreeing to share this place at all!"

"Well, it's not everyday someone comes by wanting to film here." Presley shrugged. "It's quite flattering."

"How long have you lived here?" Michelle was a Hollywood megastar herself but wanted to know more about how someone of Presley's age managed to land a property like hers. "Do you live here alone?"

Presley smiled and kicked a volleyball across the lawn for Baron to chase before she answered. "I've lived here my whole life, actually. Well, minus the four years I spent away at college that is." She shrugged and watched Baron catch up to the ball towards the water. "It's just me and Baron here though." She smiled at Michelle before her phone started ringing. Presley looked down and then turned to Phil. "I am *so* sorry, I have to take this, please, make yourselves at home, I can catch up with you on the dock if you want? This should be super quick." She offered a reassuring expression and headed towards the cottage by the water while the group continued to the dock.

"Like I said," Phil began. "Presley's going to still be living here while we're filming, she's taking up residence at the cottage over there instead of the main house though. She's got plenty of her own business to keep to I believe, so we'll all need to be mindful of each other's working hours—she's a busy gal from what I gather."

"What does she do?" Trent asked as his eyes followed Presley making her way to the cottage with her pit bull on her heels.

"Uh," Phil scratched his head. "She works at the local mill."

"Hell no." The other leading man, Pete Winters, shook his head. "I'm sure property can't be all that expensive out here in bumfuck Egypt, but there's no way she works at a mill and lives here alone." He protested while gesturing towards her massive home.

"Well, her family owns it," Phil elaborated. "They've got corporate offices in other cities too, I'm not really sure the extent of it all, but she's not hurting for cash. Plus," Phil remembered. "She said she's lived here her whole life, so it's probably a family property that's just been passed along." He shrugged.

Trent listened but watched as Presley stood on the porch of the cottage, she was animated with her hands as she was talking on the phone. She didn't look upset, but she was definitely laying down a firm hand with whoever was on the other line. She settled one of her hands on her hip and turned her back to the small group. Even from a distance Trent could appreciate her figure. As he was watching her, he noticed the loyal pit bull settled only a couple feet from Presley with his eyes maintaining watch over the group that had made it down to the dock.

"You with us, Hayes?" Michelle bumped into Trent's arm as they all walked along the dock.

"Huh?" Trent looked at her. "Yeah."

Michelle raised her eyebrows. "Watching it unfold in real-time is such a treat," she smirked.

"What?" Trent's eyes furrowed slightly.

Michelle rolled her eyes. "Okay, we'll just pretend you aren't over there developing a game plan." She decided before stepping up her pace to catch up with Pete who was peering over the end of the dock.

Trent tried to shake Michelle's comment, he might have played dumb, but he knew exactly what she was inferring.

"Sorry," Presley called out from the edge of the dock. "I see you guys made it down here just fine without me though." Her face brightened into a full smile when Trent looked at her. Despite them exchanging that pleasant look, she continued walking towards the gazebo.

The group had to part ways when Baron made his charge down the dock. He wasn't concerned about where anyone was, he was on a mission to use the dock as his own personal airstrip before he launched himself off the edge.

"Cannon ball champion, huh?" Pete called out.

Presley agreed with her head knowing her dog would need to stay away from everyone now because it was likely the group wasn't into being brushed up on by a wet dog. "Oh, he's a total showoff, for sure."

Baron swam all the way to the bank and then started making his way down the dock for another jump. Presley walked over to the coffee table under the gazebo and opened the top. She had a stash of towels in there and was preparing for Baron to settle down after his third or fourth jump.

"I want to be sure you guys feel welcome to explore while you're here too," she said as Baron splashed into the lake again. "I know you'll be working, but the lake is completely safe to swim in, I have a few paddle boards and such up in the garage you can bring down too. I try to always keep towels down here, but if they haven't moved things around too much, there should be more towels in the full bath of the main floor of the house too. And also, I'm not sure if anyone is into running or what not, but there are trails that wrap around the entire lake too."

"Hopefully our boss over there isn't a slave driver and we can take you up on all that," Michelle joked.

"Well, that'll depend on how many takes you cost us." Phil sent a little friendly fire back her way.

Presley smiled at them. "I can also take you guys up to the garage too, there's a little fitness center off the side of it." She pointed back up the lawn. "It may not suit everyone's needs," she chuckled and inadvertently looked right at Trent. "I don't power lift or anything, so it's limited to just the type of equipment I use, but you all are more than welcome to use it. Oh! I also have some lawn games stored up there with all the paddle boards."

"So, you're just the best kind of hostess." Michelle complimented her.

"I'm sure going to try to be." Presley smiled and then leaned down to wrap her dog up in a towel as it seemed like he had given them enough of a show.

"Presley!" A deep voice called out behind them.

Trent noticed Presley jump a little at the voice before turning around.

"Pres, I gotta go, got a call—you good here or you need me to send someone?" Mike called out.

"I'm fine." She assured him with a thumbs up gesture and continued to dry Baron off.

Mike kept walking down the dock to meet them anyway. "I'll be back to check on things after my shift." He looked at both Trent and Pete to be sure they heard him. "Call me if you need anything before then, alright?"

"Bye Mike." She waved before he turned around. Presley gave her attention to the group again. "Like I said," she rolled her eyes. "Things have gotten worse since Mike decided to run for Sheriff."

"Well," Phil began. "I guess we can all rest easy, the set will be safe."

Presley bent down to pick Baron's towel up. "No one is *ever* up here, you're honestly more likely to see a wild animal than a person looking to do any harm. Amazon doesn't even deliver here," she laughed.

"You seem to have your own security system anyway." Pete commented as Baron tore off down the dock towards the lawn to get his ball.

Presley only smiled and shook her head agreeing with the assessment.

"I don't mean to be rude, I know this is his house." Phil was hesitant but at the same time very concerned about Baron. "Is your dog going to mind the strangers in and out at all hours? He's a very intimidating dog."

"No," Presley assured him. "He *is* very protective of me, but he's not like aggressive, if that makes sense? Plus, he doesn't stray too far away from me so he shouldn't be a problem at all. He's not going to just run around attacking anyone if that's what you're afraid of?" She laughed.

"No, I wasn't trying to stereotype him or anything," Phil backpedaled. "I apologize."

"It's okay, I know he looks scary, but he's a big baby mostly." She ruffled the top of his head and looked at Phil. "If I stay out of harm's way, he will be a perfect host."

"Fair enough." Phil put his hands up.

"Have you had him since he was a puppy?" Michelle asked and tried to get Baron's attention.

"Yep." Presley watched her dog give Michelle the diva treatment by not going up for any kind of petting; he just wanted to join everyone on the dock while he annihilated the volleyball. "Got the little booger when he was just eight weeks old."

"I'd love to have a dog like this," Pete added. "Pure fucking muscle, he's a beast." Pete leaned down to pat Baron on his head. Baron lifted his head with the ball in his mouth and gave it an aggressive shake before resetting his feet around the now deflated ball so he could work on the hole he started.

"The physique of the breed is a big reason I picked him out," Presley admitted. "Tends to make a girl feel a bit safer when a 140-pound beast like this has your back." She smiled down at Baron.

"Probably more loyal than a man too," Michelle added.

Presley just laughed in return and motioned to make her way back up to the lawn. "You guys want to look around the house too, or did you already get a chance to check it out?"

"We did all have a chance to look around when we first got here today, but are you still going to make it to dinner with us tonight?" Phil asked. He had originally invited her to the cast and crew dinner about a week ago.

"I was planning to," Presley confirmed.

"Great, why don't we let you get to your work, and we'll see you later, then?" Phil suggested.

"That would actually work out really well because I do have a couple of things I need to do before the workday ends." Presley took two steps towards the cottage before she turned back around. "It was really nice meeting you all, I look forward to having you guys here for the next couple of months." She smiled. "And please do make yourselves at home. If you need anything, I'll just be right down here at the cottage."

There was a chorus of similar sentiments before they all parted ways.

Trent didn't know if it was all the fresh air or his overall exhaustion, but he definitely didn't feel like he had been himself the last half hour or so since meeting Presley. She was a knockout, and typically he found himself very comfortable and chatty around women like her—he had barely said a few sentences in front of her. He didn't understand his own hesitation. Rather than dwell on anything he followed his co-stars and directing team back up to the main house and picked up on a conversation between Michelle and Pete.

Two

"Bare," Presley called out as he tried to head up the back staircase. "Buddy, we can't go up there right now, c'mon." She slapped her leg. She noticed Phil watching them. "He's so confused," Presley laughed.

"Don't worry." Phil offered his hand out to Baron. "We'll give it back just the way you remember it."

Baron tried to reach his paw to Phil, he missed the first effort from his excitement but hit his hand on the second.

"We're not worried." Presley smiled and pat Baron's head.

"If you want to go check it out, by all means, please do," Phil offered.

"Are you sure? I want to respect the fact that this is your place of work right now."

Phil smiled. "I'm not worried about you guys, you're totally fine, and I don't blame you for wanting to check things out. Just be mindful there are quite a few cords running around the place."

"Presley!" Michelle called from the other side of the kitchen.

Presley turned around to the famous actress waving at her to come over. Presley took a sip of her drink and waved as she walked towards Michelle and Pete. "Hey, I was actually going to go check things out upstairs, what's up?"

"We'll join you." Michelle put her arm under Pete's and followed Presley towards the back staircase which was a secondary entrance to the second floor. "Your house is *gorgeous*!" She gawked before continuing.

"So, but, you really live in this whole big house alone?" Michelle took a drink.

Presley nodded her head again. Of course she lived alone, her town had a population of less than 5,000 people and likely less than half a percent of those people were even single males and in her age range. Further, she did virtually nothing but hang out with Baron and go to work—she had allowed work to completely consume her as of late. For a successful woman in her early prime, she didn't have much to offer in the way of an exciting life. She didn't even need her whole hand to count the number of first dates she'd been on in the last couple years. So, yes, she really lived alone, she sadly admitted in her head again.

"Ahh, I couldn't do it." Pete took a swig of beer. "I'm too used to the hustle and bustle of the city. I'd go stir crazy alone out here."

"I dunno," Michelle shrugged. "I could get away like this every once in a while. Presley, you never get bored? Or scared? I mean, you're a bit secluded out here and you live alone."

Presley shook her head. "Nope, I don't have time to be bored." She shrugged, and noticed Phil was now following them as well.

They reached the top of the stairs and Presley stopped. "Work has me pretty busy, and I don't know how anyone could ever get bored of that view." She gestured towards the large bay windows that showcased the back lawn, lake, and mountains. The four of them turned their heads to look out the windows as the sun was setting. "And don't get me wrong, it can certainly get creepy here at night, but again…," she gestured towards Baron.

Phil raised his brows in agreement.

"It *is* gorgeous," Michelle agreed. "Just crazy this is all yours, you're a damn unicorn," she chuckled.

"I'm sorry." Pete took a deep breath. "I have to ask." He looked quickly at Michelle and then back at Presley; he was animated with his hands as he continued to speak. "You're a logger, live alone in the middle of the woods basically, no man here from what it looks like," he looked around. "Do you prefer the company of women?"

Presley choked on her drink and her eyes widened while Michelle smacked Pete with the back of her hand.

"Pete!" Michelle's face began to turn red.

"Uhm, no," Presley managed. "I'm technically not a logger either, but no, definitely not a lesbian." She couldn't believe his very forward presumption considering they had just met.

"I'm sorry." Pete set his drink down. "I shouldn't have asked that. It's none of my business."

Presley looked down at Baron and then put a smile on her face to look back at Pete and Michelle. "It's okay." She shook her head. "I mean, I can understand, based on what you pointed out, why you would wonder about that. But," she turned to Pete as they approached the master bedroom, her bedroom. "I can assure you I am and have always been very much a fan of men."

Pete took another drink of his beer and gave her an apologetic nod.

"Wow." Presley looked around. "So, you guys didn't change anything at all in here?" She laughed.

Phil shrugged. "It was already perfect, we really didn't need to do much, besides adding all this equipment and a few framed photos," he added.

"My bed is even making an appearance?" Presley didn't know how she felt about that, what kind of scenes were they planning for *her* bed? It was a beautifully crafted, custom wooden piece, four post king-sized bed; but basically sharing it with the cast members—that just seemed odd.

"The set decorator didn't even look for another option, to be honest," Phil admitted. "He said why bother messing with perfection." Phil noted Presley's unreadable expression. "Don't worry though, we did move your mattress to the room down the hall and brought in a new one for us to use."

Presley felt relief come over here.

"You can thank me for all that," Michelle piped in. "I assumed some crusty old couple might live here when I heard about the property," she admitted. "So, the switches were all based on my suggestions."

"Thank you?" Presley cocked her head, not sure if it was a compliment or not.

"And this fucking bathroom is epic." Pete walked through a set of French doors. "That shower spa or whatever the hell it is!"

Presley smiled. "Yeah, that room is like one of my pride and joys on the property," she admitted.

Baron decided to make his way out of the bedroom, so Presley decided to follow; she didn't really need to inspect the place. "Sorry, if you guys will excuse me, I think I'm going to take him outside."

They all gave her a quick wave but stayed in her master suite.

Michelle waited until Presley was well on her way out of the room before she continued to scold Pete. "Seriously?" She laughed and bumped into him. "You don't even know her and you're asking if she's a lesbian?!"

"C'mon, sitting here acting like you weren't thinking the same damn thing?" Pete laughed.

Michelle simply rolled her eyes, not wanting to admit she was in fact also wondering the same thing.

"Oh, you two." Phil shook his head at them. "Don't be giving Presley a hard time, she seems like a lovely lady."

"I didn't say she wasn't lovely, but damn, rich *and* single looking like that?!" Pete's face was skeptical. "There has to be something else to all that."

Phil simply shrugged and made his way out of the suite leaving Michelle and Pete behind.

✦

Trent cracked his fourth beer of the evening and looked out onto the back patio. The view was still breathtaking, even as the sun was now covered completely by the mountains and only a sliver of light shined above them. While he was scanning the view he noticed Presley and Baron sitting on a wooden bench that ran along the covered portion of the back patio; she had her feet kicked over the side of the patio and both of their backs were to the house. He was surprised to see no one else was outside enjoying the twilight scene. Despite her casual appearance earlier in the day, Presley had changed into a nicer outfit for dinner. Trent was right about her hair being long, the soft bombshell curls of her brunette hair touched just above her waist. She had nice arms that she liked to show off because she was in another tank top. He couldn't see her shoes since she had her feet hanging over the side of the bench, but he did see her walking through the house earlier and noticed how much taller she seemed; so, he assumed she was wearing some kind of heels. Trent finally decided to make his way outside to say hello.

Baron stood up on the bench and watched Trent as he approached, his attention prompted Presley to turn around.

"Hi." Trent waved.

"Hey." Presley returned his smile and reached up to hold Baron's collar.

"You guys have the best seat in the house." He sat down next to them. "I'm surprised no one else has found it yet." Trent reached over and let Baron sniff him, so he'd settle down and give Presley a break.

"Well." Presley smiled. "The best seat is usually lakeside, but that's also where the mosquitoes like to hang out at this time of night. So, we settled for second best."

Baron hopped off the bench to walk around and sniff Trent out.

"Sorry, he's nosey." Presley began to reach for her dog.

Trent shook his head. "Don't worry about him, I don't mind a safety check," Trent warmly assured her. "He's gotta make sure I'm good. Huh, big guy?"

Baron let Trent ruffle his head.

Presley relaxed and simply watched Baron's inspection.

"Not really your scene, huh?" Trent gestured towards the house.

Presley shrugged. "I just don't really know anyone, plus, it's kind of awkward, feeling so outta place in my own house," she chuckled. "Not that it looks all that different from how I normally have it."

"It's quite the compound you've got here," Trent admitted. "I've been on a ton of sets, but nothing like your little slice of paradise."

"Thank you, I'm definitely grateful for what I have," Presley acknowledged before smiling at him.

Trent found himself struggling for something else to say, just to keep the conversation going with her, he wasn't typically so lost for words. He continued to lose himself while lingering on her physical attributes. He finally looked down and saw that Presley barely had a sip left of her drink, just before he could offer her another, he was interrupted.

"Trent!" Pete took a step out onto the porch and called out to him. Both Trent and Presley turned his way.

"Bro, come here, you gotta check this out," Pete urged.

"One sec." Trent held his finger up and then turned back towards Presley.

She smiled and shook her head. "It's okay," she looked down. "Baron and I should get goin' anyways, let you all get situated and such. We don't want to wear out our welcome, it's only day one." She grinned.

Trent hadn't even begun to scratch the surface with Presley yet—didn't even have a chance to offer her a refill on her drink and already Pete was tossing up roadblocks. Trent was busy cursing Pete in his head when Presley stood up, he followed suit as Baron took off down the lawn and towards the lake.

"So, hopefully I'll be seeing you around?" Trent asked.

Presley watched Baron for a second and then smiled up at Trent. "Of course." She wiggled her fingers at him with one hand and held her nearly empty drink with the other as she started to walk away. After a few steps she turned around and smiled up at him. "Goodnight, Trent."

"Goodnight," he put his hand up. "Presley," he quietly continued.

Three

They had been filming for almost two weeks and Trent was constantly distracted with the thought of Presley, each time he saw her she looked absolutely glowing. He hadn't noticed anyone coming by to stay with her or her going out late nights in 'date' type clothing. In fact, all he ever saw her in was athletic wear, so he started to assume that there was a large possibility she was truly single. There were a few occasions where he saw her in passing, but they never had a chance to really talk much—it was limited to quick waves and asking how the day was. He continued to linger on a day the previous week where she offered him half of her scone. Their timing was a complete coincidence that she was just pulling up to her house while he was walking towards his rental Tahoe to leave the set. He could still picture it in his mind.

Presley had slowly rolled up to him not too far from the front door of the house and asked from her car, 'Hey Trent Hayes, how would you like your world rocked?' At first his mind went in a completely different direction, but then she held up a brown paper bag and explained about the unofficial world's greatest scones. He loved their sense of ease around one another. Just the short, passing pleasantries they'd exchanged gave her the confidence to talk to him like they'd been friends for years and he was just a completely regular guy. She wasn't lying about that scone rocking his world either, it literally melted in his mouth, and he had gone to her favorite coffee shop three times since just to chase that taste high again. Today he decided to spend more time on set with the hopes of running into her while he wasn't working, and she wasn't in a hurry to go anywhere. Trent got to the house about two hours before he was scheduled for hair and makeup. He brought running clothes and decided to take advantage of the trails Presley had invited them to explore along the lake.

While on his run, Trent was thinking about how before reporting to this shoot, he was feeling like he needed a reset in life. He told himself he was going to take a complete pause and just try to clear his mind from the rush of the last few years while he was filming here. He wanted to simply keep to himself for the entirety of the shoot; he had even committed himself to a pledge of celibacy during this time as bed hopping had become his way of life on virtually every other movie he worked on. He wanted to just try some kind of solo journey in rediscovering himself or some similar bullshit people did when they wanted or needed a little rejuvenation in life. As much as he tried to keep to himself and pursue that reset, he couldn't resist the gravitational pull that was surrounding Presley. Usually when he was attracted to a woman it wasn't all that difficult to simply get her into bed. This seemed different, it was as if his heart knew something that the rest of him didn't yet. He couldn't even manage any of his trademark looks or pick-up content with her, it was like he had an invisible leash on his mouth that his heart was controlling. He figured his best option was to at least try to spend a little more time with her to see if it was simply his self-imposed pledge that was messing with his mind, or if Presley was truly something his heart wanted.

Trent had just about finished a second lap around the lake and was making his way back towards the house when he spotted Presley. He came around a slight bend in the trail and saw her kneeling down tying her shoe, it didn't take long for a slight scene of chaos to ensue. Presley jumped at the motion of Baron barking ferociously next to her and then she let out a quick, startled screech when she looked up and saw Trent coming towards them. Presley reached over to grab Baron's collar and laughed as she stood up. Trent slowed his pace but continued towards them.

"Oh man." She popped her ear buds out, still laughing she put a hand on her chest. "You scared us."

"Sorry about that." Trent took his ear buds out too.

"It's okay." She still had an ear-to-ear grin on her face. "We're still just getting used to having company around." She let go of Baron and he quickly made his way to Trent, sniffing him to be sure he meant no harm. After Baron's inspection he happily wiggled back to Presley's side.

"I can imagine, this place is like your own private sanctuary, huh?" Trent kneeled down hoping Baron would come back over and greet him again.

Presley smiled back at Trent, his flawlessly handsome attributes didn't go unnoticed by her in the least bit. She had seen him in movies with longer hair, but her favorite look was the short fade he had for this movie. He was also styled with some scruff on his face which she found overly dreamy. It gave him a more rugged and edgy appearance than his last movie where he played a lawyer. Trent was beyond a ten in Presley's mind, she was very attracted to his strapping physique and those amazing blue eyes. Presley watched as Baron went back over to him, he showered him in pitty kisses which Trent graciously accepted. As they got more comfortable with one another Trent finally got Baron on his back and started scratching his belly. After smiling at them long enough Presley responded. "It is, but it's just too pretty to keep to myself." She cheerfully shrugged. "So, I'm happy to share it."

Baron squirmed on his back, scratching it along the dirt trail before he flipped his thick body to the side and stood up. He shook off and scampered into the woods. Trent watched and then turned back to Presley; he opened his mouth to say something but Baron interrupted his line. He had a small log in his mouth and was headed towards Trent.

"Oh," Presley beamed. "You've got a new best friend now." She tried to head Baron off, not wanting him to bother Trent.

"That's for me?" Trent leaned over as Baron dropped the log. "Alright, big guy." He reached to ruffle the top of his head. "No wonder he's nothing but muscle, this thing is completely waterlogged and weighs a lot more than it looks." Trent laughed.

"You surely don't have to throw that," Presley offered. "If you get him started, he won't stop," she pleasantly informed him.

"He's alright," Trent assured her and tossed the log down the trail.

"I just didn't want to disrupt your run or anything, I'm sure you didn't have this detour on your agenda today." If Presley was being honest with herself, she hoped he didn't have to go.

"Actually, I've got some time." He flashed almost a flirtatious smile Presley's way. "If you're still in the sharing mood I'd love to hang with you guys for a bit."

Presley blushed, she looked at Baron who was headed back their way before her focus turned to Trent. "We'd love to have you."

"Perfect, we should let the big guy lead the way, huh?" He gestured towards Baron who had dropped the log for Trent to throw.

Presley laughed as Trent heaved the small log again. "You must have quite a bit of time if you're going to let him lead."

Trent smiled and continued along the path with Presley. Their conversation had little room for dead air as they cheerfully exchanged stories to learn more about one another

"No way, so you legitimately run the entire company?" Trent asked.

Presley simply nodded her head with a small smirk, she was pretty used to the shock.

"I have to admit, I kinda thought maybe you were just the face or something since I heard it was a family company." Trent was surprised to find out that she had that kind of responsibility.

Presley nodded. "I mean, to be fair, it's not like I run it all alone," she clarified. "I have like several VP's, a CFO, COO, a C3PO, and a kick-ass legal team." She looked sideways at Trent while she tried to hold back laughter.

Trent chuckled and gave her a friendly side eye. "Are you messing with me?"

"I don't actually have a C3PO, but the rest of it, nope, extra serious." She shrugged.

"No offense, you're, what, twenty…?" He was careful not to follow that with an actual guess.

Presley laughed. "Well, so you're extra brave basically asking a female her age, are we going to play a body weight guessing game next?"

"No," Trent tried to back up quickly. "No, I…," He scrambled for words until he finally settled on just apologizing. "Presley, I'm sorry, that was rude."

"It's really okay." She shook her head smiling, almost ashamed she pressed him like that. "I get that all the time, like you wouldn't even be surprised. Plus, the timber industry, especially ownership, is unofficially reserved for like old, round men who could care less about the environment. Not exactly a scene for twenty-*eight*-year-old female animal lovers." She peeked at Trent while grinning.

Trent smiled and wiped his mouth and chin. "I feel obligated to share a deep secret with you now that I know your age." He turned towards her and shrugged. "It's really only fair, right?"

Presley giggled. "Okay but not like one of the secrets where you'll have to kill me though, deal?"

"That really limits what I can share then." He acted put out. "But here it goes," he took a deep breath. "So, you know how I'm tough and brave, right?"

"Yeah, I've seen a few of your movies," she admitted with a playful laugh.

"Oh, you have, huh?" He raised his eyebrows as Presley blushed and put her head down. Trent continued despite wanting to tease her more. "Well, I'll kick the shit out of anyone out there, but I have one fear and it's completely ridiculous." Trent looked up towards the sky on the off chance there was a sign up there to tell him to stop sharing. After he had been dramatic enough, he turned to smile at Presley. "I have a fear of dryer lint."

Presley's eyes were wide and matched her smile.

Trent assumed she was ready to laugh at him so he held his hands up and opened his mouth to speak.

"Shut. Up." Presley covered her mouth with both hands. "You're making that up." She shook her head, but her eyes were smiling.

"I'm not," Trent laughed back. "Technically speaking, I guess I'm not actually *scared* of it, but on everything I won't even fucking touch it with my bare hands."

"Trent." Presley turned to him and put her hand on his forearm, she swallowed and then began. "I'm *deathly* afraid of dryer lint."

"No!" Trent was excited from her touch and shocked at her confession. "There's no way! I've never heard of anyone else being afraid of it."

"Well, who the hell admits that?!" Presley laughed. "I thought I was alone in the whole wide world with that one."

"Certainly not, I get so grossed out by it." Trent's face looked disgusted. "I've got these tongs and rubber gloves that I keep hidden with my laundry supplies, so people don't find out about my fear."

"You're so brave, I won't even do that." Presley looked down with a mix of giddiness and shame in her smile. "I'm ashamed to admit I actually have someone do all of my laundry just to avoid the lint. Like, I won't even let her keep a trash bin in the laundry room because I think she'll pile all the lint in there and it will somehow end up touching me."

"Oh man." Trent bent back and laughed out loud. "You've got it worse than I do!"

Presley just shrugged her shoulders laughing along with Trent who bent down to grab Baron's log again.

"Of all the things." He looked at her after Baron was on his way to chase down the hefty piece of wood he had just thrown. "We find that we have *that* in common, huh?"

Trent's interest and fondness of Presley was growing rapidly, he was glad he decided to finally try to get her alone. Their conversation made him feel like he'd known her for forever. She had a way of making him forget that he was famous, it was refreshing. Most of the women he had dated, or really just slept with, were all the same—gorgeous and completely interested in him because of his fame, quite literally throwing themselves at him. He never really had to put in any effort with women, his looks and fame provided an endless supply of dates. In fact, he had never known a woman of interest for an entire week without making it to bed with her; and his relationships never lasted longer than that week. He felt lost with Presley because while he found himself more interested in her as time went by, he couldn't quite get a handle on how to interact with her. Even based solely on the in-depth conversation he was finally having with her; Trent could tell Presley was different in nearly every aspect compared to the other women he had been with. She was absolutely beautiful, but he also found that he could talk to her and carry along a meaningful and enjoyable conversation. She wasn't one to simply agree with him all the time either, she challenged him which was a surprising breath of fresh air to volley a conversation with a woman. He was excited to get to know more about her, and hopefully spend a lot more time with her.

"So." Trent couldn't believe Baron wasn't tired yet, but he continued to toss the log that the trusty pit bull kept bringing back to him. "Does this trail loop around the entire lake?"

"It does," Presley's head also confirmed. "But you'll have to see if your fearless little pack leader takes the long way or not, there's a fork up here where we can keep going around, or we veer left and basically take the same route right back to the cottage."

Trent smiled at her.

"Do you want me to call him off that log?" Presley watched Trent bend down yet again to toss Baron's new favorite log. "He truly won't quit," she warned him again.

"I don't mind entertaining him." Trent looked at Presley with a smile. "Plus, tossing that waterlogged hunk of wood is definitely going to count as my work out for today."

"Well, thank you." She smirked up at him. "I appreciate you keeping us both entertained."

Trent and Presley were laughing just outside her cottage when Mike pulled up. He watched as Presley reached out and touched Trent's forearm while she was laughing at something he said. Mike didn't waste any time heading towards them. "Good morning!" He shouted as he was still pretty far away.

Both Presley and Trent turned towards him to wave before getting back to their conversation.

Mike walked quicker towards them. "Pres, you need a ride to work?" Mike offered.

"What?" Presley asked as he was still too far to hear clearly.

"I can bring you to the office if you want. I've gotta be around there for a patrol today at some point anyway." Mike was finally close enough for them to hear him more clearly.

"Oh." She smiled as he approached. "That's so nice, I may not go in today."

"Other plans?" Mike looked pointedly at Trent.

Presley ignored Mike's assumption. "I just have some things I need more quiet for." She shrugged. "And I may just head to Seattle, so hanging here is probably the best plan right now. How's your mom?"

"She was just asking about you this morning, wondering when you'll want to go get dinner again?" Mike wanted to give the appearance that Presley was already involved with him.

"I may have to try to get a hold of her for brunch in the next couple of weeks instead. My schedule may call for long days, unfortunately."

"We'll make it work for you Pres." Mike rested a hand on the hip of his duty belt and then stared at Trent before he started again. "I did bring you a donut." He swung the bag towards Presley. "A nice warm, freshly baked Boston Cream, just for you," he winked.

"Ugh, Mike, you know I'm trying to stay away from these." She laughed and accepted the bag.

"C'mon, you know you don't have to worry about that, you're perfect." His smile lingered on her even after she averted her eyes.

A very awkward moment of silence went by before Presley decided to break things up. "I guess I better go clean up." She smiled at Mike briefly. "Thank you for the donut." She then shared a noticeably more affectionate smile with Trent. "Thank you for the walk, Trent." She quickly bit her bottom lip. "And the company."

Baron lingered by Trent, leaning against his leg, begging for some kind of goodbye for himself.

"My pleasure." Trent smirked before he reached down to give Baron a sturdy pat on his chest.

Baron was satisfied with the gesture and scampered into the cottage. Presley smiled at Trent one last time before she shut the door.

Mike barely waited for Presley to shut the door. "Hitting the set early, huh?"

Trent offered a flat smile with a furrowed brow, "What?"

"Production schedule says filming starts in a couple of hours which means people aren't really scheduled to be on site for at least an hour."

Trent didn't know how to operate around Mike. He seemed completely overprotective and he definitely understood Mike wanted Trent to keep his distance, but he was too interested in Presley to allow Mike to pull this overbearing routine. He decided he'd make his stance clear from the start, if this was the start of something with Presley, that he wasn't going to be taking orders from Mike. "I rarely stick to the production schedule." Trent almost smugly offered a smile. "No worries though, I don't need security, no one really even knows we're shooting up here."

Mike scowled, Trent's security was not at all what he was alluding to. "Well, you guys are taking up enough of Presley's home, I just thought maybe you'd leave her open hours to her."

"I'll be sure to ask her if she wants me to stay away next time I see her." Trent winked at him and started to walk away. He only took about two steps before he turned back around. "Have a good one, Officer Bando." He gave him a salute-style wave.

Mike wasn't pleased, to say the least. After glaring at Trent walking away from him he decided to check around the perimeter of the house before he checked in for his official duties.

✦

Presley heard a knock at the door just as she had gotten dressed, Baron was the first down there and he was barking ferociously.

"Hey, hey," she tried to calm him with a light tone to her voice. A large part of her hoped it was Trent. "Come here." She snapped her fingers at Baron before she looked through the window, it was Mike.

"Hey Mike." Presley smiled and released Baron who quickly sniffed every inch of his shoes and then sat obediently next to Presley.

"Hi Pres, you busy?"

"Uhh, just getting my stuff together to head out, what's up?"

"Can I come in?" He took his hat off.

"Sure," She shrugged and opened the door wider so he could walk through. She decided to leave the door open even after he made his way inside.

Mike looked around, he wanted to be sure there was no sign of anyone else staying at the cottage. He set his hat on the kitchen island and then leaned against it.

Presley didn't know quite how to take his behavior. Somehow Mike had seemed to be a bit off over the last several months. Presley had been nonchalantly chalking it up to him running for Sheriff, but it was taking an even harder turn since the movie started filming. She tried to play down her concerns and instead began gathering her laptop and the rest of her work bag. "So, what's up?"

"Oh, not much." He watched her as she wound up her charger and stuck it neatly into her bag. "I just kind of wanted to check in."

Presley exhaled a small laugh. "About what?"

"Just how things are going with the production here." He adjusted his duty belt. "I'm sorry I'm not here 24/7 to make sure they're sticking to that. I don't like when they deviate, I'll talk to Marco before I leave."

"What are you talking about?" Presley choked out a small chuckle. "They've been fine, in fact, I've hardly noticed any extra noise or anything. To be honest, since they've got everything set up in there and they're already filming things have gotten much quieter."

Mike took a deep breath, he didn't want to upset Presley, but he wanted to make it very clear he took notice of Trent and his possible interest in her. "I guess I'm talking about all of them respecting the times they're permitted on the grounds."

Presley let out a full on laugh this time. "Permitted on the grounds? Mike," she turned to him. "Come on, what's with the Mr. Offish routine? Is there a creeper on 'the grounds' in particular you're worried about?"

Mike knew it was too early to call Trent out, so he lied. "I just noticed someone around front when I got here." He shrugged. "He said he was fixing a lighting issue this morning."

"Mike." Presley shook her head and smiled. "You gotta lay off some of these guys, this movie is *really* good for the town, and you know it." She turned her attention back to her bag. "I know you realize the kind of recognition and revenue this movie could bring here, it'll revitalize the place."

"We don't need that," Mike insisted. "Your family has kept this town on top for generations."

"Thanks for the plug," she continued laughing. "I'm just saying, we need to let them do what they need to do for this movie. Not only did the mayor agree but I can promise you I've had a whole legal team scour every last piece of paper I signed agreeing to this deal, only good is going to come from this."

"It's Hollywood, Pres." Mike put his hat back on. "A lot of it is all for show." He gave her an accusing look and then headed for the door.

"And when I met all of them, I made it very clear that they're all welcome to make themselves at home," she added as he was just about to the door.

"What?! Pres, you can't be serious!" Mike turned around and put his hands on his hips.

"What?" Presley was honestly confused. "Each one of them has been vetted, it's fine. I'm happy to let them kind of share the space, honestly."

Mike shook his head. "I'll be sure to make extra rounds then," he assured her.

"Bye Mike," Presley called out as he walked through the door.

Mike waved his hand and closed the door behind him.

Presley had managed to get herself ready in a little over an hour, so she started packing up the car. Baron helped by bringing his favorite toy and waiting patiently in the backseat.

"Did we finally scare you away?" Michelle approached the car as Presley set her work bag on the front seat.

"Oh," Presley smiled. "No, I just have a few things that are best done at the city office."

"Ahhh, a city office, huh?"

"Yeah, I prefer working here at the mill, but we do have a corporate office in Seattle too, so I'm heading there for a day or so." She closed the passenger door. "So, you guys aren't scaring me away, I'll be back to get in the way again very soon," Presley joked.

"You're definitely not in the way," Michelle assured her. "I was actually going to see if you have some suggestions on places to eat around town?"

"Oh my gosh, yes, there are several places you guys will love. Are you taking a huge group or just like a few of you?"

"Eh, depends on who's available and what not," she shrugged. "I saw a burger place when I came in today, is that place any good?"

"It is, you have to try their fry sauce though and also the huckleberry shake if you go." Presley dug into her purse for a pen and paper. "Here, so if you're looking for good pizza try Louie G's, we only have one bar, but the fried bar food is top tier, Chinese you'll want to go to the deli at the grocery store…," Presley waited for Michelle's laugh. "Promise, it's the best." She continued writing. "Oh, and if you need a romantic spot, there's an Italian restaurant that actually sits lakeside, it's about a twenty-minute drive from here but the food is great and it's beautiful there."

"Romantic?" Michelle nervously laughed.

Presley looked at her, she was almost embarrassed to have made that assumption when she noticed Michelle's reaction. "I'm so sorry, I didn't mean to…"

Michelle cut her off. "No, don't be sorry it's okay," she blushed.

Michelle and Pete had developed somewhat of a relationship, but Michelle thought they had been pretty discreet about it.

"I mean to say that around the twilight hour it's something to be seen—and they totally give you the whole candlelight table effect and sappy music. I go alone and grab takeout," Presley chuckled. "So, it doesn't *have* to be a romantic thing like that," she tried to clarify. "But that's how it's advertised around here."

"What?!" Michelle lightly pushed Presley's arm. "You don't have all the guys around town pining for your affection?!"

Presley laughed and continued writing. "I don't think you'd be surprised to find out that the dating scene here isn't all that happening. Plus," she looked up from the paper. "I don't typically have a lot of free time."

"Well, but you go to Seattle regularly, right?"

"I do," she confirmed. "Not to hook up with random guys though," she laughed. "I only go when duty calls, or to see my besties."

"What about Officer Macho Man?" Michelle urged. "He seems quite interested, if you haven't noticed," she smiled. "And he's pretty easy on the eyes."

"Oh." Presley shook her head and softly rolled her eyes. "Mike's just an old friend, it's definitely not like that," she clarified.

"It definitely could be, it's beyond obvious he has a thing for you."

"Yeah." Presley handed Michelle the paper. "He's just always been just a friend though," she tried to reiterate. "I do keep hoping he finds a girl, seems like he just doesn't date or isn't ready or something though," she shrugged.

"Yeah." Michelle laughed. "Not ready to give up the idea of you."

Presley winced on the inside, she wasn't hearing any of this for the first time, but she truly wasn't interested in Mike like that, she never had been. Part of her really didn't want that vibe around her since Trent may be showing some interest in her too. Rather than projecting any of those thoughts Presley simply shrugged with a smile.

"Well, thank you for the list." Michelle held up the piece of paper.

"Can't wait to check some of these places out. Maybe when you get back you can come along and we can all catch a bite?"

"I would love that." Presley smiled and put her pen back in her purse.

"I'll let ya get going, have a good trip." Michelle waved as she headed back towards the main house.

"Bye, Michelle." Presley waved.

✦

"She's definitely single." Michelle offered to Trent as she took a seat next to him for hair and makeup before they started shooting for the day.

"What?" Trent scrunched his face.

"Quit the shit, Hayes." Michelle laughed as the stylist began brushing her hair. "You know who I'm talking about."

Trent laughed. "Surely I don't." His face and tone weren't very convincing.

"Yeah, guess who's not calling *you* anytime soon?" Her accusing eyes stared him down while Trent continued to smile. "The Academy, your little oblivious act sucks."

He laughed out loud at her when Pete walked in.

"What'd I miss?" Pete dropped into his chair on Michelle's right.

"This little loser." Her thumb gestured towards Trent. "Over here trying to act like he hasn't been checking Presley out." Michelle threw Trent under the bus immediately.

Trent shook his head and tried to ignore them.

"Hayes, this is your MO, isn't it? No sense in having shame in your game now, is there?" Pete wondered. "It's a little early to do your hit it and quit it shit though, don't you think? We're filming here for several more weeks. And we're literally at *her* house."

"Yeah," Michelle agreed. "You may wanna slow down, so you don't have to keep seeing her for that long after you get her into bed. You know, you can always find a different local to keep you busy in the meantime. She's leaving for Seattle right now, we can all hit up the bar later to find someone else to tide you over?" She suggested and then leaned towards the mirror to pick something from her eye.

Trent continued to take the shots, if he was being honest with himself, he had been exactly the guy his co-stars were accusing him of being. He'd been in seven movies in the last two years and had at least triple that in movie set partners. Nothing substantial, just good times.

He nodded his head while smiling. "Keep chirping you two."

"Uh oh," Michelle swatted Pete. "Someone caught some actual fucking feelings." They both laughed at Trent.

"Fuck off, both of you." Trent smirked.

"Oh, he did!" Pete squealed.

"I'm *not* making any drastic moves, alright?" Trent's face was red and he wouldn't look up at the mirror so he didn't have to look at Michelle or Pete. "I decided before I got here that I would be slowing down and taking a break from that lifestyle."

"Call the fuckin press!" Pete nearly stood. "A female *finally* tamed Playboy Hayes!"

"Oh shit!" Michelle joined in. "This is historic." She wiggled around in her seat until Trent cut in.

"How 'bout you two keep my secret and I'll keep yours." Trent lowered his eyes to them and tried to project that he had noticed the sneaking around that had been going on between the two of them. "Yeah, those motel walls aren't as thick as you guys may think."

Michelle and Pete both blushed, and Trent continued. "Fuckin acting like, of all people, someone like me wouldn't notice?" He shook his head. "Damn rookies," he mockingly taunted.

Michelle and Pete had just begun to see each other and weren't sure it was something they wanted to share with Hollywood and the rest of the world. Trent's proposal silenced the conversation for a while until Phil walked in to check on progress and go over a few details for the first scene of the day.

Four

Presley arrived in Seattle just after two. Luckily, she was headed into the city which saved her a smidge of time compared to the pile up that was trying to get out of the city. She had drank too much water during the trip and was rushing to get to a bathroom when a text popped up on the display of her G Wagon's dash:

> **MIKE BANDO**
> Pres, just wanted to make sure you made it safe to the big city.

Presley shook her head, *Mike always with the check-ups,* she smiled and activated the talk to text.

> Yep, just about to get to the penthouse, thanks for checking in, smiley face.

Her car typed out and sent her text.

> **MIKE BANDO**
> Good, I'll keep an eye on the fort while you're away. Be safe and let me know if you need anything.

Presley didn't respond to his text after that, she was too focused on relieving her bladder.

"Good afternoon Ms. Williams." A valet greeted her when she arrived. "What a pleasant surprise to see you today."

"Hi Manny." She unbuckled her belt and grabbed her purse.

"Looks like just a couple of bags today, huh?" He looked into her backseat where Baron was wiggling to get out and greet him. "Shall I have them taken up for you?"

Presley typically took her own bags when she didn't have many, but she needed to rush to the bathroom. "If you could, I would surely appreciate that Manny, thank you." She clipped Baron's leash to his collar, and they made their way into the lobby and left Manny with the car.

Presley felt an immense amount of relief once she got into her modern and oversized, luxury penthouse. She opened a few windows and the patio slider so Baron could sunbathe on the large concrete balcony. She had a few things to do for work before heading into the office in the morning but figured she'd set up plans for the evening before getting too engulfed in those duties. She decided to join Baron on the balcony to catch some sunshine instead of hiding away in her penthouse office.

> Hey Lis! I'm in town for a day or two, are you free to get together?!👣🐾

Lisa had been Presley's best friend since middle school. She married her high school sweetheart, and the couple never left Seattle after they all graduated from the University of Washington. Presley kept in regular contact with Lisa, they made it a point to see each other at least once a month despite the geographical separation. She also found herself in regular contact with Lisa's husband as he was one of Presley's oldest and closest friends, and he was her attorney. They were all much more than friends, they had always been like family, so they didn't allow distance to keep them from one another.

> 👣BESTIE🐾
> What?! Girl, why didn't you tell me earlier?! Of course I'm down to meet up!

> I just got to the penthouse, want me to come your way or would you prefer a night away??

> 🐝BESTIE🖤
> Gah—I'd love a nice girl's night, unfortunately Bailey has swimming lessons. Can you meet at the house?

> We'll be there, just tell me what time and I'll grab dinner for everyone.

> 🐝BESTIE🖤
> Six! Can't wait to see you 🥰🥰🥰!!!!

> You too girl 😘❤️!!

"Auntie PP!" Bailey came to the door when he heard the bell ring. Presley waved feverishly at him through the decorative glass door until his mom arrived to unlock it.

"Hi Bay, baby!" Presley bent her knees and swung her arms open for Bailey to jump into. "How's Auntie's favorite boy?! I missed you!"

"Missed you." The four-year-old kissed her on the cheek and hugged her around her neck before his attention turned to Baron. "Bare!" He pointed.

"Yep, Auntie PP brought Bare." She set Bailey down to get covered in Baron kisses. "Hey girl." She turned to her best friend and they hugged.

"So glad you're here." Lisa squeezed her one last time before backing up. Lisa and Presley were precisely the same height. While they also shared green eyes, Lisa's reflected the forest while the green in Presley's eyes resembled the jungle. Lisa maintained much shorter hair than Presley with her blonde balayage hair just barely sweeping the tops of her shoulders.

"He's getting so big." Presley commented as they made their way into the house and Lisa locked the door.

"You're telling me, 'mommy uppy' is quite the workout these days." She smiled after her son who was chasing Baron into the living room.

"I brought Thai, hope everyone's hungry." Presley lifted the Wild Ginger bags up smiling.

"Is that my girlfriend I hear?" A man's voice echoed down the hall, Lisa rolled her eyes and smiled at Presley.

"Hey, boyfriend." Presley smiled at her childhood best friend. Jake, who stood just under six feet tall, made his way towards his wife and Presley. Jake was always clean shaven, mostly for work, and kept his wavy, dark brown hair in a layered cut that he could easily style to keep out of his face.

"Come here, you." He hugged her. "How are you?"

"Can't complain." She shrugged.

"Good, why don't you ladies get dinner set up and I'll go pick out some wine?" Jake headed down to the basement where he had a wine cellar.

Mike was finishing up his shift, driving through his patrol route before he headed to Presley's. He knew everyone was going to be on set and filming well into the early morning. Being as they were filming a horror movie, a lot of the shoots were scheduled for the late afternoon through the early morning. Mike parked the patrol vehicle on the road before the lane that led to Presley's long driveway. He grabbed a bag from the car and began the near mile long walk towards the house.

"Good evening." A security guard greeted Mike as he approached the main house.

"Hi there." Mike waved. "Just taking a walk through before I head home for the night, I didn't want to disrupt the set with my headlights coming in though."

"No worries at all, let me know if you need anything, sir." The guard tipped his hat.

Mike simply nodded and continued towards Presley's cottage. He was aware there was only the one guard on set that night, so he knew he had privacy and coverage in the form of the dark sky. As he got to the front porch of the cottage, he set his bag down and opened it up. Mike pulled out a small, hidden camera and looked around to be sure no one was coming.

✦

"Cut!" Phil yelled. "What the hell is going on with the lighting back there?" He motioned towards the hallway. "Someone please go take care of that!" Phil held his head and then turned towards part of the crew, including both Trent and Michelle. "You all take ten or so, someone find out if Pete's ready, and for the love of God, the rest of you fix the damn lighting! I don't want to be behind an entire day, we're already running late tonight."

"Shit, I'm making myself scarce." Michelle stood up and moved towards the hall.

"Yeah, Shell, why don't you go find Pete?" Trent smirked. "I'm getting some air."

Michelle elbowed him before she rolled her eyes. "Catching air down by the cottage, Hayes?"

He popped her a friendly bird with his right hand and headed towards the back doors.

When Trent walked onto the back porch, there were a few crew members out there smoking. He looked out onto the dark lawn and then to the lake where the moonlight was directing his attention to the dock. He took a deep inhale and made his way down there. He heard hundreds of crickets creaking along to the sound of the frogs, the air was crisp and he continued to fill his lungs as he approached the dock. There was a swing under the gazebo Presley had near the end of her dock so Trent decided to take a break there. He sat down and spread his arms across the back of the swing. An image of Presley crossed his mind as he stared out onto the lake, it made him smile. He could imagine her sitting there next to him as they cuddled each other on a perfect summer night just like this one. His vision was cut short when he felt his phone buzzing—a text for everyone to get back on set. He took one last deep breath and headed back in.

"What are you doing down here?" A voice called out.

Trent narrowed his eyes at the voice and realized very quickly it was Mike. "Good evening, Officer Bando." Trent gave him another salute style wave.

"Oh, it's you." Mike put his hands on his hips.

"Yep, just taking a quick break." He stopped in front of Mike. "Doing your nightly check?"

"Yeah, her safety is important to me." Mike crossed his arms.

"Even when she's not home." Trent smiled at him. "That's dedication to duty right there."

A scowl began to form on Mike's face, he hadn't found Trent amusing in the least bit since they were introduced, he couldn't wait for him and the entire crew to leave.

"Well, have a good one." Trent offered before continuing to the house.

Mike didn't respond, he watched to be sure Trent was really going up to the house.

Lisa came back down from putting Bailey to bed, Jake and Presley had made their way to the living room where they were laughing on the couch.

"Well, the little monkey is sleeping." She leaned down and kissed her husband as she took a seat next to him.

"So, how is the whole toddler parenting thing? I'm still envisioning the two of you killing that flour baby in health class junior year." Presley laughed. "Who knew you'd be bosses at raising babies?"

"Shit, I remember that." Jake laughed and took another sip of wine. "Babe, was it your brother who dropped it in the lake?"

"Yes," she rolled her eyes. "That's why we don't ask him to babysit."

She laughed and looked at Jake again. Presley could tell they were having a telepathic connection. "Actually, Pres, we're glad you're here because we wanted to tell you something too."

Presley's face lit up. "Are you guys pregnant again?!" She couldn't hold it in.

Jake and Lisa laughed. "No," Lisa looked back at Jake again. "Not yet anyways, I had my IUD removed last month though, I think we're ready for number two." She rubbed his arm.

"You guys!" Presley got up and hugged them both. "I'm so excited for you to have another little one!"

"Yep, she can't fuckin' stay off me." Jake rubbed his chest and took a light swat from Lisa. "So, Pres, when are you having a second kiddo." He gestured towards Baron.

"Oh please." She rolled her eyes and took a drink. "Baron would smother me in my sleep if I got a puppy." She laughed. "And I'm already your guys' third wheel, I don't want to be the third wheel in my own damn house, he's my bestie and I don't want to share."

They both laughed at Presley.

"Pretty sure he's not talking about a puppy." Lisa jumped in and popped her already perfectly arched eyebrows.

Jake sat up. "I actually was thinking… we've got a new guy at the firm." He held his hands up when Presley started to shake her head. "Okay, so I was way off with the last set-up, I'll give you that, this one might be better though."

"Might be?!" Lisa laughed. "Wow, way to reassure her that it won't be a complete waste like the last time. Just so you know, this is the first I'm hearing of this." Lisa clarified to Presley.

"Might be? As in I won't end up having to call you to come pick me up because your boy took me to a Mariners game where he ran into his ex that he realized he still had feelings for, so he ended up leaving me at the seats in the fifth inning never to return again? That kind of 'might be' situation?" Presley took a healthy swig of her wine.

"Listen, that guy was a dick, I'll admit that. My judgement was way fuckin off with him and don't think I'm not still feeling like shit about that." Jake leaned back into the couch and as he did, he propped his feet up on the coffee table. "I think this guy would be different."

"And what, you've known him for like how long? I need to know what kinds of things you could have possibly learned by now." Presley continued to laugh.

"It's going to sound bad," Jake admitted before answering. "He started last week."

Both Lisa and Presley rolled their eyes laughing.

"Jake, shut the fuck up, our friend isn't desperate." She emphasized. "Why don't you spend at least a month getting to know more about him before even bringing this up again. You can't possibly know anything about him at this point, like are you even sure if he's single?"

"That's fair." Jake nodded his head behind his wine glass before continuing. "On one condition." Jake gave Presley a smartass side eye. "I'll wait only if you're not trying to buy time to get with Officer Schmuck."

Presley shook her head and flipped Jake off. "No sir, still not reciprocating *any* of that either, thanks."

Lisa swatted Jake again. "You're such an ass." She laughed before she looked at Presley. "Seriously though, how's that been going?"

"Despite Jake's obvious obsession in wanting to see him more often." She rolled her eyes and stuck her tongue out at him. "We're still just friends. I don't see that changing in any way. I honestly can't even begin to describe how grateful I am that he hasn't flat out asked me on a date. I'm still holding hope that it's not like that and that he just thinks we're sibling-close kinda friends or something."

"You know he loves you." Lisa teased.

"Loves?!" Jake interjected. "That whackfuck is straight up obsessed, has been since middle school."

Presley rolled her eyes. "We all know that feeling has never been mutual." She reminded them before continuing. "He surely hasn't been all that subtle about it lately either." She shook her head and finished off her wine.

"What happened?" Lisa asked.

"Well, so the movie started filming like a couple weeks ago…," Presley started before Jake jumped in.

"That's right! Shit, we should go visit soon, my other girlfriend's there." Jake pumped his eyebrows at Lisa.

"You're dumb." She laughed.

"Michelle is actually pretty nice, she's a redhead for this movie though." Presley shrugged knowing Jake's dislike for what he called, 'gingers'.

"Aw, gross! never mind." He hugged Lisa around her shoulders. "Babe, I guess I'll stay with you."

"Wow, thanks." She gave her husband a firm two-finger jab to his fit torso. "So, Mike's what, like not cool with all that extra action at your house or what?"

Presley rolled her head back and forth. "Well, you know him, he's just total cop mode whenever he has the opportunity, and I think it's ten times worse since he's running for Sheriff. He *hates* Trent Hayes, I can tell you that much." She tried to disguise a smirk.

"Uh oh." Jake sat up. "If he hates him there must be a reason, huh?"

Presley blushed ever so slightly. "I don't talk to Mike like that, so I'm not sure the exact reason."

"Pres, you're hiding something." Lisa narrowed her eyes and looked at her best friend.

"What're you talking about?" Presley was able to subdue the blushing momentarily but her tone was off.

"Well, how do you know he hates Trent Hayes? Isn't Pete Winters in that movie too? Why doesn't he hate him?" Lisa asked, knowing full well Presley was never good at hiding anything from her.

"I don't know." Her eyes got wide, and it was obvious she wasn't disclosing everything. "You'll have to ask him."

"Aw shit, Pres caught Hollywood's eye!" Jake wildly rubbed his palms together. "Officer Dildo doesn't like him because he's tryna holler at you, huh?"

Presley was laughing now. "Dude," she looked at Lisa, "your hubby is delusional."

"Maybe not." Lisa was siding with her husband as Presley was acting somewhat giddy, *Jake could be right,* she thought.

"I mean, he's talked to me a couple of times." Presley shrugged and tried to mask her smile.

"What?! A couple of times and you've failed to mention it until now?!" Lisa was bouncing out of her seat. "Did you go out with him?!"

"No." Presley shook her head and furrowed her brow. "Just like in passing… a couple of times since we met." She paused wondering if she should even mention her morning. She contemplated the idea that it may have just been a total accident and a one-time walk, but the overwhelming smile she felt developing on her face encouraged her to continue along anyway. "We did walk around the lake this morning." She didn't have to wait long for a reaction.

Lisa and Jake were now both on the edge of the couch wanting to hear more. "Hold the fuckin phone! Let me get another bottle." Jake shot up and ran into the kitchen.

Presley just laughed and continued to blush; he was back in no time. "Okay, I'm back." Jake was already working to get the bottle open.

"Tell us *everything*." Lisa insisted.

"Like, there's not much to tell." Presley had a hot pink face. "I was jogging with Baron, and we ran into Trent while he was on a morning run." She shrugged, definitely trying not to think about how dreamy he was in real life if she wanted to suppress the blood rushing to her cheeks. "Like that's it, he stopped and walked with us and then Mike saw us chatting, and then Trent had to get ready for today's shoot." She finally looked up at her best friends. "That's all."

"Did you kiss him?" Lisa asked before biting her bottom lip.

"What? No!" Presley squirmed. "We walked on the same path, like it was not a kissing situation, I doubt it's even like that."

"Oh, it's like that." Jake tried to convince her. "He's a ladies' man, he wouldn't just walk with you for no reason."

Lisa swatted him in the arm. "Don't be rude."

"What? I'm not," he defended himself.

"No," Presley reassured Lisa. "It's okay, like I mean, I know about him, that's why I'm not understanding why Mike's being so territorial about Trent. Like he won't give me two thoughts and he'll be gone in a few weeks or whatever."

"Don't sell yourself short though, Pres, you're an absolute catch!" Lisa encouraged her.

"Plus, if nothing else you can take a ride on that Hollywood *D*!" Jake made thrusting motions with his hands and hips.

Both women laughed in disgust at him as he just continued with his little routine.

"I'm *not* doing that." Presley finally managed.

"Pres, you have to keep us updated much better than you have been on this topic." Lisa urged.

"I'm not hiding anything, there's nothing to hide." She insisted. "Like that walk legit happened this morning."

"What did you guys talk about?" Jake smirked and pumped his eyebrows at her.

"Just random stuff." Presley shrugged.

"Does Baron seem comfortable around him?" Lisa asked.

"Oh my gosh, they're BFFs now." Presley laughed, holding her glass out for Jake to pour her more wine. "He must have thrown that stick for him at least a hundred times this morning."

"So, this wasn't in fucking passing." Jake countered. "You guys spent some quality time together, that lake walk is at least forty-five minutes, if not more."

Again, Presley shrugged and tried to hide her face behind her clear wine glass.

"You stingy bitch!" Lisa bumped her lightly. "You're going to hold out on us?!"

Presley was turning red from stifling her laugh. "Okay, so to clarify I'm not holding out. We legit didn't *do* anything." She was still smiling. "And it was mostly just chatting about silly stuff, I mean, he asked about my work too, but nothing crazy."

"Did you get his number at least?" Lisa asked.

Presley laughed and rolled her head back. "No! You two are crazy.

I'm sure he was just being polite because we ran into each other on the trail. I also know for a fact he and I don't have the same… values… I guess you'd call it, when it comes to relationships. So, I will admit," she laughed at herself. "It was quite the treat to spend a bit of time with him this morning just chatting and laughing, but I sincerely doubt it's anything more than that. I'm sure when he finds out I'm a little square, modest, prude, who hasn't slept into the double digits, he's going to find someone else that is more open to the fling-type things."

"Hell, I'd be thinking about re-aligning my values if that opportunity presented itself to me." Lisa laughed.

"First off, what the fuck, babe?" Jake looked at his wife with his palms up. "But secondly, same, Pres, same." His nodding duck face looked at Presley.

They all laughed.

"I never said I don't think he's extremely good looking." She giggled. "I'm just saying, I don't have the heart that can just let go like that." She looked down at her wine glass. "So, while I see the appeal of re-aligning my values," she mocked. "I don't know if that's a good idea for me."

"We know, Pres." Lisa reached over and rubbed Presley's leg as she was sitting crisscross applesauce on the couch next to her. "We also just want you to be happy, so, rather than just simply 'ride that Hollywood D' like my crude husband would suggest." Lisa was sure to shoot Jake a friendly roll of her eyes. "Maybe just keep your mind and your heart open to the possibility that it's different."

Presley didn't respond, she just took another sip of her wine.

"Yeah," Jake jumped in. "They're going to be there anyway, if he pursues you to hang out, no harm in that? Stay true to you and you'll find out if that's all he's after pretty quickly."

Presley smiled, thinking about how fine Trent looked in-person. It was one thing to see him on the big screen with makeup, filters, and whatever else they did for movie editing, but in the flesh he was pretty flawless. And the way he engaged Baron was enough to make her heart melt, not to mention how easy he was to talk to.

"You guys are right," Presley admitted. "No harm in at least enjoying his company. He is actually pretty funny and so great to talk to."

"See," Lisa smiled at her. "Just go with the flow if it feels right, Pres. You'll know if it's not and you aren't obligated to give him anything."

Presley simply nodded her head before taking another sip of wine.

"But," Jake sat up straight and looked at Presley. "We want every last fucking detail as this develops!"

Presley just laughed at him, she truly had no idea where this would go, if it even went anywhere.

Five

Presley pulled up close to the door of her cottage when they got home the following night from their Seattle trip. She let Baron out who quickly bolted off into the trees.

"Bare!" She called out as it was dark and she hadn't left a porch light on at all. "Bare!" She called again until she heard his feet rustling through fallen branches and leaves. "Come here you, it's dark out and you've gotta keep me safe from the boogeyman."

Presley turned her phone's flashlight on to avoid tripping up to the cottage porch.

Her movements initiated a notification on Mike's phone, he quickly sat up and grabbed his phone from the nightstand to watch her approach her front door. *Shit!* He realized the position of the camera didn't allow him to see her typing in the door code to unlock the entrance. *Well, I'll be fixing that soon*, he rolled his eyes.

Mike watched her take three trips to gather everything from her car before she turned the porch light back off. He wasted no time in texting her when it appeared she was going to be in for the night.

> Hey Pres, wanna grab breakfast tomorrow?

PRESLEY
> Oh—thanks Mike, I just got home though. I'm so tired idk if I'll even set an alarm tomorrow lol

Presley set her phone down and then she paused, wondering how Mike even knew that she'd come home and would be in town for breakfast plans the next morning.

> Well, offer still stands if you change your mind in the morning, just lmk

> PRESLEY
> Thanks 🙂

✦

"Hey you!" Trent called out when he saw Presley on the trail. He had been running the same path as the previous couple of days hoping that she also took the same route in the mornings. He popped his ear buds out as he continued towards her.

Presley turned around smiling and then watched as Baron ran to Trent with a ball in his mouth.

Trent pat Baron on the head and then leaned down for the ball he dropped; he launched it beyond Presley and as Baron took chase Trent caught up with her.

"Good morning." She smiled at him with a cup of coffee in her hand.

He noticed she looked like she was taking a stroll more than any kind of fitness run. She was wearing her standard yoga pants that he'd mostly seen her in, but she was also wearing a knee-length hooded sweatshirt that she had unzipped exposing a very fitted cropped shirt, tennis shoes, and her hair was in a low messy bun covered by a ball cap. Even in her dressed down athletic look, Trent saw nothing but pure beauty.

"Good morning." Trent slowed his pace and instead matched Presley's once they were side by side. "I was really hoping to run into you today."

"Really?" She smiled up at him. He was just starting to form a pool of sweat on the chest of his blue t-shirt from his run. She noticed how the color of his shirt complimented his enticing eyes.

"Of course." He smiled at her. "I'm excited to see what we're going to learn about each other now since we know each other's deep dark secret about dryer lint." He laughed and used the bottom of his shirt to wipe his forehead.

Presley tried not to stare or look at all when he exposed his abs, she knew they were dreamy and didn't want to be caught staring. Averting her eyes didn't hide the blush forming on her cheeks, or the millisecond she bit her lower lip before she caught herself. Presley collected her face and joined in his laughter turning her attention to Baron who was running at full speed towards them with his ball.

"Well, what're you trying to share with me today?" She smiled at him.

"Hmmmm," he held the scruff on his chin. "We've covered deep dark fears, let's go light this time, how about favorites?"

"Like favorite what?" She smiled just before taking a sip of her coffee.

Trent threw Baron's ball. "How 'bout favorite actors?" He smirked.

Without a second passing Presley answered. "Obviously, Pete Winters." She couldn't keep her composure, so she cracked up and looked at Trent's reaction.

His face wanted to smile but he fought it, *damn*, he thought, *she's perfect*, his smile finally won and took over his face.

"I'm kidding." She kept laughing.

"It's okay." He shrugged. "You can just admit it's me, you don't have to be embarrassed that you have such great taste." He assured her.

Presley gave her eyes a hard, dramatic roll. "Aren't you Mr. Confident?" She playfully grinned up at him.

Trent didn't respond right away, he bit his bottom lip and looked into Presley's eyes. "I used to think so." He continued to hold her gaze until Baron broke things up when he barked. He had dropped the ball, and no one was picking it up to throw it again. Trent appeased him and gave it another toss. "So," he started again. "How was Seattle?"

Presley took a deep breath through her nose. "It was really good, actually." She smiled and nodded her head. "Not only did I get a lot of work done, but I got to spend some time with my best friend and her family too—always so good catching up with them."

"Oh?" Trent looked surprised.

"What?" While her tone was light, Presley had no issue in calling him out.

"I just didn't realize your best friend was in Seattle." He let out a halfhearted laugh and decided to take her temperature on the topic of Mike. "I thought maybe Mike was your bff." Trent bent down for Baron's ball.

Presley chuckled quickly through her nose and looked down. "No." She shook her head. "Mike's just a friend." She confirmed and decided not to spend any more time talking about him. "Lisa Hofner is my bestie for the restie." Her smiling eyes met his. "We've been that way since middle school."

Trent was anything but sad to hear Mike wasn't holding down that number one spot. The fact that Presley declared him to be just a *friend* was all he needed to hear though, Mike wasn't exactly a topic he wanted to dwell on. "That's gotta suck that she lives so far away though, huh?"

Presley was just swallowing another sip before she replied. "We make it work. We're really only a couple hours apart. And they come to visit here often too, so really it could be way worse." She admitted and then looked up at Trent who was just tossing Baron's ball again. "What about you? Do you have a bestie?"

Trent inhaled deeply. "Not really." He kicked a rock as he let his breath out. "I'm a bit of a lone wolf I guess."

Presley wasn't sure how far she could push him, she figured now was as good a time as any. "Lone, huh? I feel like that's *not* how I'd describe you." She started to chuckle so she hid that behind her coffee cup.

"Oh yeah?" Trent perked an eyebrow with his hands in his pockets. "How would you describe me then?"

"Well, sissy for one." She didn't miss a beat as she shot a quick smirk at him and continued. "What kind of action hero is afraid of a little dryer lint?"

Trent leaned back and buckled his knees laughing as he looked up.

"You know what?" He paused and looked at her. "I'm going to overcome that fear, just for you, Presley."

She loved the sound of his voice speaking her name. "You do that, and you'll be my perma-hero until forever." She laughed.

"I wouldn't mind that." Trent gave her a flirtatious smile.

Presley looked back up at him, she wanted to be very cautious about developing any feelings for him, but he was making it extremely difficult. She decided not to pursue the conversation anymore, she simply smiled back at him and then looked for Baron who had jumped in the lake after a small raft of ducks.

"Bare!" She called out to make sure he wasn't going to swim out too far or end up grabbing a duck.

Trent watched Presley walk down to the bank, she called out to Baron again before he grunted and paddled his way back to the shore, he was sure to shake off right next to Presley.

"Ew, you punk." She laughed and covered the top of her coffee cup. Baron jumped right back into the water so Presley gave up, the ducks were far enough away now, and Baron would find his way back to her.

"The last thing I want is him grabbing one of those poor ducks." She looked up at Trent with a giddy, animal loving smile on her face. "Did you see how stinking cute those little ducklings are?"

"I did." He smiled at the reality of her. He wanted very much to reach out to her, sweep the loose piece of hair behind her ear, rub her shoulder, hold her hand, anything; but something stopped him. Navigating himself around Presley felt different, he suddenly became very aware that everything he said and did mattered, he had to be genuine, or he'd lose any connection to her. He noticed he had just been staring at her for probably far too long, so he started the conversation again. "Are you working today?" Trent asked.

Presley lightly chuckled as she was back on the trail and matching Trent's pace. "I work every day."

"I mean like head down, can't have fun, in the office kind of working?" He clarified.

"Well, I haven't fully committed to anything today." She shrugged.

"I've got a conference call at 11, but I don't have to be in the office for that. I'd super love to stay in lazy pants all day." She admitted and kicked her foot out to point down to her yoga pants.

"Aren't you the boss?" He shrugged, trying to convince her to do whatever she wanted.

"I mean I am, but that just puts most of the responsibility on me," she pointed out. "Not that working from home in comfy clothes makes me a slacker or anything, I'm just sayin', the boss should set the best example."

"You're not wrong," he agreed. "So," Trent skipped a rock out onto the lake. "How did a pretty young thing like you end up as the President and CEO of a logging and lumber company?"

Presley laughed, she rolled her head, and it fell towards the trail. She was flattered by the compliment he slid in there. "What, like I'm the only one?"

"C'mon, no way you came home from kindergarten talking about how you wanted to chop down trees for a living."

"We happen to plant a lot of trees too, thank you very much." She sipped her coffee and took a slight hit from Baron as he ran by her to jump into the lake again. "But it's been the family business since the dawn of time, so my Paps pretty much primed me for this position." She shook her head, aside from Lisa and her therapist she hadn't talked much about her family and the tragedy that rattled throughout her childhood. She wasn't really sure how deep she wanted to dive into this conversation with Trent. They had both seemingly enjoyed each other's company and that conversation would definitely bring a storm cloud over the mood.

"He wanted to spend his golden years retired without worries of the company being taken over by some random bum then, huh? He put it in the hands of someone capable and trustworthy?" Trent asked, trying to learn more about her.

"Well." Presley swallowed hard and quickly turned her head to look out to the lake before delivering her next line. "He didn't get to do that since he passed away two years ago next month." She turned her head back towards the trail and immediately looked down. She stopped her story until she could suppress her tears.

"Pres." Trent took a step towards her. "I'm really sorry, I didn't mean to bring up…"

"No," she shook her head. "It's really okay, like you didn't know, it's okay, I'm not upset, it's okay." At this point she was reassuring herself more so than she was reassuring Trent.

He finally reached out and squeezed her shoulder a couple of times to let her know he was still there, and she could take whatever time she needed.

His touch didn't weigh heavy on her at all; in fact, she felt a slight surge of comfort from it. She located a picture of her sweet grandpa in her mind and filled her heart with joy instead of sadness before she looked at Trent again. "My Paps kind of raised me, well from about 13 or so anyway and before that he was always around. I mean I'd always lived here with him too, never knew life without him until recently." She had to pause again, she took a break from looking at Trent so she could try and gather herself a little more. She swallowed a little lump in her throat as she continued to walk. "So, it's just been really tough losing him and now taking on the company without him to consult with every 2.5 seconds when I'm sure I'm in way over my head." She kind of laughed. "Fake it til you make it, right?" She finally lifted her head again and this time tried to smile up at Trent.

He returned a flat smile to her and rubbed her shoulder. "I'm sure you're doing an amazing job, Pres; and I'm sure your Paps would be proud of you."

"Thank you." She took the opportunity to spill a little more to him, he seemed sincere and if she was being honest with herself it was refreshing to talk to him, plus they weren't even halfway through the walking trail. "He gave me so much knowledge when he was here, I just wouldn't ever want to let him down, I think that's partially why I've just thrown myself into work so much. It's kind of a lot of pressure to carry it all on. My Pap's Grandpa was the real OG." She smiled from under her ball cap. "He's the one who started tearing all the forests down around here, passed it to his son and his son and so on." She was rolling her hands along to animate her story before she looked up at him. "Then there was me," she shrugged.

"So, no siblings for you, huh?" He was building her family tree in his head.

"Nope." She shook her head. "You talk about being a lone wolf, well, here's my story in a nutshell." She checked on Baron over her shoulder and then began. "My grandma passed away giving birth to my dad, so he's an only child. I was born to my mom and dad, and then my mom I guess had enough one day and she just up and left us when I was like four; so it was just me, dad and Paps. Then the summer going into my eighth-grade year my dad had a heart attack and it was just me and Paps. That's kind of when I knew Lisa was going to be a friend for life too. And then almost two years ago my Paps was just out working at the mill, he got his hands dirty from time to time, and he fainted and never woke up. They thought it was a stroke."

"Pres." Trent was practically lost for words, he watched her as she looked down and just continued to walk along the dirt path. "Pres." He held her shoulder and gently slowed her down. "I'm so sorry, I really didn't mean to open all those wounds up."

Trent could tell she was sad and all he wanted to do was comfort her, he hesitantly stepped towards Presley, he spun her shoulder towards him and without another thought he wrapped her up in his arms. He held her firmly and didn't rock or kiss her, he just held her tightly and hoped she could find some comfort within his embrace.

Presley took a deep breath, his strong hold on her was the most comforting thing she had felt in a very long time. Her head was resting snuggly on his firm chest, near the sweat she had noticed forming earlier and it didn't even bother her. She could smell his freshly laundered clothing, but also picked up on what was either his soap or his deodorant giving off a crisp masculine scent with a hint of cedarwood. His hug had caught her by surprise, so her arms were pinned in between their bodies holding her coffee cup; she didn't mind. Trent was providing a feeling she didn't even realize she needed until that moment, she never wanted him to let her go so she closed her eyes. It felt like an eternity had passed when Baron came charging out of the water, he ran to Presley's side and let out a deep groan, unsure of the situation he sat next to her. Trent squeezed her one last time and then slowly backed away, he checked Baron and then looked at Presley.

"Pres, you alright?" He held both of her shoulders.

She nodded her head and gave Baron a reassuring smile. "It's okay." She nodded her head with more surety this time. "Thank you, Trent." She looked up into his eyes.

He watched her bright but now sad green eyes meet his from under the bill of her ball cap. "Of course," he rubbed her shoulder. "Do you want to keep walking?"

She smiled at him and nodded her head, so Trent rubbed her shoulders one last time before letting go.

They took a couple dozen steps in silence before Presley spoke up. "Sorry, you suggested going light today and I just dropped the heavy all over you." She flung her hand around.

"Oh." Trent furrowed his brow and flexed his arm. "I lift," he slapped his bicep. "So, it's alright, I can handle heavy things." He offered her an assuring smile.

It made Presley laugh. "Thank you." She looked down and then up at him, her eyes a little less sad this time. "Seriously, I appreciate you."

Trent wasn't sure what to say, or do, typically he may consider progressing the hug he just gave her. Presley had a different kind of hold on him though, he realized he actually wanted to get to know her and for the first time since he could remember, he didn't want to simply 'hit it and quit it' like Pete suggested.

"Of course, Pres." He gave her a reassuring smile.

She returned the gesture and tried to steer the conversation from her story. "Let's talk about your family." Presley suggested.

"Well." Trent bent his elbows and reached his hands up behind his head to stretch before he continued. "When I said lone wolf, I guess I wasn't referring to my crazy family." His arms came down and he exhaled a slight chuckle.

"So, your family's huge?" Presley guessed and looked up at him from her coffee cup.

"I suppose." He smiled. "I've got four siblings and I'm one of twenty-four grandkids."

"What?!" Presley whipped her head towards him. "So, you've got just a few more family members than I do." She chuckled.

"A couple." he nodded his head in agreement and walked alongside her, filling her in on his family antics.

"So, wait, your whole family lives in southern California then too?" Presley was listening along to his stories and started to realize his family was not only fairly tight knit, but they all seemed to live close to one another.

Trent nodded his head. "Yep, my parents and all my siblings live within a fourteen-mile radius of one another."

"That must be so nice." Presley imagined what it would be like to have a large family like that and be able to be so close. "Do you live within that little bubble of Hayes' too?" She asked.

For the first time Trent felt almost embarrassed to admit his living situation. "Well." He scratched his head. "I guess since you didn't judge me about the dryer lint, I'll try this one out." He smiled at her. "I am a very capable and responsible thirty-two-year-old man, who is also steadily employed, socially capable, and obviously ridiculously good looking." He rubbed his chest and let out a large exhale. "But, technically speaking, I do live with my parents." He looked at her and waited for her response.

"Really?" Presley was genuinely surprised. "I honestly thought you were going to tell me your beach house was just outside the family circle, you've got a penthouse in New York, a ranch in Texas, and just for good measure a vacation home in Greece or something." She shook her head laughing. "I was way off on my guessing game."

Trent laughed out loud at her. "What made you think I have all kinds of homes?"

Presley shrugged. "I don't know, just seems like if you're always on different sets that it would be easier to just have multiple homes? Like bounce around to the ones that are closest or something?" She laughed at herself. "Ignore me, I have no clue what it's like to live the life of a celebrity," she admitted. "But I am genuinely shocked you live with your parents." She looked up at him and then quickly clarified. "Not like in a bad way at all, I just figured you may enjoy your privacy and such."

"Well, I did have my own house. It's not like I've never lived on my own." He wanted to be sure she knew at least that much. Trent smirked down at her, even if she wasn't looking up at him. "And it was right on the beach," he confirmed. "But I was really never there. I've been so busy these last few years with work, I honestly wasn't even staying at my house for more than a night or two here and there. It really didn't make sense to have it, so I sold it a couple years ago. I asked my parents about just staying with them while I looked for a new place and basically, I just never moved from there. I figured I'd make an honest effort at looking for a house once work settled a bit, but it's been nonstop for a few years." He rolled his head. "Not that I'm complaining, it's great getting to be on so many projects, it just doesn't really afford me any significant breaks though. So, I'm not usually home for long periods. Living with them just really works and of course my mom is over the moon because anytime I'm home, she gets to see me because I live right down the hall." He laughed thinking about how much his mom struggled with the fact that she loved having him there but also ached for him to settle down. "Not sure she'd have it any other way right now."

"I mean, I would have been living with my Paps until forever." Presley shrugged. "That's why there are two masters in the house." She looked up at Trent. "So, while I'm surprised, I also totally understand wanting to be that close with family." She waited half a second. "Plus, I'm sure your mom is a dryer lint slayer."

They both laughed, but Trent cut in. "Hey, I'm not like your regular guy who still lives at home, I do my own laundry when I'm there." He clarified with his dashing white smile. "Remember, I just have gloves and tongs to get rid of it on my own." He paused. "And honestly, I always leave the lint trap for my mom to clean anyway," he fully admitted. "The gloves and tongs are for show… Or when I have a lot of laundry I have to do."

Presley laughed; she loved seeing Trent like this. He was nothing like what Hollywood made him out to be. The only things she ever saw, besides the typical trailers for his movies, were stories of Trent and his flavor of the week. She wondered how much of this he had shared with other girls, or if this was him just trying to be relatable as a way of getting into bed, as her mind wandered she couldn't help but feel all of those worries were completely ridiculous given how she felt when she was with him.

"So." Presley looked up as they were rounding the final trail before they reached the edge of the lawn. "Do you already have other projects lined up after this one?"

Trent bobbed his head along to confirm. "I have one set I'll have to be on, it's only two weeks in London and then we get to film the rest in California. But I'll also be juggling that filming with promoting another I wrapped up several months ago. So, basically running around everywhere until the end of the calendar year at the very least. After that though, I haven't selected another script, I have three I'm supposed to be reading through."

"Yikes." Presley thought about how tiring that must be. "I always feel like I'm busy, but really my traveling is pretty limited, that has to be exhausting."

Trent took a deep breath. "It is." He grabbed Baron's ball and tossed it down the trail, not as far this time since he finally seemed to be slowing down. "But with this industry I just keep having everyone in my ear about how important it is to stay relevant and cash in while you're 'it'." He patted Baron on the head when he came back with the ball but held onto it in his mouth. "Plus, I'm not sure what I would do without work right now, it's kinda become my identity." He grunted out a small chuckle. "I do appreciate being able to do what I do, so it suits me for now." He settled on with a shrug of his shoulders.

Presley felt something almost like pain in his voice, like Trent was looking for an excuse not to just be the 'Hollywood Hunk' everyone saw

58

him as; she genuinely felt for him at that seemingly vulnerable moment. "I totally understand being consumed with work." Presley agreed, she paused for a long moment before she started again. "Okay, so I'm not trying to like tell you what to do." Presley held her hand up. "But I will say that slowing down has some massive healing powers for exhaustion. So, maybe you don't have to take huge breaks if you feel that will hurt your career, but find things that will provide you with a slow moment in life, ya know? I'll be the first to admit, I don't take breaks. I'm the worst and the last time I took a vacation to unplug was like six years ago."

"What?" Trent was shocked.

"I know." Presley winced. "I just honestly love home, not really sure where I'd even want to go, and I certainly don't want to travel alone… and truly, work is a lot. So, with all of that, I just find things that slow me down around here. Like the lake." She pointed out to it as they were now walking across the lawn towards the dock. "I don't always bring my phone on our walks, so I get to just slow down and be unplugged."

"Honestly, just being here in your town has helped me slow down a bit. I mean, I know I'm working and all, but this place has been so revitalizing." Trent admitted.

Presley smiled up at him. "I'm glad you've liked it so far—it is quite special here."

"Am I interrupting your slow moments by joining your walks?" Trent asked.

Presley reached for his forearm and lightly held it. "Oh my gosh, of course not." She assured him before taking her hand back. "Honestly." She only held back for a split second before continuing with her genuine sentiment. "You are a very welcome addition to our super exclusive morning trail club." She smiled.

Trent fondly nodded his head. "Good, because I was trying to join again tomorrow." He tried to catch her eyes as he smiled. "As long as you aren't just using me to entertain Baron, that is." He teased her with a wink of his amazing blue eyes.

Presley gently tugged on the bill of her hat and laughed. "I mean, that's the primary reason, obviously." She turned on the ball of her foot towards him and held his forearm again which he loved. "But secondary to that, I have legitimately enjoyed chatting with you."

"Me too." Trent caught and held her gaze. "So, I'll be here." He reached for her hand and gently rubbed it. "Same time tomorrow, Pres?"

She blushed and confirmed with her head just before he let go and walked up the lawn. She watched him for a few steps and got caught staring when he turned around. "Have a good day at work." he waved.

"Thank you, you too," she waved back.

Six

Mike was getting ready for his shift, he had his clothes laid out and was about to get showered. His mom had just left for a few errands, so he decided to go down to his basement before starting his morning routine. There was a combination lock on the door to his basement and a chain to lock himself in once he was on the stairs. He walked down the rickety wooden stairs and pulled an old cord to turn a fluorescent light on. Mike rotated a load of laundry and leaned back against the dryer while checking his phone. He figured Presley may be coming back from her morning walk soon and he wanted to catch a glimpse of her before work. Since he didn't see any movement, he took a key out of his pocket and made his way to a locked room in the basement.

In his secured room, there was a single, leather reclining chair set up on a light-colored oriental rug facing a television; he sat in his chair and looked around at the sanctum he had created over years of collecting. The walls were plastered in pictures of Presley, many of which looked like surveillance photos. There were hundreds of them where she wasn't smiling at, or even aware of, the camera—particularly the pictures of her laying out by her lake. He had an infinite number of pictures from high school to present. Mike's pride and joy was a photo of he and Presley in their bathing suits, the picture was very clearly cropped as it was originally a group of people posing on a boat.

Mike looked around and took a deep breath, besides anytime he spent with Presley, this was his favorite place to be. He had known

Presley since he could remember, in fact, he didn't have any memory of a childhood without her. They shared the same classes throughout elementary school and were even on the same tee ball and soccer teams for a couple of seasons. Mike acknowledged that Jake had always been Presley's best friend back then, but he also watched how welcoming and kind she was to everyone at school. She was like a burst of sunshine every time he saw her, she was always smiling or laughing. Presley was also the one to include everyone when they were playing at recess, and her sharing heart was constantly looking for ways to help whether it was splitting her lunch with anyone who may have forgotten theirs or letting everyone use her box of crayons since she always seemed to have the largest selection. Mike even remembered a few times when Presley intentionally pushed her spelling test towards him to copy, knowing full well Mike always struggled with his letters.

He could pinpoint the first time his fondness of her transitioned from watching her with friendly eyes to the infatuated ones that had developed over the last sixteen years. Mike hadn't been brave enough to ask Presley to the sixth grade Valentine's Day dance, but he could still clearly visualize Presley walking into the gym with Jake that night. She was in a blush pink dress that draped just below her knees with spaghetti straps. Jake's mom had helped Presley with her hair. Mike couldn't recall ever seeing Presley's hair curled before that night; half of it was clipped back with a heart shaped barrette and that was the moment Mike felt his body project him into puberty… And the night he decided he would spend his life with Presley.

Since that night Mike had made it a mission to keep her close until they could be together. Life had separated them from time to time, but he knew they'd always end up finding their way together. Mike was convinced he had been aligning everything for them over the last couple of years and this was going to be his year to solidify what had been initiated back at that dance when they were kids.

He leaned down and picked up a box that was next to his reclining chair, inside the cardboard box were various trinkets he had managed to obtain. He sifted through to find his favorite bathing suit bottoms of

Presley's that he remembered plucking off the clothing line on a group camping trip their senior year. She had three different suits that trip so he figured she would get over having lost one pair of bottoms. He reclined his chair as he held the bottoms over his nose. Once he was reclined, he rubbed them on the front of his pants. Mike's eyes found a poster sized picture on the far wall of Presley lying on a beach in Cabo in her swimming suit. He had taken that photo from Jake's Facebook page from a trip she took with him and Lisa. It didn't take him long to pull his sweats down and grab a bottle of lotion from the side of his recliner.

Seven

There were a couple weeks of scheduled nighttime shoots and the time they'd be filming at Presley's was dwindling with each passing day. Trent had been enjoying their unofficial routine morning walks around the lake. While he learned a little more about Presley each day, and had yet to find anything about her he didn't like, he genuinely craved more. In addition to his steadily increasing interest in her, Trent felt relaxed enough to truly be himself around Presley—something he wasn't able to do with anyone aside from his immediate family. So, while he loved their walks, they weren't enough; he wanted to establish something more official with her. He made his way to the set even earlier than normal that day and his biggest hope in going over there was that she was home, secondary to that was that Mike wasn't around.

Trent walked through the main house and out onto the back patio to look for Presley. He immediately noticed her sitting on the end of the wooden dock with Baron lying beside her soaking up the sun. It made him smile and he didn't hesitate to continue towards them. He could feel his nerves building as he crossed the lawn.

Baron lifted his head once Trent stepped on the dock; he slapped his tail in recognition before he hopped up to greet him. Fortunately for Trent the dock was pretty long, he had at least another thirty feet for his nerves to settle before he reached Presley. She didn't react to Baron getting up, she was focused on her laptop. Trent reached down and pet Baron but only briefly because the pit bull excitedly made his way back to Presley. He shoved his face under her arm while she was typing and nearly knocked her laptop into the lake.

"Bare!" Her reflexes saved the laptop from taking a dip. "You nut, why'd you do that?" She pulled her laptop to the right of her and let him continue sliding under her left arm. She kissed the top of his jubilant head before he bathed the side of her face in kisses. Presley pushed away from him pretty soon after he started, and she wiped her face. "Your breath is dang stinky, homey!" Her chuckle was a mix of disgust and adoration for her lovable dog.

Trent laughed under his breath and decided it was time for him to make his presence known to her.

"Sorry, he's probably just tattling that I was sneaking up on you guys." Trent was just steps away from her now.

Presley jumped slightly when she heard his voice. "Hey, Trent." She smiled and turned around, battling Baron who was trying to get on her lap now. Presley was finally able to push his foot off of her thigh and scurry out of range from any more Baron kisses. She stood up and turned to face Trent. "Hi." She giggled at her struggles.

"Hey, sorry, I didn't mean to get him all excited." Trent tried to stifle his own chuckling.

"Oh, no, he's a goof, it's fine." She ruffled the top of Baron's head. "Shoot, I must've looked at the wrong schedule. I didn't think you guys were filming until a bit later today, I better get packed up." She noticed the bouquet of flowers Trent was holding but suddenly felt almost embarrassed. So, she tried to avoid staring at them and instead knelt down to pick her laptop up.

He waited until she looked at him again. "We aren't, I wanted to come by early." He inadvertently looked down at the flowers he had brought before extending the bouquet to her. "These are for you, Pres."

"Trent, these are beautiful." Presley wasn't exaggerating, the over-sized bouquet was colorful, and she counted at least ten different types of flowers at first glance. "This is really sweet of you, thank you." She looked up at him and decided to hug him. Not only did she want to hug him, but she also found it to be a good tactic for hiding her flattered face that was turning pink.

Trent welcomed her embrace and took in the sweet scent of her hair while she was briefly against his chest.

"You're welcome." He responded as she was slowly backing away from their hug. "Do you have work to finish right now?"

She began shaking her head from side to side. "Nope, everything I have will be here for a while."

"I was thinking we should go do something together soon, you know, something where it's not just saying hi while in passing." He threw his hands up smiling. "Don't get me wrong, I have *thoroughly* enjoyed our morning walks." He wanted to make it very clear to her. "And I hope I can still spend that time with you too."

Presley blushed and looked down at the flowers before she could answer him. "Me too." She nodded her head along. "So, I think maybe you're on to something." She tried to hide the smirk that was sneaking up on her, but her eyes gave it away.

Her giddiness made Trent smile. "Would you like to spend some time together this Saturday? I noticed there's an annual festival this weekend, something about logger games?"

Presley giggled and finally smiled up at him, she loved the simplicity he flashed every now and again. He had his Hollywood persona, but she really enjoyed the funny, and down-to-earth guy she had gotten to know more about over the last couple of weeks.

"I'm sure you've been to it a trillion times or more, but I thought maybe you wouldn't mind showing me how to fully enjoy the logging games." He smiled in anticipation of her answer.

"I'd love to, that sounds like a lot of fun." She bit her bottom lip. "It's called the Mason Loggers Jubilee, officially, but the cool kids just call it the Jubilee." She smiled.

Trent looked genuinely excited that she accepted. "I certainly want to be a cool kid, so what time should we plan to be at the Jubilee?"

"Is nine too early to meet?" Presley asked.

"Not at all, we actually have the day off, which is so rare. Why don't I come pick you up?" Trent offered.

"That's sweet." She blushed. "So, just meet me here at nine Saturday?"

"Sounds like a plan to me," he agreed. "Is there a dress code so I don't show up looking like a Jubilee rookie?"

"Not at all," Presley assured him. "It's supposed to be hot as Hades Saturday though, so there's that." She continued along. "Oh, and it's basically in a bit of a rural area so no cement really, you'll want some shoes that you don't mind walking in grass, dirt, and gravel with. It's definitely not a black-tie affair."

"Oh, so leave my heels at home?" He teased.

"I'll seriously have to reconsider going with you if you show up in heels," she laughed.

Trent bit his bottom lip. "That's reason enough for me not to wear them." He smiled and glanced at the flowers she was fondly clinging to. "I can't wait… I guess I'll let you get back to work though." Trent offered a gentle rub of Presley's shoulder before he turned around.

Presley let Trent get about two steps in the opposite direction before she called out to him. "Trent?" She waited for him to turn around. "I do have time for a walk." She tilted her head to the side with her glowing face. "I mean, if you want."

Trent smiled. "You know I'd love to."

✦

Presley texted Lisa the very second she was back in the cottage, alone with Baron.

> Your bestie for the restie has a date Saturday 🙈💕

"Girl!" Lisa immediately called her and was shrieking into the phone. "Shut up! Please tell me you're talking about Trent Hayes?!" She didn't even let Presley respond before she continued along in increasing pitch and speed. "I am literally walking into a meeting, so I have like 2.5 seconds but oh my gosh, are you for real?!"

Presley laughed. "Well, I won't keep you, but yes! Trent just came by the house. Lis, he brought me flowers and asked if I'd go to the Jubilee with him this Saturday."

"Oh shit!" Her voice was muffled now but still filled with excitement. "Pres, I can't even!! I'll call you after work today, okay?"

"Okay," she laughed. "Love you girl."

"Oh my gosh, love you too!"

Eight

"Good morning." Trent greeted Presley as he stepped out of his rental Tahoe just before nine that morning.

Presley was walking towards the garage, pulling a wagon. "Good morning." She excitedly waved.

"Here, let me help you with that." Trent jogged over and took the wagon from her.

"Thank you." She turned around, presumably looking for Baron since Trent hadn't seen him yet.

He gave her a once over because she looked like an absolute doll. "You look beautiful," he smiled.

Presley laughed and did a quick spin. "You like my weekend hick-wear?"

She was in a pair of cut-off jean shorts with a form-fitting white top and an unbuttoned blue and black flannel which she completed with black platform, low-top Chucks. Her hair was pinned up with a white claw clip and a pair of gold rimmed Aviator sunglasses were sitting on top of her head.

Trent loved the effortless look of her beauty. "I do," he confirmed. "Very much so."

Presley blushed and Baron came scampering by. He had been going too fast to be able to greet Trent, so he made a wide turn to come back around. He passed him to dip his head into the wagon and grab his ball which he dropped at Trent's feet.

"I don't get a greeting? Just a demand to throw the ball?" Trent lightly scolded the excited pit bull but catered to his request, holding Baron's ball up in one hand and reaching his other out to him. "At least dab it?" Baron slapped Trent's fist with his paw before waiting in anxious anticipation for him to throw it.

Presley laughed when Baron took off. "He's trained you so well."

Trent smiled and kept walking towards his truck.

"Trent," Presley stopped him. "I was actually going to see if you wanted to park in the garage, we usually take the truck to the Jubilee."

"Oh." He locked the Tahoe. "Sure, Pres, I don't want to squash tradition," he smiled. "We can just leave this parked out here though."

They walked over to a man door on the side of the garage and Presley keyed in a code, she hit another set of numbers and Trent could hear one of the bay doors opening as well.

Trent had already seen Presley's G Wagon, but as he looked around the garage, he noticed she also had a 1960s cherry red Mustang and in front of the bay door that was opening was an absolute unicorn.

"Are you kidding me?! Pres, this truck is sick!" Trent touched the fenders and admired the classic. "What year?"

She smiled and opened the tailgate. "It's a 1930 Model AA." She watched as he inspected and gawked at the truck. "It was my Great Grandpa's—there's a guy in town who keeps it up for me too."

"I can't believe you take it out! I'd waste something like this keeping it couped up in a garage."

"She gets out at least once a year, the Jubilee ya know." She rolled her head around. "Weather permitting, of course, I don't bring her out in the rain."

Presley grabbed the small cooler out of the wagon to set in the bed of the truck, Trent stopped his gawking to pick the entire wagon up and set it in the truck.

"Thank you," Presley giggled and tried not to linger on the thought of how Trent's muscles weren't just for show.

"Packing for a full day, huh?" He smiled at her. "I wish I would have asked, I could have brought stuff."

She swished her hand around. "Oh, most of this is Baron's," she laughed. "He's a bit of a diva." She reached down and scratched the top of his head. "Are you okay with hanging for a while, or do you have a time you want to be back?"

"Absolutely down for whatever," he established with an edge of excitement in his voice. "I was hoping to spend some time with you, so if this becomes an all-day date, then perfect."

Presley blushed at the word date. It wasn't as if he hadn't made it very apparent that that's what they were going on; he showed up with flowers to ask her and was planning to pick her up, of course she knew it was a date. Hearing the words from his mouth just hit different.

"Well, since you left the heels home and all, I guess I'll still go with you." She fondly gestured at the Vans he was wearing.

Trent reached out and rubbed her shoulder. Presley enjoyed his touch, it was comforting, protective, and intoxicating all at the same time. He shut the tailgate for her before turning to continue admiring the truck.

Presley could see the love of cars in his eyes when he looked at the mint condition classic. "Do you want to drive her?" She held the key out.

His eyes went wide. "I couldn't." He shook his head. "No way," he chuckled.

"C'mon." She got in through the passenger's side and dangled the keys. "Plus, if this is a date, you should be driving me, right?" She smirked, waiting for him to get in and take the driver's seat.

Trent got in and looked like a kid with his giddy smile.

"You're sure?" He asked as he took the keys.

"Absolutely," she smiled. "I mean, you *can* drive a manual, right?"

"You've seen all my movies," he offered a sly grin as he turned the key in the ignition. "So, I know you've seen me drive."

Presley rolled her eyes laughing as Baron settled himself across her lap as best he could. "I thought maybe that was your stunt double doing all the driving."

"A guy like me doesn't need a stunt double." He confidently replied as he put the truck in gear and headed out of the garage. "I am a guy who needs directions though," he admitted with a smile as they were driving along the nearly mile-long driveway.

"Take a left onto the highway at the end of the drive, tough guy." She rolled her eyes smiling back at him.

Trent laughed and followed her directions.

"You can feel free to stretch her legs, she's got some giddy-up to her still," she assured him.

"You're sure? You don't want me to be driving Ms. Daisy right now?"

"I mean, don't be straight up reckless." She laughed and pushed Baron's foot off of her exposed thigh as he was trying to get to the open window. "But you can use the speed limit as a bit of a suggestion." She shrugged and ended up sliding closer to him on the bench seat so Baron could fully enjoy the window.

Trent gave her a sly smirk before he changed gears and gradually hit the gas to cruise down the highway. Presley dropped her sunglasses down and rubbed Baron's back. The wind blowing through the cab as Trent accelerated loosened a few pieces of Presley's hair. A loose piece ended up tickling Trent's ear; he turned to look at her and she was gazing out Baron's window as she nonchalantly tucked a few of the flying pieces of hair behind her ear. He wanted very badly to touch her, reach down to rest a hand on her leg, hold her hand, put his arm across her shoulders, or even kiss her; but he hesitated.

✦

They found parking in a large gravel field, Trent was grateful for the heads up about footwear, his Vans would be easily replaceable.

"Who knew such a small town would draw this kind of crowd?" Trent looked around at the thousands of patrons making their way around the festival.

"See," Presley shrugged. "That's why I was also sayin' the hat and sunglasses may help conceal your identity for the day." She shook her head, "I mean, you don't have to hide from people if you don't want to, I just wasn't sure if you wanted to be obvious and out in the open like that."

Trent lifted the wagon from the back of the truck and then he turned to Presley. "I just don't want any of our time together compromised." He reached for her hand, squeezed it and then winked before he pulled his sunglasses down. They were soon following Baron's lead towards the Jubilee.

"So, what are you going to dazzle me with first?" Trent smiled down at Presley.

"We always swing by the Lumberjack games schedule first to make sure we don't miss our favorite events."

"What's your favorite event?"

Presley looked up at Trent with a smile in her eyes. "I'm a sucker for a good birling," she admitted.

Trent laughed. "So, this is one reason why I acquired the expert for my first Jubilee; I have *no idea* what birling is."

Presley touched his forearm and giggled. "Okay, it's also called log-rolling to you city folk."

"See," he shrugged. "That's all you had to say, and I totally would have been on the same page." Trent ran his feet around as if he was on a spinning log in water.

Baron barked at his movement and danced around him until he stopped. "Alright buddy, I won't enter the *logrolling* contest then." He sarcastically rolled his eyes at Presley.

She overly exaggerated an eye roll herself before she continued. "Also, there's an epic fireworks show around 10 tonight, I don't know what time you were…," Presley stopped when Trent jumped in.

"We're going," he declared with a warm excitement in his voice. "I have to get the full experience to make my final determination on where this festival ranks. Plus, that gives us more time to spend together, which was the goal, you know." He tipped his sunglasses down to look Presley in her intense green eyes.

Presley blushed and bit her bottom lip before continuing. "If you're trying to get the *full* experience then we absolutely need to go get some fried food," Presley insisted. "And definitely wash it down with Mama Mabel's famous Arnold Palmers—you know she uses fresh squeezed lemonade and true sun-soaked tea?"

"Wow, that does sound pretty hick," he joked. "I mean pretty authentic," he laughed.

Presley giggled along but bumped into his shoulder slightly. They approached the event schedule, and it didn't take long for a small scene to develop.

"Oh my God!" A girl screeched. "You're Trent Hayes!" She bounced over to him. "It's you, isn't it?!"

The girl couldn't have been more than fifteen, she had on daisy duke shorts and a crop top. Her round, small sunglasses covered part of her face while her French braid pigtails flew around behind her during her approach. Trent was politely smiling as she arrived in front of him with two friends directly behind her.

"Hi," he waved.

She tapped her feet quickly and held her chest. "I *love* you! Oh my God, can I have a picture?!"

Trent chuckled. "Alright, but let's keep it down, I'm in disguise today."

The girl looked like she was about to explode. He didn't mind meeting fans, but he also didn't want to take time away from his date by posing for pictures and signing autographs all day.

She jumped up and down and made a zipping motion over her mouth. Her friends also wanted pictures, but they amused their friend and allowed her to take a few alone first.

"You ladies have a good day." Trent allowed her to hug him when she excitedly went back towards him with her arms out.

"Bye Trent!" They all feverishly waved and were immediately on their phones the second they turned around.

"Sorry." Trent rubbed Presley's exposed shoulder, now that she had taken her flannel off and tied it around her waist. Trent noticed how perfect the fitted white tank top was on her, it flattered her on every level, clinging to her like a second skin and tastefully showcased her chest. He also noticed a small tattoo poking out just barely to the left of her spine. It didn't look like it took up much of her back, but what he did see peeking over her tank top was what looked to be part of a white, feathered wing. He was interested to know more, but didn't mention it.

She bashfully noticed his hand resulting in pink cheeks when she finally looked up at him. "It's okay, I did find out that birling won't start for a couple of hours though, so we can go make our way through food and the market if you want?"

"I'll follow you." Trent slowly removed his hand from her shoulder, gently caressing her with the backs of his fingertips all the way down her arm.

His touch sent goosebumps down Presley's arm and back and she inadvertently let out a small, shy giggle that she hoped Trent missed.

"You're not on some kind of strict eating regimen right now, are you?" Presley looked back at Trent who had fallen a bit behind when Baron decided to switch which side of Presley he'd walk by.

"Not especially," he slowly admitted.

"So, dessert first," she decided. "How do you feel about deep-fried candy bars?"

"I'm down to try whatever you suggest." He assured her with a smile.

"Okay, let's go this way." She led them.

"Hi Presley!" An older woman was wiping her hands with a towel she had securely folded over her apron. "It's so good to see you, honey."

"Hi Joan." Presley leaned over the table and hugged her. "How are you?"

"Still kickin'," she laughed and looked at Trent. "And this," she raised her brows at Presley. "Who's this handsome, burly young man?"

Presley's bashful smile took a minute before she was able to look up at Trent. "Oh," she exhaled a small giggle.

"I'm Trent." He jumped in and held his hand out to Joan.

"Ohhhhh," she shook his hand and cocked her head at Presley. "Trent, huh? I didn't realize you had a gentleman friend?" Joan continued. "How great do the two of you look together?"

Presley's face turned a special kind of red and she tried not to look at Trent at all, unsure of what his reaction would be.

"Trent's never been to the Jubilee, I'm trying to get in the best of the best for him." Presley cut in before Joan could say anything else on that topic.

"So, you need the sweet sampler, I'll put it in one dish for you two." She winked and then turned around to prepare their dessert.

Presley tried to wipe the embarrassment until she saw Trent beaming and poorly attempting to hold back his laughter. She shot a sarcastically angry face at him until he rubbed her shoulders. Laughter took Trent over once Presley stuck her tongue out at him.

"You're a rude boy." She playfully shook her head before turning her back to him.

Trent didn't let her pout for long, he put his arms around her to hug her from behind. The embrace took her by surprise, but she absolutely loved it, it felt so natural. Trent rocked her a bit before letting her go when Joan asked her if they wanted chocolate and whipped cream on the side of their dessert.

While Joan was preparing their food Trent watched as Presley was a magnet for attention, it made him smile to think he was the celebrity to the rest of the world but here in Presley's corner of the globe everyone seemed to know her. She was all smiles and knew every single person's name that greeted her.

"Man, I'm feeling pretty invisible next to you." Trent leaned into her after a family had said their goodbyes.

"What?" She smiled up at him.

"*Everyone* is coming to say hi and I'm over here like chopped liver," he shrugged.

"Oh man, is someone jealous?" She bit her bottom lip.

"No." He furrowed his brow and puffed his chest out. "Trent Hayes doesn't get jealous."

"Oh," she laughed. My b." She rolled her eyes and turned to Joan who had their sampler ready. "Thanks so much, Joan!"

"Bye sweetie, you two enjoy," she winked.

"I'm just sayin' maybe you're the one who needs the hat and sunglasses," he smirked.

"You forget about this guy," she pointed to Baron. "He gives me away every time." Presley picked up the kabob looking dessert and dipped the end of the fried treat into the ramekin of hot fudge. "Here," she held it up to Trent to taste. "You get the first bite since you're the newbie."

Trent was surprised at every corner with her, she had confidence beyond his expectation, and he happily leaned toward her to try the delicious smelling treat.

"Oh my God." He felt a drop of chocolate on his mouth, so he wiped it and continued with his bite. "This is amazing," he declared after swallowing. "What is that?"

Presley examined his bite before answering. "Looks like a Milky Way," she smiled.

"You just keep showin' me the way around the food here and I think we're going to be just fine." He took another bite as she held the stick out again.

"Presley!" A sturdy voice called out.

Both Presley and Trent turned their heads to see Mike just a few yards away.

"Hey, Mike." Presley waved.

"I swung by your place; didn't realize you were already here." Mike gave Trent an accusatory once over.

"Yeah, we needed an early start since this is Trent's first time." She tried to ignore Mike's frigid demeanor towards Trent.

"You visited Joan already, huh? You need me to check the birling schedule?" Mike offered, mostly to show Trent how well he knew Presley.

"We stopped there already, got a couple hours." Presley smiled.

"Trent, where's Michelle?" Mike asked.

Trent gave him a puzzled look. "Uhh," he laughed. "I'm guessing off with Pete somewhere?"

"Huh," Mike nodded his head. "I thought the two of you had been spending lots of time together, I noticed you guys out to eat when Pres was in Seattle."

Trent laughed to himself; he knew exactly what Mike was trying to do. "Yeah, we all grabbed a bite at the pizza spot Pres suggested. They let me be the third wheel a lot," he gleaned back.

"Wait, they date?" Presley looked shocked. "TMZ sure isn't up on their Hollywood couples," she chuckled under her breath.

"They've got some catchin up to do, that's for sure." Trent took another bite of their shared dessert and made eyes with Mike. *Let's get that tape measure out, bro*, he thought to himself.

"Pres, where're we headed next?" Mike asked.

She looked at Trent quickly and then back at Mike, trying to mask her confusion. "Oh, uhm," she stumbled. "I think we were going to eat our way around here until birling." She shrugged. "And if we get full, maybe hit up the market."

"Great," Mike invited himself. "I'd love to get you some Mama Mabel's."

Trent laughed under his hat and continued walking along. "So, not on duty today, huh? You here with anyone, Officer Bando?"

Mike didn't answer, he simply glared at Trent and then forced a smile when Presley looked his way.

"Oh yeah, is your mom here?" She asked.

Mike shook his head. "It's going to be too hot for her today, she'd love to see you again soon though, so we'll have to make that happen."

"Yeah, we can do that." Presley picked up another fried treat and took a bite. "Oh man, try this one!" She smiled at Trent and held it out for him.

"Why's this one darker?" He hesitated.

"Just try it!" She cocked her head to the side and laughed.

Trent happily gave in and took a bite. "Holy shit." He rolled his eyes back. "That's delicious, is it brownie? Or is that Oreo?"

"It's both!" She bounced beside him and held it out again.

"Officer Bando," Trent wiped his face and swallowed his second bite before continuing. "Man, you want in on these?" He snickered at the thought of Mike biting the same dessert he was just eating from.

"I've had it before, thanks though." Mike narrowed his eyes at him and watched as Presley carelessly took a bite off the same one Trent just had in his mouth.

Trent bit into the lightest colored treat on the plate. "This tastes like chocolate chip cookie dough, try this one, Pres." He held it out to her, and she took a bite.

"Okay that one and the brownie Oreo are my faves, hands down."

Trent smiled at her glowing excitement. "Oh, for sure those ones are top tier," he agreed.

"Oh my gosh!" Presley quickly tried to swallow the second bite he offered. "Do you like corn dogs?!"

"Who *doesn't* like corn dogs?" Trent laughed.

"I don't." Mike chimed in.

"Oh, Mike," Presley joked. "You just don't like these ones because of who sells them."

Presley wasn't wrong, Mike didn't like the Grundley family because they were always somehow caught up on the wrong side of the law.

"What can I say?" Mike shrugged. "Can't trust people like that to make something I'm eating."

"Well," Trent took another bite. "Whatever you wanna eat, I'm game, Pres. This one," he pointed to their dessert, "is bomb. I trust your food choices."

"Corn dogs?" She smirked at Trent.

He nodded his head to confirm. "Corn dogs."

"I'll grab some Mama Mabel's." Mike offered.

"Thanks, Mike." Presley didn't look at him, she and Trent were headed to the Grundley's wagon.

Presley ordered three corn dogs so Baron could partake as well. "What do you put on yours?" She asked as she brought them to the condiment station.

"Mustard of course." He rolled his eyes and then smiled at her.

"Me too." She pumped the mustard into the corner of her tray. "I'm a dipper, not a spreader."

Trent laughed at her word choice but knew what she meant. "Me too." Trent smiled. "Can't be getting anything on my face and end up lookin' like a schmuck."

Presley laughed. "That's exactly why I dip."

"Are there two hotdogs in here, or what? These are fucking huge!" Trent bathed a portion of his tray in mustard.

"They dip them in batter, then crushed up corn flakes, then dip them in batter again before they're fried." Presley informed him.

"What?!" He looked at the corn dog again. "So, how is that family not morbidly obese? I can already tell this is going to be slappin', this is probably all I'd eat if I were them."

Presley giggled. "I'm telling you, small town folk know how to throw down in the kitchen."

✦

Typically, Mike was obsessed with Presley's smile, he couldn't get enough of it. Today, however, he was less than thrilled to watch her smiling with Trent. In Mike's eyes Trent had been nothing but a smug asshole since the first day they met. How dare he come in here and just think Presley was his, he probably went through women quicker than rolls of toilet paper. The last thing he wanted was Trent tainting Presley—she was his and he didn't want Trent touching her. And what was Presley's deal? She had been more or less single for the past two years; he only knew of a couple dates she'd even gone on in that time span. It all seemed wrong, and Mike had to figure out a way to slow them down because he didn't like where this could lead.

"Hey," Mike bumped the arm of a local high school girl; he recognized her as the student body president and from the homecoming court that year. "Did you see Trent Hayes is here?"

"What?!" Her eyes were as big as saucers and she looked around before tapping her girlfriends around her.

"Yeah," Mike peeked to be sure Presley and Trent weren't paying attention to him. "You know he's shooting a new movie at the Williams' grounds, right?"

"Oh my gosh, I heard that but like we're not allowed around there right now." Her excitement began to deflate thinking he meant Trent was 'there' in general.

"Well, yeah," Mike confirmed. "But it's your ladies' lucky day because guess what?" He checked Presley's direction again. "Trent Hayes is here at the Jubilee." Mike pointed towards the corn dogs. "He's right over there in that hat, with the sunglasses on top, standing next to Presley."

"Holy shit!" She ran over with her friends not too far behind.

Mike took a sip of his Arnold Palmer and watched as a crowd formed around Trent, *perfect*. He smiled knowing that the crowd would only get larger, and the attention would cut into the time Trent was trying to spend alone with Presley.

Trent and Presley paused when they saw a couple of girls hastily jogging their way squealing like giddy tweens. Their scene began catching the attention of others around them and soon there was a small crowd headed their way. The girls began talking a million miles an hour when they reached him. The sudden, loud crowd made Baron nervous, so Presley hooked a leash on him and pulled him next to her. Trent still had a hold of his corn dog he hadn't been able to taste yet, and Presley was slowly getting pushed away from him.

"Pres, you alright?" Trent looked at her as she was now standing behind a couple of the girls.

"I'm okay," she assured him.

He gave her a look, but she just nodded her head.

Phones were flashing at Trent from all angles, he wasn't even sure where to look or who to talk to because of the girls jumping and gabbing around him. He tried to smile for as many pictures as he could but there were too many people, he looked around for Presley again and he finally caught eyes with her. She mouthed 'Are you okay?' when their eyes met.

Trent shook his head back and forth, but he didn't look scared or worried. Presley looked around for Mike, who was walking towards her with their drinks.

"Hey Mike, who's on duty here today?"

"What's up?" He smiled, knowing full well what he had just done.

"Well, I think Trent needs a little help, that's a big crowd." Presley instructed Baron to hop into the wagon as more people were joining the crowd.

Mike looked at Trent's direction. "Eh, he's fine. Pres, he eats that shit up. Guys like Trent love that kind of attention."

"I don't know," Presley disagreed. "He looks a bit overwhelmed."

Mike just watched as his plan was working out better than he could have imagined. They were barely able to see Trent anymore when Mike offered Presley the drink he bought her.

"Thank you." She accepted and then pulled Baron and the wagon along with her. "I'm going to go see if I can get Trent out of there."

"Pres, don't go in the middle of that, that's a lot of people." Mike was worried about her getting moshed.

"Well," she looked at him, trying to be nice but firm. "It's either fine or too many people, you just said it was fine."

"Fine for Trent," Mike clarified, but Presley was already on her way in there.

"Pres!" Mike jogged after her.

"Mike, you can either get a hold of whoever's on duty, or I'm going in there." She hoped he'd make the call because she didn't love the idea of dragging Baron into the middle of that crowd.

Mike rolled his eyes and got on his cell.

Just then the mayor was walking by, so Presley grabbed his attention as she noticed an officer with him.

"Hey Jude!" She waved.

"Presley!" He smiled and walked over with his arms open. "How are ya, sweetie?"

"Hey, good, sorry to have to ask." she tried to look for Trent again, she saw him, but it didn't look like he noticed where she was. "Do you think you guys can get this crowd thinned just a bit, please? Trent is in there and I just think there are too many people, and more are coming."

"Trent Hayes?" The mayor, of course, knew all about the movie. "I didn't realize he'd be here today, that's great! But I agree, we need to at least get a little order around here."

"Can you guys just help me get to him? I can bring him to the lumberjack trailers to lay low for a bit," she suggested.

"Officer Bando," Jude said and then looked to the other deputy. "Jerry, I need both of you to help make a path, let's go grab Trent out of there. Presley, you wait here, we'll try to funnel him this way."

Presley agreed and watched them make their way through the crowd.

Not too long after they went in, Trent was making his way towards her. Once they made eye contact, his eyes got big and then he smiled at her. Presley was relieved that he was okay. He finally made it to a more open area and continued to head towards her and Baron.

"Come on," she encouraged. "I've got a little secret spot we can go to for a bit."

"I lost my damn corn dog." Trent said as he reached for the wagon knowing full well it gained about a hundred and fifty pounds since Baron was in there. After they walked a few steps he put his arm around Presley's shoulder to stay together.

"Sorry, I tried to get help as soon as I could, that was a little crazy," she admitted.

"I've had larger crowds, but not like that without security and some barriers. That was a little wild." He laughed.

"And don't worry about your corn dog, there was no way I was about to finish mine on my own." She laughed. "And we can always grab another in a bit too."

Trent smiled at her. "Thank you, that crowd would've chipped hours off our date today."

She wasn't able to hide her smile from him so instead she took the tea out of the cup holder on the wagon and handed it to him. "Here, try this."

"I'm just waiting for you to give me something that isn't delicious," he laughed.

"It won't be anytime soon, because look at this corn dog." She smiled up at him offering the corn dog. "And it's still warm of course."

"You don't want the first bite?" He looked at the corn dog she was trying to hand to him. "You know that's usually the best bite."

"I do," she smiled. "But I've had these ones before, so you need the first bite."

They traded the corn dog and tea.

"Holy shit," Trent drew out. "I'm not sure if I can even share this with you." He dipped the corn dog again and then gave her a playful side eye before he reached it towards her to take a bite.

Presley shook her head smiling and accepted a small bite. "Hey, I deserve at least two bites for helping out back there." She defended herself.

"You're right, that was pretty clutch."

"Presley!" Mike called out.

They both turned around to see Mike headed their way again.

"Presley, hey," he continued. "So, gonna need Trent to sit over with the lumberjack trailers for a bit until a few extra officers can get here." He gave Trent a flat, irritated look, despite the fact that he was actually the one who had just created that stir.

"Yeah," Presley started. "I was already planning to take him that way, thought we could meet a few of the guys and lay low for just a bit before going out again."

"You don't have to stay in there, Pres." Mike clarified she wasn't the one who was confined to the temporary playpen. "We can drop Trent off and then I can take you back out to the festivities until the extra officers arrive."

Presley let out a scoff-like laugh. "Mike, I'm not just dropping him off like some kid who needs to be babysat."

Trent didn't bother cutting in, he smiled at Mike, Presley seemed to have it handled. The least of his worries was that Presley would consider ditching him for Mike.

"I thought you wanted to hit up the market too?" Mike asked.

"I'm okay doing whatever works. We did plan to go to the market, but we aren't on any kind of time schedule, we'll be fine." She tried again just as Trent held the corn dog out for Presley.

Mike had a look of disgust and confusion on his face that they just continued passing that same corn dog back and forth. *How could Presley be so careless*, he thought, *Trent is probably a walking talking STD.*

"You hanging with us for the day, Officer Bando?" Trent asked after he took another bite.

"Yeah, Mike," Presley looked at him. "Don't worry about us. If you've got extra guys coming, we'll hang out with the lumberjacks for a bit. I don't want to hold you up from anything."

"I'll need to let the guys know where you are when they get here. They're going to have to be keeping an eye out so your presence doesn't cause any more scenes today." Mike looked flatly at Trent. "So, I think it's best if I stay close."

"Great." Trent managed, he watched Presley snag the tea from the wagon and she took a sip before offering it to Trent. "Thanks for the tea too." Trent smiled at Mike, knowing full well he hadn't bought it for him and certainly not for him to share with Presley. "I've never had anything like this, it's delicious."

Mike wanted to slap the grin off his face so badly, nothing at that moment would give him anymore pleasure. "I'm surprised she's sharing—Mama Mable's is her favorite drink here."

Trent rubbed Presley's shoulder as he took another healthy drink. "I'm happy to grab her another one later today."

"Staying all day?" Mike more or less demanded.

"We rode here together so I'm down as long as she is." Trent smiled.

Just then Mike's cell began to ring, he rolled his eyes at Trent before answering. "Bando here," he greeted. "Yeah, we're headed towards the lumberjack trailers." There was a pause. "Uh huh, okay… Well, just meet us on the north end of the trailers. Yep, bye."

Neither Presley nor Trent stopped when Mike took his phone call, so Mike jogged a bit to catch up. "The other officers are here; we're going to meet with them in just a few minutes."

"Do you need us for that?" Presley asked.

Trent looked at Mike, she had a great point, why would they all need to meet with the officers?

"Well, it may be easier for logistics." Mike attempted to reason with her just so he could continue to interrupt any alone time Trent was going to have with her.

"Trent and I don't have to hangout with the officers though, right?" She politely declined another bite of the corn dog from Trent before continuing. "I mean, I really appreciate their assistance, but we can manage now."

Trent swallowed the last bite of the corn dog and nodded his head in agreement. "Yeah, she's safe with me and if they're going to be around then I guess they can help break up any other large crowds that gather. I'll certainly be trying to avoid us losing any more time together today." He smiled at Presley.

Mike rolled his eyes, to his dismay, he realized Presley saw him do it. She gave him a look but then she smiled at Trent. "There are a couple of the mill guys who participate in some of the games, I'd love to introduce you to them."

"Show me the way, Pres." Trent tossed the corn dog garbage in a nearby can and continued to follow her while pulling the wagon. Baron was thoroughly enjoying his ride as he had his head resting on the side of the wagon and had his legs sprawled out in front of him.

"Want me to pull the wagon? I know it's not light." While she laughed, she also shot him a guilty flash of her teeth knowing full well her dog was on the heavier side with his powerful frame.

"Are you kidding me?" Trent almost laughed at her. "First of all, hell no are you working hard around me, and secondly, this is light work for me." He smirked, before continuing. "In fact, if you want to hop in too, I'll pull both of you."

Presley laughed and reached up to caress his arm, which Mike noticed. Mike could feel the hatred projecting on his face, rather than get caught again making an unpleasant gesture, he decided to remove himself so he could regroup. "I'm gonna go meet up with the guys. Pres, I'll give you a call when we've got a plan in place for moving around the Jubilee safely."

Presley didn't even think twice about it, she waved her hand. "Bye, Mike, thank you!"

"Officer Bando." Trent turned to wave at him, but he was already speed walking in the opposite direction, offering no acknowledgment to either of them.

After being thoroughly amazed by the speed climbs and various block chop events, Trent was excited it was finally time for the birling. It had to be quite the spectacle if this was Presley's favorite event when the others had already been pretty exciting. They found a spot on the grass, it was in the restricted access area, at the recommendation of the security team that was now trailing them through the Jubilee.

Trent noticed Mike had kept his distance since separating right before they met a few of the lumberjacks—he wasn't disappointed Mike wasn't hanging out with them anymore. He looked a few yards away and noticed Mike watching them, so he waved. Mike wasn't amused, but it did discourage him from continuing to stare.

"That's James." Presley leaned into Trent and pointed to one of the lumberjacks before they began. "He works at the mill, he's like defending his third or fourth birling championship this year here."

"That's pretty impressive." Trent ruffled Baron's head as he sat next to him on the grass. "Have you ever tried it?" He gestured towards the two men as they began out on the water.

"Uh, no." She shook her head with wide eyes. "Have never wanted to either, it's too much fun to watch. And I like my teeth, I feel like I'd end up slapping my face against a log if I even attempted that."

Trent chuckled as he watched the two burly men finesse their feet along the large tree trunk. "Yeah, I'd probably end up getting a stunt double."

"Oh, so you're selectively without a stunt double, huh?" She lightly bumped into him.

"When my new birling movie comes out, you'll get to see my very first stunt double." He assured her.

Presley lingered on his shoulder. "Can't wait to see that one," she lightly chuckled.

✦

Trent was thinking about how grateful he was to be a guy when he had to use the portable restrooms. The one that became available when he was next in line was about twenty degrees hotter inside than it was outside and smelled exactly how he expected it to; but he didn't have to sit on or even lift the lid of the toilet seat. He was gasping for as much fresh air as he could when he stepped out to look for Presley. He found her waiting at a safe distance from the stench and she had an ear-to-ear grin on her face, which made him smile too.

"So, I saw this and couldn't pass it up." She was holding something behind her back and her tone was giddy. "Since we're staying for fireworks, and it can get chilly once it gets dark around here, I got you a hoodie." She was giggling when she held it up for him.

Trent laughed out loud from his gut the second she had it fully visible to him.

"Isn't it so perfect?! I've never seen one of these here!" She was ecstatic to have found it.

Trent reached for the forest green hoodie that had a white silhouette image on the front of it. There was a lumberjack figure who was holding an ax and standing next to a stump and a fallen tree. The text at the top of the hoodie read, 'I DO ALL MY OWN STUMPS'. The bottom, in much smaller font read, 'MASON LOGGERS JUBILEE'.

"Pres," he tried to stop laughing. "I fuckin' love it, this is perfect."

"Right?!" She bounced in agreement.

As he accepted the hoodie from her, he wrapped her up in his arms. "Thank you."

When they released each other, Presley felt weightless from his touch and she looked up at Trent. "You're welcome."

Trent folded the hoodie back up since the hot summer sun was still beating down on them.

Presley reached for the folded hoodie and put it in the wagon. "I couldn't let you leave your first Jubilee without a proper souvenir."

"I'll cherish it always." He assured her while rubbing her bare shoulder.

Mike had been on his way to talk to Presley since he noticed her alone for the first time that day, he slowed when he saw Trent's approach though. He was really disappointed in himself for not having interrupted them before he watched Trent hug her. He had an unobstructed view of Presley's face as it was pulled against Trent's chest, her eyes were closed, and she had a smile casting across her face that he had never seen before. Initially, he felt a small stab in his heart until resentment and anger took over. He called the head of the security team to let them know he was out for the evening, and they'd be on their own. He couldn't even bring himself to say goodbye to Presley before he left.

"My second favorite part of a good fireworks show is about to happen." Presley projected an ear-to-ear grin towards Trent. They had created a comfortable spot near the water amongst a few hundred onlookers. Presley brought a large blanket for them to sit on and a couple smaller ones in case they got cold.

"Second favorite?" He shot her a bewildered look while sporting his new favorite hoodie. "And what's that?"

She paused for a brief moment, suddenly, the artificial lights around them began to shut off. "See," she smiled. "Once the lights are all off you can see the stars." She looked up at the millions of little bright lights glimmering in the summer night sky.

"This is insane." Trent joined her gaze and looked up to see at least double the number of stars he thought were in the sky.

"And now for my favorite part." Her teeth quickly trapped her bottom lip, and excitement was in her eyes when she looked into Trent's briefly before tipping her glance back into the sky.

His stare lingered on her even after her gaze had moved on, his desire to lean in and kiss her was overwhelming. Just before he leaned her way, he froze when Baron sat up, almost as if he knew what was running through Trent's mind. Trent instead smiled at Presley and then looked into the sky as the fireworks took flight. It wasn't long before Trent noticed Presley's right hand as it was gently rubbing the back of Baron's head. His tongue was hanging out of the left side of his mouth and a waterfall of drool was making its way down. Trent was patient and didn't want to stop her from showing affection to her dog. Baron took a deep breath and then laid down in between them. Presley's hand followed him but simply laid on his back in between his shoulder blades now; her focus on the fireworks didn't break, she continued to watch the show and rested her hand on Baron. Trent tried to look at her through his peripheral, she didn't appear to be paying attention, so Trent moved his hand on top of hers. He only set it on top of hers for a second before he interlaced their fingers. He waited for Presley to bend her fingers as well before he began caressing her hand with his thumb. As the grand finale began, she loosened their hands, he was worried until he realized she was only loosening them so she could turn her hand over to touch their palms and have a better hold on each other. He responded by giving her a quick squeeze.

The final boom lit up the sky and then a roar of the crowd echoed across the lake. The lights slowly began to turn back on around them and the crowd was rustling to gather their blankets and coolers. Baron didn't seem to want to get up yet, so Trent and Presley stayed seated.

"Will these lights stay on for much longer?" Trent broke the silence.

"Well, probably." She looked around. "They won't go off until everyone is gone, and the trash is all picked up. Why do you ask?"

Trent rubbed Presley's hand and gave it a squeeze before starting again. "I was going to see if you wanted to lay here and watch the stars with me." He turned and looked into Presley's eyes.

She looked at their hands smiling. "I've got a better place to do that if you're interested?" Her gaze slowly lifted from their hands to his inviting blue eyes.

Trent got himself up, never losing contact with her hand, he turned to face her and held out his free hand. Presley accepted it and allowed him to help her up, he pulled her up, so they nearly touched chests. He was now holding both of her hands as he gazed into her eyes. "I'm *very* interested."

Mike was pacing back and forth as he waited for a notification on Presley's front porch camera. He had left them at the Jubilee hours ago and was more than upset that she wasn't home yet. He didn't even want to think about what Trent could have possibly convinced Presley to be doing this late at night. A guy like that could not be trusted. He figured they would have stayed for fireworks, but even at that, she should have been home by now. He would wait another fifteen minutes before he drove by the motel to see if that's where she had found herself.

"You aren't taking me somewhere to chop my body into unidentifiable pieces, are you?" Trent joked as Presley was behind the wheel and somehow navigating through basically the forest. Trent hadn't seen a light, sign of life, or an actual road for a solid ten minutes.

Presley laughed at him, continuously checking for little markers she used to guide her way through the wilderness. "No, I'm trying to give you the best view for stargazing." She offered him a sneaky smile.

"It's a good thing I trust you." He tried to look at her, despite the darkness. "I don't know how you're navigating through here, it's dark as hell."

"You aren't scared, are you?"

"Hell no!" He laughed.

"Good, we're here." She put the truck in park and Baron stepped across her lap to ensure he was first out the door. "C'mon," she eagerly encouraged him and pushed her flashlight on.

They brought a couple of the blankets with them and Trent followed Presley to her secret spot.

He thought he saw a clearing ahead of them so he figured they must be close. They stepped over a fallen tree and were suddenly on a ledge that overlooked endless mountains and trees, the light of the moon shined down just enough for Trent to see they were literally in the middle of a forest. The night sky was scattered in stars, it looked almost like glitter, and he could very clearly see the Milky Way. He couldn't stop looking at the sky around them, looking at the celestial spectacle made him feel very small.

"Here." Presley had laid out a blanket for them while Trent was gawking at the sky. "We can sit here, I don't want you walking off the cliff." She chuckled as she gestured towards the blanket she laid out. "That's a for sure way to death or at the very least complete paralysis."

"This is unbelievable." Trent finally sat down, he had never seen anything quite like this.

"See," she smiled. "The lake is a nice place to watch them, but you simply can't beat this view—it never disappoints and always takes my breath away."

"Pres," he turned to her. "Thank you for sharing this with me."

Presley nodded her head slowly. "Of course," she smiled. "It wouldn't be fair to keep it a secret forever."

"Is this like your hiding spot?"

"Kinda," she shrugged.

"It doesn't scare you to be way up here alone?"

"No one comes way out here, it's like impossible to find pretty much." She continued looking up at the stars and took a deep breath while rubbing Baron's belly. "Plus, I've got my personal security with me."

Trent laughed. "True," he looked down at Baron. "How'd you stumble upon this hidden gem?"

Again, Presley shrugged. "We do enjoy a good hike from time to time. But I really needed some space and quiet one day and we weren't too far from this spot when Baron took off after something so we ended up walking out on this ledge. It was so pretty during the day, I just had to check it out at night, and I've been coming back ever since."

"I've got no hiding spots at home." Trent looked up. "Always something or someone." He took a deep inhale and shook his head.

"I realized it's just not sustainable for me, a reset and refresh is good for the soul. Baron and I were coming up here almost every night for a few months—it's even better since there's no service up here."

"I can't remember the last time I was completely unavailable to the world." He joked, "probably never."

"Well, in addition to finding things that slow your day down, I highly recommend making yourself unavailable from time to time." Presley welcomed Baron onto her lap, she laid her head on his back and patted his chest.

"He's got the routine down huh?" Trent chuckled as Baron looked up into the sky to coax Presley into scratching his head.

She didn't say anything, she just smiled warmly back at him and then looked up into the wondrous galaxy. Trent wasted almost no time before he reached for her hand to interlace their fingers. Presley felt more and more connected to Trent, she still fought with her feelings because of his 'playboy' reputation; she wasn't interested in just being another notch in his belt. In her heart she knew she would never get that close to someone without the intention of pursuing more than just a quick physical connection—she wanted more. She didn't know how to vocalize that to Trent quite yet so instead she just sat there, holding his strong hand as it stroked hers, and enjoyed the view and the company. They both noticed a shooting star flash across the sky.

Presley smiled. "Fun fact, did you know shooting stars travel at over 100,000 miles per hour?"

Trent looked at her with a smirk on his face. "Damn, really? You're a little star guru, huh?"

"Not really, I do spend a bit of time looking at them, but I just know the basics really." She started again with a higher inflection in her voice. "And technically speaking, shooting stars aren't actually stars."

Trent listened along to her, spewing a bit of her knowledge like how stars take four years to be seen, Icarus being the farthest star from Earth, and then she started pointing out different constellations to him.

She paused after a couple of constellations and motioned for them to turn around. "Okay, so, if you're brave enough, sometimes I push the blanket closer to the edge over here and then lay with my head that way."

"Of course I am, let's do it." Trent got up smiling.

They spun the blanket around and moved it closer to the edge, there was a good 20x20 or so area, so they weren't in much danger of falling to their ends.

"Holy shit." Trent laid on his back and looked up. "This is like you're in space or something." Laying the opposite direction and looking up gave the illusion that there were no trees around them at all, it was only the dark night sky sprinkled in stars and shooting meteors, now that Trent had been educated on shooting and falling stars.

"I could never see this at home." Trent was still in amazement.

"You'd probably have to search quite a ways up north at the very least, and even then, I'm not sure much can compare to this. It's the pollution and such that hinders the view, not just always city lights."

"Little science genius over here." He smiled.

"Hardly." She rolled her eyes, not wanting to disclose science was almost always her weakest subject in school.

Trent was about to tell her how hot it was that she had a nerd side, but then realized that's something he'd say to all the other girls. Presley wasn't all the other girls; she was something special. Trent was beyond falling, he was crashing into the feeling of how just being in her presence gave him so much joy. She was always glowing and easy to talk to, he felt like he could expose any part of himself to her and she would cherish it. For the first time in a long time, he had to be much more mindful of his words.

"You are full of surprises, Presley Williams." He fondly shook his head. "I love that I get to learn something new and addictive about you every time we talk. And I look forward to uncovering a little more of you every day."

Presley didn't know what to say, she could tell he wasn't looking at her, so she didn't feel pressure to look at him. She knew she couldn't just sit there and not respond, she had to say something.

Her brain tried to stop her, but her heart went rouge. "Spending time with you really has been an amazing surprise, Trent Hayes. I'd be lying if I said I didn't want to keep showing you more," she admitted.

Trent turned his head and looked at Presley; the shifting of her head was delayed, but when she was finally facing his direction, she was met with a sincere gaze projecting from his enticing blue eyes.

They stared into each other's eyes before Trent started again. "You're so damn attractive and that extends far beyond the surface, Pres." He reached for her face and tucked a piece of hair behind her ear. "All of your unknowns are completely intoxicating to think about."

Presley tried to calm her breathing. This scene was something out of a movie and her brain kept warning her this can't be real. Just as she took another controlled breath Trent leaned towards her. His movement was slow, but she knew the intent. He slid his body closer to her until their faces were nearly touching, he only paused for a moment before moving in with his lips and closing his eyes. Presley slowly closed hers and waited for their lips to connect. Trent pressed his softly against hers before backing up and then repositioning his lips once again for a longer peck this time. He wanted more than just their lips touching, but he suppressed that urge because the last thing he wanted to do was move too fast with Presley. He gently pulled away and as he did, he immediately reached for the side of her face to caress it. She slowly opened her eyes and found his charming blue eyes which were confident and delighted to have finally made that move. Trent kissed her forehead and then pushed his arm under her neck and pulled her in; Presley was suddenly cuddled snuggly between his arm and his chest with her head resting on his shoulder as they were both looking up at the stars.

Mike drove by the motel for the third time, still no sign of Presley's truck or the Tahoe he knew Trent had been driving. He checked the camera again and rolled it back to the last ten minutes just to be sure he didn't miss a notification. *It's fucking 1:30 in the morning, where could she be,* he thought to himself. As an officer of the law, he had room to pry in the motel room or go to her house and look around but he didn't want to get caught. The thought of driving back to the grounds where the Jubilee was had crossed his mind as well. Again, if she was there, she would surely see him as the only way in or out was a two lane highway and she knew his car. He was sweating heavily and could feel the palpitations pounding to get out of his chest. He decided to go to the station.

✦

"I had an amazing time with you, Presley." Trent looked at her after she parked her truck in the garage. "I would really love to see you tomorrow." He didn't want to be too forward in inviting himself to the cottage or suggesting they do anything else for the evening. The gentleman thing to do was to say goodnight now and terrorize himself with a sleepless night until he could see her again.

She put her hand on his and looked into his eyes with a coy smile on her face. "This has been the best time I've had in a long time, Trent. We can definitely see each other tomorrow."

"Perfect." His smile projected his genuine delight that she had agreed to see him again. "I should let you get some sleep then, huh?"

She squeezed his hand and then reached for the handle on the door. They both walked around the truck and through the large garage door. Baron took off towards the cottage, not waiting for anyone else.

"So, he's not going to walk you to your door?" Trent laughed.

She fondly watched her dog continue running. "Oh, he'll come back, he just gets excited."

Baron fulfilled Presley's prediction and ran right back to them after making a full lap from the garage to the cottage and back.

"See." She pat Baron on his chest as he sat down and leaned his weight into Presley's leg.

Trent kneeled down to say goodbye to him. "Can I trust you to walk her safely to the door, big guy?" Trent knew Baron was more than adequate as an escort, but he battled the feeling of wanting to be the one to walk her to her door. He knew he should, based on etiquette alone, but walking a lady to her door also suggested a possible invitation inside and he didn't want Presley to feel obligated. Everything between them needed to stay genuine and he wanted to project as much respect as possible. Baron licked his face and offered him a paw while still pushing against Presley's leg.

Trent stood up facing Presley and reached for her hands. "We're shooting at 8 tomorrow night; I have to be here by 6 though. Why don't I let you sleep in and then we can catch lunch or something together?"

Presley blushed and looked down at their hands. "Lunch sounds good, should I pick a local spot, or what did you have in mind?"

"I'll be here to pick you up around 1 and you can show me another secret place around town, how does that sound?" He rubbed his thumbs gently across the back of her hands.

"That sounds perfect," she agreed.

Trent loosened one of his hands and placed it under her chin, he admired her gorgeous green eyes before slowly moving in to settle a soft kiss on her lips. "Goodnight, Presley." He whispered as they disconnected.

Presley was holding on to his hand with both of hers, she gently stroked her thumbs on the back of his hand and looked at him in his handsome blue eyes. "Goodnight, Trent."

Baron trotted a few steps ahead of Presley as they made their way onto the porch. Baron's movements triggered the camera, and a notification popped up on Mike's phone. He was driving home from the station and swerved when he reached for his phone. After straightening the car out he slowed down to watch the video feed.

Presley approached her door and waved to Trent as he had turned the truck on to offer his headlights to guide her down the dark lawn.

He gave her two quick honks before she reached for the door to enter her lock code.

✦

Mike watched as she hit the numbers, the picture wasn't as clear as he would have liked so despite having moved the camera, he still wasn't able to clearly identify the code. *Shit.*

✦

Presley shut and locked the door behind them, she dug in her purse for her phone. She acknowledged that it was well after two o'clock in the morning but she texted Lisa anyway.

> He kissed me.

Presley was happily lost in her thoughts as the feeling of Trent's lips against hers was lingering. Their late evening was even more magical than the day had been, and she was consumed by the sensation of laying under the stars with him affectionately holding her. Presley couldn't deny her feelings for Trent. She would certainly continue to try and suppress them until she was more confident that whatever was developing was genuine, but there was no denying that she was cautiously falling for him.

Nine

"Hey, Lis." Presley's tired voice answered the phone and then quickly laid her head back on her pillow.

"Shut up!" Lisa screeched into the phone at just before seven in the morning. "Tell me *everything*!"

Presley laughed and rolled to her back. "Lis," she smiled. "Yesterday was beyond amazing, like from start to finish." She held her head trying to overcome her giddiness. "I just can't even."

"Shit girl, give me something! Jake and Bay are eating breakfast right now, so I have all of ten minutes before they start yelling for me." She laughed and continued with increasing speed. "So, *he* kissed you, you didn't kiss him?"

"Which time?"

"Presley Marie Williams!" Lisa squealed in a high pitch voice followed by all kinds of giddy giggling. "I have to know, pecks or are we talking full on make out sessions?"

Once Presley could talk without laughing, she started, Lisa could still hear the smile in her voice. She left no detail unrevealed from the second he got to her house, through the Jubilee and fireworks to the stargazing and his gentlemanly goodnight.

"Pres, girl, I can't!" Lisa held her mouth and then started again. "That sounds like the most genuinely sweet time, girl. I'm so happy for you!"

"I haven't felt like this before, Lis… It's scary. I don't know if it's just because he's like super famous or what, but this seems like a dream I'll end up sadly having to just wake up from one day."

"I know, girl, just take things at your own pace, Pres. And follow your gut." Lisa wanted to offer her the best advice she could. "Your brain will be too rational and your heart too reckless, trust the gut. I'm telling you."

"Thanks, Lis." Presley could hear Bailey in the background yelling for her. "Sounds like Bay is coming," she smiled.

"Gah, he always finds me, somedays I want to change my name." She joked, "I'll change it to Dad."

"It's okay, we can talk later." Presley looked at the clock and knew she'd have a couple more hours to sleep if they got off the phone soon.

"Okay girl, call me later tonight?"

"Of course I will." Presley assured her.

"Bye Pres."

"Bye."

Baron started scratching at the door just after 10, he was ready to go outside even if Presley wasn't. She reluctantly rolled out of bed, she didn't care to do much to just walk the lake, so she threw a pair of jogger sweats on with chucks, a baseball hat and a button-up sweater before she slumped down the stairs to get her cup of coffee.

Just as she sipped her coffee her phone was notifying her of a text from Jake.

> BOYFRAAN 👯 🖤
> Hey hot lips! Heard you had a good night 😏 💬

Lisa didn't waste any time sharing that story, Presley laughed to herself before replying.

> Wouldn't you like to know 💅 🙊

She smiled down at their exchange before setting her phone on the counter.

Baron danced around her feet. "Alright, alright, bossy." She headed for the door. "Let's go, your highness." She gestured her hand for Baron to go outside first. The second they walked out the front door Mike was notified so he headed straight for her house. Presley followed Baron to their trail.

✦

"Hey, Pres." Despite Mike being upset with Trent's interest in Presley, and their ridiculously long night together, he projected a smile and pleasant demeanor.

"Good morning, Mike." She waved and then kicked Baron's ball as they walked up the lawn back to the cottage.

"What're you up to today?" Mike asked as they approached one another.

Presley shrugged initially, she didn't want to seem available for plans but didn't know how to respond to him, she sipped her coffee and continued along towards the cottage.

"Hey, so, I know it's short notice but do you wanna grab brunch today?" He fished for her daily agenda. "Or we can even do dinner instead, I got the day off." He smiled.

"Oh." She forced a flat smile. "That's really nice Mike, I don't think today's going to work out though."

"Working?" He pressed.

She shook her head and kicked Baron's ball again when he dropped it at her feet.

Mike didn't like the shortness in her replies, he knew there were several hours of the evening where she spent time alone with Trent and he needed to know where things were stacking up. "How was the rest of the Jubilee?"

She smiled and tried to hide it behind another sip. "Good," she finally answered after taking her sip. "It was fun."

"Trent stay for fireworks?" He tried to sound nonchalant but his distaste for him was very obvious.

"He did," she very quickly answered. "That show was better than last year actually, they had two finales this year which was nice."

Mike dismissed Presley's commentary on the fireworks show. "Hopefully he found his way back to his own hotel last night, I thought I saw his car off on a side road out there when I went to the station last night."

"I haven't talked to him today." Presley shrugged. She knew full well where Trent was all night and his car was parked at her house until the wee hours of the morning. "You didn't stop? Kinda odd a car just sitting on the side of the highway, isn't it?"

"Well, I wasn't on duty." Mike cleared his throat. "Plus, I didn't want to walk in on anything, you know how he is with the ladies." Mike accused and looked directly at Presley for her reaction.

Presley chose not to respond, instead she followed Baron— definitely wanting to be back inside, taking a nap before she needed to get ready.

"What about tomorrow?" Mike called out.

"Huh?"

"Tomorrow," Mike reiterated. "We can grab a bite tomorrow if you're free?"

"Oh?" Presley didn't know how else to say no thank you at this point. "Uhm, I'll see?"

"Yeah, let me know, I'll be back later to check on everything tonight." Mike waved. "We can talk about it then?"

"Okay, yeah." Presley agreed even though she wasn't all that interested in doing anything that may suggest she wanted to be with him. She typed in her key code while Mike was standing on the porch, this time, he was able to see each entry clear as day.

"I'll catch you later, Pres." Mike's attitude was re-energized knowing that he was now going to have full access to the cottage.

"Bye, Mike." She waved as she and Baron walked into the cottage. Presley locked her door and then cuddled on the couch with her loveable pit bull before drifting off to sleep.

"Well, well, well." Michelle put her hands on her hips when she saw Trent leaving his motel room. "Look who came home." She shot an accusing look at him while slowly shaking her head smiling.

"What do you mean? I've been here all night?" He laughed.

"No, I don't remember seeing your car when I last looked outside, which was around 1 this morning." She pointed out.

"What were you doing looking outside at 1?" His smile was accusatory, and Michelle just smiled in return before Trent continued. "See, I didn't get back until a little after 2, so that's why you didn't see me." He informed her.

"Oh. I see, and what exactly were you up to?" Michelle loved their sibling-like banter and Trent was always a good sport about it; she more or less demanded that he just admit he had a thing for Presley. If nothing else, it was so she could continue teasing him through the entire shoot.

"Honestly?" Trent walked towards her, so their conversation was more private. "I was having an unbelievably bomb ass date with the most amazing woman I've ever met."

Michelle's eyes were wide and she looked at Trent for a long minute before she could think of a reply. "Are you pulling my leg?" She narrowed her eyes.

"No." Trent shook his head, but he was smiling.

"So, you got some, huh?"

"No." He put his hands up. "Honest, I was a perfect angel, Shell." He maintained his friend's inspection.

"You're telling me you just spent all day *and* basically all night with a girl and you weren't able to seal the deal? Are you losing your touch, Hayes?"

He shook his head again. "Don't get me wrong, I *definitely* want to." His eyes were wide when he continued. "A girl like that doesn't deserve that version of me though, she's different."

"What?!" Michelle shoved his shoulder. "Who are you and what'd you do with Trent Hayes?" She had heard plenty about how Trent operated, and this didn't track with any of the rumors she had come across. Of course he had been with many women, but none of her sources ever mentioned him vocalizing any kind of genuine feelings. He had a reputation of being a smooth talker to get with the ladies and once that happened, he pretty much lost interest.

Trent smiled. "I found someone worth working for." He turned to make his way to his truck before he looked back at Michelle. "I think this is the Trent Hayes I was meant to be." He shrugged and continued towards his truck.

"Well shit, I'm proud of you." She called as he was walking away. "Where're you off to now, we don't have to be at the set until later tonight?"

"Can't meet a lady for a date without some fresh flowers." He opened the car door and smiled at Michelle as he got in.

She smiled and waved at him. Michelle remembered all the other times she'd been around Trent since they met a few years earlier on a red carpet, he did seem different. It had been about a year and a half since they had seen each other prior to working together on this film, but even so; Michelle wondered if Trent was truly turning over a new leaf or simply improving his game now that everyone was wise to his antics.

Trent rolled up to Presley's just before 1, as planned. He checked in the rear-view mirror that his hair was right and there was nothing on his face or in his teeth. The last few hours were agonizing anticipation of seeing Presley again, he didn't even have a way to get ahold of her besides going to her place. His normal playbook would typically consist of getting a phone number, begin texting, picture sending and sooner than later, sexting. He couldn't use the playbook with Presley though, he would eventually want all of those things, but it was too soon. He picked up the oversized bouquet of peonies he just bought and headed for the cottage.

When Trent got to her porch Mike's phone alerted him of the movement. Mike's face developed a smear when he saw who was there, and he was even more upset to see the flowers. Presley opened her door with a bright smile. *Oh Pres*, Mike rolled his eyes, *don't fall for his fake ass shit.*

"Hi, Pres." Trent smiled and tried not to give off any offensive vibes as he was checking her out. "You look gorgeous." He commented on her spaghetti strapped denim dress that stopped halfway up her thighs. It had a plunging, more form-fitting neckline in the front and then just above her waist, the skirt was less restrictive.

"Hi, Trent." She gleamed.

"These are for you." He handed the bouquet out to her and as she reached for it, she leaned in with her free arm to hug him which he was fully receptive to.

"Thank you, these are beautiful. And how did you know I love peonies?" She smiled at him over the bouquet as she smelled them. "Please, come in, I still have to put some shoes on."

Oh, hell no, Mike gritted his teeth as he watched them leave the frame.

"Please, make yourself at home. I'll put these in water and get my shoes—I'll hurry." She assured him.

"No worries, Pres." Trent looked around. The cottage was much smaller than the main house, but he could tell she set it up knowing it would be home for a couple of months. It had the layout of a guesthouse but it definitely had the 'Presley' touch to it, complete with pictures of Baron and who he assumed were friends and family. *Huh, no Mike pictures,* Trent happily noticed. He looked down when he felt Baron pressing into his leg.

"Hey, buddy." Trent reached down and rubbed his massive head.

"Oh, Bare," Presley called. "Come here, sorry, he's been a drooling machine today."

"He's fine." Trent shook his head and wiped the slimy shoestrings from Baron's jowls with his right hand.

Presley was shocked that he was willing to touch Baron's drool like that, she stopped what she was doing and simply watched them. Once Trent had wiped Baron's mouth clean, he stood up and walked towards the kitchen sink where Presley was standing to fill a vase with water, he smiled at her.

"Uhm," she let out a quick chuckle. "Thank you for cleaning him up."

"Of course." He stuck his hands under the faucet and then pumped some soap into them. "I couldn't let that drool get on you, you look too perfect."

Presley looked up from the flowers and into Trent's eyes as he was drying his hands now. He was already waiting for the moment, so he set the towel down before sliding his hand along her jawline and leaned towards her to kiss her lips. Both Presley and Trent repositioned their mouths several times during the exchange, Presley was not ready for their tongues to meet so she continued to be very soft. She was the first to slow down, as she opened her eyes, she tried to suppress a smile by biting her bottom lip.

Trent flashed a full smile, grateful that she put a stop to their kiss before he was tempted to do anything else. "Why don't I find a place for those, and you can get your shoes so I can take you to lunch?" He bargained.

"You've got a deal," she agreed and handed him the vase.

✦

Mike watched as they walked out of the cottage, they were all smiles, and it made him clench his fists.

"I know you probably wanna flex a bit more with your sweet ass truck, but how 'bout I drive us this time?" Trent teased her as they walked up the lawn. "I'm taking you on a date and all, it should be the full experience." He smirked.

Presley rolled her head and laughed.

Trent reached for her hand, he didn't let go of it until he was opening the door for her to get into the Tahoe.

"So," Trent started the car. "Where to?"

Mike wasted no time in heading to Presley's, he assumed he had at least an hour or two before Presley would come back home. His hope was that Baron wasn't going to give him any trouble, he had never been near him when Presley wasn't around. Mike gathered four more cameras and got into his truck.

"Alright, so what's this place?" Trent asked as he opened the Tahoe door for Presley.

She took his hand as he helped her out of the truck. "I know it looks a little run down, but seriously, they've got the best diner food you could imagine, and also, the scenery isn't terrible." She rallied for the little shack that they were approaching.

The diner looked like a fusion of a rundown rambler and an old cabin, it had logging for siding, a long wrap around porch, and the roof was completely covered in moss. There were two very wide and uneven stairs from the dirt to the porch which Trent approached with caution. He could see what she meant about the view not being terrible when they walked in, the entire back wall was open to the river that the diner sat next to. The windows were floor length and when those ended a mod podge of sliders filled in, half of them were open allowing a breeze to flow through and push the fried filled air throughout the restaurant.

"Presley!" A very sweaty cook came around the counter and headed towards them, his apron was covered in food and Trent noticed the sweat marks on his arms and large belly. Presley didn't seem to be turned away by the man's appearance at all, she hugged him when he got to her and then he planted a kiss on her cheek.

"Hey, Walt," she greeted him. "How are you?"

"Can't complain, still kickin' ya know!"

"I see that. Man, you guys have done a little bit of remodeling since I was last here, huh?"

Trent looked around, slightly confused as it looked to have been untouched since 1970 something.

"You noticed?!" The man looked surprised and proud at the same time. "I finally got around to painting, and then the tables outside got a sanding and a fresh coat of stain. Oh!" He walked them towards the back porch seating. "And, I found these old umbrellas too lying around in the garage, cleaned those up too." He took pride in all the work he had put in.

"Well, it looks really good, I guess I need to come around more often." She smiled at him and then turned to Trent. "Trent, this is Walt, owner of this little gem and master chef to the best biscuits and gravy anyone's ever had."

Walt reached his hand out. "Nice to meet you." He offered a sturdy handshake and a smile. "Why don't I show you guys to a table out on the patio here." He gestured towards one of the sliders and allowed Presley to go first.

They sat down and Walt headed back inside.

"Wow." Trent looked beyond the patio and out towards a river that was running by them. It was fairly quiet, and the bank looked like the water had gone down a bit for the warmer season. "This *is* a pretty hidden gem, huh?"

Presley laughed. "I know it's probably not exactly what you're used to, but it's extra local, the owners are amazing, and I promise you the food won't disappoint."

"Pres." Trent reached his hand across the picnic table they were sitting at, he looked at the red and white checkered tablecloth as his hand reached hers. "This is perfect, time with you could never disappoint."

Mike approached Presley's about fifteen minutes after they'd left. He sat in his truck for a minute, scanning the property for signs of anyone on the property. *Alright, I better get started,* Mike thought to himself, knowing he had to possibly contend with Baron and also set up several cameras before Presley came back.

Mike confidently keyed in the code he watched Presley use earlier that day, he heard the lock pop, and he slowly opened the door. He could hear Baron's nails clicking against the hardwood floors as he raced to the door. Mike kept the door cracked to greet Baron safely in case he was in guard mode. Mike reached his hand near the crack of the door and greeted Baron, "Hey, bud." He smacked his lips a few times at Baron. "Are you a good boy?" The inflection in his voice was high.

Baron let out a deep groan, but Mike watched as his body wiggled. Mike slowly opened the door a bit more and Baron tried to get out, Mike put his knee up to stop him and instead came in and shut the door behind him. Baron sniffed his shoes and up his legs before he looked at the door again, he seemed confused and continued to moan. Mike saw a cookie jar on the counter and assumed he may have treats in it. "You wanna cookie?"

He was right, Baron's treats were in there so Mike tossed him one and then shoved a couple in his pocket. Once it seemed like Baron was more settled Mike began to look around for spots to set his cameras up. He only had four and wanted to be strategic about their placement, so he headed for the bathroom first. He wanted to view as much of the bathroom as possible, but his focus was ultimately on the shower. So, he found a spot that would capture her entire vanity on the right of the frame and as he looked to the left, a water closet door, the shower, and then the door to the bathroom. It was going to give him basically a full view of the bathroom; well, minus the toilet if she used the restroom with the water closet door closed. He figured it would be polite to give her that privacy though. As he finished verifying that the camera feed was working, he noticed the hamper Presley had in her bathroom. He hoped there was something in there he could take for his collection, so he opened the top of the hamper and began to dig through her clothes. He moved aside a hoodie, some socks, presumably her pajamas from the night before, nothing he was able to take without her noticing yet. Just as he picked up a skimpy cotton nightgown, he spotted a pale blue, lace thong. Mike picked it up without hesitation to examine them, they had double strings that went over Presley's hips, Mike pushed himself down in his pants thinking about what they looked like on her. He rubbed the thong between his hands for a minute until he wadded them up and put them in his pocket.

Mike walked out of the bathroom and into Presley's bedroom. The shades were all open and the room was filled with sunshine. To his left there were two large windows on either side of her queen-sized bed. Below the windows were twin nightstands, Presley didn't have anything on them, but he was curious what she kept in her drawers.

Mike walked over to the plush bed and took a seat on the cream-colored comforter. He could smell Presley, and he felt a high from her scent pulsing through his body, he leaned back to lay his head on her pillow. He laid on his side and stroked the opposite side of the bed just imagining Presley lying next to him. It didn't take him long to sit up, realizing his time there wouldn't last forever since he didn't know when they were coming back. Mike reached for the nightstand drawer, truly hoping to find some kind of secret stash of bedroom toys. The drawer was empty, so Mike got up to look in the drawer on the other side of the bed. Presley kept a few remotes in there along with an iPad and presumably her current read, which he had never heard of. Nothing all that interesting caught his eyes in the bedroom so he decided to scope out a place for the two cameras he wanted to set up to watch the room.

Trent and Presley were watching the river when Barb approached the table with their food, "Okay sweetie." She set a plate down in front of Presley. "Biscuits and Gravy for you, side of fruit. And for you, dear," she set two plates down for Trent. "The house special." She wiped her hands on her apron. "Anything else I can get you kids?"

Presley shook her head smiling. "Thank you, Barb."

"No ma'am, this looks great." Trent looked at Barb and returned her smile.

"Well, I'll let you get to it then." She turned to a table near them to bus it since the family that was seated there had just left.

Trent shook his head, examining both of their meals, he smiled and looked at Presley. "I really need to know how you don't weigh 600 pounds. The amount of good home cooking that you have readily available is unreal. I'd be Two Ton Trent if I lived here."

Presley laughed. "Uhm, thank you?"

"Sorry." Trent held his hands up. "That was *definitely* meant as a compliment." He clarified.

Presley just continued to laugh, she pushed her biscuits and gravy aside and grabbed her fruit before looking up at Trent.

"Stop!" He rolled his eyes laughing.

Presley laughed too and grabbed her biscuits and gravy instead. "C'mon, I wasn't going to let these go cold!"

"I don't even know where to start." Trent admitted while scanning both plates of the greasiest, most delicious looking breakfast food he had seen in recent memory.

"I would recommend either those bacon hushpuppies you have or the biscuits and gravy." Presley offered.

Trent smiled. "You haven't steered me wrong with food yet, so I'll take you up on that recommendation."

Mike was securing the last camera in the living room; he found a decorative piece above the fireplace that offered a perfect view of virtually the entire first floor. He was excited to have managed that angle since it was his last camera given he had one set up in the bathroom and two in Presley's bedroom. Unlike the camera on the porch, the interior cameras all had audio as well. He did a quick test on all five cameras now to ensure everything was in proper, working order. Mike took a deep breath and looked around, his eyes zeroed in on the two bouquets he knew were from Trent. *Fucking poser*, he shook his head glaring specifically at the bouquet of peonies, *how'd he know those are her favorite?*

Without thinking about it Mike swatted the vase which broke all over the kitchen, Baron barked at the shattered glass and then looked up at Mike. Mike snapped his fingers. "Go lay down!" He pointed to the couch. Baron didn't move, he tilted his head from side to side and looked at the vase and then at Mike. *Shit,* Mike thought, *I can't clean it up now, that would be obvious that someone was here.* He stood there for a minute, considering knocking the second vase over as well. The glass from the first vase had made its way around the kitchen, large and small shards everywhere and the peonies lying in a pile over a pool of water. Mike looked at all the glass and then at Baron.

"Stay out of it!" He warned. Baron simply watched him until Mike walked towards him snapping his fingers. "Go on, get!" He pointed towards the living room. Baron reluctantly backed up and quickly walked away from Mike towards the couch. "Get up there." Mike told him. Baron was no stranger to making himself comfortable on the furniture, so he did just that. Mike put his hands on his hips and looked around the cottage once more before he let himself out the front door.

※

"I still have quite a bit of time before shooting today." Trent pointed out when Barb picked their plates up. "Can we continue our date, or do you have plans?"

"I mean, I cleared a whole twelve hours because I know how you like to go on long dates." Presley tilted her head smiling at him since their first official date was just over sixteen consecutive hours. "What did you have in mind though?"

Trent grinned at her, not regretting the length of their last date in the least bit and knowing she too enjoyed it. "Well, I'm loving all these places you've shown me, plus, I want to get to know more about you." He reached across the table and rubbed her hand. "Maybe we can go grab Baron and do a town tour or find a spot to explore together?"

Presley smiled at their intertwined hands. "You just always have the best ideas, don't you?"

"I mean, is this like the first time he hasn't been able to come along?"

"No." Presley shook her head with a slight chuckle. "I do try to give him a break from me sometimes, so he's been home alone before. He doesn't miss out on much typically though." She admitted.

"Well then let's go get him and find our next adventure." Trent slipped more than enough cash on the table and took her hand to get up.

Presley opened the door to the cottage and immediately ran to Baron, there was blood tracked all over the floor and he was lying on a rug licking one of his front feet that had a pool of blood around it. She cried out and knelt down by him. "Bare! What happened, buddy?" She started sobbing.

Trent's eyes were wide, there was a lot of blood, and he noticed the shattered glass vase on the kitchen floor. He knew they had to get him to the vet.

"Pres," he crouched down by them. "Pres, sweetheart," he held her face and very calmly spoke to her as tears were streaming uncontrollably down her face. "I need you to get us some hand towels, okay?" He held her gaze. "I need to get this bleeding stopped so we can bring him to the vet."

Presley's head slowly moved up and down while she held her dog tightly around his neck.

"Pres, can you get those towels really quickly, please? I'll stay with him, I promise, c'mon." He held his hand out and helped her up.

Presley reluctantly got up, once she snapped back to Trent's voice, she knew she needed to get what he asked for. She ran into the kitchen, crunching over all the glass she grabbed a handful of dish towels.

When she came back Trent was down on the floor trying to inspect Baron's foot as the blood continued to flow. Trent moved one of his pads and Baron yelped.

Presley went straight to her knees and hugged him around his neck again.

"Pres," he started while her head was buried in her dog's neck. "Pres, I need you to look at me." He asked gently.

Presley lifted her head and turned it to Trent.

"Pres, I need you to keep him as calm as you can." He stroked her head. "That means you have to try to stay calm too, okay? I have to pull the piece out and it's not going to feel good, he's gotta stay as still as possible."

Presley's eyes didn't look like they were focusing, all Trent saw were tears.

"Pres." He pushed again and rubbed the side of her face. "I need you right now. Can you keep him calm?"

"Yes." she finally croaked out. "Trent, please help him."

"I will." He looked very deeply into her eyes. "I can get this bleeding stopped but it's going to hurt him, it has to be done so we can move him though." He waited for her to approve. "Are you ready?"

She wiped her tears on Baron and nodded her head again.

"Hey, buddy." Trent pat Baron who was breathing heavily and was hesitant to stop licking his foot. "You're a good boy." He stroked his neck and slid his hand down to Baron's foot again. Trent knew he'd have to put his face in a position that left him exposed to Baron biting him; but there wasn't another way, so he laid down on his side and continued to talk to Baron in a calm voice. He picked his foot up and Baron whined. "Pres, he may be more comfortable on his side for this, do you think he'll lay down with you?"

She confirmed by nodding her head as she rubbed her dog. Presley laid to the side of him and then pulled his head towards her, Baron initially fought her but then gave up and let out an exasperated breath. Baron and Presley were now laying on their sides. He was in front of her and he had his head resting on her arm as she rubbed him up and down his side to try to keep him calm. With his paw much further away from his head now, Trent went in again. He was seated now and put Baron's foot in his lap, when he pulled on the glass Baron screamed and tried to lift his head. Presley held on tight and the scream made her cry even more.

"Okay, sorry bud." Trent said calmly. "It's in there deeper than I thought." He stroked Barons's head. "Pres, I am just going to try to make a little tourniquet and get him wrapped up, we need to get him to the vet."

Trent was quick with the tourniquet and then continued to wrap his foot enough to keep the glass from moving around.

"Pres, I gotta pick him up so he isn't shoving that glass further into his foot and we need to go to the vet. Can you take my keys and open the cargo area?" He handed them to her. "I'll drive but I can't lift him and open the door."

Presley kissed Baron's head and gave him a squeeze before she got up. She rushed out the front door and clicked the car unlocked, she was relieved to see the back was already clear and had plenty of room for her and Baron to sit back there. When she turned around Trent was already right behind her with Baron in his arms. Trent, as carefully as possible, set Baron into the SUV.

Presley looked at him and then reached for Baron.

"Pres," he said gently. "Do you want to be back here with him?"

She nodded her head and wasted no time to climb in the back.

"I just need directions, okay?"

Presley got Baron settled enough to lay down again and then she looked at Trent. "Okay."

He felt a sharp pain in his chest looking at the tears in her eyes, he made sure nothing was in the way before he shut the cargo door.

"Right out of the driveway." Presley called out when Trent started the truck.

◆

"Uh oh." The receptionist greeted them when they walked into the vet. "What happened to Baron?" She looked at a distraught Presley.

"He cut his foot really bad." Presley looked visibly upset but wasn't crying anymore.

The woman could see the blood slowly seeping through the towel around his foot. "Has he been bleeding for long?"

"We don't know, we came home and his foot was already cut." Presley admitted.

The woman shook her head and then went through a swinging door that was behind the counter, she quickly came back with another person and a gurney. "Here, why don't you set him on here and we'll take him in the back?"

Trent had Baron in his arms like a bale of hay, he set him down on the gurney and was thanked with a lick from Baron. "You're a good boy." Trent patted his head.

"Can I go with him?" Presley reached for her dog.

"I'm sorry, it's best you stay up here, okay?" The woman felt bad telling her no. "But I promise we'll take good care of him, and we'll let you know as soon as we figure out what we need to do, okay?"

"Whatever you need to do, stitches, shots, bandages, medications, please, whatever you need to do," she pleaded.

"It'll be okay." The woman reached for her shoulder.

Presley leaned down and kissed her dog. "I love you buddy, be brave, okay? Mom'll be right here waiting for you, bud." She assured him.

Trent and Presley watched as the veterinary staff pushed Baron into the back.

Trent didn't wait long before he pulled Presley in and kissed the top of her head, for a moment he just held her tight. "Pres," he kissed her head. "He's gonna be okay, alright?"

She nodded her head while it was hiding in his chest.

"He's a tough guy, they'll get him stitched up." He kissed the top of her head again.

Presley wiped her eyes and then looked up at Trent. "Trent, thank you so much." She looked down. "I don't know what we would've done without you there today."

"I'm glad I could help." He rubbed his hands up and down her back. "I'm sorry, I shouldn't have put the flowers on the counter there."

"No." She shook her head, "No, he's *never* gotten anything off the counter, that vase was flung off there, I have *no idea* how that could've happened."

Trent took some relief in knowing he wasn't directly at fault, it's not like he put the vase right on the edge either, he was trying to figure out how Baron even reached the vase with his stocky stature.

"Sorry for freaking out," she started. "That was *a lot* of blood and Baron's never been hurt like that before."

"Don't be sorry or embarrassed, Pres." He continued to rub her back. "I know what Baron means to you. Do you want me to go back and clean things up?"

Presley looked up at him. "I'd like it better if you could stay with us."

Trent hugged her tighter. "I'm not going anywhere then." He kissed the top of her head. Trent noticed a vintage waiting room loveseat that was unoccupied. "Here, let's go sit." He put her under his arm and walked them to the seat. "Come here." He encouraged her to lean into him and he put his arm around her.

Shit! Mike rolled the living room footage back, *fuckin pushed her right into his damn arms.* He was upset with himself because now Trent looked like a superhero, and he was the one who set him up to look that way. He was kicking himself for having ignored all the notifications of Baron moving around the cottage. He hadn't noticed the porch camera go off at all, so he knew it was only Baron. If Mike had been more attentive to his new unrestricted access, he could have been at the cottage to comfort Presley instead of Trent. While this seemed like a momentary failure, he wasn't completely discouraged because his cameras would soon allow him unfiltered views of Presley's private life.

✧

"Presley." The veterinarian walked into the lobby almost an hour after they got there. "Hi dear, how are you?"

Presley sat up. "I'm okay, how's my Bare?"

He smiled and took a seat on the coffee table near them. "Your guy is going to be just fine." He assured her. "Now, he had one gash that was causing most of that bleeding, so we did have to give him quite a few stitches."

Presley's head nodded along, and she felt Trent rubbing the small of her back.

"He's a tough guy though, he'll get those out in a couple weeks if he's good with them." The veterinarian smiled at her and then at Trent. "I gave him some fluids too, he seemed to be very dehydrated, probably just the stress and the blood loss, but I'm putting him on some antibiotics to keep the germs away and then I'll send him home with some pain killers. He's going to be a bit groggy for a while too from the drugs we gave him to clean him up and do the stitches. The other smaller shards of glass didn't really cause any kind of cut we can really treat, so that just got cleaned up and any of those knicks will heal on their own."

"Thank you so much." Presley leaned forward and hugged him.

"Of course." He smiled. "These things happen, just something we deal with when we've got active pups. Speaking of, I need him to be less active for the first couple of days, definitely no running or rough housing. After that go easy on the walks and jumping just to be sure he doesn't tear through those stitches."

"Okay," Presley agreed.

"Do you have any questions?"

"Uhm, when can we take him home?" Presley asked anxiously.

"I just need to get his prescriptions in order and then give Jennifer the charges and you'll be on your way." He patted her shoulder before leaving.

"See." Trent hugged her around her shoulders. "He's going to be totally fine, no better place to recover than at home with you."

Presley looked up at Trent and gently kissed his lips, which he wasn't expecting but happily accepted. "Trent," she whispered as she backed up. "Thank you." Presley looked into his chest. "I'm sorry the day ended up with an emergency type adventure."

Trent reached for her hair and tucked a piece behind her ear, before sneaking another quick peck. "We can raincheck another adventure if you'd like? I'm just glad Baron's alright."

"I'd love that." She smiled as the receptionist called her name. Presley pat Trent on the leg and got up. As she was walking over she realized she didn't have her purse or any means of paying.

"Jennifer," Presley was quiet. "I uhm…," she was red. "I didn't even grab my purse from the house when we left, can I call you with payment when we get home, please?"

"Oh honey, of course!" She waved her hand and set Baron's file down. "We aren't worried about it at all, you guys just get settled in and call when you think of it."

"Thank you, I'm so sorry about that." Presley took a couple steps from the counter when she saw the door swing open, it was Baron. "Hi, bud." Presley crouched down and opened her arms. He was very wobbly and staggered over to her with a hefty limp. Once he got to her he sat down and leaned all his weight into her, she reached for the leash from the technician. "Thank you." She smiled and then kissed Baron.

Trent walked over to them, he could tell from Baron's eyes that he was still pretty out of it. "Hey, tough guy." Trent kneeled down.

They spent a moment petting him before Presley started to stand. "Want to go home?" She asked Baron who tried to get up but very quickly went back down to sitting.

"I can pick him up, Pres." Trent offered.

Presley was again very grateful that Trent was there to help her with him. "Would you?"

"Of course." He leaned down close to Baron and lifted him just as he had before.

Ten

Mike watched as Trent walked through the doorway with Baron in his arms, he was on the edge of his seat waiting to hear their conversation once they were inside.

"I don't want him in the glass again, can I set him on the couch?" Trent waited.

"Oh, sorry, yes." She rushed over to make sure it would be comfortable for Baron, "Here, he can lay down up here." She gestured to Baron's normal spot.

"Why don't you settle in with him and I can clean up?" Trent suggested.

Presley was moving pillows around and helping Baron get comfortable. "Oh no," she shook her head. "No, you don't have to clean at all," she declined. "But thank you."

"Pres," he smiled. "I'm not going to just let you clean all this up alone."

"Well, let me change at least and we can clean up together?" Presley was still in her dress that was now a mess.

Trent agreed, he looked down at Baron who was already sleeping. "Alright, I'm grabbing different clothes from the car then too and I'll help."

Trent headed for the door and Presley walked upstairs to grab other clothes.

At least one good thing's going to come from today, Mike concluded knowing his cameras covered all the possible places Presley would change up in her bedroom area. He watched as she dug through a drawer where he knew she kept her tank tops, she pulled a white one out and then grabbed a pair of cropped joggers that were hanging on the back of a chair. To his dismay, she pulled the sweats on before removing her dress. Once her sweats were on she reached for the bottom of her denim dress and pulled it up over her head. He had seen Presley in a bathing suit before, but never just a bra. It was a blush pink lace bra that plunged in the front and he wondered if she had matching panties on. Presley turned to grab her tank top so the show was over. Mike's heart was racing as he watched her, just thinking about when he was going to have the opportunity to watch her get into the shower. He didn't like that she adjusted her bra, once her tank top was on, to plump up her chest, but he was quickly and pleasantly surprised when she threw a light zip up hoodie over her tank top. She put her hair up into her signature messy bun and walked down the stairs, Trent had already found a broom and was sweeping up the kitchen.

Presley smiled at him. "Thank you." She approached, noticing he was already wearing different clothes. "Can I wash your clothes for you?"

Trent furrowed his brow and shook his head smiling. "You don't have to do that."

"I want to, seriously, it's the least I can do." She urged him.

"They do all of our laundry for us, besides," his eyes widened, "who's going to clean the dryer lint if we do our own laundry?"

Presley laughed. "You're right."

They carried along conversing and cleaning all the blood and glass up from around the cottage. Presley was constantly checking on Baron while they worked. Trent came back in from taking the trash out and they looked at each other, he scanned the room and everything looked to be back in order. He walked towards her, Mike was watching and considering whether or not he should go over there. He told Presley he'd be back later but a couple hours wasn't exactly later, plus he preferred to get her alone.

Trent finally reached Presley, they were facing each other standing only a step away. Trent held on to both of Presley's hands and intertwined their fingers. Presley was the first to move as she closed the gap in between them. Trent responded by placing her arms around him and then putting his around her. They stood in silence for a moment, Trent noticed the clock on the microwave, it was just after 5, he didn't have much time at all before he was to report to the set.

"Pres," he petted her head before kissing the top of it. "I'm going to have to hit the set in a little bit." He kissed her head again. "I'd prefer to stay here, but I can't."

Presley exhaled deeply. "I know, today didn't go quite like we planned, did it?" She looked up at him.

"No." He smiled. "But I did get to spend my day with you, and Baron's going to be okay, we can't complain too much about that now, can we?"

"You're right." She smiled.

"*And*," he emphasized. "I can check in if we get breaks, or we can always spend some time together tomorrow too."

"Trent," she looked into his eyes. "Do you want to relax on the couch before you have to go?"

Trent's mind flooded with the thought of where that could lead, he knew it wasn't the right time for 98% of those thoughts, but he decided to test himself and take her up on the offer. "Sounds perfect." He followed her.

Mike watched in the camera, it was directly facing them as they were cuddled on the couch. Presley was in between Baron and Trent. She didn't sit long before leaning forward to grab the remote off the coffee table to turn the tv on. Mike quickly realized that the tv cut off all his audio, all he heard was the tv. *Shit.* He was making mental notes of everything he needed to adjust.

Trent had his arm around Presley and continued to rub her shoulder as they sat comfortably relaxed next to each other. Presley wanted to kiss him; she didn't know if those feelings were magnified by the day's events and Trent saving Baron, or if she was truly falling for him. Despite trying to avoid developing anything deep with Trent, she continued to get caught up in him. He seemed too real to have a hidden agenda. Presley left the channel on *The Golden Girls* and they sat back, leaning into one another.

"Is everything alright, Pres?" Trent pecked the side of her head.

"Huh?" He caught her off guard.

"You're staring at the fireplace," he smiled. "And there's no fire."

"Oh." She chuckled, embarrassed that he noticed.

"Damn." His eyebrows heightened. "Must be thinking about something deep."

Presley didn't answer him, instead she pecked his cheek. When she pulled back, Trent reached up and caught her chin so she would look at him.

"Is there something you want to talk about, Pres?"

This was her opportunity, she should ask him about his intentions, she opened her mouth to say something but quickly stopped herself.

"Whatever it is," he rubbed his thumb on her jaw. "You can tell me, I hope you know that."

She moved her head up and down but she wasn't completely convinced she should say what was on her mind. Noticing her hesitation, Trent leaned in to her, he held her chin lightly and connected with her lips. He tilted his head slightly and pressed back into them, his hand found itself behind her ear as he continued to kiss her. Presley rubbed her hand across his chest and returned his gesture. Her head was screaming for her to stop while her heart was settling in for the long haul. *Lisa said to trust the gut*, she remembered. That wasn't helpful because all she felt were butterflies. If Trent had made a move that very second, she may have completely given in to him. Knowing this, Presley slowly pulled away and tilted her chin down. Trent opened his eyes, he scanned Presley's face wondering if he'd done something wrong.

"Trent," Presley swallowed. "I can't have a meaningless fling with you." She shook her head. "That's not me."

Trent realized how much he wished he could take the years of dating around all back. His reputation and the plethora of women he had gone through could very well prevent him from a woman he truly wanted to be with beyond the bedroom. He very much wanted her to see herself through his eyes so she could understand his intentions were different than any time before.

"Pres," Trent turned towards her and held her hands. "Presley, I don't want that either." He kept his focus on her face. "I'll admit, I've been so shitty, I really have, but I do *not* have that intent with you." He squeezed her hands. "I know that sounds like a line, but on everything, Pres, you're different."

Presley wanted to believe him. She had to admit she was judging him based on tabloids and media, not based on what she'd seen or felt the last couple of weeks. She weighed all the good things in her mind that were combating the 'playboy' side of Trent. He had spent a substantial amount of time with her in the last couple of days which she could appreciate, he saved Baron that day, they connected on a lot of different topics, he had been a great kisser so far even though their kissing hadn't progressed into anything too risqué, *and* he was afraid of dryer lint—the most random coincidence she could think of.

"Pres," Trent was worried as she hadn't responded, all he saw were the wheels turning in her head. "I get that I'm asking you to trust me and it's a lot, I know that and I don't take that lightly. I do truly want to spend more time with you." He rubbed her hands. "I've enjoyed getting to know you and I really think we could be great."

His last comment made Presley smile, she took a deep breath and then looked at him. "As long as we're both on the same page." She rubbed his hands. "Trent, I'm not asking for a marriage proposal or whatever right now." She let out a nervous exhale. "I'm just quite traditional when it comes to…," she slightly rolled her head. "Like I just, well, my heart just looks for something deeper than just a one-time physical connection." She looked down. "And I don't participate in anything but monogamy."

Trent noticed Presley wasn't looking up at him, he truly didn't intend to hurt her or 'hit it and quit it' as his reputation would suggest. "Presley," he slowly rubbed her hands. "I'm truly sorry to have given you that impression. And I'll admit that your comments are warranted, not that I feel real great about it now that I'm looking at what I could possibly lose because of what a shitbag I've been." He waited to see if Presley had anything she wanted to say, she stayed quiet and was still just looking at their intertwined hands.

"Pres, you're special to me." He squeezed her hands. "And I promise I'll go as slow as you need me to to show you this is different," he assured her. "Trust me," he exhaled a laugh. "I *want* to progress with you." His eyes were wide and he tried not to make it too uncomfortable. "But you're far too important to me now to rush anything we're both not ready for. I care about your feelings and I want to do this right."

Presley bit her bottom lip, he was an actor after all, but something just told her to take that leap of faith towards him. She had never felt uncomfortable or like he was pushing anything; he seemed sincere. She definitely wanted to progress with him as well and even more so now that they had this conversation. Rather than talking about it she leaned in towards Trent and kissed him, he released her hands and instead put one hand on her lap, softly gripping her upper leg and the other he used to massage her head. They teased each other by getting dangerously close to escalating the type of kissing they'd become accustomed to; the pecking was pushing the envelope.

Just as Presley was leaning further into him and they were opening their mouths up wider, the doorbell rang. Baron barked and tried to get up but Presley turned to him and encouraged him to stay where he was. Presley blushed at Trent as she got up to see who was at the door, it was Mike.

"Hi, Mike." Presley greeted him.

Trent rolled his eyes, *of course it's that fuck with the bad timing*, he tugged on the front of his sweats and readjusted how he was sitting on the couch.

"Hey, can I come in?" Mike smiled widely, still catching his breath from running down the lawn when he saw Trent and Presley kissing through his secret camera.

Presley's eyes went wide. "Uh, sure." She opened the door wider and let him in.

Oh hell, Trent was even less thrilled about his arrival now.

"Oh, Trent, didn't know you were here." Mike's attempt at surprise was poor. "Am I interrupting?"

An awkward exchange quickly happened as Presley blushed at Trent and then immediately looked down to try to hide her smile.

"My truck's right out front." Trent pointed out when Mike's stare lingered on Presley too long for his comfort.

Mike completely ignored Trent. "I brought you your favorite flowers because I heard the big guy had a bit of a scare today." Mike handed her the bouquet and then made his way towards the living room. When Baron was able to make out who it was he let out a low growl. Presley didn't hear it at first but Trent and Mike certainly did. It was constant and Baron had his eyes fixed on Mike.

Trent looked back and forth between Baron and Mike, he finally reached over and patted the top of Baron's hip.

"Thank you." Presley looked at the flowers. "Who did you hear that from?"

"Oh," Mike had actually watched the event go down. "You know how the town gets to talking." He shrugged and looked at the bouquet Trent brought her that was in a new vase. "Did you go to the market while you were in town today? Those other peonies almost look fresh too."

Trent laughed under his breath and continued to stroke Baron as his growl was going away.

"Trent brought me those." She smiled at Trent and proceeded to put Mike's flowers in a different vase.

"Isn't that nice." Mike looked smugly at Trent.

Trent flashed his million dollar smile at him which only made Mike more upset.

Mike walked towards Baron to check in on him. "Hey, big guy." He motioned to pet him and Baron growled even louder this time.

"Is he growling?" Presley looked surprised.

"Yeah." Trent was quick to answer. "Hey bud, you're alright." He tried to calm him down and discourage him from getting up.

Presley walked over to them. "Bare?" Her tone was more of a question. Baron responded by slapping his tail on the couch and looking at her. "Sorry Mike, he's had a long day and he's full of drugs."

"Yeah, no worries." Mike put his hands up and sat down on the chair across from the couch. "So, don't you have to work soon?" Mike was ready for Trent to leave.

"Yep." Trent stretched. "We're starting at eight so I need to be there at six."

"That's only fifteen minutes from now, what a bummer." Mike looked at Presley. "I was hoping to go catch a bite, Pres, are you still coming?"

"What?" Presley didn't remember making actual plans with Mike, she had very clearly told him maybe and what she had actually meant was no.

"Remember when I came by this morning? We talked about it then?"

"Oh," she scrunched her forehead. "I'm sorry, did we make plans?" She searched her brain but knew she surely didn't make any with him that morning. "I don't remember making any plans, I'm sorry, Mike."

"It's okay, I can wait while you get ready." He smiled at Trent.

"Thank you, but I'm going to stay in with Baron tonight."

"We can order in." Mike shrugged. "I don't mind helping out with the big guy." Mike tried to reach for Baron again, he barked and then his growl followed, low and lingering.

"I don't think he's into you, bro." Trent thoroughly enjoyed watching Baron push Mike away.

Mike glared at him but sat back down. Once Baron stopped growling he looked at Trent's hand that was placed on his hip, he stretched to lick it. "You're alright, buddy, good boy." Trent gently ruffled the top of his head.

"Yeah," Presley looked concerned. "I don't know what's up with him." Presley leaned down and kissed her dog. "He may just need some time alone with his mom tonight." She pecked him again and then sat in between Trent and Baron.

Trent wasted no time in rubbing the small of her back, he didn't look at Mike this time, he was checking Baron's demeanor. Suddenly, Baron was trying to get up, Presley stood up and was ready in case he was still too groggy to stand straight.

"Oh baby boy," Presley watched as he limped towards the door, she followed him and they went out onto the front porch.

"Looks like it's time to go, huh, Officer Bando?" Trent reached for his shoes.

"I'll leave when I'm ready." He looked up at the clock. "Seems like you need to go though."

Trent smiled at him, which Mike hated. "I'll be invited back though." He shrugged before following Presley and Baron.

Trent went out the front door and left Mike back inside the cottage. He walked up behind Presley as she was standing next to Baron who couldn't decide where he was going to relieve himself.

"I sure wish I didn't have to leave." He hugged her from behind.

Presley smiled as she leaned into his comforting embrace and put her hands on his arms. "I'd love to get that last ten minutes back with you." She admitted while settling her head on his shoulder.

"Really?"

"Yes." she turned to him. "Trent, I'm sorry about Mike, he's... he's," she was lost for words. "He's Mike," she shrugged.

"He doesn't get to me like that." He pecked the side of her head. "But if you're uncomfortable or want me to, I can always ask him to leave?"

Presley squinted. "I really actually appreciate that offer and I don't super love that he just shows up... Or invites himself to hang, but I think you saying something to him may not be a good idea." She looked up at Trent. "But if Baron is still upset like that when we go back in I'll probably have to be the one asking him to leave—I don't know what's up with him? He's always been pretty indifferent about Mike, certainly never any growling or anything."

Trent knelt down and patted Baron on his head as he made his way to them. "You're a good boy." Trent assured him. "Take care, big guy, get some sleep." Trent looked back at Presley. "Pres, if you guys need anything please let me know, okay?"

"Trent, you've done so much for us already, I really appreciate you." She rubbed her hand up and down his forearm. "And, plus, I don't want to interrupt your work." she laughed.

"Do you have your phone on you?" Trent squeezed her shoulder affectionately.

"I do...?" She pulled her phone from her pocket.

"Here." Trent took her phone. He smiled as his fingers raced across the screen and then gave it back to her. "Now you can get a hold of me anytime."

Presley looked down and giggled, Trent had texted himself from her phone.

> You want to go out tomorrow?

Trent leaned down and kissed her firmly on her lips. "To answer your question," Trent slowly pulled his lips away. "Yes, Presley, I would love to go out tomorrow, thanks for asking." He winked at her.

Presley swooned at his gesture as Trent headed for the main house. He only got two steps from her before he turned back around and wrapped her in his arms; he planted another firm kiss on her lips and then smiled at her.

"I wish tomorrow was now," she giggled. "Have a good night at work, Trent."

"I sure hope it flies so I can see you again sooner." He pecked her once more and this time he did leave for the house.

Presley watched him walk up the lawn for a bit. She never fully appreciated his backside until seeing it in person, and each time she had a view she appreciated it even more. After he was well on his way to the house, she turned to Baron who was sitting next to her. "You ready for dinner, bud?" She leaned down and kissed the top of his boxy head. Baron slowly walked with Presley, favoring his front paw.

"Hey, Bare." Mike tried again to greet him when they walked in the house. Baron made his way back to the couch but hesitated so Presley walked over to help him.

"Exciting day, huh?" Mike watched as Presley sat down.

"I guess you could say that." She shrugged. "I'm just trying to figure out how he knocked that vase over in the first place."

"At least he's on the road to recovery now." He tried to reach over and pet Baron but he was met with a threatening stare so he thought better than to touch him. "Do you wanna grab dinner with me?"

"Oh." She rubbed Baron's head. "I don't want to leave him again today."

"I can pick something up? Or we could order in?"

"Lisa's supposed to call me in about an hour or so, so it would have to be before then." She shrugged.

"Well, we'll make it easy, I'll order us pizza." He pulled his phone out and Presley heard hers going off.

> BESTIE
> Hey girl—Bay is coming down with something and is being a total monster tonight.
> Can I call you tomorrow instead?

A text from Lisa, Presley was bummed because it would have given her an excuse to tell Mike he needed to go. She felt almost uncomfortable having him there given her developing feelings towards Trent. Presley continued to be kind to Mike even though she knew his intentions; she thought she had been clear with him, but dreaded an actual conversation on that topic.

> Oh no, poor baby!! Alrighty, yeah let's touch base tomorrow.

🐾BESTIE🐾
Can't wait to hear about 😊 Mr. Movie Star!!!!

> Lol 😊💕

"Do you want another piece?" Mike was walking to the kitchen to grab another slice of pizza.

Presley shook her head. "No thanks, I'm stuffed." She truly wasn't even hungry given the late lunch she had. The single slice of pizza she forced herself to eat was more than enough. Presley kept a watchful eye on Baron who seemed to be very unsettled about having Mike there.

"Lisa should be calling soon, isn't she?" Mike bit into his slice as he walked back to the loveseat.

Presley considered lying to him just so he'd still think he had a curfew. "Well, she texted me, I guess Bailey's sick so I'm not sure when she'll be calling exactly." She felt okay with that line, it wasn't completely a lie.

"So, should I head out soon?"

"I do want to catch up with her, so I'd like to be available when she calls." She rubbed her hand up and down Baron's side. "And I think he's had too much excitement today, I think he just needs some quiet time, so I don't want to like kick you out." She let out a quick laugh, trying to ease her delivery. "But, yeah, I don't know." She shrugged.

Mike caught her drift, he had wanted to stay as late as possible into the early hours of the morning and have Trent watch him leave, but instead he figured he'd at least be able to go home and still see Presley. "Yeah." Mike carefully watched Baron. "He's been a bit off tonight for sure, it's like he's upset." Mike looked at Presley. "Do you think he's getting more territorial around another male?"

"Trent?" Presley very pointedly asked.

"Yeah, I'm sure he picks up on his intentions and he's trying to protect you." Mike had to take the opportunity. "We're all trying to protect you."

Presley laughed. "I surely don't know what you're talking about." She rubbed Baron's head. "And Baron absolutely adores Trent, so I'm positive that's not Baron's issue. He had a rough day himself."

"You don't know what I'm talking about?" Mike accused. "Pres, it's obvious that he's got you on his hit list."

"I wouldn't call it that, that's not fair, Mike." Presley disagreed.

"C'mon, you know what a player he is, everyone knows." Mike's voice was getting louder.

"Who's everyone?" She shrugged. "And to be fair, do you really know him?"

"Do you?" Mike threw his hands in the air and slapped his thighs.

"I'm getting to know him. And I think it's just not right to judge him like that when you don't know him." She shrugged. "And it doesn't seem like you're willing to give him that chance either."

"Presley," Mike moved towards her and tried to sit on the floor next to her feet. Baron didn't like his proximity and he snapped. "Oh, shit." Mike jumped back.

Presley put her arm out so Baron stayed on the couch. "Bare!?"

Mike slowly backed away and instead returned to the loveseat staring at Baron.

"Sorry, Mike." Presley rubbed Baron's chest. "I really don't know what's gotten into him today?"

"It's okay." Mike tried to be understanding, seeing as he was the one who ultimately caused Baron's injuries. "I get it, he's not feeling himself today." Mike had his elbows resting on his knees and he looked down. "You know," he began. "I already know what Trent's about and I know what he's interested in. Pres, I just care about you and don't want to see you get hurt. What happens when the circus leaves town and he's already gotten what he wants?"

"Mike, I appreciate your concern but I really honestly think you're not giving him a chance." Presley was slightly irritated on the inside because truth be told this was none of Mike's business.

"So you really like the guy then, huh?"

Presley didn't want to answer him, she stared at Baron for a long minute before she started. "Mike, I understand your concerns and I hear you, but I'm not sure I want to talk about Trent with you. Honestly, you should get to know him versus making assumptions or getting information through me."

Mike didn't like her protecting that information, he was impatient for it and knew if he waited until he saw things develop on his cameras he would be too late. He stood up. "I don't see that happening, but who knows?" Mike took a deep breath in and out. "I'm going to head out and let you two get some rest."

Presley popped right up, she had been waiting for him to leave.

Mike headed to the door and opened it for himself. "Goodnight, Presley."

Presley had one hand on the door knob ready to close and lock it behind him. "Goodnight, Mike."

Presley didn't even have time to move, Mike stepped towards her and put his arms around her, they didn't typically hug to say goodbye to each other, but Mike went in and took this hug. Presley was frozen for a second until Mike tried rubbing his hands up and down Presley's back, when she felt that she began to back away. As their bodies disconnected she felt Mike's mouth on her neck. Presley was in shock and all she wanted to do was shut the door, she looked down and waited for Mike to take a step back so she didn't completely shut it in his face. After locking it she immediately reached for her phone.

> Girl ... Mike is on a whole other level lately .... 😳 😳

💅BESTIE💅
> Oh shit, what happened?

> I can call you in about ten to fifteen?

> Please do

Presley walked back into the cottage and checked on Baron before she started picking up the kitchen. It wasn't too messy, just a pizza box and a few cups and plates. She was disturbed and distracted by the unsettling feeling that lingered on her neck from Mike's presumptuous gesture. He had never crossed the line like that with her. There was no doubt in her mind that he was indefinitely bound to the friend zone, and he was even testing his limits with that status after what he'd just done. It wasn't like she had never hugged him before but that hug and certainly the kiss just made her feel gross. After she picked up the kitchen she walked over and gave Baron a peck on his head; he looked to be recovering from all the drugs alright but she still felt bad for him. He stayed on the couch as she walked up the stairs to take a shower— she hoped that would help wash the feeling away before Lisa called her.

✦

Mike walked to his car but thought he'd take a lap or so around the grounds before leaving, he too was feeling the hug and the kiss he gave to Presley but in a very different way. He thought about the scent of her body and the taste of her skin when his tongue touched her neck, it excited him and he decided to pull his phone up while he was walking. He checked the living room camera and didn't see Presley so he quickly tried the bedroom cameras and didn't see her there either, his heart raced as he checked the final camera that was mounted in the bathroom—and there she was.

She had taken off her sweats and zip-up and she was standing in front of her mirror pulling her hair out of the messy bun it was in. Her panties did in fact match the blush lace bra she was wearing and Mike thoroughly enjoyed the cheekster style she had on. Presley's hair fell down her back and she rustled her fingers through it a couple of times before she walked over to the shower to turn it on. When she leaned over Mike's heart skipped a beat, he really wished she would have had her tank top off as well. Presley reached her hand under the falling water to make sure the water was warm enough. She turned around and was taking her tank top off while walking towards the hamper, Mike's camera was tucked in a frame that was hanging from her wall right over that laundry basket. He was anxious that she'd remove her bra right in front of the camera so his view was as close as if he were standing in that bathroom with her. After she tossed her tank top in the basket she removed her panties and then turned to take her bra off. *Shit!* He thought.

She slid her bra off and walked back to the shower, setting it down on the vanity and Mike watched the mirror to get a full front view of her before she opened the glass door to get in the shower. Although the doors were clear glass, the heat of the water had already created steam so he wasn't able to clearly see her in there. He stopped when he reached the driveway of the main house and he bent his knee and kicked his leg to readjust his pants. Even though he couldn't clearly see her he wanted to wait for her to get out, he'd surely get another unobstructed view if he just waited.

"Good evening, Officer Bando." A security guard approached him.

Mike fumbled with his phone and tried to shut the screen off, his sound was still on so he looked at it again and cut the feed before putting the phone back in his pocket. "Oh, uh…," he cleared his throat, "Good evening." Mike turned around and it wasn't just the security guard, it was Michelle too.

"What were *you* watching?" She pumped her eyebrows and smiled at him.

Mike tried not to show his nerves. "Oh, nothing." He shook his head.

"Didn't sound like nothing." She laughed. "Sounded like a shower."

The security guard looked down, he was just as embarrassed as Mike.

"No." He furrowed his brows and continued to shake his head. "No, it was just a video."

"Well, can we see it?" Michelle pushed.

Mike wiped his forehead and stuck his hand in his pocket to make sure his phone was still there. "Sorry, I can't let you do that." He squeezed his phone. "Official police business."

"Oh," she laughed. "Alright then." Michelle looked at the security guard and then back at Mike. "Well, I'll let you get back to that *official* police business then."

"Goodnight." The security guard waved to Mike and continued to walk with Michelle to her car.

Mike waved and then turned his back to them. He could feel his face burning with embarrassment, *that could have been worse*, he shrugged; *it could have been Trent… and he could have seen what I was watching.* He decided to cut the walk around short and instead headed for his car to go home and finish watching in private where he didn't have to worry about anyone catching him; he could just imagine he and Presley were alone together.

> We're about to start shooting but there was no way I could start work without telling you I really have enjoyed getting to know you Presley. I can't wait to see you and your gorgeous face again soon. I hope Baron is settling in alright, give him some extra loves from me, get some rest and I'll see you tomorrow morning. 😘

Presley smiled as she read the text from the number she hadn't saved yet. Trent definitely had a way with words and she had to admit that seeing him again couldn't come soon enough.

> 😊 🐾 I'll give him allll the loves and tell him it's from both of us. Thank you so much for helping to save him today—that really meant a lot. And thank you for spending so much time with me lately Trent, I've absolutely loved getting to know you and I'm really looking forward to seeing you soon. Have a good night at work. 🐾 🐾

TRENT HAYES 🖤

"Hey girl," Lisa sounded tired. "I'm sorry I didn't call earlier, I don't know what's up with Bay, I think it's an ear infection or something. He's been a real treat, Jake and I are back to taking shifts all night."

"Oh man, I'm sorry," Presley grimaced. "We can catch up later, why don't you get some sleep, Lis?"

"Like I can sleep without knowing what all went down today!" She practically yelled into the phone. "I'm grabbing a pint of ice cream and I want every last detail, don't you dare hold out on me."

Presley laughed. "I guess I'll just go in order of the day then because it was straight *cray*." Presley began and then dove into the day starting with sleeping in and then her morning walk with Baron.

"Girl, he likes you, like legitimately likes you." Lisa put her spoon down as she had finished the entire pint of ice cream while listening to Presley's day. "He *has* to. Pres, this is insane! Trent fuckin Hayes." She shook her head in waning disbelief. "When can I come meet him?"

Presley laughed. "As soon as possible! Lis, you really think it's like that?"

"Yes!"

"I think so too, but I want you guys to meet." Presley leaned closer to Baron. "And if you could come out and visit that'd be really great."

"What's wrong?" Lisa could hear something different in Presley's voice.

"What do you mean?"

"You sound almost sad?"

"I just...," Presley held her head. "I just also want you to come and see Mike too."

"Pres, what happened?" Lisa's voice was protective. "You need me out there or you need Jake out there? You know we'll be there in a heartbeat for you."

"It's not like an emergency—I don't think...," She slightly regretted saying anything. "I'm interested to see your take on him. Lis, he got kinda weird tonight."

"I'm about to get packed right now, Pres, what did he do?"

"No, please don't. Stay with Bay and Jake." She assured her. "He's been acting really protective and possessive, like he showed up at like the worst possible moment tonight, unannounced, and then he was dropping like... you could tell, smug comments Trent's way. Then, in front of Trent, he made it seem like he and I had dinner plans tonight."

"He is *psycho*, Pres, that's not okay!"

"Well, so like he stayed after Trent had to go to work, it was weirdly uncomfortable—I felt like I didn't want to be alone with him." Her voice suddenly remembered how Baron acted. "Oh! And Baron was like growling at him all night, he legit snapped towards him when he tried to sit on the floor by me when Bare and I were on the couch."

"Why was he trying to be a creeper and sit on the floor like that?" Lisa's voice was an even mix of disgusted and pissed.

Presley rolled her eyes. "He was trying to convince me that Trent is a bad guy who only wants one thing."

"*He's* a bad guy! Pres, *Mike's* a bad guy and Mike only wants one thing! I'll tell him to take a hike."

"I don't know if that would make things worse or not though." She shrugged. "I don't even know if I should tell you the worst part now."

"Shit, you can't say *that* and not tell me. Pres..."

She cleared her throat. "So, Mike got like oddly upset or something and he was leaving, so I walked him to the door so I could lock it. It was fine like he said goodnight but then he hugged me. It wasn't like a normal hug, it felt wrong and then he started like… rubbing his hands up and down my back slowly so I pulled back and he leaned into my neck and kissed it." She quickly continued. "But not like a peck, Lis… he like softly sucked it or something—I felt the inside of his lips and his tongue. I felt just… just gross, like disgusted and I didn't know what to do."

"Presley." Lisa was fuming. "That's absolutely unacceptable behavior, he *knows* you're not into him! He *knows* you and Trent have something going on and he knows you're too nice to say anything. *Nothing* about that is okay. It's okay for you to feel gross about it but that's it. I want to kick his ass right now."

"Then maybe you shouldn't tell Jake, I don't want this to get outta hand. I don't even know what he was thinking?"

"Pres, you can't just keep it a secret and pretend it never happened. What about Trent, are you going to tell him?"

"No! They already clearly hate each other. Before Trent left tonight he told me he'd tell Mike to leave if I wasn't comfortable… I should have let him." Presley considered the appearance of keeping a secret from him. "I don't want to seem like I'm trying to hide something with Mike though either as like 'our little secret' or something. Honestly, I don't know what to do."

"Pres, I'm going to come out there, okay?" She could hear Presley try to cut in. "No, hear me out. I'm coming out there Thursday night, okay? That's four whole days away girl, I can't get over there and stay for any extended period of time any sooner; but I'm coming out and I want to see all this. I want to see Mike and I also don't think you staying alone where he can just come by whenever is okay."

"Lis, I don't have another local place to go though."

"You can stay with Jake's parents. Just say you need a one story place for Baron right now, it'll be easier for him than climbing up and down stairs. I know he follows you up there to go to bed and you're not sleeping on that couch all week. I'll call them in the morning and set it all up."

Presley considered Lisa's idea, it wasn't a bad one. Mike could continue to do his 'routines' at her house, she didn't need to be there—and he wouldn't show up at Jake's parents for a legitimate reason. Even she and Trent were going to be on opposite schedules for the week with them shooting at night, so they only had time to meet up for a couple hours at a time and weren't at the point of staying over with one another.

"I suppose you're probably right, that is a really good idea," Presley agreed. "Lis, are you sure you can come out this weekend?"

"Stop, of course I can, I can bring Bay and Jake too if you want? That's totally up to you."

"Yes, I'd love for all of you to meet Trent." A smile grew on Presley's face.

"It's settled then, four more sleeps, Pres. Alright?"

"Okay, thank you so much Lis, I love you guys."

"We love you too girl. Please call me if *anything* gets weird or you don't feel safe tonight. I'll call you in the morning after I talk to Jake's parents."

"Thank you."

"Of course, girl, sleep tight."

"Goodnight, Lis."

Presley hung up and opened her texts from Trent. She wanted to text him but didn't want to seem too clingy, they had just texted and she would be seeing him in a few hours. She decided to get Baron outside for his last potty break of the night before they went to bed.

Eleven

Presley's alarm rang loudly at 6:30am. She wasn't ready for the morning, she had tossed and turned all night on the couch and all she wanted was a few more hours of sleep. Duty called, however and she thought about how much better she'd sleep at the Hofner's than on the cottage couch with Baron basically on top of her all night.

"Alright buddy, let's go potty outside and then mom needs to get ready for work." She pat Baron who didn't bother to move. She managed to get herself out from under his muscular body and allowed him to sleep in—she'd get ready first. Presley watched him as she climbed the loft stairs to get in the shower.

✦

Mike was awakened at the sound of a notification on his phone, it only took him about two seconds to register the noise before he scrambled for his phone. He was pleasantly surprised when he opened the camera to see Presley standing in front of the mirror with nothing on; she was plucking at her eyebrows. He could tell the water was on because the mirror was beginning to fog, Presley walked over to turn the fan on, when she did he got a full frontal view and seized the opportunity to take multiple screenshots. Presley then turned around to get into the shower and he took a few more. He laid in bed caressing his chest; he watched her for a minute since the shower hadn't completely fogged over yet. Her first order of business was wetting down her hair. Mike felt his pants pulsing as she leaned back massaging water through her hair. She reached for the shampoo bottle and Mike was disappointed to see she was turning into a hazy silhouette because of the steam in the bathroom. He wanted nothing more than to watch her hands washing her entire body. To his pleasure, Mike didn't see a towel or a robe near the shower so he knew her dripping wet body would have to come get something from across the bathroom when she was finished. Not knowing how long her shower would take, Mike dropped his boxers and began to slowly stroke himself. He didn't grab anything to help him with the release quite yet, he was just patiently caressing himself until she got out of the shower.

"Good morning." Presley smiled when she answered her phone.

"Good morning, beautiful." Trent replied. "We're wrapping up and I noticed a couple lights on down there, you up?"

Presley's heart skipped a beat at 'beautiful'; she was trying to suppress the giddiness in her voice when she responded. "Yep, just getting a few things together and then hittin' the office for the day, how much longer will you be?"

"Oh, you're trying to see me, huh?" Trent flirted.

Presley laughed. "Uhm *you* called me, so maybe you're trying to see me, huh?"

"I am," he fully admitted. "And now that you gave me your number and asked me out today I'm just trying to see if you wanna have breakfast with me?"

Presley just kept laughing, he was good, she enjoyed his charm and couldn't get enough of it. "Well, breakfast would be the obvious choice because then we'd get to see each other the soonest. So, what time's breakfast?"

"How 'bout I come down there in about 45 minutes and we'll go get something to eat?"

"That sounds perfect, can't wait to see you."

"You too, Pres. See you soon."

As soon as Presley hung up the phone her smile started to fade, she thought about the chances of Mike coming by before Trent was able to get down there. She checked through her bedroom window and didn't see his car yet. She almost felt like she needed to hide from him. Instead she quickly made sure her bags were all packed for the week and then put them in her car. When she got back into the cottage she coaxed Baron up with a treat. She knew he shouldn't walk too far, but they could go down their trail a bit and find a little hidden spot by the water to wait until Trent was ready.

Trent walked down towards the cottage and he smiled when he saw Presley sitting on the lawn staring out at the lake. She was rubbing Baron's side as he laid in the grass beside her.

"Good morning." Trent spoke softly as he approached since Baron didn't notice him coming up on them. They both jumped but were quick to recover when they noticed it was Trent. "What are you guys doing out here?"

"Oh," Presley smiled and looked up at him. "We took the shortest walk down there and he just kinda stopped here, so we're resting."

"I'll pop a squat then." Trent sat next to her, he leaned over and kissed her cheek when he sat down.

Presley looked behind them towards the driveway. "Do you mind if we go soon though?" She hesitantly asked.

Trent felt something odd in her voice. "Of course, is everything alright?"

"Yeah," she tried to assure him. "I just…," she looked down at Baron and decided she didn't need to say anything about Mike. "Yeah." She forced a smile up at him.

Trent knew something was wrong but he didn't push her anymore. He put his hand on the side of her face and then leaned in to kiss her, it was a prolonged kiss and he caressed her face with his thumb. He slowly backed away as they opened their eyes. "We can head out now." He smiled.

Presley pecked him once more and then motioned to get up. Baron felt ready to join them so he also slowly made his way up to follow them.

Once they were both standing Trent reached for Presley's hand and intertwined their fingers. It didn't take long for Presley to lean into him a bit and rest her head on his strong shoulder. Presley felt at ease with Trent, the tension she had built worrying about Mike showing up was starting to release because she knew Mike wouldn't dare touch her with Trent there.

Trent helped Baron and Presley get into their car before he got into his. They planned for Trent to follow Presley into town for breakfast in case they needed to split right after. As Presley was driving away from the house her phone notified her of a text from Lisa.

> Pres—sorry girl the morning is getting away from me. I did talk to Jake's rents though and they obviously would LOVE to have you for the week. Pack your bags girlfriend and get ready to see your besties this weekend. We love you, have fun with Trent, and I hope Bare is feeling better.

> THANK YOU girl, love you guys and can't wait to see you. Omw to breakfast with Trent and then I'll stop by their house before work to touch base and drop my stuff off.

Trent and Presley were sitting outside at a small iron bistro table near the sidewalk off Main Street; another little hole in the wall eatery that continued reminding Trent how truly small town this place was.

"Thank you for breakfast." Presley reached over and rubbed Trent's hand. "You know, one of these times I want to take you out, you don't always have to pay."

"That's not how this works," he informed her. "I *am* happy to hear you're onboard for more dates though."

Presley laughed and then started blushing.

"Don't be embarrassed." He held her hand. "I certainly want to take you on more dates, Pres."

Presley finally looked back into his eyes. "Well, perfect."

"So, let's just have a standing breakfast date until I can get off this damn night schedule," he proposed. "And, when you're extra missing me, we can plan to hang out when your workday is over too."

Presley's face didn't hide her amusement. "Oh, so there isn't a scenario where you would be extra missing me?"

Trent let out a soft laugh. "I didn't say all that." He looked into her eyes. "I haven't been able to stop thinking about you when we're apart." He continued to play with her hand until he interlaced their fingers. "So, I just wanted to see if you're on board spending the free time that we do have together for the foreseeable future."

Presley smiled. "I'd like that a lot, actually." They continued to play with their intertwined fingers. "I also…," she stuttered. "I mean, just so you know," she cleared her throat. "I uhm… I won't be at the cottage for the next few days." Her face was more serious as she looked down at their hands.

"Seattle?"

"Oh no, I'll be at the mill," she confirmed. "But I'm going to stay with Jake's parents for a couple of nights." She didn't allow him time for follow up questions just yet, she tried to lighten her voice to hide any worry. "He and Lisa are coming this weekend but they offered me to stay there for the week." She looked away from Trent and shrugged her shoulders. "It'll be better for sleeping arrangements for Baron since they live in a rambler. We had a slumber party on the couch last night and my back doesn't feel so great. So, just for a couple days until he's better about stairs and such."

Trent nodded his head, he still wasn't convinced something wasn't wrong, whatever it was Presley was terrible at trying to cover up the whole story.

"I just wanted to let you know though, even though I'll be staying the night there, that doesn't mean at all that I don't want to see you. I won't be just right next door when you're shooting this week, but Trent, I still would very much love to spend our free time together still."

Trent looked at her for a moment, trying to read her expression that didn't seem to match her tone. "And you're sure?" Trent tried to be more serious. "You're sure nothing's wrong? And you're okay?"

Presley realized then that Trent knew something else was up, she still didn't want to make a big deal out of the Mike situation with Trent, she didn't know how that'd go over. "Yeah," she looked at him. "Just need a couple days in the rambler." She tried to assure him.

"Pres, you can talk to me," he assured her. "Don't be afraid to tell me, or ask if there's anything I can do." Trent pulled her hand towards him and looked her in her eyes. "Okay?"

"Thank you, I appreciate it." She smiled. "Spending time with you is more than enough, I kinda like having you around."

"Only kinda, huh?" He laughed, and then reached across the table to push a piece of her hair behind her ear. "You know I kinda like you, right?"

Presley blushed and looked down. His stare wasn't going anywhere despite her obvious bashfulness, she finally decided to look up at him. "I know." She shrugged and tried not to laugh but failed miserably.

Trent caught her chin and leaned in to kiss her, she set her hand on his leg and kissed him back as she leaned towards him as well.

When their lips separated Presley was the first to speak. "I kinda like you too, Trent Hayes." She smiled.

He kissed her once more before taking her hand and walking them back towards their cars so Presley could get to work.

"So, you have a busy day today?"

"Definitely have plenty to do." Her head bobbed around. "Such is life though, there are a few big issues going on, so I've got some decisions to make here pretty soon." She let out a large breath.

"I don't know much about the logging industry, but if there's anything I can help with I'd be happy to." He swung their hands back and forth. Presley didn't answer, he could see the smile on her face. "Do you want me to take you to work? We can drop your car off at Jake's parents so I know where to pick you up for dinner tonight."

"Oh, we *are* getting dinner then, huh?" She bit her bottom lip and looked up at him.

"Let's be clear." He held his hands up. "*I'm* taking you out to dinner, you're not paying for anything."

"I mean, I don't want to be keeping you from anything else," Presley teased him.

"Please!" He laughed. "If anything, work is keeping me from you." He looked at her. "And I don't like it."

Presley gushed up at him. "Then yes, let's grab dinner tonight." She rubbed his hand with her thumb. "You just call me when you wake up, does that work?"

"Absolutely."

Twelve

"Thank you for taking me to work today, you're such a gentleman." Presley leaned over the console to peck him while he drove.

Trent reached over to hold her leg. "It's not a problem at all, anything I can do to sneak some extra time in with you—plus I'm looking forward to seeing your office." He smiled.

"Well, here we are." She pointed to the left where Trent could park the car. "C'mon, bud." Presley encouraged Baron out of the car.

"Do I get a tour, or do you need to hit the ground running with work?" Trent asked.

Presley smiled. "I will always have time for you, Trent Hayes."

Trent happily followed Presley to what looked to be the main office building on the property.

"Hey Baron!" A woman called out as they walked through the front doors. "Come here, bud, I haven't seen you in a few days!"

Baron trotted over and sat for the woman who was holding out a biscuit for him.

"Good morning, Alicia." Presley smiled.

"Hey, Pres." She looked up from Baron and took a quick look at Trent as well. "Hi." She bashfully waved.

"Alicia, this is Trent." She gestured towards him. "Trent, this is Alicia, she's the administrative rockstar around here."

Trent held his hand out. "It's very nice to meet you, Alicia."

She was giddy the second their hands touched. "Nice to meet you." She quickly said before turning to Presley. "I don't have any messages for you, but I will ruin your day by letting you know that bastard Jeff brought in those damn homemade cinnamon buns again! I think his goal is to add about eight inches to everyone's waistline this year."

They laughed. "Well," Presley started, "I appreciate the heads up. I'll probably try to avoid the lunchroom today."

Presley led Trent through the lobby and up the stairs towards her office. "I just want to set some stuff down, then I can show you around the mill." She smiled.

She unlocked a door and flicked a light on.

"This is your office?" Trent looked around at the small, outdated office that didn't even have a window with a view. The desk looked old, but not in a nice, vintage kind of way and the two chairs she had for company in front of her desk were straight out of the 70s.

Presley laughed as Baron settled on his bed in the corner, the newest, nicest thing in her office and she set her purse and laptop on the desk. "Not as fancy as you pictured?"

"Not even close." Trent laughed.

"Well," she continued to hook her laptop up. "I'm not always here, so it doesn't make sense for me to hog the nicer, larger offices." She shrugged. "Plus, I do have a fancy office in Seattle."

"That's pretty nice of you to let the others have all of the new stuff." Trent took a seat carefully on the old wooden office chairs.

"New stuff?" Presley laughed. "So, the mill has a bit of a different vibe than the city office. We did update the lobby, and a conference room, but not all common areas or offices got much of an update. These guys around here are straight clowns sometimes and they don't treat the office like an office, if you know what I mean. So, we get to work in a time warp until stuff is actually too old to use, or they all grow up." She looked at Trent and began to shake her head. "I'm not holding my breath for any of those boys to grow up anytime soon though."

"As long as work is getting done, I guess." Trent shrugged.

"Oh," Presley was starting her laptop. "Absolutely, I don't mind them having fun at work, in fact, I encourage it. I'm pretty lucky to have the group I do, truly they all work so hard, I rarely have to worry about anyone here at the mill. The stressful things are almost always coming from the outside, so at least there's that." Presley looked at Trent. "Ready for a tour?" She smiled.

"I'll follow you." He reached out for her hand.

✦

Trent had seen nearly every inch of the mill when they finally made their way back towards a smaller, brick building that was just off the main office. Presley had to use a key to get into the building, a waft of old air hit them as they walked through the doorway. She walked over and pulled on a chain to turn a light on and then made her way to the back wall to lift a few of the shades which immediately lit up the one room building.

"This," Presley smiled, "is my favorite place at the mill." She looked proud.

Trent looked around, the building was about the size of a modern day two car garage and it didn't appear there was any real rhyme or reason for the items in the shop. In one of the back corners were two large, old looking pieces of industrial-style equipment that had gathered quite a bit of dust. He noticed a worn velour couch that was set up right in front of the machinery. There was also a large workbench that spanned the length of one of the walls, and countless framed pictures were hung randomly above the workbench.

"These," Presley walked towards the machinery, "are the first steam powered saw mill and boiler that my family started the entire company with." She swiped a bit of dust off of one of them.

"Wow." Trent walked over to get a closer look. "Your family managed to create a bazillion dollar company and just started with these two machines?"

"We haven't quite hit the bazillion dollar mark yet." She laughed. "But I do love that we've managed to keep these beauties." She patted the side of the saw mill. "My Paps actually reduced the size of the original structure and then closed in the walls, because this used to just be like a carport looking thing way back when, and he used this place as his own little office and workshop." She smiled. "I used to love coming out here and working with him; sometimes we'd just sit in here and play cards or just chat." Her smile softened and she looked over at the wall of pictures. "I really miss that," her voice was soft and trailed off.

Trent walked over to her and hugged her from behind as she was looking at the pictures. "Thank you for sharing this with me, Pres." He kissed the top of her head.

They stood in silence for a moment until Trent spoke up. "Is that you with your Dad in that one?" He pointed at an 8x10 gold frame with a black and white photo of a young girl in pigtails on the shoulders of a dark haired man with a full beard.

Presley smiled. "It is." She rubbed Trent's arms that were around her. "That was actually taken at one of the Jubilees. I was probably like five or six in that picture."

Trent pecked her head and continued looking at all of the photos.

"That must be the man, the myth, the legend over there, huh?" Trent pointed to a wood framed photo that was resting on top of the workbench. It was a more recent looking picture of Presley leaning down to a seated older man with her arms around his neck and their cheeks touching.

"Yep, that's Paps." She confirmed and then reached out to pick up the frame and bring it closer for them to see. "He was always the ultimate wedding date." She lightly shook her head. "Paps got his online ministry certificate to be the officiant for this wedding." She chuckled and tapped the frame. "It was actually at our foreman's wedding, the one you just met, Greg."

"That guy's married?" Trent kind of chuckled.

Presley returned the gesture. "Believe me, we were all just as shocked when he announced he was engaged. I honestly can't imagine how he got so lucky because his wife is like the sweetest little thing imaginable, and *so* pretty."

Trent rubbed his hands on her and got closer to her ear. "I know of someone in this room that's even luckier."

Presley smiled and squeezed his arms before turning to look at him.

"Yeah," Trent continued. "So when you want to share your secrets of being so lucky, you let me know." He kissed her ear through her hair.

Presley laughed, squirming in his arms. "You are *such* a rude boy."

"I'm just playin'." He moved her hair with his nose. "You know I'm the lucky one in this equation."

"We can both just consider ourselves lucky." She suggested with a smile as she hung snuggly in his embrace.

Trent continued to look at all of the pictures, holding Presley as she gripped the frame she had picked up and was still looking at the wall as well. He kissed the top of her head as they stood there. He could tell how close she was with her dad and grandpa, he also enjoyed taking in all of the pictures throughout her family's history. Presley and her small town continued to pull Trent in, he had always run at a much faster pace throughout his life with his family being so large and his career taking him all across the globe; it was like a calling to slow down with her.

Trent was leaning down to kiss Presley's head again when the ringing of her cell phone interrupted their slow moment.

"Ugh," she complained and set the frame back down. "I am not ready for work today." She looked at the phone.

"Pres, babe, I can head out so you can take care of business." He brushed her hair behind her ear.

Presley's heart fluttered at his touch and the sound of him calling her 'babe'. She turned the ringer off and stuffed the phone into her back pocket. "I'm sorry, Trent."

He laughed. "You don't have to be sorry that you've got work to do." He reached for her hand. "I'll go grab some sleep so I can pick you up from work later."

Presley rose onto her tiptoes to connect their lips. "That sounds perfect."

Thirteen

Mike hadn't seen Presley at her house since she left Monday morning. He knew she'd been in town because he noticed her car at the mill throughout the week. He had been able to hold her, watch two showers and now nothing, not even a glimpse of her. It worried and infuriated him all at the same time. He wanted to confront Trent because he knew that's who was stealing all of Presley's time and keeping her from her normal routines. Something drastic had to happen so he could gain her attention, he wanted Presley to need him. Mike's desires for Presley had cascaded over their peak just before Trent and his circus moved into town; he wouldn't allow this playboy roadblock to stop him any longer from getting the wife and the future with her that he deserved.

As Mike was walking back up from the cottage during yet another tour of voyeurism disguised as an official security patrol, he noticed Trent on the back porch of the main house. Trent was posted up leaning on the bar top attached to the porch with his phone in his hands. He could see the ear-to-ear grin on Trent's face as he looked down at his phone.

"Officer Bando." Trent more or less greeted Mike when he got closer, although he didn't bother much to look up from his phone.

"Done for the day?" Mike reached the final step up onto the porch.

Trent continued texting during his reply. "Done shooting until later tonight, yeah." He finally looked at him.

"I'm sure you'll find something to keep yourself occupied with until then." Mike sharply replied. "I want to talk to you though."

"Yeah? About what?" Trent had a pretty solid idea what Mike wanted to talk about, but he wasn't going to make it easy on him, not when it came to the topic of Presley.

"Oh, I'm sure even you can guess." Mike put his hands on his duty belt and continued to glare at Trent. "You got a couple of minutes to talk?"

Trent felt his phone buzzing and knew it was Presley's reply so he smiled when he reached for it and looked at the screen. "Not anymore I don't, I've gotta head out." His fingers flew across the screen of his phone. "You have a good one, Officer Bando." Trent headed back into the house.

Trent wasn't even two steps into the house when he turned back around. "Let's do this again real soon, Officer Bando. I'm sure we'll be seeing you around—we always do."

Smug fuck, Mike thought as he watched Trent leave. *He's gonna pay soon, he's about to realize how quickly he can be replaced.* Mike decided then and there that his next plan for separating Presley and Trent would be put into motion that night.

It was just after two in the morning when Presley's phone began to ring; it woke her from a dead sleep, "Hello?" Her muffled voice answered the phone, she didn't even look to see who it was before picking it up.

"Presley, it's Mike, there's been a fire," he started. "Are you able to get to the mill anytime soon?"

She was wide awake now and getting out of bed. "What?! Are you serious? Is it out? I'm on my way." She didn't wait for a response, she hung up and started to get dressed. She tried to quietly scramble around the room looking for a hoodie and some shoes to slip on, Baron nervously followed her. Presley tried to be as quiet as possible walking down the hall so as not to wake up Jake's parents. Her mind flooded with the possible destruction—the entire mill was nothing but a giant tinder wonderland. She was grateful there wasn't, or shouldn't, be any of her employees there, so it was likely no one was hurt. She then ran through the last time they had a safety inspection on the alarm and sprinkler equipment and remembered that it had all been very recent, so maybe the damage would be minimal.

Presley's heart sank as she pulled up to the mill. Thinking about the history of her family's business and seeing the fire fighters still putting out the last few flames of her Pap's little shop blew a crater through her heart and drew instant tears. That little shack was where her family started it all, she had spent countless hours with her Dad and Paps there, the sentimental value alone far exceeded anything Presley owned and everything inside of that shop was absolutely irreplaceable. Her breathing became irregular and she felt like she couldn't take in any oxygen. Presley put her car in park and told Baron to stay. She saw Mike and tried to dry up her tears, she didn't want him touching her.

"Pres," Mike started when she got out of the car. "I'm so sorry."

"What happened?" Presley was shaking and her knees wobbled, nearly losing her footing from the shock.

"We're all lookin' into it." Mike took a closer step towards her as he noticed she was unsteady. "We'll know more when we can get the Fire Marshall out here."

She grabbed her head and just tried to breathe, she stood helpless while the last flame went out and all she saw was destruction. She jumped when Mike put his hand on her shoulder.

"Sorry," he rubbed her shoulder again. "I didn't mean to scare you."

His hand weighed heavily on her, she couldn't stop staring and didn't register anything else Mike was saying to her, she knew he was talking, but all she heard was the water coming from the fire hoses and blurred shouting from the fire fighters.

Presley covered her mouth thinking she could swallow the feeling, but before she knew it she was bent over, puking her guts out.

Mike took the opportunity to rest his hand on her back. "Pres,"

Mike pulled on her ponytail to keep it from the next heave that was coming from Presley.

She reached down deep for any strength she could manage to take her ponytail from Mike and work a few steps away from him to finish emptying her stomach. Tears were now flowing down her face uncontrollably. Presley finally stood upright and then tried to wipe her face as she slowly made her way towards the fire fighters.

"Pres, I can't let you over there." Mike reached for her arm and held it.

She didn't look at him, she tried to keep walking. Mike wouldn't let go so she pulled her arm. "Please don't."

"Pres, it's not safe," he insisted.

"Can I help you, miss?" A firefighter approached her.

"Uhm," Presley's voice shook. "I own the mill, do you know how this started?"

The firefighter shook her head. "I'm sorry, we're going to have to conduct an investigation, we just don't have any answers right now."

"What can I do?" Presley managed.

"Honey," the firefighter put a hand on her shoulder. "Maybe you shouldn't be here, are you okay?"

Presley didn't answer, she just stared at the smoke that was now hovering around the remnants of Pap's shop. Between the suppressed hysterics and the thick smoke in the air, Presley could hardly breathe.

The firefighter gave her a moment before she started again, realizing Presley wasn't going to just simply turn around and go home.

"Well, you'll need to contact your insurance company. It looks like this building is far enough away from the others, you should be okay to conduct business, but we'll go ahead and caution off the area that needs to be avoided." She could see the distraught look in Presley's eyes. "Honestly, I know you want to be here tonight, but you should try to get some rest. We can take care of this." She turned to Mike. "And you'll be able to be on duty here until we can get the investigation started tomorrow? It honestly looks like arson versus an accident based on my experience."

Presley's mind flooded with terrorizing emotions, she tried to take a deep breath but the taste of the smoke in the air elicited another round of puke; this time, however, she didn't have anything but bile to expend. No chance this was some business competitor, they would have gone for something that would shut down or slow production at the very least—not an old building that housed a lot of sentimental history. No, if it was truly arson it was someone who wanted to absolutely rip Presley's heart right out of her chest.

"Pres." Mike again tried to put his hand on her back as she rested her hands on her knees waiting for another episode of panic to take over. "Pres, are you alright?"

Presley again managed to stand upright enough to remove Mike's hand from her, she wiped her face with her forearm and just shook her head. She took a couple of steps away from them and towards the shop.

Mike decided he wouldn't follow her, she was still close, and if he was being honest with himself, he had done enough that night. He turned his attention back to the firefighter. "Yeah, I can secure the scene tonight. How much longer will you guys be? Do I have time to take her home?"

Presley shook her head. "I'm alright. I don't need a ride, thank you though."

"Pres, I promise I'll come right back and be here all night, the mill will be fine." Mike stepped towards her.

"I can drive myself." She insisted.

"I sincerely don't...," Mike started as he reached for her.

Presley cut in. "I'm fine," she snapped more than stated. She turned to the fire fighter, with tears in her eyes. "Thank you, I appreciate you guys getting here and stopping it when you did."

"Sure thing." She offered Presley a flat smile.

"Thank you for calling, Mike." Presley didn't look at him as she made her way back to her car. Baron was waiting patiently when she returned.

Presley pulled out of the mill as quickly as she could so she could park on the side of the highway, out of sight from anyone who was at the scene. Baron let out a low grumble when she pulled over. Presley looked at the steering wheel for a split second before crashing into a full on meltdown; she sobbed into her hands until she felt her loyal pit bull nudging her arm. Presley opened her arm and pulled Baron into her and sobbed into his neck. He whined and pushed his snout further towards her chest while she cried.

"I know, buddy," she finally tried to focus on breathing. Presley wiped her face with her sleeves a couple of times so she would be able to talk on the phone. She called the movie production's assistant director to find out the possibility of getting into her basement that evening; she had all of her important papers in the safe there and wanted to have everything she needed as soon as possible, she wasn't going to be able to get any sleep anyways. Her basement safe also happened to have a lot of pictures, which she thought may help comfort her from having just lost so many. To her surprise, they were more than welcoming about her being there despite their shooting schedule.

"Come on in Pres." It was Phil who greeted her at the door when she got there. "I'm sorry to hear about the business, how are you?"

Her face showed her sorrow, he could tell she had been crying.

Presley looked up at him. "Uhm," her voice cracked. "I'll be okay, thank you so much for letting me sneak in here tonight, we'll be quick and quiet." She wiped her face again.

"Don't even worry about it, do what you need to do," he assured her.

"Thank you." She tried to keep her face down so Phil didn't see the full extent of her grief.

Presley walked through the entry and Baron's nails were clicking on the floor right behind her.

"Pres!" Trent saw her and jogged up behind her, he wrapped her up in his arms. "I heard about the mill, are you alright?" He could smell the fire on her.

Presley took a deep breath, but it was too late, his embrace released another sobbing episode. By this time she was so exhausted that she luckily wasn't going to puke or hyperventilate.

He started to stroke her hair as he held her tighter. "I'm sorry," he kissed the top of her smoke filled hair.

"Pap's shop is gone." She couldn't look up at him. "It's gone, like there's absolutely nothing left of it." She buried her face deeper into his chest as her knees began to falter.

"Oh Pres." His chest tightened for her loss and he pulled her in securely when he felt her knees giving out. "Sweetheart, I'm so sorry." He rocked her. He could feel her tears starting to drain through his shirt so he simply continued to stroke her hair and kiss her head. Presley stayed comfortably on his chest; she didn't see Phil poke his head around the corner motioning to Trent he could take some time. Trent nodded his head with a flat smile, fully appreciative of Phil's understanding. He could feel her jagged breathing so he rubbed his hands up and down her back to help calm her. He didn't know what else to say to her, there was nothing that would make that loss feel any better. So, he simply held her. Suddenly, they heard a loud crashing noise; it made Presley jump and Baron barked.

"I guess I should go down and get what I came for." She lifted her head from his chest.

"Pres." Trent held her shoulders and tried to look at her face. "Are you sure? I'll go talk to Phil about cutting out of here."

Presley shook her head, and her drained voice replied. "No." She reached for his chest and held her hand gently on his pec, she softly gripped his shirt and sniffled. "I really appreciate that, but I'm going to go look for some insurance papers and try to clear my head." Tears steadily flowed down her tired, puffy face.

Trent rubbed her shoulders as she wiped her face yet again with her soaked sleeves. "Thank you, Trent."

He reached down to hold the sides of her face, he was gentle when tilting her head up. "Pres, if you need *anything* just don't be afraid to let me know, okay?" He reached down to meet her lips with his, he gently held them together while he stroked the back of her head. Presley took comfort in their lips touching, after a moment she softly pinched his chin and pulled her head back.

"Seriously, thank you." She pecked him again.

"Of course." He held her face and wiped a couple of tears with his thumbs. "Pres, I'm here." He assured her, "If you want to talk or you need anything you just let me know."

Presley gently nodded her head, she could feel tears welling up in her eyes again so she looked down and then squeezed his hand before her and Baron continued to make their way to the basement.

Trent watched them walk away with an ache in his heart. He remembered the look on Presley's face when she was showing off Pap's shop; she was so proud, he could tell she lost another piece of her heart with the fire tonight.

Presley settled into the safe room under her house. She took a deep breath and began to cry from the lingering scent of her Paps that somehow still clung to that room. The timing of the fire and the upcoming anniversary of his death created a resurgence of her grief. She took a seat on the old couch sitting in the room and held Baron, just letting her tears flow freely for the third time that night.

✧

Mike was finally alone at the mill; it was dark, quiet, and the air was riddled with the distinct scent of fire. He walked the grounds with his flashlight in hand, it was like a ghost town now since the fire department had left. He headed for a large garage that housed the company vehicles, Mike looked around before he went in. When the firefighter suspected arson Mike felt a cold sweat up his back, he thought he was more careful than that. He went back to the garage to ensure he had wiped everything down and hadn't left a trace of himself on anything they'd test for accelerant. As long as he could avoid suspicion, he'd be the one spending more time with Presley as they'd surely need to question her. There was a small part of him that felt bad for taking something so special away from her, but it was all going to be worth it when she realized she belonged with him. He'd be there through the investigation and the rebuilding to comfort her—she would soon see the light, he decided. Her devastation would be lifted once she found out Mike had pulled several of the pictures out of the shop before he burned it down. Those selected photos had already made their way to his basement shrine and were not lost to the fire as Presley had assumed. Mike checked the camera feeds from the cottage on his phone, no movement, just as it had been lately. *Where could she have gone to?* He decided more cameras around the property needed to go up so he could see when she was coming and going. The sun would soon be rising, so Mike decided he should continue his watch over the mill until his relief came. To help pass the time, Mike pulled up the album he had on his phone of the recent screenshots he'd taken of Presley since he installed the cottage cameras. His favorite, by far, was a photo of Presley in the bathroom with absolutely nothing on, facing the camera so he could see every inch of the front of her body; he zoomed in on her chest and waited for the light of the morning.

Fourteen

Presley was startled awake at the sound of her phone, she lifted her head and noticed she had fallen asleep in the safe room.

She had no idea what time it was, she squinted her eyes and looked at her phone, it was Trent which lightened her mood.

"Hi baby," Presley answered in a soft, muffled voice.

"Pres, oh babe." Trent put his hand on his chest as he let out a relieved sigh. "Good morning, are you alright?"

She rubbed her eyes. "Is it morning?" Her voice was still very soft. "I don't even know what time it is."

"Pres, I was so worried about you. I've been texting and calling, I didn't know what happened to you and I went to Jake's parents, the mill, the cottage." He let out another sigh of relief. "Are you sure you're alright?"

"I am." She sat up and realized it was after 8, they had been meeting for breakfast around 7. "Trent, I'm *so* sorry." She held her head. "I had no idea what time it was and I fell asleep, oh my gosh, I'm so sorry."

"Don't be sorry, I'm just glad you're alright." He took a deep breath. "Shit, I was getting really worried. I know last night was tough on you, sweetheart. Should I let you get back to sleep?"

"No." She stood up and grabbed all of the papers she had collected the night before. "I really do want to see you if you're still up for it—gosh, I feel terrible."

"Of course I still want to see you," he assured her. "I'll come get you, where are you?"

"I'm still at the house," she admitted.

"Oh shit." He grabbed his head. "I didn't even see your car or anything, you never left?"

She shrugged. "Apparently not, I fell asleep on the couch down here."

"Well, I'm just in front of the cottage, I'll run back up to the house and meet you there."

"Sounds good, thank you, Trent."

Mike glared as he watched Trent leave the cottage porch, it was the second time the motion detector went off that morning and it was him instead of Presley. He had a long night at the mill himself and was just waiting for Presley to return, preferably without Trent. He was kicking himself for not putting a camera with audio on the cottage porch, he was interested in hearing Trent's phone call. Mike didn't need the audio to make the likely assumption that Trent had been on the phone with Presley and he knew exactly where she was. Mike had burned an entire building down, was the first to notify her of trouble at the mill, was there for her when she showed up on the scene and somehow he still wasn't the hero; Trent got in the way. Had he known that, he wouldn't have burned down Pap's shop, he would have gone for something else. He thought if her heart hurt enough she'd come running straight to someone familiar and consistent. Instead Trent pounced on the opportunity to smother her, Mike *had* to come up with something else to push Trent out of the picture.

As Trent was jogging up the lawn Presley walked out of the back doors of the main house. Trent quickened his pace when he saw her; Baron greeted Trent out on the grass before he found a place to pee.

"Hi, sweetheart." Trent spoke softly and opened his arms to Presley as they approached one another. "Come here."

Presley put her arms around him. "I'm really sorry, I didn't mean to scare you or miss our breakfast date. I can't believe I didn't hear your other calls and texts."

"Don't even worry about it." He kissed her head. "I'm just glad you're safe."

They stood there holding each other for a long minute before Trent broke the silence. "What do you want to do this morning? I'm fine with whatever you need."

"Well," she lifted her head. "Did you eat yet?"

"Of course not." He put a piece of hair behind her ear. "I was hoping to eat with you."

"I kind of want to get cleaned up, would you mind eating after that or are you in a hurry?"

"I can wait, c'mon." He held her hand and motioned towards the cottage, assuming she would want to just get ready down there.

Presley hesitated and didn't move forward with him. "Uhm…," she looked down and then up at Trent. "I don't…," she stumbled, and looked towards the driveway. "Can we go? All my stuff's at Jake's parents'."

"Oh." Trent turned to go the other way. "Sure, we'll go wherever you need to go."

"Will you ride with us?" She squeezed his hand.

Trent didn't like her demeanor, she looked and sounded scared. "Of course I will."

As they walked to the car Presley looked down at her phone, eight missed calls from Mike. It was his personal cell rather than a department number and it was followed by several texts asking how she was, so she closed her phone and ignored all of them. Once she put her phone in her pocket Trent reached to her, it made her jump at first and then she leaned into him to rest under his arm.

"Pres," Trent started slowly. "You seem unsettled, are you sure you're alright?"

Presley shook her head as if she was physically removing something from her brain. "Yeah, sorry, I just have a lot on my mind and I feel like I didn't sleep much." She shrugged and unlocked her car.

"We can reschedule?"

"No," she held his hand. "I really do want to spend time with you." She tried her best to smile at him. "I need something good in front of me right now."

"Well, I'm right here." Trent smiled at her and pressed his lips firmly against hers. He rubbed his hands up and down her back and pulled her tighter to him with each stroke. "And why don't you hand me the keys, babe, I'll drive."

Presley exhaled relief that Trent was such a strong and comforting presence. She handed him the keys and he walked her over to the passenger side of her car.

◆

"Hi Presley, honey." Mardele, Jake's mom, opened the screen door. "Come on in, I was wondering about you dear, I heard about the mill." She hugged her and rubbed her shoulders. Mardele looked up at Trent, "Hi honey, you must be Trent." She walked over and hugged him. "Please come in and make yourself at home."

Trent appreciated her nonchalant behavior about meeting him, her focus was on Presley and didn't give him the normal Hollywood reaction.

"It's nice to meet you, Mrs. Hofner."

"Oh please, call me Mardele." She insisted and then turned back towards Presley. "Honey, I was just going to start cooking breakfast; Ron's out back tinkering in the yard, why don't you kids have breakfast with us? I'm sure you have a busy day, honey." She held Presley's shoulder.

Presley took a deep breath. "I'm pretty sure I do, they think the fire was arson, and I've missed about a dozen calls from Mike this morning." She rubbed the side of her head.

"Arson?" Trent and Mardele gasped in unison.

Trent understood even more why she was so upset and seemingly jumpy.

"Honey, you go take a shower and get some fresh clothes on, I'll take Trent into the kitchen and we're going to all have breakfast and chat about that, okay?"

Presley gave them a flat, sad smile before giving Trent's hand a quick squeeze and then she headed for the bathroom. To Trent's surprise, Baron followed him and Mardele into the kitchen.

"So, Trent, do you like coffee?" Mardele headed for her coffee station that was tucked in the corner of the kitchen.

"I do, thank you." He smiled.

"How do you take it?"

"Just black is totally fine." He replied. "Thank you."

"How's the movie going? The town sure is excited about you guys being here, of course all the girls, certainly." She smiled at Trent and handed him a cup of coffee.

"Thank you. Yeah, I figured that when Pres and I were at the Jubilee." He laughed remembering the mini mob that wanted pictures and whatever time they could get with him.

"You guys have been spending some time together, huh?" Mardele picked up on the 'Pres' and had heard chatter about Trent and Presley being out and about around town. Not to mention her kids had given her enough of a recap from what they knew for her to determine they were an item.

"Trying to." Trent smiled behind his coffee cup.

"Hi, love." Mardele greeted her husband when he came in from the back door.

Ron kicked his boots off before walking into the kitchen. "Hey, sweetie." He sounded a bit short of breath.

"Breakfast is cooking." She smiled and walked over to peck him. "Presley and Trent are going to join us this morning. Honey, have you met Trent?"

"I haven't had the pleasure." Ron walked towards Trent.

Trent stood up and was half a foot taller than the older round man donning overalls. "It's nice to meet you."

They shook hands and then Ron took a seat while his wife brought him a fresh cup of coffee. "Oh hey, buddy." Ron laughed and pat Baron when he climbed onto his lap with his front end. "Where's your mama?"

"Poor thing had a rough night so I sent her to shower and freshen up before breakfast." Mardele had her back turned to them tending to the eggs frying on the stove.

"Rough week from what it sounds like." Ron pat Baron on his side one last time and then sent him to lay down.

They heard a ringing on the kitchen counter, it was Presley's phone. Ron got up and looked at it. "It's Mike." He narrowed his eyes at his wife.

Mardele put her hands up and shook her head. Trent didn't know how to take that.

"Hello?" Ron's voice sounded stern. "Michael Bando, this is Ron Hofner."

There was a pause. "Uh huh," Ron continued. "She can't come to the phone right now but I'll give her a message… Uh huh, alright." Ron nodded his head. "She was?" Another long pause went by. "I don't think so, I didn't see her this morning." A quick pause went by. "Yeah, she's here at our house."

Great, Trent thought, *now Mike will be joining us for breakfast too*.

Ron continued after a brief pause. "No need…," he was cut-off by Mike but continued anyway. "You don't need to come by; no, one of us will bring her by the station later." He put his hand up. "No, we insist. Yep. Bye."

Ron pushed the screen to end the call and then looked at his wife, they exchanged an awkward look before Ron sat down.

"So?" Mardele waited for more. "What did he want?"

"To talk to Presley of course." He took a deep exasperated breath. "Also, he said she needs to meet him to answer some questions about the fire."

"*At the station* I hope." Mardele put a hand on her hip. "And what kinds of questions, she clearly wasn't there when it happened?"

"I told him one of us will bring her by the station later." Ron stated.

"He's always up to something." He shook his head. "I don't want that punk at my house and I'm not sending Presley along with him alone, she's gone through enough for now."

"I'd be happy to take her." Trent offered. "I don't want to step on toes, but I don't mind."

"I think the only toes you're steppin' on are Mike's." Ron laughed. "Monopolizing the time of his imaginary girlfriend, I suspect."

"Oh Ron, honey, that's not very Christian-like." Mardele lightly swatted her husband with a dishtowel.

Trent tried to stifle his laughter behind the coffee cup Mardele had given him.

"Hey, so how's she doing?" Ron took a sip of his coffee. "According to Mike she had quite the breakdown at the mill last night, threw up all over and was hysterical when she saw what happened."

"What?" Mardele put her hand on her hip. "She did look a little rough when she came in this morning, but I didn't know she had been throwing up."

Trent's heart hurt to know how physically and emotionally upsetting the fire had been for Presley, she did look pretty awful the night before, but he had no idea she had been puking.

"I didn't know that either." Trent admitted. "She looked exhausted last night and was still crying, but she didn't mention anything else."

"Well, let's all just try to be really gentle with her when she comes back from the shower." Mardele suggested.

"Presley likes to keep things close to the chest." Ron admitted. "That girl is made of something different than the rest of us. I think it'll be good for her that the kids are coming out this weekend." He set his coffee cup down and looked at Trent. "And of course good for her that you're here, Trent."

Trent smiled and offered a quick nod of his head.

"The kids tell me you two have been spending quite a bit of time together." He raised his eyebrows. "Are you guys dating?"

"Ron," Mardele lightly hissed. "Leave him alone, you sound like your son." She set some toast on the table. "Besides," she turned around.

"I already let him know we've noticed how much time they've been spending together."

Trent just laughed again.

"Honey," Ron countered. "I'm just trying to prepare him for when your son's in town." He looked at Trent. "Presley is like a daughter to us because she and Jake have always been so close. She's the girlfriend Lisa lets him have." He chuckled. "In the most unromantic way though, those three are thick as thieves."

Trent nodded his head after taking another sip of coffee. "It's good to have those friendships," he agreed.

"Mike isn't one of those friends, just so you know," Ron clarified. "Just because he's been around doesn't mean he's part of the crew."

Trent smiled. "Officer Bando doesn't worry me like that." He considered not saying anything else but felt comfortable with the Hofners so he got a bit more serious. "I don't get jealous, but it seems like he makes Presley uneasy and that's something I won't tolerate."

Ron's smile spread across his face, and he gripped Trent's shoulder. "I knew I liked this kid." He shook his shoulder and looked at his wife.

Fifteen

"Trent," Presley held his hand firmly as he drove them to the Sheriff's station. "Thank you for taking me, I really appreciate it."

He lifted her hand to kiss it. "Absolutely, anything you need, Pres."

"I know you need to sleep today too, so…," she was interrupted.

"Don't you worry about me." He offered an assuring smile. "I'm more than fine and there's no place I'd rather be than with you."

"Thank you." She rubbed his hand with her thumb.

Mike was waiting anxiously for Presley to get to the station. He knew either Ron or Mardele would be with her after having talked to Ron on Presley's phone earlier that morning. It also gave him a bit of relief to know she had likely been staying with them all week since he hadn't seen her at the cottage. Just as he was looking out the front doors again, he noticed Presley walking up the steps. *Ah fuck, what's that piece of shit doing here?* Mike thought as he watched Trent open the door for them with Presley under his arm.

"Hey, Pres." Mike walked around the front counter with a folder in his hand. "How are you?" He didn't so much as acknowledge Trent. *Why the fuck is he just always around?!*

Presley's head lightly bounced. "I'm okay."

"Officer Bando." Trent rubbed Presley's shoulders but did his best to be cordial with Mike.

"Trent." Mike didn't so much as look at him. "Pres, can I get you coffee or anything?" Mike asked.

"No, I just…," she fidgeted under Trent's arm. "I just want to do whatever we need to do and go."

"Well, why don't I take you into one of the rooms?" Mike picked up his coffee cup from the front desk and gestured towards a hallway.

They both started walking and Mike stopped them by holding his hand up. "Just Pres for this." He was firm with his statement.

Presley didn't leave the comfort of Trent's arm, he felt her gripping the back of his shirt.

"Is she being interrogated, or is this an interview?" Trent asked.

Mike shot him a bit of a death glare. "Listen, this is a sensitive topic, and she doesn't need an audience." He tried to meet Presley's eyes, but she was looking down, so he addressed Trent. "So, no, it's not an interrogation, but this is what I do for a living, and I think I can handle the sensitivity she needs."

"Oh, I'm sure," Trent sarcastically agreed. "But seeing as it's just an interview, if Presley wants me to, I'll go ahead and sit in." Trent had observed how anxious Presley had been since the fire. He knew she could typically handle her own and would likely push through this interview alone if she needed to, but why make her do that, in a room alone with Mike, if he could be there to comfort her through it? Her body language gave no signs that she wanted to be anywhere but under his arm and that's exactly where he would keep her until she indicated otherwise.

"Pres." Trent gave her shoulder a comforting rub and turned his head down towards her. "I'm more than happy to go with you, but if you prefer I stay out here, that's okay too. What will make you most comfortable, sweetheart?"

Presley slowly lifted her gaze from the floor to Trent. "Thank you," she nodded her head ever so slightly. "Can you stay with me?" Her grip around him tightened slightly.

He caressed her chin before answering. "I'm not going anywhere," he assured her.

"Great." Mike didn't want to be subjected to a kiss, this was enough as it was. "The room is this way." He turned his back and walked down the hall, stopping at the final door on the right.

The room was small, there were four wooden chairs situated around a rectangular shaped table that was made of metal. Trent walked Presley around the far side of the table and pulled a chair out for her, he confidently scooted a second chair right next to hers and took a seat. He picked up her hand, intertwined their fingers and set them on his lap. Presley gave Trent an appreciative look.

Mike set his folder down and clicked a pen. "Pres, how was your night?"

She felt Trent rubbing her hand. "Not great," she honestly answered.

"I know, I'm sorry, you know I'm here for you." He expected her to look up, but she didn't.

"So, I talked to the Fire Marshall this morning and he said it was definitely arson," Mike disclosed. "So, I need to get a bit of a rundown of your recent activities and associates." Mike scribbled something quickly on his notepad. "Can you remember what you've done the last week or so, Pres, and who you've been with?"

Mike tried to keep his disgust at bay when Presley continually mentioned she was alone with Trent at 99% of the activities she was describing.

"So, let's go back to the part where Trent was at the shop." Mike scooted his chair. "Was there anything he took particular interest in while you guys were there?"

"What?" Presley looked at him as though she misheard him.

"Well, he's the only outsider who's been in there, right?" Mike pushed.

Trent tried to keep his movements calm, and a half deadly grin formed on his face as he directed his attention to Mike.

"Trent isn't an outsider," Presley stated. "What does that even mean, Mike?"

"Just looking at all possible scenarios." He set his pen down and focused on Presley. "It is out of the ordinary to have shown him something so special to you and then days later it's the only thing that you lost at the mill." Mike was almost giddy when he discovered Trent had toured the mill so he could plant a seed of doubt in Presley's mind. He didn't want to let up now that he felt he was gaining a bit of traction to the theory he was trying to spin. "And it's no secret that he's taken an unusual interest in you since he got here."

"Unusual?" Presley's brows furrowed and her mouth formed a frown.

"This is sounding more personal than it is professional," Trent warned. "You and I can have a conversation if that's the route you're planning to pursue, but you're not going to sit here and treat her like this." He realized the hold on Presley's hand had tightened, so he tried to relax before he continued. "You know she doesn't deserve this, especially right now."

Mike glared at Trent who was maintaining it.

"Do I need to schedule a time to come back here?" Trent finally asked after their stare down had gone on long enough.

Mike finally broke his gaze when he closed his folder. "You know, I'll have to follow a few of my leads then I'll be letting you know."

"Wait, you have leads?" Presley sounded hopeful and Trent worried for her, he could tell Mike was just toying with her because his main goal was to make Trent look bad.

"Nothing I can disclose right now, Pres." Mike tried to offer her a look of sympathy.

Presley just looked down, disappointed.

There was a short moment of silence where Presley simply stared into the table.

"Are we done?" She almost whispered.

"Pres." Trent squeezed her hand. "Do you want to leave?"

She barely moved to nod her head, and Trent was already getting up to pull her chair out.

"Well, hold on." Mike stood up.

"No." Trent shook his head and pushed Presley's chair in after she stood up. "I may not be a cop, but I do know that she's here as a courtesy for an interview, you can't make her stay here. She's ready to go, so I'm going to take her out of here."

Mike glared at him while Presley took a half step closer to Trent who noticed her movements and quickly put his arm around her.

"Okay, well, if I have more questions, where will you be, Pres?" Mike asked, desperate to know where she was going to be.

"Her cell." Trent cut in. "You can give her a call on her cell, that's where she'll be." Trent made sure to keep his body in between Mike and Presley, she was tucked under his arm and he moved them towards the door. Once they were through the threshold Trent turned around to look at Mike. "And you can let the head of our security team know if you need to schedule an interview with me, I'll be around." Trent didn't wait for a reply, he walked Presley down the hall and out of the station.

✦

Presley felt like she could finally breathe the second they were outside, it felt like it had been more than twelve hours since the last time she was able to just breathe. Trent had gone in there ready to stand in front of anything that was headed Presley's way, he didn't let Mike slip up at all with her and appeared to be very attuned to her emotions the entire time. She wasn't used to being spoken for, and prior to today, very much hated the idea of anyone speaking on her behalf. However, Trent's presence and demeanor during the interview, and his genuine care and concern for her overall, encouraged her to let her guard down. Where she had allowed doubt to live in her mind the last couple of weeks based on Trent's past, she felt it vanish somewhere in the sheriff's station. They reached the car and when Trent opened her door Presley turned towards him and threw her arms around his neck. Trent caught her and held her firmly, one hand on her back and the other gripping the back of her hair. She was on her tiptoes but could feel Trent also holding her up.

"Thank you." She muffled into his shoulder as they held each other.

"Babe," he spoke softly into her ear, "I've always got you." He brushed his fingers through her hair. "I know you're strong as shit, but Pres, I will do the heavy lifting around here, you don't have to."

Presley peeled her head back from him to look him in the eyes. "Thank you, Trent." She reached up and their lips connected. Trent wanted very badly to give her more, but he had promised to go slow. So, he left the kissing at just their lips, having no idea that Presley was willing and waiting for him to make that move. When they separated again Presley lowered from her tiptoes and slid her hands down to hold Trent's waist. He reached a hand down to tilt her chin and give her one more peck.

"You should get some sleep today, baby." Presley rubbed her hands on the small of his back.

Trent smiled at her. "I will get myself some sleep once you're somewhere comfortable and resting as well." He massaged her shoulders.

"I'm supposed to be calling into a meeting for a pretty big work issue in a bit." She sighed. "So, I do need to get somewhere to touch base with Jake to figure out what's going on with all of that." She wiped her face. Trent continued massaging her shoulders, wishing he could just remove all of her stress.

"Do you want to go home for that?" Trent suggested, he couldn't imagine she wanted to be at the mill.

She shook her head. "No, I don't even think anyone is there right now, so maybe just...," she let the mill enter her mind for a split second but quickly shut that out when she knew what it would do to her. "Can you just bring me back to the Hofner's, please?"

"Of course I will." He agreed and shut her door once she was in the truck.

Trent pulled out of the parking lot. "I'll get you settled in over there and then I'll hit the motel for a little nap so you can do some work if you want?"

"We can do that." She smiled and reached for his hand.

"I can pick you up for dinner before I hit the set too," he offered.

"Why don't you sleep?" Presley's face scrunched in concern. "I feel like you haven't really slept," she encouraged him.

Trent made his way through town, Presley loved that he was more familiar with all of the local spots. "That doesn't mean I don't *want* to see you," she assured him. "I just want to be sure you're taking care of you as well."

"I'll only agree to this plan if you let me take you to breakfast the second the shoot is over in the morning." Trent countered.

"That's a deal," Presley agreed.

"And," Trent pulled into the Hofner's driveway. "You have to promise to call me if anything comes up or if you need me."

Presley looked at Trent in his eyes when he parked. "Trent, I promise."

Presley looked at the clock and knew she had less than an hour before her meeting. She could manage with just her laptop and phone, but desperately needed to talk to Jake to be sure they were on the same page. She had forgotten to bring her phone when they went to the Sheriff's station, so her first move was to go find that. A plethora of texts and missed calls covered the phone's screen.

MISSED CALL FROM BESTIE
MISSED CALL FROM BESTIE
MISSED CALL FROM BOYFRAAN
MISSED CALL FROM MIKE BANDO

BESTIE
Pres are you okay?! Jake's parents just called and told him what happened!! Girl I have a class but I'm calling you tonight. I'm so sorry and I can't wait until we're there. Love you girl take care and I will talk to you soon.

MISSED CALL FROM BOYFRAAN👫❤️

BOYFRAAN👫❤️
Pres my rents just called —are you okay? I'm so sorry about the shop. I don't want you to worry about anything with the work stuff, I'll handle the meeting today—I have a little surprise for that fucking bitch. Keep your pretty little chin up, we can't wait to see you this weekend. 😘

MISSED CALL FROM 👯BESTIE💕

👯BESTIE💕
Just in between classes and thought I'd check on you, love you girl. 💗

MISSED CALL FROM MIKE BANDO

MIKE BANDO
Pres, I know today was rough, I'm sorry. Let me know if you'd like me to pick you up later, I'll bring you over to see mom and have dinner. 💜

Presley was about to call Jake back when her phone indicated another text, it was from Trent, so she smiled and opened it.

🤠TRENT HAYES💕
Try to get some rest today sweetheart. I'll be counting down the minutes until I get to see your beautiful face, hold you in my arms, and smooch on those lips! Call me if you need anything 😘

She replied, knowing full well she'd be on the phone with Jake for a bit and didn't want to wake Trent up by a text later.

I will try to resist waking you up because I too will be counting down the seconds until all of that. Trent thank you for today, I can't even explain how much I appreciate you 🫶🫶

TRENT HAYES🫶
🙂♥️

Sixteen

Mike knew he had about an hour before anyone from the movie crew showed up at the house. Fortunately, since he was offering his law enforcement services to keep the set safe, he had full and unrestricted access, and no one would even ask questions if they did see him around. Mike brought a few cameras with him hoping he would also have time to hide them on the off chance that Presley had been spending time at the main house with Trent. All in all, it had been a difficult week for Mike—his attempts to separate Presley and Trent resulted in them spending more time together. As he was walking through the house scouting out the best spots for cameras, Mike landed on what he thought was a genius idea. He stood in the living room staring at one of the cameras from the film crew, he wondered if they actually left all of the film on-site. To his delight, they did. *Trent can't possibly spend time with her if he's working,* Mike thought and then he began removing as much film as he could find. Removing film took much longer than he anticipated and left him with only time to install one camera near the front entry of the house, he figured at least he'd be able to see who was coming and going and when it was happening.

◆

"What the hell?!" Phil threw his head set and was yelling in the main house. "Who the hell was here after we shut down yesterday morning?! Who was the last to leave?" He looked around the room.

The crew was silent and looking around, finally the first assistant director spoke up. "I locked up with Suzan, Keith and the guard on shift last night—I *promise* you, everything was here, all of it."

"It was," Suzan hesitantly concurred.

"Well, it's not here now. Someone's going to need to find that missing fuckin footage or heads will fucking roll," he warned. Phil stormed off towards the makeshift dressing room in the second master suite. "Hey." He walked in as Trent, Michelle and Pete were getting their final touches done by the costume designer. "So, change in plans, we need to get these first two scenes done quickly tonight, we may be re-shooting everything from yesterday."

"What?" Michelle whipped her head around. "What was wrong with the takes from yesterday?"

"All of the film from yesterday is gone." He threw his hands up. "I've got *no* explanation from anyone down there. They better fuckin find it, but re-shooting is plan B for now." He looked at the two set costumers. "I need everything we used yesterday ready to go as early as the end of the scheduled shoot tonight." He turned back to the cast. "And you all better buckle in for a long shift, I need everyone's A-game tonight to keep this on schedule."

Trent rolled his head back and took a deep, irritated breath before reaching for his phone.

> Sweetheart you know I'd love to see you for breakfast in the morning like we planned but it sounds like we may run late tonight .. Film from yesterday is gone. Can I still check in with you when we're done though?

PRES

> 😢 💜 I was definitely looking forward to seeing you too. I understand though, you can absolutely call when you're all done 💋💋 I'll get some work done tonight so I can hopefully have more time tomorrow.

> You're amazing 😊. And I'm sorry definitely wasn't planning to extend my day like this today.

PRES
> You don't have to apologize—I hope your night gets better 😊💕.

> You too beautiful 😊

Trent wasn't finished talking so his fingers raced across the screen.

> Hey ... if I'm outta here in time, can we have breakfast somewhere we don't get cell service tomorrow?

PRES
> Planning to cut me up into unidentifiable pieces??

> 😆 Definitely no! It just seems like it's been a long week and if we can't answer our phones maybe we can spend some uninterrupted time together. I wanna have a slow moment with you sweetheart we both need it.

Presley giggled, alone time after the week she had sounded like a fairytale.

PRES
> 💕💕 Just call me when you're ready?

> I will 😊

Presley pulled her laptop out to see if she could get ahead of a few things to better clear her morning. It had been a long week, and she couldn't imagine falling asleep knowing she was going to see Trent in several hours.

✦

"Hey, beautiful." Trent smiled when he pulled up and Presley was waiting outside of her G Wagon. "Did I keep you waiting long?"

"No." She smiled as he turned the car off and got out. "Good morning." She looked up at him and they kissed. Their lips were active, and Presley could swear she felt the tip of Trent's tongue. Baron interrupted them when he whimpered for his greeting.

Trent chuckled. "He's jealous." Trent looked over Presley's head and into her SUV. "Hey bud, I didn't forget you." He pecked Presley's head and then went to the window to give Baron a friendly chin scratch.

Presley watched them love on each other; she adored these moments. Despite her busy, worried mind, it seemed like being around Trent always cleared it.

"You two are just exactly what I needed." He pulled Presley in so he could kiss both of them. "Thank you for waiting for me." He rubbed Presley's shoulders.

"Of course." Presley pecked his lips. "You are exactly what we need too, Trent Hayes."

They stared into each other's eyes, Trent rubbing Presley's cheek with his thumb, and Presley rubbing her hands along Trent's strong chest.

"So, how do you feel about a breakfast picnic?" Presley interrupted their moment.

Trent opened her door, smiling. "I've never been on one, and I'm with you, so of course I'm extremely open to it." He shut her door for her and walked around to get into the driver's seat. "So, should I stop at the grocery store, or do you want to pick something up to go for our picnic?"

"Everything's packed." She confirmed and reached over the console to hold his hand.

"Pres?" Trent squeezed her hand. "You already packed it?"

"Uh huh." She rubbed the top of his hand with her thumb.

"Babe, you didn't have to do all that." He lifted her hand and kissed it. "But thank you."

"Of course." She smiled. "Sometimes I get to try to take care of you too, baby."

Trent looked at her, he could tell her heart still hurt, but he had to admit she looked much better than she had. "Pres, how are you?"

She nodded her head a few times and finally turned to smile at him. "I'll be okay."

"Let's try to get you better than just okay." He suggested with a smirk.

Trent enjoyed that time slowed down when he was with Presley, he was even beginning to fall for her small town. He wasn't ready to turn his back on L.A., but he had a soft spot for her little Pacific Northwest Mountain town. Presley instructed Trent to pull to the side of the road right off the highway to park.

"A little hike next?" Trent smiled.

"No, I don't want Baron walking too far. We're close though, is your phone working?"

"Nope." He smiled. "It's currently 'searching'."

He followed her to a small rock ledge that sat overlooking a large creek. The creek was calm, and you could only tell it was moving when you looked at it and listened carefully. There were so many trees that they weren't exposed to the morning sun besides the sporadic rays that fought their way through the branches.

"You've got all the spots, huh?"

Presley laughed and proceeded to get their breakfast out as Trent fixed their blanket. "This all belongs to the mill, so I kinda have to know it."

"You own more of the world than anyone I know." He smiled at her.

Presley just returned his dashing smile with one of her own.

"What time do you need to be back, Pres?" Trent took a drink of water.

"Well, the Fire Marshall is going to be at the mill at 1." She wasn't overly excited to be at the mill, especially in the daylight when she'd be able to see the full impact of the fire.

Trent rubbed her shoulder. "Have they given you any answers yet?"

She shook her head. "They've found zero leads, as far as I know, as to who the arsonist could be, but they're convinced that's what it was." She shrugged her shoulders and looked down at the picnic basket. "They keep asking me and I honestly have no idea who would actually do something like that or like why they'd hit that building. I could probably put together a short list of names if the actual business was what got hit," she admitted. "But everything else was completely untouched, that's what's making it extra hard for me to understand why it would be arson?"

Trent took a deep breath, he felt for her. "It's been a rough week." He scooted closer to her and put his arm around her. "I'm sorry." He squeezed her around her shoulders and kissed the side of her head.

"Yeah," she sighed. "You've made it much easier to digest though." She looked up at him. "Thank you, Trent."

He smiled back at her and brushed the side of her face, it didn't take long for their lips to connect for a quick peck. Trent caressed her cheek with his thumb and looked into her eyes before he moved back in. This was the first time they were able to truly be alone with no interruptions since the night of the Jubilee. Trent decided it was time to progress their kissing, so he opened his mouth wider when they went back towards each other, Presley allowed him to lead. Trent consumed the side of her face with his hand and slid his tongue past her lips, he softly moved his hold to the back of her head and continued to kiss her. After a few exchanges of their tongues Trent began to lean Presley back, she went with him until they were both lying on their sides. Presley reached out and put her hand on Trent's chest and caressed him as he slid his hand up and down her side.

"See what happens when we're not constantly interrupted or short on time?" Trent whispered as their faces parted slowly.

Presley blushed and bit her bottom lip.

Trent smiled at her and reached for the small of her back to pull her as close to him as possible, he wasted no time in continuing to show her how much he appreciated the alone time. Their kissing was interrupted when Baron bumped into them, he was on his back wiggling about on the blanket next to them. They both watched him as he tried to scratch his back. "Hey thanks, man." Trent lightly pushed him.

Presley giggled before she pecked Trent, she sat up and pat Baron's belly. "He's probably trying to just remind me that I still have to be a responsible professional today," she sighed.

"I really wish you didn't." Trent rubbed her lower back as he was still lying on the blanket.

"I know, I'd love to just spend all day with you." She set her hand on his leg. "But besides meeting the Fire Marshall I've got *a mountain* of work that needs to be done. I just want to be able to take a true weekend while the Hofners are here." She held his hand and smiled down at him. "I'm really excited for you to meet them."

Trent returned her smile. "I can't wait, babe." He sat up and held her head to kiss her again.

Presley enjoyed that he was more consistently calling her by little pet names. She also thoroughly enjoyed their new style of kissing; Presley was caressing the back of Trent's neck when he tried to lean them back again. Presley giggled and broke their rhythm. "That's probably an extra bad idea right now." She looked into his eyes and held his chin. "Because I don't think I'd ever make it to work today if we keep going."

"C'mon, no one's called looking for you yet?"

Presley laughed. "Crazy how that works since we're intentionally out of cell phone range."

"I know." Trent laughed and then hugged her. "Any chance I can sneak one more kiss out of you."

Presley certainly didn't mind tasting his lips again, so she turned back towards him, and they made out. Trent remembered she stopped when he tried to lie her down so this time, he made sure to keep her upright in hopes their kissing would last longer.

Seventeen

"Bay! Hi baby," Presley ran up to his window when Jake and Lisa pulled up.

"Hi Auntie PP, look I got." He held out his Paw Patrol sunglasses.

"Those are so dope!" She opened his door and started to take him out of his seat. "Can Auntie PP try those on?"

He held his arm out to her and offered her to take them, which she did and put them on to make him laugh. She still had them on when she picked him up out of his seat and turned to Jake, who had been driving.

"Auntie PP's a dork, huh Bay?" He laughed.

Bailey laughed and feverishly nodded his head in agreement, so Presley stuck her tongue out at Jake.

"Don't be mean to my best friend!" Lisa warned. "I'll spank both of you."

"Don't tempt me with a good time." Jake laughed and slapped her butt.

Lisa walked over to Presley and hugged her tight, sandwiching Bailey in between.

"I'm *so* glad you guys are here; you don't even know." She kissed Lisa's cheek.

"Where's mine?!" Jake complained and leaned towards her tapping his check, Presley laughed and pecked him before quickly catching Bailey on his.

"Auntie PP!" Bailey laughed.

"Babe, do you need both of these bags?" Jake asked since Lisa was going to stay the night with Presley for a little sleepover and the boys were going to stay at Jake's parents for the night.

"Yes, please." She grabbed her purse, and they all headed for the cottage.

"When do we get to meet him?!" Jake jumped up and down while they walked up the porch.

Presley laughed and rolled her eyes. "*Please* get that all out now, I'll die if you embarrass me." She kept laughing.

"You know I'm just teasin', Pres." He set Lisa's bags down next to the couch and then headed to the kitchen.

"Looks like you've settled in here quite nicely, huh?" Lisa looked around.

"Yeah it's actually not so bad, plus I'm closer to the water." She set Bailey down who ran towards Baron.

"I'm glad you've been able to stay here though, closer to the set." Lisa winked and then shrugged.

Presley kept laughing and the red raced to her face.

"Yeah, don't make me and Bay stay here too long with you two, I don't want to get stuck in the braid train or have manual labor forced upon me giving you two a mani pedi."

"Love, you're not getting rid of us that easily, we're all having dinner at your parent's tonight." Lisa reminded him.

"Ah shit, that's right."

"Unless they've had enough of me?" Presley laughed.

"Are you kidding me? They love you, Pres," Jake assured her. "They'd probably trade me for you if I didn't have Bailey." Lisa swatted him. "Oh, and my beautiful wife too of course."

They all heard the doorbell ring, so Baron started barking. Presley looked surprised because she wasn't expecting anyone, she smiled as she opened the door—it was Trent.

"Hey." She hugged him. "I wasn't expecting you, come in." She smiled.

"Hi, sweetheart." He reached out to hug her and planted a quick kiss on her forehead. "I know, sorry to bust in, I know you guys just got here."

"Oh my gosh, don't worry about it." Lisa flicked her wrist and gushed at Trent's greeting to her best friend.

"I'm working all night, but I just couldn't wait to meet you guys when I saw that you were here." He held his hand out to Lisa first. "I'm Trent."

Lisa blushed. "Lisa," she started. "I've heard wonderful things."

Trent grinned back at Presley who was beginning to blush. "Oh yeah?" He kept smiling and then turned to Jake. "Nice to meet you, Jake, right?"

"Hey yeah, you too, man." Jake returned the gesture, but not in an aggressive way like Mike had when they first met.

"And you must be Bailey?" He kneeled down to Bailey. Baron couldn't decide who he wanted to kiss more so he went back and forth offering kisses to both Trent and Bailey.

Bailey ran behind his mom's leg and put his thumb in his mouth.

"Bay, you can say hi, can't you?"

Bailey smiled and then hid his face.

"It's alright, I know we won't be strangers for long." He stood back up but not before patting Baron on the head.

"So, you guys are going to dinner soon, huh?" Trent asked as he rubbed Presley's lower back.

"Yeah," Jake made sure to clear his throat. "My parents would kill us if we didn't spend some time there too while we're in town."

"Is everyone still down for breakfast tomorrow?" Trent wanted to be sure he'd still have the opportunity to get to know Presley's friends.

"I'm pretty sure we are." Presley looked to her friends for confirmation.

"Yeah." Jake and Lisa said almost in unison.

"Perfect." He looked at Presley. "I only had a minute; I better get back." He looked at Lisa and Jake. "I'm glad I came down; it was great to meet you guys."

"We'll see you tomorrow morning." Lisa waved.

"Bye, nice meeting you." Jake waved too.

Presley turned to walk him to the door, Jake and Lisa stayed but they were definitely eavesdropping.

"Trent, thank you so much for coming down." Presley stood in the doorway and Trent was on the porch.

"Of course." He reached out and stroked her hand. "I knew you were excited for us to meet so I wanted to make that happen as soon as possible."

Presley smiled; Trent wasn't sure if she wanted to be kissing in front of her friends, but he leaned towards her anyway. When Presley leaned into him as well, he grasped her chin gently and planted a PG-13 rated kiss, with his tongue just barely touching the tip of hers, before leaving. "Have fun tonight."

"Thanks." She blushed. "Have a good night at work."

Trent winked and jogged back up to the main house.

Presley didn't even have time to shut the door before Jake and Lisa started howling, smacking their lips and cat calling. She laughed and then covered her blushing face.

"Hot lips 24/7 these days huh, Pres?" Jake poked at her.

"Girl! TRENT HAYES just kissed you!!" Lisa squirmed and then quickly started again. "OH MY GOSH *I* just met Trent Hayes!!"

"Don't get your panties wet you two." Jake rolled his eyes pretending he had to calm them down.

Lisa swatted him and then reached for Bailey to put her hands on his ears.

"Oh please." He rolled his eyes and laughed at his wife.

"Let's head to dinner." Presley suggested, still trying to get her face back to a normal shade.

Bailey's face scrunched as he pointed to the door. "Him kiss you?"

Everyone started laughing and Presley bent down to pick him up and hug him. "Oh," she squeezed. "You are too cute for words!"

> Trent that was so sweet and I can't wait to see you for breakfast tomorrow 😘💕

Presley was still glowing from Trent coming down to the cottage, even though it was brief.

> 💚TRENT HAYES💚
> I'll be counting down the minutes babe. 😘

Trent quickly replied.

✦

Mike watched as old high school friends were reuniting; he was upset he hadn't talked to Presley very much that week and then wondered why she never mentioned the Hofners were coming to town. Also, despite his efforts over the last week or so, it seemed like Presley and Trent were getting closer and that pissed him off above and beyond. He really didn't love the kiss he watched on the porch, he determined it was more than a peck and he wanted to rip Trent's tongue right out of his mouth for it. He shut the feed down and set an alarm for later in the evening when he estimated Lisa and Presley would be back.

Eighteen

"So," Lisa settled into the couch once they got back to the cottage after dinner. "I want the nitty gritty now that Jake's not around."

Presley laughed and shook her head while filling their wine glasses.

"Don't act like you're going to hold out on me now, you bitch!" Lisa threatened with a smile. "I've been patient all damn day."

"I know." Presley kept laughing.

Mike was excited that they hadn't turned the tv on, he could hear everything clear as day.

"What do you want me to say?" She shrugged with a bright pink face.

"Hell, I wanna know how he is in bed?!" Lisa screeched.

Presley covered her face laughing. "C'mon Lis." She rolled her eyes, "We haven't done *that*, you know me better." Presley kept laughing and leaned over to turn music on.

Shit! Suddenly all Mike was going to be doing was watching them as their conversation was now private.

"Yet." Lisa was sure to point out.

"I wouldn't even know how to get there." Presley shamefully admitted.

"What? What do you mean?"

"It's intimidating to think about." She shrugged.

"Because of who he is?"

"I mean, that's part of it." Presley's head rolled around deciding what she was going to say next. "Like, let's be honest for 2.5 seconds, he is like a worldwide celebrity *and* according to the media, he's had his fair share of girlfriends."

"Yet here he is paying extra attention to you, girl."

"Plus, I'm just not that experienced, especially compared to him, he's going to laugh at me and wonder if I've ever even had sex."

"Shut. Up!" Lisa laughed. "He's not going to think that at all, he's going to be too into you, literally." Lisa laughed while Presley planted her face in her hands. "He'll show you the way and you just roll with it, Pres."

"You sound like your husband right now." Presley laughed at her friend.

"If you feel like that for him then you need to just go for it when the occasion arises, I'm telling you, Pres." Lisa took a sip of her wine. "Seriously, girl, you've got this sparkle in your eyes, if you feel ready then I think you need to be open to that idea if it comes up."

Presley blushed. "I mean, we've kissed a bit," she admitted. "It's been nice, especially lately."

"What kind of kissing?" Lisa prodded.

Presley got giddy, it wasn't as though she'd never had these conversations with Lisa, she just hadn't felt like this about anyone before. "The kind where we may or may not have had our tongues down each other's throats."

"Presley Marie!" Lisa laughed. "Any cookie kissing?"

"Oh my gosh, no!" Presley laughed. "Nothing even remotely close to that," she further clarified. "We only started kissing like *that* very very recently." Presley sipped her wine. "He's actually been quite the gentleman."

"Really?" Lisa asked.

Presley laughed. "I've been a little surprised as well, I honestly was nervous that he'd be hitting the gas pedal day one."

Lisa blinked her eyes feverishly and then rolled her hand in the air a few times wanting Presley to elaborate.

"Well," she blushed. "I did tell him this week that I'm not the kind of girl who does flings or non-monogamy…"

"How did he take that?"

Presley nodded her head around slowly. "He was actually so sweet about it, truly. He more or less told me any of the assumptions I had from his playboy behavior were spot on." She scrunched her face a bit. "But then he said he will give me as much time as I need before we progress because, while he does want *that*," she giggled. "He wants more than that with me."

"Pres," Lisa reached for her hand. "That does sound super sweet and genuine. I mean, he took ownership of his previous lifestyle." She shrugged. "Being honest with that has to be something, he could've just tried to gaslight you on that subject to try to ease your mind." She continued. "And I also know how high your damn walls are, so if you're letting him climb over that shit, then I know it's real."

Presley smiled and reached her hand to rest it on Baron's back as he was sitting next to them on the couch.

"So, do I need to be sure you're stocked up on condoms before we leave this weekend?" Lisa asked as Presley was taking another sip of her wine.

Presley had to slap her hand on her mouth to avoid spitting all over the couch. "Oh my gosh!" She swatted lightly at her friend.

Lisa just laughed and then changed the subject a bit. "So, what did you guys do all week?"

"Well," Presley took a deep breath. "It was just non stop this week,

I swear, we could barely sneak in any alone time." She shook her head. "If it wasn't one thing, it was another." A smile formed on her face. "But Lis, he's legit like…," she struggled to describe him. "…He's pretty damn perfect."

"That's so sweet, Pres." Lisa smiled.

Presley rolled her head a bit. "I know I'm not the easiest person to get close to, like I keep busy and especially this week I was somewhat distant, but he just has a way of just…," Presley searched for the words. "Like when he's around or when I talk to him on the phone it's like we're just in our own little world. He just eases my mind and makes the bad not as bad."

Lisa smiled at her best friend.

"Like when he touches me it's just different too." She shrugged. "We ended up kind of talking about family the other day and like I started talking about Paps." She paused to swallow hard and then she forced a smile to finish her story. "He ended up just holding me. The comfort I felt in his arms was like nothing I've ever felt. He didn't like make it creepy or turn it into feeling me up, he legit just put me in his arms and just held me." Presley could almost feel his arms around her at that very moment. "And each time he's put me in his arms since then, it just feels… Right."

Lisa took a drink from her wine glass and let her friend continue.

"Lis, please don't think I'm crazy, but he treats me like he would literally walk in front of a moving train for me. The emotional effort he's put in these last couple of weeks, I know he's an actor, but can someone really fake that?"

"Pres," Lisa cut in. "First of all, I don't think you're crazy; secondly, what does your gut say about it?"

"That treacherous bitch just keeps tossing around butterflies, the gut has been zero help." She rolled her eyes laughing into her wine glass before taking a quick sip. "But I'm telling you, his touch is like magic; I feel an immediate sense of calm and comfort from it." She held her forehead, "It's scarier than shit."

"I know, girl." Lisa rubbed her hand. "It's scary because you've never felt it. Sure, your Dad, Paps, and even Jake would move mountains for you, but Trent provides a different kind of… comfort." She was sure not to use the term, 'love'. "You've carried enough, you've been through enough on your own that you should consider letting Trent help take care of you, Pres. If just his embrace gives you relief, that *has* to mean something."

Presley was staring off into space with a smile in her eyes. "Just something about how he takes charge too, like I don't even have time to consider the million scenarios, Trent's already got our path cleared and he's got me on his back just moving us forward. It's almost like I can just shut my brain down and know everything will be fine, better than fine really."

"Presley," Lisa tried to emphasize the sincerity. "That's exactly the type of man you need. Trent sounds like he's good for your heart. And trust me, no man is putting in that kind of effort if he isn't interested. You told him you're not down for the one-night stand thing and yet here he is, daily, making sure the punches being thrown at you don't even have a chance at landing." She continued. "Not to mention he said he'd wait and go slow with you. Pres, you see that, right? He's going slow with the physical stuff, but he hasn't just separated himself from you until you give him a little booty call when you're ready. He's still here, he's still making sure he meets your friends the second they show up at your house, he's still coordinating date nights with you, still isn't just hoeing around town to get his dick wet while he waits for you." That made Presley laugh. "He seems real. And believe me when I say, I really did have my doubts about him. His reputation isn't easily ignored, and I obviously want to see some things for myself, but everything you've told me, that man is more interested in you than you realize."

They remained silent for a moment before Lisa reached out and held Presley's hand. "Pres, don't let the bullshit going on around you right now make you skeptical of something good. You can't be consumed by worry and angst all the time, if it feels right with Trent, follow that."

Presley nodded her head.

Nineteen

"Good morning, sweetheart." Trent greeted Presley by leaning down to kiss her. "I brought you some flowers." He held out a bouquet of pink peonies. "Apparently the last ones didn't look fresh." He laughed.

Presley laughed and kissed him again. "Thank you, and for the record, all the flowers you've given me have been beautiful," she assured him. "Breakfast is almost ready."

Trent smiled and walked into the cottage to Jake and Bailey coloring at the table and Lisa helping Presley finish breakfast.

"Hi!" Bailey yelled and waved at Trent.

"Oh hey, bro, we're good now?" Trent asked as he ruffled his hair.

Bailey just handed him a crayon and then picked a new one to color with.

"Smells great in here." Trent told the girls and then stuck his hand out to Jake who shook it.

"What's up, man?" Jake greeted him.

"Bay baby, it's time to put the colors away because we're going to eat," Lisa instructed him.

Bailey furrowed his brows and crossed his arms.

Jake leaned into Bailey and whispered. "Mommy's a fun-killaaaaaaaa," he teased.

"Mommy you're fucknilla." Bailey gave her a toddler death glare.

"Nice." Lisa rolled her eyes at Jake while Presley and Trent tried to stifle their laughter. "Come here, baby." Lisa picked up a now pouting Bailey and brought him to the bathroom to wash his face and hands.

"You're a brat." Presley shook her head, laughing at Jake as she finished picking all of the coloring supplies up from the table.

"What?" He held his palms up.

"Jake's acting up because we drank all his wine last night." Presley sat down next to Trent.

Trent laughed and looked at Jake for his response.

"Fuckers drank all *five* bottles I brought!" His head was shaking back and forth. "Pres, you know I was looking forward to trying that pinot."

She smiled. "Would it make you feel better to know that was the last one we drank?"

"Fuck no." He shook his head, acting as if he were mad.

"I'll let you pick out whatever you want from my cellar then to make it up to you." She promised.

"Fuckin' better." He replied and then smiled at Trent.

"Look, Daddy." Lisa came back in with Bailey holding her hand just behind her. "The four-year old ears are back in the room."

Jake made a zipper motion over his mouth while rolling his eyes.

✧

Mike couldn't get to Presley's soon enough, he was leaving her favorite donut shop in town and raced towards her. He would have typically waited until a bit later, but he didn't want to miss any more of breakfast since Trent was there.

✧

"No way, bro, you're wild, Rubble is the coolest." Trent tried to convince Bailey.

Bailey laughed. "No! I like Chase."

"Okay, well, Chase is cool too, but c'mon, Rubble on the Double has all the sweet tools!"

Bailey laughed and hid behind a piece of pancake he picked up.

"Bay, honey, don't play with your food." Lisa told him before taking a bite and turning to Trent. "You're a regular Paw Patrol expert, huh?"

Trent looked back down at his plate and hooked a piece of fruit on his fork. "I have a niece and nephew who live and die for that show," he explained. "So, I have to be well versed."

"Oh, how old are they?" Lisa asked.

"Those ones are actually twins, they just turned five a couple months ago."

"Are those your only nieces and nephews?" Jake asked.

Trent smiled. "Not at all." He looked at Presley, she knew he had a large family, but they hadn't discussed nieces and nephews yet. "I have eight and a half. My younger sister is due at the end of the year with her first. They all range from seventeen to not even a year old yet."

"Holy shit." Jake commented. "How many siblings do you have?"

"Four. I have two older brothers, an older sister, then a younger sister."

"Wow." Lisa wiped Bailey's hands before he got syrup everywhere. "I had no idea you had such a big family, are you guys all pretty close?"

"I'd say so, I mean, obviously they all spend a lot more time together than I do because I'm just gone a lot for work, but we're pretty tight knit."

"Are all of your siblings married?" Lisa asked.

"They are." Trent confirmed and then took a drink of orange juice. "All married and either have kids or are actively baking them in the oven." He smiled.

"So," Jake couldn't resist. "You like the uncle lifestyle, or are you trying to be a husband and a dad too?"

Trent exhaled a chuckle. "I do love the uncle status. But if my mom had it her way, each of her kids would be married with four to six of their own. I've always told her not to hold her breath waiting for me to fulfill that dream of hers." Trent reached down to gently hold Presley's leg before he continued. "I honestly never thought that lifestyle was in the cards for me until very recently."

Lisa's eyes immediately shot towards Presley who was already looking down at her plate and blushing.

Jake was just about to open his mouth when the doorbell rang. Lisa watched Presley as she reluctantly got up from Trent's hold, she rubbed him on his shoulder and then headed for the door with Baron on her heels. She wasn't shocked when she got there and saw Mike, but she wasn't particularly happy to see him either. She had been able to mostly avoid him since his awkward hug and neck incident.

"Hey, Mike." Presley greeted him.

"Good morning, just about to go to the station and start work for the day." He looked beyond Presley into the house and then back at her. "I haven't seen you much this week though so thought I'd check in."

They all heard Mike's voice, Jake didn't wait at all, he shot his wife a quick scowl and got up to head towards the door.

Trent didn't know what to think about that and when he looked at Lisa she just smiled. "This oughta be fun." She pumped her eyebrows and slayed a piece of pancake on her fork.

"Yeah, it's been a crazy week." Presley agreed and put her foot out to Baron who was growling and trying to walk by her to Mike.

"So," Mike wanted an invitation to stay. "I saw a new car out front too, everything alright? Did you get a new car?"

Suddenly Jake was at the door too. "If it isn't the next Sheriff of these here parts," he joked.

"Hi Jake, I didn't realize you guys were in town?" Mike reached for his hand to shake it.

"Really? I waved at you yesterday when we passed each other on the road near my parents?"

"That was you?" Mike tried to pretend. "Now I see the connection." He pointed at their new Jeep Wagoneer that was parked in front of Presley's cottage.

"Yeah, here for the weekend."

"Oh, alright." Mike held up the bag containing Presley's donut. "Well, I only brought one donut today, but I can bring one for everyone tomorrow, is the whole family here?"

"Why don't you come in?" Jake gripped Mike's shoulder harshly, he wanted to witness firsthand what Mike had been acting like.

"Sure, for a minute." He shrugged and gave Presley her donut.

"Thanks, Mike."

Mike's lip began to smear when he saw Trent chummy with Lisa and Bailey.

"Hi, Lisa." Mike smiled.

"Hi, Mike." Lisa waved and put on what Presley knew was a fake smile.

Bailey ducked behind Lisa, trying not to make eye contact with Mike.

"Officer Bando." Trent nodded his head and then turned back to Bailey who was making his way to Trent and continuing to hide.

Mike didn't care to acknowledge Trent's presence. "Looks like quite the morning spread, did you girls do all this?" He looked back as Presley was making her way to the table.

"Yep, taking care of their boys." Jake returned to his seat to finish breakfast. "You can certainly join if you wanna grab a plate?"

Trent tried to conceal his smile, Jake had what seemed like a bit of an edge to his voice now, he could swear Jake's comment was also pointed at the fact that Mike was *not* one of the boys and had no claim whatsoever on Presley. Trent's smile faded when Mike decided to take the chair at the head of the table, which was also closest to Presley's seat.

Presley cut her Boston cream donut up knowing that Bailey loved them too, she came over and set a large portion of it on his plate. She took her seat back next to Trent and as she sat, she grazed his shoulder; he responded by setting his hand back on her lap once she was settled. When Bailey was brave enough to look up, he saw her smiling at him and the donut waiting, he ran back over to his seat to pick his plate up.

"Bay, honey, where are you going?" Lisa asked.

The toddler didn't respond, he carefully, with both of his hands, walked his plate onto the other side of the table to the bench Trent and Presley were sitting at. Trent helped him push the plate securely onto the table and then Bailey held his hand out for Trent to help pull him up to the bench seat.

Trent smiled at him. "Here, bro." He made sure his new little friend made it safely onto the bench. He ruffled his hair, and the toddler wasted no time in feasting on his donut.

"Can you tell Trent thank you?" Lisa reminded him.

He didn't vocalize any kind of gratitude, he held his fist up for Trent to dab, which he did. Lisa shook her head, smiling. "That's a Jake thing." She rolled her eyes. "What about Mike?" Lisa reluctantly pointed out. "Can you tell him thank you for the donut?"

Bailey hid his face behind Trent and told Mike 'thank you' in his monster voice which had everyone chuckling.

"You're welcome, big guy." Mike smiled even though he couldn't see Bailey's face.

"Bay!" Lisa tried to get his attention. "You are going to get chocolate all over Trent."

Trent looked down. "Oh, he's fine, honestly, I'm no stranger to toddler hands." Trent grabbed a napkin. "Hey man, you want some help with your face there? You're missing out on so much chocolate, epic party foul for sure."

Bailey didn't respond, he put his donut down and then stood on the bench to face Trent. He closed his eyes and leaned towards him demonstrating he was fully trained for the face wipe.

Presley smiled at them. "Bay, do you like Trent?"

Bailey waited for Trent to be done with his face before he nodded his head. "Yep." He sat down and immediately dug back into his donut. "Auntie PP, you like Trent?" he asked.

Presley blushed as the table was now trying to suppress their laughter and looking at her for an answer.

"Yeah, Auntie PP." Trent turned to her. "You like Trent?" his hand started to slide towards her inner thigh, but he stopped before it was too suggestive.

Presley giggled and held on to Trent's arm, she battled the rose-colored embarrassment that was still on her face. "Yes, Bay, Auntie PP likes Trent too," she managed.

Bailey was intently inspecting his chocolate covered fingers when he responded. "Yep, and him kissed you." He clearly stated and then sucked the chocolate off his thumb.

The table roared and Presley buried her head in Trent's shoulder. Mike was definitely not amused, but Jake reached his fist out to bump with his son all while Presley squirmed. Trent reached his free arm towards Presley and held the side of her head against his arm as he planted a kiss on her forehead.

Mike decided he had seen and heard enough so he cut in. "I saw Michelle leaving the set when I pulled in this morning, do you need a ride to your motel, Trent?"

Trent was still rubbing the side of Presley's buried head when he laughed through his nose at Mike. "I don't typically ride with her and Pete, but I appreciate the offer. Aren't you headed into work soon? Because I probably won't leave before you need to be on duty." He looked right at Mike and smiled.

"I don't mind going in late, I'm sure these guys have plans today, it's not every day we get the Hofners back into town." Mike smiled at Lisa to try to connect with her.

Lisa's face didn't disguise her feelings about Mike's behavior, she looked at Presley and then at Jake before going back to watching Bailey.

"I've got the Tahoe here still too." Trent continued to reassure him a ride was not necessary.

"We've got him." Jake jumped in. "Unless your crush is that big?" He joked. "Seems like everyone's starstruck, but I think you'll have to arm wrestle Presley for extra time with Trent though." He laughed.

Mike wasn't amused, everyone else took the opportunity to laugh and Presley blushed before looking back up at Trent.

Trent was grateful that Jake was so outspoken, and even more grateful Presley was closer to being his.

"No." Mike shook his head. "Just trying to help out." He was finding it difficult to keep his composure while Trent appeared completely smug. He could just imagine hopping the table and laying Trent out right then and there, he wanted to just pull his duty weapon and rid Presley of him at that very moment, he realized his face may be showing his hatred, so he snapped out of it and looked at Jake. "So, you guys wanna have dinner tonight or something? I can try to get a few guys from the ol football team out too? Or we can all go out to the bar later in the night, I'm sure the guys would love to see you two." Mike thought he could further exclude Trent because he'd be working, and he also wasn't part of their football memories.

"Maybe," Jake said. "Why don't you text me later after you talk to some of the guys? I'm sure the girls don't want to get drunk with the team all night reminiscing about the glory days." He laughed.

"I can just text Pres, I don't have your number." Mike shrugged.

"Well here, what's yours?" Jake pulled his phone out. "No sense in having a go-between." Jake looked up from his phone before Mike was able to respond. "Trent, what time do you have to work again tonight? You'd love a good guy's night, wouldn't you?"

Trent was about to answer until Jake continued. "I gotta get some bro time in anyway while we're here." Jake pointed back and forth between Trent and Presley. "I see what's going on here and that's my girl so, you know." He shrugged and looked back at his phone. "Mike, what's your number?"

Mike fumbled and then gave his number to Jake.

"Actually." Trent was trying hard to wipe his smile. "I'd really love to join but I'm not sure what time I'll be able to sneak out of there tonight, I can keep in touch about it though, if it's before the bar closes count me in." He agreed.

"Fuck yeah." Jake nod.

"Jake!" Lisa gestured towards Bailey.

"Babe." He rolled his eyes. "He hears you say that all the time."

Lisa shook her head. "You lie." She laughed before catching her son's attention. "Are you done eating, bud? You ready to go down to the lake?"

"Swimming?" He asked.

"In a little bit, we're going to walk first so it can get a little warmer out, is that okay?"

He rattled his little head feverishly and then rushed to his backpack to put his shoes on.

Presley stood up and started clearing plates.

"Nope." Trent got up. "You made breakfast." He smiled at her. "I'll clean up."

Presley laughed. "You're not cleaning the kitchen."

"I'm not above it." He pecked her cheek and walked into the kitchen.

Presley's smile was glowing, she shook her head, looked back at the table, and then followed Trent to help.

Mike didn't wait long, he followed Presley so as not to give them any alone time.

Lisa lightly swatted Jake. "He's off his damn rocker."

"I don't like this." Jake looked back at his wife.

"Two helpers, huh?" Trent commented when he saw Mike walk in.

Mike mostly ignored him. "Pres, I'm gonna head out, shift starts soon." He put his hand on his duty belt before offering Trent a dirty look.

"Alrighty, thanks for the donut and for stopping by." She waved. Presley didn't want a repeat of Mike's extra feels like several nights ago. She watched out of the corner of her eye as Mike's hands began to leave his duty belt, she assumed he may be coming towards her for a hug, so she quickly went to Trent's side at the sink, making space between where Mike was standing, to help with the dishes.

"Maybe I'll see you tonight?" Mike didn't want to leave. "I can pick you up if you want to come out?"

"Oh." She rinsed a plate off and smiled quickly at him. "I'll see what Lisa's planning; I want to spend as much time with her as I can while she's here."

"No worries." He held his hands up. "I was just sayin' it'd be nice to spend time with you tonight."

Presley was looking down at the sink, but her eyes got wide.

"I'll be here." Trent butt in. "I can always try to swing down here and see where you're at if you want to come with me." He gave Presley a reassuring smile and then looked at Mike. "If I'm able to go, that is. Then you won't have to drive back out here." Trent shrugged.

"Or that." Mike rolled his eyes.

"Yeah, I'll see." Presley reached for the soap to lather her hands in hopes she would avoid any kind of contact with him.

"Alrighty, I'll see you later, Pres." Mike took one step towards them.

Trent noticed and took the opportunity to switch them places. "Babe, you're not washing these, I will." He smiled and moved himself to now be in between Mike and Presley. "You just rinse, remember you do the light work around here."

Presley let out a sigh of relief and took another small step in towards Trent, practically under his arm, "Okay, be safe today." She waved.

"Bye, Officer Bando." Trent chimed in.

Once Mike was out of the kitchen and they both heard Jake walking him to the door, Trent looked at Presley. "Do you want me to say something to him?"

"I'm so sorry, Trent," Presley shook her head.

"Why are *you* sorry?" He looked puzzled.

"That can't be comfortable." Presley continued to look into the sink. "I don't have some kind of secret something with Mike, like sure we're old friends, but…"

Trent cut her off as he laughed and reached for her. "Pres, you don't have to justify anything, I understand. I'm not upset you guys are friends, what upsets me is you look uncomfortable when he's around. If that's for my sake, then don't worry about that." He held her face.

Presley reached for his lips and connected with him, he rubbed her chin with his thumb and gently slipped his tongue into her mouth. They massaged each other's tongues until they heard Bailey charging into the kitchen. "I'm ready!" He announced as their lips separated.

"Hey." Presley put her hand on her hip. "Those are my sunglasses!"

"No way, Jose!" He countered. "Trent, look these shoes I got!" Bailey stomped around until he got to the sink.

"Light up Paw Patrol shoes?! So rad!"

"Rad." Bailey repeated before he scampered out of the kitchen.

Presley didn't waste much time when Bailey was out of earshot again. "Thank you, Trent." She looked up at him with gratitude projecting from her eyes.

"Absolutely, sweetheart." Trent leaned down to connect their lips for a quick peck.

Twenty

"Do we get to know *anything* about the movie?" Lisa prodded as they were making their way around the lake. "I know it's supposed to stay sorta under wraps and all that, but is there anything you can tell us?"

Trent smiled. "I can share some details, certainly not the entire storyline." He chuckled. "It's a horror movie, my first." He briefly put his hand to his chest before continuing. "And actually, I'm playing the villain."

Presley whipped her head around and looked at him. "I didn't know that." Her face was nervous.

"It's… different," he admitted. "We were watching playback the other day and it was almost eerie to see myself like that."

"I will basically have nightmares after seeing the movie then?" Presley laughed.

"Oh Pres," Jake called out. "I'm sure Trent will put those nightmares to rest *real* quick." He pumped his eyebrows.

"Jake!" Lisa scolded him while Trent stifled his laughter.

Presley blushed but was eased when Trent reached for her hand.

"I mean, there are some scenes that I'd rather not associate myself with." He rolled his head. "But, overall, the script is amazing, and I think it'll end up being a really good film." He shrugged as he was intertwining his fingers with Presley's.

"When does it come out in theaters?" Jake asked.

"Oh." Trent scratched the back of his head. "It'll be almost a year, and that's including our time here shooting."

"Wow, that long?" Lisa scrunched her face.

"Actually," Trent laughed. "This is the quickest shoot I've ever been a part of." He squeezed Presley's hand. "Unfortunately."

Presley blushed and immediately looked down which prompted Trent to loosen their hands and put his arm around her.

"So, Lisa," Trent looked towards her for a moment. "I know you are an educator, but Jake." He turned to him. "What is it that you do for work?"

"Oh," Jake smiled, "*I* am a partner at a pretty large law firm in Seattle." He wiped his shoulders.

Lisa rolled her eyes, smiling.

"Wow, a partner?" Trent was genuinely impressed. "You're a pretty young guy to be making partner."

Jake rolled his head a bit before giving credit where credit was due. "Well, I will admit, it did help my chances that two of the old partners retired about a year after I came on board, I sat in on two massively successful wins during my first year, had an obnoxious caseload on my own…,"

Presley was sure to clear her throat in the most obvious way to remind him about her part in the deal.

"Aaaand," Jake continued, after smiling at Presley. "When they were considering their potential new partners, it definitely did help me that this little lady was shopping around for new representation."

Presley smiled. "I was beginning to think you'd leave me out of that one."

"Never." Jake assured her as he picked Bailey up. "You know you're my girl, I've always got your back."

"Which is why I could only trust you to help keep me out of white-collar prison." She laughed.

"Pres," Jake started, "not that I actually enjoy bringing this up, but we do need to have a chat about our little *friends* too."

Presley rolled her head back and took a deep inhale.

"Probably sooner than later." He reluctantly suggested.

"Yep," she exhaled deeply. "Later today?"

"Sure, we actually got another proposal from those wonderfucks this morning." Jake's mouth went flat. "I know what I'd like to tell them, but we need to be sure we're on the same page because honestly the stakes just got higher with this recent bullshit. I think part of it's my fault for being such a dick at the meeting this week."

She just shook her head as the group continued to make their way around the lake.

Trent began to think about what Presley had already been going through that week and Jake's comments made it seem like work was much worse than Presley's general comments about just being busy. She didn't divulge a lot of details from her workdays with him, but he assumed it was because he had zero knowledge of the industry she worked in so she wasn't trying to bore him. He now began to wonder what else Presley was silently dealing with and how much he wanted to offer his support. It was becoming clearer that Trent would maintain a slower pace with Presley physically, because she had requested that, but emotionally, he could be there for her. He wanted to be there for her.

✦

They were walking back up the lawn from the lake when Jake started. "Hey." Jake had his arm comfortably around his wife's shoulders. "Remember after the regional game Senior year Paps let us come back here and have that huge ass party?"

Presley smiled and looked down at the lawn, she nodded her head remembering that very same night. "I do."

"That was the night we convinced him to get up on the keg!" Lisa quickly remembered. "Oh my gosh, Trent, you would have loved it! Paps had to be pushing just past 70 at that point, Jake and someone…" she thought for a moment. "Shit, I don't remember who else, but you two had his legs, I nearly wet myself. I was laughing so hard."

"This backyard was *fucking* covered," he emphasized. "Ended up with like six kegs, not to mention I don't know how many fifths we gathered. We didn't even know who half those people were that showed up." Jake laughed.

"It was the other team." Presley bit her bottom lip wishing she wouldn't have brought that team up.

"Oooohh," Jake pumped his eyebrows. "That's right, Pres had a thing for that quarterback."

Presley dropped her head and immediately turned red.

"Oh, quit telling stories Jake." Lisa bumped into him knowing Presley didn't want that story going any further.

"Unless you wanna start talking about the story where we all saw your bare ass jumping off that dock over there that night." Lisa laughed.

"Yeah," he squeezed Lisa and looked at Trent. "And you've been tappin' that ass ever since."

"Jake!" Lisa pushed away from him laughing.

Trent fought back a yawn in the middle of laughing as they worked their way towards the cottage.

"Are you tired?" Presley reached over and held his hand.

Trent laced their fingers immediately and smiled down at her. "I'll be alright, I can always sleep later." He assured her.

"You're more than welcome to take a nap at the cottage, we'll be down at the lake, so it'll be quiet up here, I certainly don't mind."

Trent would have rather spent time in Presley's bed *with* her, but a nap sounded great after his long night of work. "I don't want to ditch out on the party." He smiled before sneaking a quick peck to the side of her head.

"Trent, we all know you had a long night, no one will blame you." She assured him.

He bit his bottom lip and looked at her. "Then maybe I'll lay down for just a minute." His smirk was cut off by another involuntary yawn.

Jake was out in the car grabbing things he needed for work and Lisa was helping Bailey with his swim trunks in the bathroom when they got back to the cottage.

"Do you have a different pillow I can borrow, sweetheart?" Trent asked as he pulled a blanket off the back of the couch to lay down.

Presley laughed. "You don't have to sleep on the couch!" She took the blanket from him and placed it back where it was. Presley reached for Trent's hand and led him up to her room. "You can sleep in my bed."

"I always knew you wanted to get me in there." He rubbed his thumb on her hand and waited for her to turn around, it took her a second, but she playfully rolled her eyes at him. "I'll admit," he continued. "This is starting out much different than I had imagined."

Presley continued to shake her head at him as they entered the bedroom.

✦

Mike's phone notified him of bedroom movement, so he checked the camera. *What the fuck did I miss?* He watched as both Trent and Presley were in the bedroom. He turned the volume to the maximum setting, wanting to hear every last word.

✦

"Here," Presley drew the shades. "These are blackout curtains so you shouldn't have any sunlight sneaking in, I'm going to grab a few clothes real quick." She walked to the dresser. "Are you going to be alright, or do you need any more pillows or blankets or anything?"

Trent looked at the bed and then back at Presley who had a bathing suit and some kind of cover in her hands when she turned around. "Thank you, Pres." He walked to her. "I think I'm good on pillows and blankets." He held her chin. "But I'll sleep better with a goodnight kiss," he informed her with a devilish grin.

Presley slowly lifted herself on her tiptoes to meet his lips, she held her clothes and Trent put his arms around her. They escalated right to twisting their tongues. Trent wanted to lift her up and take her to bed with him, he squeezed her for a moment and then remembered he vowed to take things slow, so he let up and instead rubbed his hands up her back and then grasped her hair.

Shit! Mike paced, *no fucking way this is happening already. Pres, do not let this happen*!

Presley began to giggle when he pulled her hair. "I better tuck you in," she whispered when she separated their lips.

Trent reluctantly agreed with a deep exhale. "You're probably right, although," he smirked. "If you wanted to take a nap with me, I'd be alright with that too."

Presley blushed. "Soon," she winked.

Trent's face lit up, *a promise to sleep together soon?*

Presley took his hand and led him to the bed. "But for now, I'll just say goodnight."

They smiled at each other as Trent crawled into bed.

Presley pecked him. "I'll be right back." She went to the bathroom to change.

Mike's heart rate was going down since realizing they weren't actually planning to do anything. He didn't watch her make her way to the bathroom for long before he was checking in on that camera instead. His heart rate began to climb as he watched Presley removing her clothes. His lips curled up into a sneered smile knowing Presley was changing in the privacy of her own bathroom instead of letting Trent see her body.

He felt excitement in his chest, and his pants, as he watched Presley struggle with her top. She had lost her grip on the ties several times which just resulted in her breasts popping out over and over, he screenshot each occurrence.

✦

Trent took his shirt off and then made himself comfortable in bed, he set his alarm, and when he looked at the nightstand, he noticed a phone charger so he plugged his phone in. He was getting the pillows situated when the bathroom door opened, Presley walked towards him and his heart skipped a beat at her sheer bathing suit cover which exposed the fact that she was in a two piece.

"You're not asleep yet?" She joked and continued towards him.

"I couldn't possibly fall asleep without a goodnight kiss from you."

Presley leaned down to him, he could see directly down her cover when she leaned over. He tried not to stare at her perfect chest that dangled in front of him; he didn't have to worry about it too much since Presley was soon touching his lips. They were active on each other, and he felt Presley reach down to place her soft hand on his bare chest, she wasn't on the bed with him, but this was a pretty amazing conservative compromise in his mind. He figured she would slow them down when it became too much, but thought it was worth testing just a little, so Trent tried to pull her into bed with him.

Presley immediately smiled and slowed their kissing. "I can't do all that." She rubbed the side of his face.

"I know," he admitted. "Soon," he winked and laid down.

Presley leaned down for one more peck before she shook her head smiling at him and then left the room.

✦

"Did you get him all tucked in?" Jake pumped his eyebrows at Presley when she came down the stairs.

"Shut up," she blushed.

They all walked towards the door to spend a few hours at the lake.

The second they left the porch, Lisa started. "Well." She smiled at her best friend. "I love him." She shrugged. "He for sure has my endorsement."

Presley was still blushing, but she returned her best friend's smile.

"He's even hotter in person too," Lisa added.

"What the fuck?!" Jake exaggerated. "I'm still standing right here, you two didn't manage to get all that out at your slumber party last night?"

"I can assure you," Presley shot a sly grin at Jake before turning her attention back to Lisa. "His chest and arms are as firm as you'd expect them to be after watching that movie when he played that Viking *God*."

Lisa rolled her head back. "Girl!"

"There's a child within earshot." Jake continued to complain while pointing at Bailey who wasn't paying attention to anything but racing Baron down to the dock a few yards ahead of them.

"Oh whatever, Love." Lisa rolled her eyes. "As long as Bay can't hear us, I think the biggest child can take it."

Jake shot a finger up at her as they all laughed.

Twenty-One

"Hi, guys." Presley looked up from her lounge chair as Michelle and Pete made their way down the dock.

"Hey, girl." Michelle replied and then waved at Lisa.

"Michelle, Pete." Presley gestured towards her best friend. "This is Lisa, my best friend in the world."

"Hi," Lisa got up from her chair and reached her hand out. "It's really nice to meet you guys."

"Same to you." Pete smiled.

They noticed Jake, Bailey and Baron down the bank of the lake, but didn't see Trent. "Is Hayes not around?" Michelle asked.

"Oh," Presley smiled. "He's taking a nap; he joined us for breakfast this morning so he hadn't really been able to sleep since yesterday."

"His car is here though?" Pete observed.

"Yeah, he's uh," she stumbled. "He's taking a nap up at the cottage."

"Oh." Michelle smiled; she didn't dwell on that very long as she noticed Presley begin to blush. "Are you guys doing a private thing down here or do you mind if we join?"

"Oh gosh, absolutely, please join us." Lisa stepped in.

"We were thinking about paddle boarding. Presley, is your inventory still open for sharing?" Pete asked.

"Absolutely." She got up from her chair. "Here, let me go grab them."

Pete stopped her. "Aren't they in the garage up there??"

"Yep." Presley confirmed as she put her cover and shoes on to make the trek back up the lawn.

"Well, don't worry about it, I'll go grab everything, we just wanted to check first."

"I don't mind helping." Presley started but Lisa cut in.

"Pres, I'll ask Jake. Jake!" She called out.

Her husband turned around and saw she was gesturing to him, he also saw two more people on the dock and based on the figure and the red hair of the woman, he guessed it was Michelle and Pete.

> I hope I don't wake you, but wanted to let you know Pete and Michelle are down here now too— If you wanted to join us after your nap. 😌 💤

Presley texted Trent, but she wouldn't hear back as he was sound asleep.

✦

About an hour after Michelle and Pete arrived, Baron excitedly hopped off the lounge chair he was hogging from Presley, he scurried his way down the dock as best he could. Presley smiled when she noticed what Baron was chasing. After Baron made it to him, he turned back around and ran down the dock for his tennis ball. Trent smiled at the pit bull as he approached and anxiously dropped the ball at Trent's feet. Trent bent down and then gave the ball a toss into the water which Baron wasted no time in retrieving.

Trent finally made it to the end of the dock. "Hi, ladies." He acknowledged Lisa and Michelle before he leaned down towards Presley. "Hi, gorgeous."

He softly pressed his lips against hers and caressed her cheek. He was stunned and appreciative of the bikini Presley was wearing, even more now that the cover was gone. He didn't want to make things awkward in front of Lisa or Michelle so instead he took a seat by Presley's legs on her chair.

Michelle smirked at him when he finally took his gaze off Presley.

Lisa projected her eyes as wide as she could towards her best friend gesturing at Trent in nothing but a pair of swim trunks.

"Sorry, I missed out on the fun, I fuckin crashed in there, probably could've slept another 12 hours." He rubbed Presley's legs.

"That's okay, you were up for a long time yesterday." Presley assured him. "Do you want a drink?"

"Yeah, shit, look at this little bar out here." Michelle stood up and walked over to a mini fridge they had been depleting the last hour.

"Hmmmm, maybe just a water?" He replied.

Michelle tossed him one.

"Thanks." He took a drink and then looked out onto the water at the paddle boards that were almost to the opposite bank of the lake.

"The guys took Bay on a little adventure." Lisa smiled.

"That sounds fun." Trent noticed a dripping Baron headed their way, he stood up and met him before he got too close to the girls because he knew he'd take the opportunity to shake off on them. "Me and Baron don't mind holding down the fort with the ladies." Trent tossed the ball off the side of the dock again.

"Those guys should actually be headed back soon, we're due for makeup in a little over an hour." Michelle reminded Trent.

"Oh shit." Lisa looked down at one of the side tables. "Jake doesn't even have his phone."

"Neither does Pete." Michelle held his phone up.

"Are you hungry?" Presley lightly glided her fingers across the bottom of Trent's back. "I can go put something together before you have to go?"

Lisa noticed Trent's nipples hardened at Presley's touch and she bit her lip and tried to look out on the lake instead of at her friend.

Michelle didn't care, she smirked at Trent.

"I'm actually still full from breakfast, if you can believe it." Trent patted his washboard abs. "Plus," he looked at Michelle. "I think I've got a scene to shoot tonight where I really can't be bloated at all."

"That's right." Michelle laughed. "Hayes adds a demand in every one of his contracts to have his shirt off in at least one scene per movie."

"Fuckin' lies." Trent flipped her off smiling.

Presley smiled. "Michelle, are you hungry at all?"

Trent butt in. "Yeah, Shell, are you hungry or are you trying not to be bloated either? Why don't we talk about the scene you've got tonight?" He pumped his eyebrows.

She returned his previous gesture.

"It's why I get to leave the set earlier than the others this evening." He took another drink. "They don't need me in that one."

Michelle continued to blush. "Hayes, you're lucky I like your girl, wouldn't want to embarrass you in front of her." She couldn't stop laughing.

Lisa and Presley exchanged looks.

"I'm not embarrassed of my scene tonight; you know the box office triples when I'm shirtless." He shrugged. "A shower sex scene though? You guys might end up being responsible for pulling in the cash on this one."

"Fuck off." Michelle laughed.

"Oohh!" Lisa cut in. "I'm not trying to embarrass you Michelle but is it in Pres's master?! That place is like a literal spa." She emphasized. "The world is going to want to know her contractor when they see that damn shower."

"Hey." Presley finally cut in. "I should actually be getting a lot of the credit for that bathroom; those were my ideas and design selections." She reminded Lisa.

"That's true, my B, girl." Lisa agreed.

"That's probably the biggest shower I've seen in my life." Michelle admitted. "And honestly part of the reason that scene in particular is going to be so damn awkward." She narrowed a friendly gaze at Trent. "Despite you suggesting I'm embarrassed of a sex scene; everyone knows I've already done them before." She shrugged. "But typically, in a bed or something that doesn't make me feel as exposed. That shower could quite literally allow eight other people around us, that's what's making me nervous for this shoot, *zero* hiding anything at all."

Trent narrowed his eyes back at her, understanding where she was coming from but also skeptical that she may also be nervous because she and Pete had been doing more than just a shower scene these last few weeks. He could imagine how awkward that would be keeping all of that private and then having to act out a mostly choreographed sex scene in front of the crew. He chose not to say anything else that may embarrass her, she'd been a good sport already.

"Maybe they'd consider using one of the other showers?" Trent suggested.

"Psh," Michelle rolled her eyes. "And miss out on including that dope ass shower in the movie? I doubt it."

Trent repositioned himself to lean back in the lounge chair with Presley, he put his arm around her shoulder. Presley adjusted slightly to be snuggled under his arm so her head could rest on the front of his shoulder. Trent bent one of his legs once the sensation of Presley's nearly naked body against his skin really hit him, he wasn't trying to let everyone know how her sweet touch made him feel. Holding her under his arm was so natural at this point, he hadn't really thought about his shorts tightening when he had leaned back to lay with her. He tried to bring up a topic to occupy his mind before he got hyper focused on Presley and her body.

"Lisa, how old's Bay?" He asked as they noticed the paddle boards were making their way back to this end of the lake.

"He will be 5 this December."

"About time for a little sibling." Michelle suggested.

Lisa smiled. "We think so too, so that's the plan."

"Aww." Michelle's bottom lip went out. "I love babies, my problem is I need to capitalize on all these nudey, sex scenes before I start poppin' 'em out."

Lisa laughed. "Bay is absolutely the reason I choose not to assault anyone with a two piece."

"Stop!" Presley rolled her eyes. "You're still a hottie boombalottie!"

"Yeah," Michelle agreed. "You absolutely do not have a mom bod, not even close."

"It's the stretch marks I'm not willing to put on display." She laughed. "That kid was responsible for what I think looks like some kind of albino bacon grilling along my midsection."

"Oh no!" Michelle joined everyone in laughter. "Okay, well now that does make me nervous, but I'm still ready for at least two."

"Does Pete want kids?" Lisa asked.

Michelle choked on her drink and Trent tried to suppress his smile.

"What?" Lisa looked at Presley and then back at Michelle. "I'm so sorry, I," she stuttered, "Are you guys not together?"

Michelle was wiping her mouth trying to recover from choking.

"Sorry, I, it just seemed like maybe you guys were together." Lisa was visibly embarrassed.

Michelle collected herself and was still red in the face. "Well," she started, feeling slightly uncomfortable because she didn't know Lisa and Presley all that well and she and Pete did want to make sure what they were doing was much more serious before they let the cat out of the bag. "I mean, technically speaking, we are seeing each other." It was the first time she had said those words out loud. She had more or less confirmed with Trent already but never said the words. "We haven't exactly talked about kids though." Michelle looked at Trent who was still biting his lips to suppress his smile. "And you can wipe that shit eating grin off your face, Hayes." She playfully warned.

"Shell," he chuckled. "All I'm gonna say is I told you so." Trent held his hands up, "I tried to tell you, you two were not as sneaky or discreet as you thought."

"Okay, based on that logic." She turned to Lisa. "What made you think we were dating?"

"I caught him looking at you a couple times and it's a look that you don't just give a friend." She nodded her head towards Presley. "My husband loves her more than life itself, calls her his girlfriend all the time, but the way he looks at Pres is much different than how Pete looks at you. There's just something about the eyes when you're in love." She shrugged.

Trent and Michelle locked eyes, Lisa used the 'L' bomb.

"We've only been seeing each other for a few weeks." Michelle clarified.

"Love doesn't have a timeline." Lisa shrugged. "Plus, I saw you two kissing on the porch at the main house before you came down here today."

Michelle's face went scarlet. "Coulda led with that one, Lis!" She laughed.

Trent rubbed his hand up and down Presley's arm, she had been pretty quiet since he got there. Suddenly a phone was ringing, it was Jake's.

"Ugh," Lisa looked down at it. "It's the firm, even on his dang days off." Lisa shook her head before silencing the phone.

Just as soon as Lisa set his phone down, Presley's started ringing. She leaned across Trent to grab her phone from a side table, he tried not to think about her breast squishing against his chest, he'd prefer to fully indulge in that sensation when they were alone. During her reach he finally got a nearly unobstructed view of the tattoo that peeked over her tank top a couple weeks ago. She actually had two birds on her back, both no taller than about four inches a piece. It looked like she had both a dove and a raven placed around the middle of her back.

Presley looked at Lisa. "It's Jake's firm."

"Hello?" She answered, Trent could hear a loud voice on the other end but couldn't quite make out what was being said.

"Excuse me?" Presley had her hand to her chest, and she sat up, she continued to listen for another minute. "Like hell." She stood up and grabbed her cover. "No, that's absolutely not what was discussed this morning."

She took a few steps down the dock while putting her robe style cover back on. "Actually, you know what, no." She put her hand on her hip and stopped. "I'm not even entertaining this until Jake's on the phone too because he's the only one I trust to get it done."

Another pause.

"That's too damn bad." She started walking again. She wasn't yelling, but her voice was firm as she walked down the dock. "You *know* that's not what we talked about this morning. And no, I'm absolutely not okay with that at all."

"Is everything alright?" Trent asked Lisa as he gestured his head towards Presley.

Lisa let out a large exhale and looked at Presley before she started. "I think it must be that dispute she and Jake were talking about earlier today, they've been working on it for weeks. Quite honestly, I'm not sure how she's been holding herself together lately."

"What happened?" He asked.

"I don't know all the details; this issue has really been a Jake thing more than her talking to me about it." She watched her best friend with sad eyes, and then turned back to address Trent. "To make a very long story short, her useless sack of shit mother fluttered back into her life about two years ago because she coincidentally married the CEO of a competing logging company. A pretty sizable one, not as big as Pres's, but enough to make problems."

Trent thought back to when he and Presley were talking about their families, she mentioned her Paps passed away about two years ago as well.

"So, that bitch and her new husband have been battling Pres for ownership and if not that, they want a portion of the assets earned since like 15 years ago or something dumb, like it's completely ridiculous that she has to even entertain this. They have to fight to keep ownership first and the next step is that those Jackoffs are going to come after the assets and wealth Pres's company has made since her mom split basically."

"Why since then?" Michelle asked.

Trent couldn't look away from Presley, she was pacing at the end of the dock and her face was flushed.

"Well, when that dumb bitch just up and left her husband and Pres when Pres was like Bay's age, they were still married! Unfortunately, Gary never filed for divorce and neither did the snake queen, so they were still married until his death."

Presley was making her way to the cottage, still on the phone with Baron now on her heels.

"Shit." Trent finally looked at Lisa. "So, she lost Paps and then mom decided to resurface."

"Within days," Lisa glared. "Acting like some long-lost hero and then the day before his celebration of life that dumb bitch had someone serve Pres with papers, she wanted the fucking house. She must have been watching for a while because she knew when to strike Pres. She never wanted to tangle with Paps, he would have buried her alive somewhere in the wilderness and not even given it a second thought. Paps did not play when it came to Pres."

"Should I go talk to her?" Trent asked. "That can't be easy, that's a lot to deal with. I had no idea."

Lisa exhaled and noticed her husband, Bailey, and Pete were just about to the shore right next to the dock. "Honestly, you may wanna let Jake take the first shift." She looked at Trent. "I promise, it's absolutely nothing against you. It's just really likely they'll have to call the firm together and I'm not sure if she'd even want me consoling her right now. Pres gets in this work mode where she has to just boss up. She doesn't like to show weakness because she works with basically all men, so she puts those big girl panties on and handles shit. I will say though, when the dust settles is when she truly needs help finding her breath again."

Trent wanted to respect what Lisa determined to be best for Presley, but it sure felt like shit to know what she was going through and just let her continue along.

"Mommy!" Bailey shouted as he was running down the dock. "Look I got!!"

Lisa got up and opened her arms for her boy to jump into. "Hi baby, did you have so much fun?!"

Pete and Jake were deep into a friendly conversation as they caught up with Bailey. Pete continued to walk over towards Trent and Michelle, he dabbed Trent as he passed and then stood a semi-respectable distance from Michelle.

"These guys all know." Michelle shrugged. "So, no need to hide here."

Pete looked around with a smile on his face. "You're sure?"

Michelle laughed at him and pulled him by the shirt to kiss him.

"Hey, love." Jake leaned beyond Bailey and kissed his wife on the lips.

"Hey." She lowered her voice a bit before continuing. "The firm called; I think it was Dan."

Jake walked to the table where he had left his phone.

Lisa started again. "Pretty sure he called Pres right after he tried you… She got up a minute ago and didn't sound like a happy camper, I think whatever was discussed this morning wasn't getting through or working out for someone."

"Shit, where is she now?" Jake didn't look up from his phone.

"She took the call up to the cottage."

Jake didn't waste any more time, he grabbed his phone and jogged to catch up with Presley.

Lisa noticed Trent still watching the cottage, so she reached out to him and patted his arm. "Pres is a tough cookie," she assured him. "But she does need support too, something to pull her out of that world on her shoulders feeling, ya know? Whatever you do, I just suggest waiting a bit to check in with her."

"Lis." Trent scratched the back of his head and slid his hand down firmly to grip his neck. "This isn't really my style, just hanging back for my girl to deal with everything alone."

"Trust me." Lisa set Bailey down. "I know that feeling, she's so damn independent it's tough to allow it because she carries a fuckin lot for one person."

Trent looked at the cottage again.

"Trent." Lisa rested her hand on his shoulder. "You'll have to find your own groove with Pres, but I know for now you're her light. Whatever you do, please just keep being that tether to the light for her."

Trent nodded his head. He was beginning to realize what an impact he was having on Presley's life; he wasn't accustomed to caring enough about anyone but himself to really take on any kind of responsibility for others' emotions. He had watched countless times as his behavior had crushed women, he had never made promises to any of them, but the implied desire was there anytime he slept with someone new. He could only recall maybe two occasions where he even felt any kind of remorse for his non-monogamous and extensive dating history. But now, after spending time getting to know Presley for a couple of weeks, he couldn't imagine hurting her. Trent knew he had to have his shit together this time around, he couldn't pile anything else on Presley's overflowing plate of trauma and stress. He ached to take away any negativity that was haunting her, and he wanted to be responsible for her emotional and physical well-being. And that was fucking scary.

After yet another glance towards the cottage, Trent finally responded. "Lis, I promise you, I've got her." He gave her a reassuring look that wasn't quite a full smile.

Pete and Michelle had taken off for alone time before the shoot started that night and Lisa was just walking up the lawn towards the cottage to change Bailey out of his swimming gear. Trent looked around at the mess they'd all made that day, so he started to pick up the dock a bit.

He was carrying the paddle boards back up to the cottage when he saw Presley walking his way.

"Hey." Presley let out an exhausted breath as she approached Trent.

"Hey, everything alright?" He set down the paddle boards just before she reached him. Trent massaged her shoulders for a quick second and then pulled her into his chest.

"I wouldn't say alright quite yet, improving... hopefully." She closed her eyes as her temple was resting perfectly on his chiseled chest. "Sorry for taking off like that."

Trent kissed the top of her head. "That's the last thing you need to worry about," Trent assured her. "I get it when duty calls."

Presley took another deep breath. "It's crazy how worry tends to melt away here."

"Well, it is quite beautiful out here," he agreed.

"No," she laughed and looked up at him before she responded. "In your arms."

Trent smiled at her and then bent down to connect their lips.

"Let the worry melt, sweetheart." He continued to hold her while he rubbed his hands up and down her back in a comfortable rhythm.

Presley had been carrying an obscene amount of emotional baggage for a while—the last two years being the worst of it. Her stress level was at a constant state of unnerve on top of all the loss she'd experienced in life. Projecting positivity and developing a rocksteady presence in the boardroom was exhausting, Presley hadn't even been on a real vacation since her senior college trip to Mexico. Somehow winding down and taking breaks had just simply passed her by and she just buried herself in work. The problem with work recently was that she was dealing with unnecessary and draining legal issues with the woman who birthed her. Even with all of that going on, Presley felt comfort and relief with Trent. She had gone slowly getting to know him and took caution initially, but now, in his arms, when her mind felt at ease, she felt like she was home.

Trent was still rubbing her back when he started up again. "Pres, the shoot starts soon." He hated having to say it at that moment. "But I've got time to sit down at the dock and hold you for a bit."

"I would honestly love that." She looked up at him. "Even if I only get you for a bit longer."

Trent gave her a final squeeze before holding her around her shoulders and walking her back down to the dock.

Trent sat down first and pulled Presley into him, she was situated in front of him and his arms engulfed her immediately as she sat down. Presley curled her legs and relaxed her head onto Trent's shoulder.

"Do you want to talk about anything, Pres?" Trent held her firmly.

Presley took a deep breath. "Another time." She rubbed her hands on Trent's strong legs that were extended on either side of her. "We don't have a lot of time right now and I just want to soak in this slow moment with you." She turned her head to look at him. "If that's okay?"

"Of course it is." Trent kissed her forehead. "Just know, I'm here for you."

Presley rubbed her hands across his strong biceps that were still holding her.

It didn't take long for Baron to hop up on the sunbed and make himself comfortable on top of Trent's right leg. Trent reached one hand down to rub Baron's neck. It made Presley smile; she reached a hand to lay gently on the top of Trent's as he continued to rub Baron.

"Thank you, Trent." Presley turned and kissed Trent just under his jaw on his neck. The placement of her lips sent a quick shiver throughout Trent's body.

Twenty-Two

> Babe, I just finished up here, are we still planning to go out?

Trent texted as he was gathering his things since he had finished his scenes for the evening.

> **PRES**
> Of course!! 😊😊 Lis and I just dropped Jake off at the bar—Bay is having a nuclear level meltdown with Nana and Papa rn so we're going to check-in real quick.

> Should I head there to pick you ladies up?

> **PRES**
> That's sweet baby, but idk if it's a quick fix—he's supposed to be getting his booty in the bathtub lol 😬😬 I can give you the code to the cottage to hang and we'll come get you after or if you want to head to the bar I know Jake would wet his pants to have you there without me. 😂🤣

> Definitely not a goal of mine to get Jake's pants wet lol but I don't want you to have to drive back out here so I'll meet you at the bar gorgeous.

> **PRES**
> I can't wait to see you 🥺

> Then tell Bay to buck up buttercup because Auntie PP's got a hot date to meet!

> **PRES**
> 🥺❤️🥺❤️

✦

"Hey, I wanna talk to you." Mike had a few drinks in him and took the opportunity to have a conversation with Trent after following him into the Men's room.

"Didn't think the interview would be taking place in here; are you here to chat about your theory of what happened to Pap's shop?" Trent pointedly asked.

Fuckin poser, Mike thought, *where does he get off referring to Paps as if he knew him?* "Not exactly."

"Oh, then perhaps the conversation you were trying to have the other night?" Trent nodded and shrugged his shoulders at him. "Sure, what's up, Officer Bando?"

"You know very well what's up." Mike rolled his eyes. "And I'm telling you now to *back off*," he firmly warned.

Trent laughed, completely dismissing Mike with his body language and then continued towards the urinal.

"Don't fuckin act like it's a joke." Mike followed him.

"Look, you've had plenty to drink and I'm sure you're not ready for this conversation with me." Trent put his hands up and shrugged. "Because there's no way you're this delusional."

"Oh, I've been ready since the day you slithered into town." Mike glared. "I've watched you since the second you met her." He let out a small hiccup. "That fuckin playboy shit isn't going to fly; you're not going to get yourself into those panties."

"I don't know what you're talking about." Trent shook his head.

"Presley. I'm talking about Presley and how you've been trying to get it in since you got here. It stops now." He pointed his finger at Trent, just less than a foot from his face.

Trent laughed while taking a firm wipe of his mouth and chin. "I'm sure you've heard it before, but I'll say it again; she's not yours," Trent's expression and tone warned Mike. "And you don't know anything about me. You just keep your dirty fuckin thoughts away from her."

"*My* dirty thoughts?!" Mike choked out. "We all know you're just looking to score." His face turned into a scowl. "Just score a piece of that ass."

"Don't you *dare* talk about Pres like that." Trent got closer to his face. "I don't give a fuck what you do here, I'll lay your ass out."

Mike scowled back at Trent but didn't say another word.

"And don't ever come at me like I cut you in the lunch line; Presley's never even allowed you a spot in line from what I can tell." Trent held a glare on Mike. "I'll respect that the two of you have a *friendship*, but you don't own her and you sure as shit don't know me so you can mind your own fucking business."

"I know *her* though." Mike defended his position. "You don't get to show up and hurt her—you'll *never* deserve her."

"And neither will you," Trent spat. "So, leave her the fuck alone from now on." Trent's face hardened and he continued to lay out Mike's boundaries in relation to Presley. "Don't come by uninvited, stop trying to start shit with me in front of her, and you don't need to continue bringing her shit. I'm more than capable of taking care of her."

They stared at each other briefly until Trent started again. "I'm done here." He walked up to one of the urinals. "You gonna watch, Officer Bando?"

Mike's face was fuming, he slapped his hand against the bathroom door and walked back into the bar.

"Mikey!" one of his old teammates called.

Mike tried to hide his outrage while he walked over to his old high school buddies. His conversation with Trent was spewing through his mind and he couldn't register any of the friendly commotion around him.

Trent came out of the bathroom soon after Mike. He wasn't all that excited about being at the bar anymore, he could've been sleeping or better yet spending alone time with Presley. He knew Mike hadn't liked him since the moment they met; he didn't give a shit about that. The way Mike behaved in relation to Presley was making Trent feel like he needed to rip the guy up by his shirt collar instead of simply blowing him off with smug gestures all the time. He headed straight to the bar to order a drink.

"So, what'd that little fuckhead want?"

Trent turned around and his face lightened when he saw it was Jake. "What?" Trent laughed.

"C'mon," Jake lightly elbowed him. "I saw him basically follow you in there, did he actually talk to you?"

"Yeah." Trent nodded and then turned to the bartender. "I'll take a double of whatever your best bourbon is, on the rocks, please."

Jake laughed. "That kinda convo, huh?" He sipped his beer. "Hey, let's go out on the patio?" He suggested and swayed his head towards the door. "Get a little air, huh?"

It didn't take Trent long at all to agree, he grabbed his drink, thanked the bartender, and followed Jake outside.

"Mike looked fuckin' *pissed* when he came back out." Jake smiled. "Do I get to know what you said to him?"

Trent wasn't as amused by their conversation, but he liked Jake and knew his intentions weren't out of malice. He took a sip of his bourbon and then leaned on the rail. "He obviously doesn't like me," he shrugged. "And he's delusionally in love with Pres."

"Yeah, that little schmuck's been chasing her for years," Jake rolled his eyes. "I don't know if it makes you feel any better, but they've never done anything beyond spin the bottle in like the ninth grade." Jake started laughing. "But, hell, we all kissed that night so that couldn't have meant anything to her." He shrugged and took another swig.

"Hey," Trent put one of his palms up. "History is her business; Lord knows I've fuckin' got mine." He admitted as he hung his head looking into his glass.

Jake moved his head side to side. "Yeah," he nodded in agreement. "We've all heard those rumors too, man."

"The shitty thing is the rumors you've heard about me are probably very true." He looked out beyond the patio and into the darkness of the woods near the bar.

"Maybe, but that's history too… right?" Jake looked at Trent for an answer.

"That's not my plan for Presley, if that's what you're asking?" Trent stood taller now instead of leaning on the rail. "I know I deserve that kind of question since I've been such a total fuckboy, but it's honest to God not what I'm doing right now."

Trent rolled his glass around and watched the ice as it bobbed along through his bourbon. "I have never felt so small as I did when Pres told me she couldn't just have a meaningless fling with me." He took a drink. "That was like a fuckin magnified mirror of horrors; the look on her face about killed me, and I know it took her everything to even say that to me. I hadn't realized truly how bad my reputation was until I saw the fear and sadness in that woman's eyes."

Jake watched Trent and simply nodded his head up and down, agreeing to take his word for it, despite any of the playboy rumors he had heard. "I'm sure that lifestyle is a lot of Mike's problem with you too, he's not wanting anyone to touch her but him. And he's afraid, given your past, that you'd have a real good shot at just getting yours and taking off." Jake guessed. "But I also don't like how he is with Pres."

"Shit." Trent shook his head. "You and me both. He literally comes by her place at any hour and mostly at the worst possible time, like he knows we're together or something." He took another drink. "And bringing her shit, *constantly*. Do you know that every single day, with the exception of one, that I've spent time with her, he's just randomly shown up while we're together?"

"Yep, sounds like Mike," Jake concurred.

"I don't get jealous, that's not my issue at all with him. In fact, I prefer to be around when he shows up." Trent shook his head. "Because something just doesn't sit right with me when he's around her. He very clearly makes her uneasy and I just won't with that shit."

"She'd never be outright mean or admit it to him, but I know she feels a shit ton of discomfort around him too, especially since you've been around."

"Wait, *I* make her uncomfortable?"

"No! Sorry, no," Jake clarified. "I just mean that Mike's behavior has made her even more uncomfortable with you around because she doesn't want you thinking they have something going on already and she doesn't want to come across like she's hiding anything from you. Not to mention, Mike's been over the top with her lately."

"Oh." Trent completely understood, it wasn't that he was an actual problem, Presley was more concerned about losing traction with Trent because of Mike. "He doesn't scare me in the least bit, and she has absolutely nothing to worry about as far as Mike pushing me away from her. Anything going on between them is limited to what that douche has made up in his head."

Jake laughed and shook his head in agreement.

"Honestly though, Pres has struck something in me." Trent looked down at his glass of bourbon again. "I honestly didn't expect any of this, not even when she took my breath away the first time I saw her. I've never been this interested in just fucking getting to know a girl—the whole talking stage is something I've always tried to avoid." He paused. "But now, I just want to know anything and everything about her." He tipped the bourbon glass on the railing and balanced it while rocking it in his hand. "And I have this… Urge to just make sure she's happy and safe. All I want to do is make her feel…," He paused again, carefully choosing his words he finally continued. "…Special. She's special to me."

"I could've told you that, hell, anyone around here would tell you that." Jake laughed and then got more serious. "Pres is family, man, and we absolutely love her, I mean, what's not to fucking love? While Lisa holds the best friend title, I've actually known her since Kindergarten, we go way back and have always been close." He checked Trent's reaction before continuing. "Just know beyond that sweet little lady guard that she exudes, she's a strong ass, boss bitch and she won't take any shit."

Trent's smile turned into a laugh. "I kind of get that impression too, she seems to handle her shit, that's for sure."

"She does." Jake nodded his head up and down. "Despite what I've seen her go through, I still didn't even give her the breadth of credit she deserves for that strength until I saw that woman in the boardroom discussing a heated business deal." Jake smiled. "Don't get me wrong, she is also very emotional and sensitive, but good fucking luck seeing that side of her. When she gets knocked down, she usually does her best to hold it together and cry about it later when there aren't any witnesses." Jake took a drink before turning back to Trent. "She just has trouble putting Mike in his place. I think she's always felt bad he does whatever for her, and she does enjoy his mom, but she still doesn't have those feelings for him." Jake shrugged. "Like I said, he's been chasing her since middle school, and she's *never* reciprocated any of his romantic feelings. And shit," Jake admitted, "I've seen plenty of guys shoot their shot, myself included back in the sixth grade." He laughed. "But Mike's been the only one who hasn't been able to just take the hint, he still thinks there's a chance. I'm not sure what needs to happen for him to let go of that shred of hope he somehow continues to cling on to?"

"Well, now that I've said my peace to him, I'll go ahead and kill the fuck outta him with kindness." Trent took a healthy swig of his bourbon. "Until she gives me even the slightest indication that I have the green light to kick his fucking ass."

"That's one way of going about it," Jake laughed.

Trent didn't want to linger on the Mike topic, the conversation with him already put him in a pissy mood and he wanted to change that before Presley got there. "Also, back this all up," he waved his hands. "I need to hear about this sixth-grade story." He smiled at Jake. "You two seem like the best of friends, fuckin thick as thieves; I want to be sure I don't find myself limited to that friend circle, how'd you slip up?"

"I didn't slip up," Jake almost shouted out his laughter. "I went at it like a fucking legend." He popped his collar.

"Okay, legend," Trent mocked. "How'd you get your shot blocked then?"

Jake took a deep inhale and puffed his chest out. "It was just before the sixth grade Valentine's Dance, so the first dance any of us had ever been to, pre-Lisa too, she hadn't moved into town yet," he clarified. "And Pres was obviously the cutest girl at school, so I was trying to ask her to the dance. I mean, we were already friends, right?"

Trent had a smile just thinking of little sixth grade Presley and likely a very awkward, prepubescent Jake.

"Anyway, I get some flowers, daisies of course because I'm like twelve and have no damn clue, I put my tie on… with my favorite Seahawks jersey, of course, slicked the fuck out of the bleached buttcut I had, grab my boombox and head over to her house."

"Noooo." Trent was laughing now.

"Her Dad answered the door, he loved me and knew what I was scheming, so he goes and gets Pres and the second I see her I hand her the flowers. She was giggling and eating that shit up and then I hit play on that sweet ass boombox I carried over… That's when the giggling ended. Her Dad was dying of laughter and Pres turned from smitten to embarrassed real damn quick."

"Oh shit, please tell me what song you picked?" Trent covered his face.

"Well, Pres and I were raised on classic rock, so you know Styx?"

"Of course."

"Yeah, I played 'Babe'." Jake admitted.

Trent laughed out loud at him; he slapped the bar top a few times but couldn't stop laughing.

"Okay, so I thought I was bad as fuck." Jake shrugged. "I was like what girl wouldn't love to be asked to the Valentine's Dance like this?! But I stood there letting the song play for a bit, after like the first chorus in comes Paps. And Pres was always Paps' baby girl, so he storms out to the porch and was like 'what the hell is going on out here?'" Jake smiled remembering the moment. "He saw the flowers and my fucking handsome ass and just stared me down, arms crossed and all, standing right behind his little Pres. But I was a man that day and I asked her all proper like, in front of both of them mind you, if she'd like to go to the dance with me." Jake shook his head, still in disbelief sixteen years later. "In front of her dad and Paps, you know what this bitch hits me with after all my thoughtful fucking planning?"

Trent just shook his head, still laughing at the story.

"She says," Jake's voice heightened in pitch. "'Thank you for these pretty flowers, Jake but if I go to the dance with you, you know that doesn't mean I'm your girlfriend, right?'"

Trent reached out and patted Jake's shoulder. "That's rough." He laughed before recovering enough to continue. "But did you guys still go to the dance?"

"*Hell* yes we did!" Jake bounced his head with authority. "And the night of the dance I told her it was just as good she didn't want to be my girlfriend because I only asked her so none of the other honies I had lined up would be fighting over me."

"Okay, well," Trent managed. "I see why the two of you get along so well now, two fucking peas in a pod." He chuckled.

Jake smiled. "I mean, honestly back then I did have a little crush on her for a minute. But then Lis came to town the following year and talk about someone taking your damn breath away. I knew I loved Lisa the second she sat down in homeroom," he happily admitted. "She and Pres hit it off immediately. I wasn't as confident approaching Lis as I was with Pres, so, lucky for me Pres and I had the relationship we did because I was able to let her know how bad I was crushing on Lis. Pres is wing woman of the century, she pushed us closer and closer together until my balls finally dropped and I could ask Lisa out myself. I'll be forever in her debt for that one because now I have everything I've ever wanted." Jake fondly smiled into the distance. He allowed a short pause before he chimed in again with a little more excitement in his voice. "And just a heads up, everyone and their mom fucking knows about my whole 'Babe' routine, so Pres and I have embraced it and that's our jam.

Lis actually had a surprise set up for us to dance to it at our own damn wedding." He shook his head. "Fucking bittersweet living a life with those two fuckers."

Trent loved it, he couldn't wipe the smile from his face thinking about all of the happy memories Presley had with her friends who were really more like family. He thought about how much he would love to create a future where he could be looking back and recalling such fond memories with her. He was already more than interested in her, but Jake's story just made him even more drawn to his gorgeous and glowing, green-eyed interest.

Jake felt like enough time had passed and Trent hadn't offered anything more than a smile; he definitely had his wheels turning though. "Bro, I wouldn't worry at all about Pres putting you in any kind of friend zone, I've seen that routine plenty and that's not what's happening with you." He laughed. "I'd be lying to you if I said I didn't have some reservations about you when she first told us she met you." Jake admitted. "But, from where I sit now, as long as your intentions are genuine, man, I would be more than happy to welcome you into our little circle." Jake leaned back down to rest his forearms on the railing. "So, I'll be corny as fuck about it and say it anyway, I officially offer you my blessing with Pres."

Trent looked back down at his now empty glass, for the slightest moment he resented the comment regarding his intentions until he realized his past behavior really didn't offer any assurances he was capable of genuine feelings, even despite what he'd told Jake that night. The weight of Jake's approval started to sink in. He hadn't asked for it, but he knew it was an enormous token of trust. He was at a point where either Presley was worth proving all the doubters wrong, or he could venture down the path of familiarity and just settle for his usual game. Thinking about Presley and even the sliver of her she had shown Trent, he knew he couldn't live with the second option. Trent didn't know exactly what to say in response yet, so he just reached over and gave Jake's shoulder a confirming pat.

"You need another?" Jake interrupted his thoughts.

"Maybe a beer this time, still want to be able to have a coherent conversation, can't keep drinking like that all night." He admitted before grabbing Jake's full attention. "And, Jake, I appreciate who you are for Pres, and the way you protect her." He made sure his face was as sincere and reassuring as his words. "I don't expect to have everyone's trust right now, and that's okay, I get it. I'm going to do everything I can to make her happy. I promise you I don't have any intention to hurt Pres in any way, I understand what a privilege it is to have your blessing."

Jake just nodded his head in approval as they headed back into the bar. It was a little more crowded now, but Trent noticed Mike was still there tipping back drinks. Trent formed a scowl as they walked to the table, but that look completely disappeared when he heard Jake.

"Oohhhh shit!" Jake hollered. "The baddies are in the house!" He spotted his wife and Presley walking in through the front doors. Jake met Lisa with a long kiss to her lips and then leaned over and pecked Presley on her cheek. "You girls were missin' me, huh?" He laughed and rubbed his chest.

"Hell no." Lisa looked at him. "We heard Trent Hayes *and* the high school state champs were in town."

Jake laughed and grabbed her to kiss her neck.

Presley walked up to Trent who was occupying a barstool just behind Jake at the opposite end of the table from Mike. "Hi," she spoke softly.

Trent smiled as she approached. "Hi." He reached out for her hands and pulled her into him. Their lips connected, and Presley squeezed his hand as they kissed. She could taste the booze on his lips.

"I'm glad you're here." He held a lock of her brunette blowout when they finished their kiss.

"Me too," she smiled. "Didn't want to miss out on some extra time with you." She bit her bottom lip, "Sorry we're late."

Mike watched from the other end of the table and was fuming.

"It's okay, but Bay owes me big time though for making me share our time tonight." He winked. "What can I get you to drink, Pres?" Trent pecked her once more as he stood up. "Lis, can I get you a drink too?"

"Oh what?" Lisa smiled. "Move over, love, Trent Hayes wants to buy me a drink." She playfully gripped her husband's butt as she passed him. Lisa and Presley followed Trent to the bar, Trent led them with Presley's hand in his.

"Hey, I got next round!" Jake laughed.

✦

"Hi, oh my gosh!" The bartender walked around the bar with his arms wide open. "It's the dynamic duo back together, huh? Come here you two." The man had each one of them under one of his arms and traded off kissing their cheeks.

"Hey Stan, how's it hangin'?" Lisa asked after squeezing him one more time.

"Well, the ticker's gettin' quite the shock this evening to see all you kids in here together." He motioned towards a few of the football players. "It's not every day we have a Hollywood superstar in the mix either!" He smiled at Trent. "What can I get you girls? On the house, my treat."

"No." Presley and Lisa shook their heads in unison.

"Thank you, Stan, you don't have to do that," Presley insisted.

"But I'd like to," he insisted.

"Anything but vodka Red Bulls for them!" Jake warned. "No shit shows tonight." He laughed at Lisa remembering the last time she and Presley got drunk off those together.

"Oh yeah?" Trent grinned. "What happens with vodka Red Bulls?"

"Jake!" Both Presley and Lisa warned in unison.

"Bro," Jake's eyes were wide. "This beezie right here pissed all over her fuckin romper in the bathroom at a nightclub." He grabbed his wife who was trying to cover his mouth. "Because this one," he pointed at Presley. "Convinced her she could just slide it to the side instead of taking it off, *but*," he emphasized while trying to battle his wife's attempts to stop the story. "The kicker to that is when I walked in to check on them in the bathroom, since they'd been in there for like fifteen minutes, Presley had her romper around her ankles so she could pee without incident." He rolled his eyes. "So, this one is pissed soaked and this one is half naked, in her bra and underwear, dragging her romper all over the floor when I walk into the ladies room. And there's just paper towels *everywhere* because they were cleaning up the pee and everything else on the fuckin floor!" Jake had finally managed to subdue his wife for the moment so he could finish his story. "Presley was hovering over the toilet and sliding paper towels around with her foot as my wife is sitting on the ground next to her, *fucking shit show*. Not to mention," the inflection in Jake's voice increased. "We were at my fucking celebration party for making partner!"

Presley's face was buried in her hands, Lisa had been struggling to cover Jake's mouth up but clearly lost and Trent had an uncontrollable belly roar.

"I hate you," Presley laughed and managed to get out towards Jake.

"So, absolutely anything besides vodka, please Stan," Jake begged. "I don't want to have to do another load of bar bathroom laundry."

"Well, geez," Presley finally looked up, still red from embarrassment. "After that story, I'll have water please, Stan."

"I haven't worn a romper since," Lisa admitted.

"I haven't had any kind of energy drink *or* vodka since," Presley added to their confession.

Stan laughed along with them. "I'll mix somethin light up," he assured them.

Trent rubbed Presley around her shoulders, still shaking from his laughter, but gave her a comforting smile that he wasn't repulsed by the story.

"And you don't hate me," Jake lightly pushed Presley's arm. "You fucking love me," he smiled.

Presley just rolled her eyes and smiled back at him. "Just know I have plenty of my own embarrassing stories to share on your behalf, Jake."

"Oh," Jake had an ear-to-ear grin. "Don't worry about embarrassing me, *babe*—Trent's been getting a history lesson all night."

"Has he now?" Presley cocked her head at Jake. "That's interesting you'd be so willing to educate him, Mr. Sloppy Shorts."

"Pres," Jake's face skipped red and went straight to white. "You swore on our friendship."

Presley looked up at Trent and giggled, she took a step towards Jake and hugged him. "You're lucky I love you and that friendship, *babe*."

"You're a motherfuck." He flipped her off as she backed away from their quick hug.

Presley blew him a kiss as Stan was handing the girls their drinks and slid a couple of beers out for Trent and Jake. She picked up her glass and turned to Trent. "Cheers," she smiled.

He clinked her glass and then was greeted by the Hofners' glasses as well before he reached down to connect his lips with Presley's.

✦

They were at a large table with mixed company from the football team. Everyone was sipping on their drinks and enjoying the evening when Jake cut in. "Darts?" He looked right at Trent.

Trent had his arm around Presley as she and Lisa were working on a basket of pull tabs. "You like getting your ass kicked?" He smirked.

"Oh, shit, you play?" Jake grinned.

Trent shrugged. "I'm not the worst."

"Anyone else?" Jake scanned the table before he walked over to erase the previous score on the chalkboard.

"Not me," Lisa declined.

"Preeesssss?" Jake smirked. "I know you want in."

Presley smiled, looking down at the pull tab in her hand while replying. "You boys don't want a warmup game before you invite me?"

Jake made a face while flipping Presley his favorite finger.

"Just put 'Dubs' where my name would go on that scoreboard over there, Sparky." She pointed up at the chalkboard.

Trent bit his bottom lip; he liked the sassiness. "Sweetheart, I won't be taking it easy on you."

Presley walked right next to him to grab her darts, she turned so they were facing each other and put her hand on his chest before looking up at him. "Baby, I'd be upset if you held back." She reached up to press their lips together.

"I'll go first," Jake claimed.

Trent looked at Presley. "No ladies first around here?"

Presley shook her head. "He likes getting points on the board first, so he isn't trailing the *entire* game." She smiled at Jake.

"You can kindly, fuck all the way off, Pres." Jake tossed a dart to start the game, he left with a tick for seventeen and another for nineteen.

Jake was marking down his score and hollered over his shoulder. "Trent, you up, bro?"

"Sure." He smirked at Presley. "Take notes, sweetheart."

She rolled her eyes at him and wasted her first look watching his form as he hit a triple eighteen. The next toss she took full advantage of checking out his ass, which looked so good in his jeans; another eighteen to rack up points. His final toss was a four, no points. He was sure to look back at Presley before he walked over to pull his darts from the board. "So, you rookies better catch up on those eighteens otherwise I'm about to run up the score."

"That was super cute." Presley watched him write down his score before she took her turn. Her first toss was a bullseye, Trent beamed. Her second toss closed out the twenties and her final toss hit an eighteen.

Trent had an ear-to-ear grin across his face as Presley walked to the chalkboard.

"Fucking showoff." Jake shook his head.

As Jake was throwing Trent grabbed Presley by her hips when she walked by him. "Should we put something on this game?" He suggested once he got her close enough to whisper in her ear.

Presley was now standing in front of him with her back to his chest, she smiled and pulled his arm around her. "Oh, you're still that confident after that masterclass you just witnessed?"

Trent laughed. "I can't get enough of you." Trent kissed her neck, and they watched Jake hit a double seventeen to close them out for himself.

"If I win," Presley started, still leaning her back on his chest. "You have to let me start paying for some dates."

"Hell no," Trent argued. "That's already a well-established law that can't be changed or bet on." He kissed the side of her head and got up to throw his turn.

Presley laughed. "See, no confidence, you already know I'm going to win."

Trent marked his score, another eighteen, and a double fifteen.

"Jake, you better start closing in on these eighteens." She threw her first dart, triple eighteen. "Otherwise, it's going to be real ugly, real quick."

Trent smiled at her.

"You guys are assholes." Jake looked at the board.

"Oh, Love," Lisa laughed. "You can play me in pool later, you always destroy me in that."

"Yeah because I be droppin balls in your pockets, girl." He made thrusting motions at his wife.

"Jake!" She laughed.

✦

Trent and Presley moved like magnets throughout the evening, taunting each other after every turn at the dartboard; when they weren't playing darts, Trent's arm would quickly find its way around Presley's shoulders, or her hand would find his leg under the table.

Lisa came in clutch a few times requesting all kinds of pictures of everyone. She got action shots of their extended party, a couple of group photos of the football team, and to Presley's enjoyment, quite a few of just Trent and Presley. Presley sent them all to Trent as soon as Lisa had airdropped them. She watched Trent on his phone just after she hit send, he had a smile on his face, and she assumed he was flipping through all of the photos. After a while, he leaned over and showed her his new lockscreen, it was a photo of them standing in front of the scoreboard of their first Cricket game. Trent was holding Presley from behind and Lisa had snapped the photo right when Trent was teasing Presley about her almost win by tickling her neck with his mouth. His arms were wrapped completely around her waist and his face was buried in her neck while she had her arms reaching up behind her and around his neck with a vibrant smile across her face.

"This is my new favorite picture." He pecked Presley's lips.

"Because you have proof that you barely beat me?!" She smiled.

"A win is a win, sweetheart." He pecked her again. "But no, it's my favorite because of how damn perfect you look."

Presley leaned back in towards his lips, but she did so with her mouth slightly open, Trent didn't realize she was the PDA type but who was he to deny her? So, he matched her mouth and they quickly shared a saucy kiss at the table with their tongues slowly dancing together.

✦

Mike had been keeping a close watch on Presley all night, just waiting for the chance to talk to her alone. He thought he had found his opportunity earlier in the night, but Jake had grabbed him and asked to take a shot right before he patted Presley's shoulder for her attention. She was simply dressed, just in a cropped white tee shirt and black skinny jeans, but he thought she looked so damn good tonight. He wanted very badly to just touch her. He ordered another shot when he saw she and Trent basically making out at the table not too far from him. *What a fuckin tool pushing her to be a floozy, that's not my innocent Presley*, Mike thought.

"So, Mikey," one of the old football guys, Aaron, took a seat next to Mike and grasped his shoulder before sitting down. "How's the cop life treating you? Got any little shits to deal with like poor old Sheriff Harry did when we were kids?" He laughed.

Mike was still glaring towards Trent but gathered himself enough to turn his attention towards Aaron. "Eh," he rolled his head. "A couple of burnouts at the high school, but mostly just graffiti and dumb shit like that, nothing like what we were doing back in the day."

"Yeah, I don't imagine with all of the shit getting posted online these days that much of what we were doing would really fly today." Aaron took a drink.

"Fuck no, not on my watch." Mike finally started to loosen up. "I don't know how we weren't locked up from half the shit we pulled." He shook his head. "Fuck, we set that one car on fire and pushed it down into the damn grange."

"Yeah, that shit was pretty fuckin dumb." Aaron laughed into his beer mug. "I sure had a damn blast doing it though."

Mike agreed with a smirk on his face before he scanned the bar again. Presley had made her way onto Trent's lap now, he had his arms around her waist, and they were sitting at a table, with plenty of chairs he noted, talking to the Hofners and two of Lisa's old cheerleading friends.

Aaron noticed Mike's face starting to form a glare, so he turned to see what Mike was looking at. "Hey, so, have you met him yet? You're at the set all the time, right? How about Michelle Bennett's fine ass, you meet her?" He pumped his eyebrows.

Mike finally broke his stare. "I've met all of them." He took a deep inhale. "That one," he shot his finger towards Trent. "Is a fucking problem."

"Trent Hayes?" Aaron furrowed his brow. "I've never heard anything about him being in trouble with the law?"

"Not that kind of problem." Mike said with an edge.

Aaron laughed. "Mikey, bro, you cannot possibly be worried about him and Presley? You still hung up on her?"

Mike glared at him.

"Listen," Aaron held his hands up. "I'm not saying she's not fuckin something, I'm just saying you know how he is—who the fuck cares? So, maybe he gets lucky or whatever, shit'll be over when he leaves town."

"It's just not right," Mike countered.

"Honestly, bro, and I mean no disrespect, but given the week we all heard she's had, she could probably really use a good lay." He shrugged. "Shit, we all could." He clutched Mike's shoulder again and gave it a firm shake. "Not sure if you've noticed, but there is a small group of fine ass women who have been out on the patio almost all night, they're begging for someone to bring them home. If you're not down for all that, at least come be my wingman for a bit?"

Mike wasn't overly interested in bringing anyone besides Presley home, but it would give him a break from being subjected to the Presley and Trent show. He was also feeling his buzz and some fresh air seemed like a good idea, Aaron had always been good company too, so he decided it was best for him to go along on this side quest for a while.

✦

Later on in the evening, Mike was in luck when he was washing his hands in the Men's room, the door was cracked and he heard Presley walking down the secluded restroom corridor. "Yes, girl, order one for me too please, I'll be right back!" He knew if he just waited, she would come to him.

✦

Presley was looking in the mirror tousling her hair before leaving the bathroom, she was having an amazing time; Trent meeting her friends was even better than she could have imagined. Whatever Stan was giving them all night was very mild, so she wasn't feeling drunk, just a nice little buzz, she gave her hair one last fling and then walked out of the bathroom. As she rounded the corner, she very nearly ran right into Mike who was leaned up against the wall. "Oh!" She screeched. "Sorry," she began to chuckle at the noise she made.

"It's alright, Pres." Mike leaned his arm up above his head onto the wall creating almost a barrier to prevent Presley from getting by him. He stood there and simply looked at her for a moment before continuing. "Having a good time tonight?"

She nodded her head; it had been nearly a week since she and Mike really had any 'alone' time; she had done her best to avoid being alone around him since his presumptuous hug and neck grope. "Uh huh."

"I wanted to tell you how good you look tonight." Mike leaned towards her.

Presley could smell the alcohol on him, and she tried to be discreet in her movement away from him, "Thank you."

"Pres," Mike let out a hiccup and then recovered and looked into her eyes. "He's not good for you."

"Mike…," she started before she got cut off.

"You know I only want the best for you, I'm telling you, it's not him. He doesn't deserve you."

"Mike, we already had this talk." Presley just wanted out of the little corridor at the very least.

"But you didn't hear me, I think you're making a mistake with him, and I don't want you to get hurt."

"I appreciate your concern Mike, but that's not your decision." She tried to take a step around him.

Mike pulled his arm down from the wall and stepped to the side with her. "Pres," he reached out and held the sides of her arms. "I'm only trying to look out for you," he pleaded his case.

Presley stiffened and contemplated yanking back from his grasp, but she didn't have anywhere to run to besides back into the empty bathroom.

"I'll always watch out for you." His thumbs rubbed her bare arms as his grip tightened. Mike exhaled before continuing. "I would be so good to you Pres; we would be good together."

"Pres!" Lisa walked around the corner. "Girl, your drink is…," her voice tapered off when she saw Mike.

Presley didn't respond vocally; she just wanted her friend to get her out of there.

"What are you doing?" Lisa looked pointedly at Mike and walked right into the middle of them, breaking any kind of hold Mike had on Presley.

"Nothing," he smiled at her. "We're just chatting," he shrugged.

"Well, not anymore." Lisa reached down for Presley's hand and pulled her right by Mike and back out into the bar. She waited until they were back in the bustling bar with the music blaring. "Are you okay?"

Presley's head moved up and down slowly.

Lisa didn't want to sound off too many alarms, so she tried to clear the pissed look off of her face. She knew her husband well and knew he would cause an unruly scene if he had been the one to catch Mike basically trapping Presley. She could only imagine what Trent would have done… Not to mention, she continued to contemplate, *everyone* was drinking.

Her thoughts were interrupted by an almost inaudible Presley.

"I think I'm ready to go home, Lis." She looked down. "Like, I just don't want to be here anymore."

"Of course, Pres." Lisa nodded her head. "We can go."

Twenty-Three

A car dropped all of them off at Presley's house.

"Thank you," Trent opened the door and was the first to get out followed by Presley.

"Pres." Lisa slid over on the seat. "We're going to go back to his parents for the night."

"Oh," Presley looked surprised. "You guys can stay if you want, it's no big deal."

"I know, girl, but I didn't stay with Bay last night and Jake's bound to pass out soon, we're just going to get home now. But we'll see you tomorrow for sure."

"Okay," Presley leaned down to hug her. "Text me when you get home?"

"Of course, girl." She got a little more serious and her voice lowered. "You good?"

Presley knew she was following-up on the Mike scene Lisa had saved her from, so she just nodded to confirm she was alright.

Lisa accepted the small gesture and then smiled. "Bye Trent!" She waved.

Trent waved to both Lisa and Jake, Jake did look like he was about to fall asleep.

The car drove away and left Trent and Presley in the moonlight.

Trent looked down to Presley. "Pres, I can call for a cab if you're tired too?"

"I'm okay," she smiled up at him. "That is, if you want to come hang out?"

"Of course I do." He reached for her face and cradled it before leaning down to kiss her. Trent quickly brought his other hand up as well, so both of his hands were holding her head. Presley's hands found themselves on Trent's chest, but they didn't stay long, she slid them across his chest and then down his sides and around his back to hold him.

Trent slowed down first. "You're not drunk making out with me, are you?" He grinned.

Presley giggled. "Not unless you are."

Trent tugged her hair and then kissed her once more on her lips. "Should we go see Baron?"

Presley agreed with a smile, and they walked to the cottage.

Baron trotted towards the door when he heard the lock pop.

"Hey bud," Presley kneeled down to greet him. He quickly said hi to both she and Trent and then went outside. "He must need to go potty." Presley shrugged. "Are you up for a quick walk?"

"With you, anytime and all the time."

"We're going to go back to shooting during the day for a bit." Trent informed Presley.

"Really?" her face lit up. "So, we'll have similar schedules, that will be so much better."

"Yep." He put his arms around her.

"I mean, were you telling me that because you wanted to spend time together?"

Trent rolled his head back and laughed. "Stop it, of course I was, sweetheart."

Presley loved the sound of him calling her sweetheart, each time he said it her heart swooned.

"Do you want to go see the set?" Trent laughed. "I mean, it's your house and all, but I can show you around my office?"

She bit her lip and reached for his hand. "Let's go."

✦

Presley looked around. "I still can't get over the fact that everything still looks so normal."

"Well, you've got an ideal set up already," Trent shrugged. "Besides all this equipment lying around." He motioned to a few cameras and lighting equipment. Baron galloped around the house, sniffing every inch, it was almost like it was a foreign place to him now.

"And my couch is going to be in this movie, huh? Do you know how much I love this thing?" She sank into the oversized leather sofa, it still looked new but had also been loved based on the creases that were just barely visible.

Trent smiled as he walked towards her. "You look like you're at home on it, that's for sure."

"Well, come sit with me." She patted the couch next to her.

Trent was more than willing to take her up on the offer, he sat next to her and put his arm around her. Baron was next to hop on the couch and he needed no invitation.

"Bare!" Presley tried to wiggle out from under his foot as his nail was digging into her thigh.

Trent lifted Baron off of her and then pulled her towards him while Baron found a spot to lie down. Trent kissed the side of Presley's head and began rubbing her shoulder.

"Trent." Presley broke the silence.

"Mm hm?" He responded during his next peck to her head.

"Did you think it was going to be like this?" She paused. "When we first met?"

Trent kissed her head again before answering. "No," he answered very honestly.

A moment of silence went by before he said anything else. Presley began to worry, she thought about her question again and suddenly had feelings of regret for asking in the first place.

"I mean, don't get me wrong," Trent started. "You took my breath away the first time I saw you." He kissed her head again. "I just wasn't expecting all this."

Presley decided to leave it at that, she could read between the lines and didn't want any more of a commitment that evening, everything was perfect as it was for the moment. She laid against him and stroked his arms. The next kiss Trent planted on her was to her neck, it sent goosebumps down Presley's side. She responded by turning her head and connecting their lips for a few quick pecks until they were in full on make out mode. Presley soon found herself facing Trent straddling him, their lips never separated. Trent pressed against her butt with his hands pulling her closer to him, he had a rhythm going when Presley picked up on it and joined in. Trent noticed and it intensified his hold on her. Her hands massaged his shoulders a few times before she wrapped her arms around his neck. Trent's hands were momentarily relocated when he began rubbing her sides, his fingers caught her shirt a couple of times and nearly lifted it, this made Presley slow down. Her hands came back around to hold his face as she slowly pulled away from him.

"Trent," she looked down. "I don't want to go too far after drinking so much tonight." She looked ashamed she had let it go even that far.

Trent rubbed his hands calmly up and down her back, he wasn't accustomed to any pumping of the brakes, and he wasn't sure if he needed to say something.

Presley finally spoke up. "I'm sorry, Trent." She still hadn't looked him in his eyes since halting their passionate exploration.

"Pres, no," Trent's eyes were wide. "Babe, don't ever feel sorry for something like that." He reached for the side of her face. "I told you I'd go as slow as you needed, I promise you that's more than okay."

Presley softly nodded her head but hadn't found the courage to meet his eyes quite yet.

"Don't get me wrong, I am ready and fucking willing to give you so much more, Pres." He smiled. "But that's not all I'm after, so if we need to slow down then we can slow down, okay?" He caressed her face with his thumb.

Presley was shy about sharing her feelings, but the alcohol she consumed that night gave her the ounce of courage she needed. "Trent, I do… want more too." She tried to conceal a smirk. "I just don't want that on a night we've both been drinking as much as we have." She finally looked into his eyes. "That's just not very pure in my mind and I…"

"Pres," Trent cut in. "This is exactly one of the reasons you're so damn special." He gripped a handful of her hair that had fallen in front of her shoulder. "I totally agree, and you don't have to worry at all. We both need to be ready and confident in that next step." He brushed her hair behind her shoulder. "Should we call it a night?"

"You don't have to leave. I understand if you want to… or need to, I didn't want to make you feel like you had to go." She rubbed his chest with her thumb of the hand that was already resting on it.

"I don't want to leave yet." He squeezed her sides. "So, how about I just agree to stay on my best behavior?" He smiled.

Presley smiled back at him. "I'll be sure to stay on mine too."

Trent gripped her cheeks to pull their pelvises closer together and then reached his lips up and began kissing her again, neither one of them had much restraint this time around, despite their conversation. Their only saving grace was that the jeans they were both in didn't allow much pleasure even with Presley straddling Trent. Presley giggled when one of Trent's hands slid itself from her left cheek, around her hips, under her shirt and up to cup her left breast. He was soon massaging her breast in his hand and Presley couldn't help but giggle a little more. "Trent Hayes, is this your version of practicing your best behavior?"

Trent didn't stop, he applied slightly more pressure as he continued to massage her. "It is," he smirked. "As you can feel," he whispered. "I've stayed on top of your bra." He kissed her neck a couple of times before continuing and speaking softly in her ear this time. "And, despite having every fucking urge to do so, I haven't put my mouth on these perfect breasts, yet."

Presley's body shuddered in pleasure, his hands were already doing plenty, just the thought of what he was describing had her sincerely considering if she needed to reevaluate the stance she had just taken.

"So, are we just going to play a game testing the limits of our best behavior tonight?" Presley nibbled his neck and then reached down and suggestively rubbed the front of Trent's jeans from his inner thigh to the top of his zipper and back down, she could feel they had already tightened quite a bit on him.

"Ha ha, oh fuck." Trent was rarely caught off-guard; he loved it, but his hand quickly receded down to her rib cage. He looked at her in her beautiful green eyes. "I can see that game would be a very bad idea." He touched their foreheads. "In the best kind of way." He pecked the side of her head. "So, we'll call it a draw."

Presley leaned into him, just inches from his lips as both of her hands were holding his hips. "The only reason I didn't win outright was because even over my bra, your boob fondling had my eyes rolling to the back of my head." She got up slowly, smiling but didn't look back at him when she got up.

Trent had slammed himself into the back of the couch and was covering his smiling face with both of his hands. He was desperately trying to erase what she just said to him, so he didn't pursue something they had just discussed they weren't going to do tonight. He could feel his heart trying to beat right out of his chest and the smile under his hands wasn't disappearing anytime soon. Trent finally got himself up off the couch and tried to readjust his jeans. He looked up and didn't see Presley, so he went to find her.

She was rummaging through her pantry as Trent walked into the kitchen. When she turned around and looked at him, he was still speechless, so he just took her in.

"Don't some chips and salsa sound so good?!" She held up an unopened bag of his favorite brand of tortilla chips.

Trent laughed, it was almost three o'clock in the morning and her second wind had obviously hit. "Actually, it does, and those chips are bomb."

"Right?! They're my favorite." She turned the light in the pantry off before coming out. She went to her cabinet to grab a couple of glasses. "What do you want to drink?" She smiled at him.

Trent leaned in to kiss her. "What are you having?"

"Bourbon." She quickly answered.

Trent laughed again, but noticed she was absolutely serious as she was digging through her freezer and pulled a bottle out.

"You keep a $400 bottle of bourbon in the freezer?" Trent laughed.

Presley smiled. "It's the best way to sip it, with a little ice of course."

He shook his head. "I'll try it," he agreed with a smile.

They had been sitting on the couch mowing down chips and salsa and throwing back bourbon during a very rounded conversation all about life when the first light of day started to appear.

"Fuck." Trent wiped his face and looked out the window. "It's almost daytime."

Presley slowly turned around to confirm, she was far beyond buzzed now and maintaining a pretty sizable state of drunk.

"Come here, sweetheart." Trent started to situate himself against the arm of the couch so he could look out the large back patio windows. Presley crawled over to him and leaned in between his legs, Trent wrapped his arms around her once she was settled and then began stroking her hair. "This is perfection," Trent stated.

"Trent, I've had so much freaking fun with you tonight." She smiled as she reached down and rubbed his leg. "Thank you." She squeezed his quad a few times.

He grinned. "Thank *you*, gorgeous."

Presley's eyes shut for a moment before her drunk mouth popped off. "Trent, I feel like I need to tell you something while I'm drunk." She leaned her head closer to his chest. "Because I don't know if I'd ever say it out loud while sober."

Trent rubbed her arms. "Hmmm, are you sure? Maybe if it takes this much liquid courage you want to just keep that secret for now?"

He worried she would regret saying whatever it was she felt the need to share at that moment.

"No." She slowly rolled her head side to side. "I think it's something kind of important too and also very embarrassing."

Trent lightly chuckled, he wasn't exactly sober either but appeared to be doing much better than Presley. "I promise you can back out now, babe. If it's embarrassing you don't have to tell me, I'm worried it'll upset you when you realize you've shared whatever it is."

"I mean, you'll probably find out anyway and telling you before anything happens might be better so you can run away first instead."

"Runaway?" Trent tilted her chin to look at him. "Sweetheart, what could you possibly be afraid and embarrassed to tell me that would make me run away from you?"

Presley shrugged and tried to break eye contact. Trent gently held her chin to try to maintain it, but didn't want to force her.

"Can I at least hide my face a little when I spill?" Presley giggled. "It's so you can just understand."

Oh shit, Trent thought, *she's so drunk, I shouldn't be letting her talk anymore, she's talking gibberish.* But just as he was silently reflecting on their current conversation Presley started.

"I'm scared that I...," she stuttered. "Uhm, like I'm not really good at things like you are... This is..." she started playing with his fingers as he listened as intently as he could. She decided closing her eyes would help her put a full sentence together. "Trent, you should know I talk a big game." She giggled. "But I don't have the experience you do."

Trent started to realize what she may be preparing to disclose.

She fidgeted, her legs were tucked with the bottoms of her feet on the couch, and she started to sway them slightly. "I haven't." She covered her face. "Shit." She squirmed, completely embarrassed to be sharing. "I think our habits have been quite different with our bedtime friends." She quickly blurted. "Lisa said I don't need to be embarrassed about that, but I feel like I needed to prepare you because..."

Trent stopped her from saying anything else, he pulled her closer to him and rubbed his hands up and down her arms before kissing the side of her head. His lips lingered on her head, and he took a deep breath of her sweet scented hair before he said anything.

"Pres, baby." He kissed her again. "That's nothing to be embarrassed about, at all. If anything, I'm the one who should be ashamed and embarrassed. And don't worry, that doesn't make me judge you or want to run away from you, not even close."

Presley finally looked at him again, she didn't smile, she just assessed his sincerity.

"Sweetheart," Trent spoke softly and tucked a piece of her hair behind her ear. "Is that why you want to wait, because you're afraid we've had different experiences?"

Presley scrunched her face. "Maybe a little bit of it… Or a lot of it." She rolled her head towards his chest again to hide her face. "Trent, it's almost like things are just brand new with you, you won't laugh at me if I don't know or remember what I'm doing?"

"Pres." Trent was a little more forceful with turning her now, he made sure to look her in the eyes so she could see the concern as he was talking. "Are you kidding me?"

She didn't respond right away; her face was red and Trent wasn't sure if that was more from the alcohol or her embarrassment at this point. "I really have just enjoyed you so damn much and if, like when that happens, I just don't want you to be disappointed…" She couldn't even finish her thought because she was immediately cut off by Trent.

"Stop." He pulled her closer to him. "You are worrying about nonsense, babe, I promise you. You have plenty on your plate to worry about; this, *us*, should never worry you." He kissed her firmly on her lips. "You don't have to be embarrassed or scared with me, ever, about anything. And you could *never* disappoint me—I've seen too much of your heart already, Presley." Trent kissed her again. "Sweetheart, I want to make you feel cherished, wanted, worshiped, appreciated, and safe, always safe, Pres." Trent held her face in his hands. "Okay?"

"Trent," Presley reached up and rubbed the side of his face. "You've been so good to me." She looked into his eyes for a long moment. "Thank you."

Trent rubbed her chin. "You don't have to thank me." He laughed. "Do you have any idea how special you are? You deserve the world, Pres." He smiled into her eyes. "And I'm going to work on getting that for you, starting with a special little something that I think you're long overdue for, and that's a damn promise." He leaned in to kiss her and led with his tongue.

Twenty-Four

Baron was barking as he hopped off the couch, it wasn't long before there was shouting, and Presley scrambled to see what he was barking at.

"Bare, leave it!" She called out and tried to lift herself off the couch while her head spun.

"Babe, you alright?" Trent asked with a groggy voice from under her. They had fallen asleep on the couch in the main house and the crew was starting to trickle in. Baron was alerting them to a security guard and two of the prop masters walking in the front door.

"Good morning." The security guard waved first. "Sorry to startle you, we didn't realize anyone would be in the house."

They could just barely see Presley's head over the back of the sofa from their angle, so they definitely hadn't seen Trent yet.

"Come here, Bare." Presley tried to untangle her legs from Trent's so she could stand. "I'm so sorry, I didn't realize what time it was, we fell asleep." She stumbled a bit when she stood and then reached down to her pit bull's head when he came back to her side. Trent was also rolling off the couch at that point.

"Oh," the security guard stuttered, "Mr. Hayes." He greeted him while one of the prop masters chuckled under his breath. "Good morning, sir."

"Marco," Trent waved and then rubbed his eyes. They looked like a drunken mess; their hair was disheveled and they were still in their full outfits they had gone out to the bar in. Presley wasn't sure if she should be embarrassed, or how Trent felt about being caught on the couch with her. She looked down at the coffee table and remembered they had also decided to crack open a bottle of bourbon at some point last night, no wonder she was so disoriented.

"Well, we should," she stuttered, "I should…" Presley began gathering their mess from the coffee table. "Sorry, I'll get all this picked up and head out."

Trent smiled at her, she was acting like they were going to somehow be punished, they hadn't even done anything. He picked up his phone, but it was dead. "Do you know what time it is?"

One of the prop masters spoke up. "It's almost 9am."

"Shit." Trent rubbed Presley's shoulder before he bent down and picked up the bag of tortilla chips and half eaten container of salsa they had paired with their early morning bourbon.

"Are you going to be in trouble?" Presley whispered to Trent, trying to turn her face away from their guests to conceal what she was saying.

Trent laughed and rubbed her back this time. "Pres, no." They noticed the prop masters and security guard were already on their way to take care of their duties. "What are you worried about?"

Her arms were full of the nearly empty bottle of bourbon, glasses and her shoes; she shrugged. "I don't know, like were we supposed to be here, and are you going to be late for the shoot this morning?"

Trent kissed her forehead and smiled at her. "Pres, this is your house, so you're not getting into trouble." He assured her. "But I do need to get my ass in gear because I'm supposed to be ready by 9:30."

She shook her head in agreement. "Not sure what all is going on in the bathrooms here, but if you need a shower or whatever, you're welcome to come down to the cottage to get ready."

"Really?" He raised his eyebrows at her and shot a sly smile her way.

"Of course." She reached her lips up to his. "I'll make you something for breakfast while you're getting ready."

He bent his knees and rolled his head back. "Shit." Trent smiled as he followed her, that wasn't what he had in mind when thinking about showering down at the cottage.

They were about to walk out the back door when they heard Michelle. "Well, well, well, what's this I see?"

Both Presley and Trent stopped in their tracks, Presley was too embarrassed to turn around at first.

"Morning, Shell." Trent greeted her. "Chips and salsa?" He held up the food.

"What the hell are you guys doing?" She laughed as Pete walked in and tried to catch up on the scene in front of him.

"About to go get ready." Trent said and Presley finally turned around.

"My my," Michelle laughed when she saw the bourbon in Presley's arms. "What kind of morning did you two have?"

"You two pull an all nighter, or what?" Pete laughed and leaned down to pet Baron when he walked over to them.

"We just got back from the bar really late and then fell asleep up here." Presley admitted and then quickly clarified they were on the couch.

"Oohhhh." Michelle drew out.

"Don't make me start asking about how that shower scene went last night you two." Trent smiled and then put his arm around Presley for them to head to the cottage. "I need to go get ready or I'm gonna be late," he called back to Pete and Michelle before he shut the door.

✦

Mike barely heard the notification go off on his phone, there was movement at the cottage. He wasn't able to lift his head yet, so he decided to listen if the motion would continue, this was likely just the porch camera anyway.

✦

"You can help yourself to whatever's up there, the towels on the rack are all clean too." Presley set the bourbon and glasses down on the kitchen island. "Oh, and there's like a plethora of brand-new toothbrushes in one of the drawers up there, and different soaps and such if you don't like what's in the shower."

Trent set the bag of chips down and then put the salsa in the refrigerator before he made his way back to her. "Thank you, beautiful." He pressed his lips against her forehead. "And just so you know, you're more than welcome to join me." He winked.

Presley blushed and put her arms around his neck. "Well, first of all, I'm quite positive I'm still drunk." She reached up to him on her tiptoes and was just inches from his lips. "And," she said softly. "You'll likely need more than fifteen minutes if I join you."

Trent's hands rubbed down Presley's back as he leaned back and laughed. "I sincerely doubt that." His hands reached her cheeks, and he squeezed just as he connected their lips. After their tongues massaged each other for a bit, it was Trent who slowed down first. "And to clarify, I wouldn't *need* that long, but I'd *want* longer in there with you." He lifted her up and set her on the kitchen island with her legs on either side of him. Trent gave her one last, juicy kiss. "I'm going to go get ready before I run out of all my good behavior." He winked.

Presley reached down and gave his cheeks a squeeze. "I'll get something together for you to eat for breakfast." She smiled at him.

Mike's notifications were going off again so he decided he could muster up the strength to take a look. It took an unusual amount of effort to sit up because his head felt like it weighed about eighty pounds. Once he located his phone, he dropped right back down to having his head on his pillow. His eyes stayed open long enough to see it was the bathroom camera that was alerting movement, so he forced himself to focus on the screen. To his dismay, when the feed appeared on his screen, he was getting a side view of Trent completely naked while brushing his teeth. It looked like he had turned the shower on, so the room was starting to steam, but from the angle he had, he could still see plenty. Mike had seen many of Trent's movies, and he had also already seen him in person without a shirt, so he knew Trent was muscular, what he wasn't aware of was how well-endowed Trent was. He only had a side view of him so far, but it was clear Trent was of more than adequate size below the waist. Mike decided to look at the other cameras in the cottage instead, he didn't want to look at Trent any longer; the guy pissed him off to no end and his resentment only increased seeing the size of him. His only hope in looking at the other cottage cameras was that Presley wasn't headed for the shower as well.

Twenty-Five

"Auntie PP!" Bailey came running into the cottage a couple hours after Trent had left for the set.

Presley didn't lift her head from the couch, she was lying on her back, with sunglasses on. "Hi Bay, baby." She smiled.

"You're sleeping?" He asked as he got closer.

"Auntie PP better not still be sleeping." Jake walked into the living room. "Oh hell, Pres, what happened to you, girlfriend?" He laughed.

Bailey had made his way up on the couch with her and was now laying down next to her petting her hair. "Me and Bay are going to stay here today, just like this." She was appreciative of Bailey's gentle brushing.

"Pres," Lisa made her way to everyone. "I didn't realize you had that much to drink last night, I feel fine."

Presley still had her eyes closed under her sunglasses. "I wasn't that messed up after the bar." She hugged Bailey when he laid his head on her chest. "However, my dumb butt pulled the bourbon out when we got home and next thing you know we were watching the sun come up this morning."

Jake and Lisa were both laughing. "Shit," Jake started. "I thought I had it rough this morning."

"Do you want to just sleep for a bit, Pres?" Lisa offered.

"Auntie PP, you're not coming with us?" Bailey leaned up towards her face and put his hand on her forehead.

"Bay, Auntie PP is going to come with you," she assured him. "She just needs some medicine, a gallon of water and the biggest chunk of carbs your Daddy can find in the kitchen." She smiled.

Jake and Lisa exchanged glances. "I'll go get the aspirin from the bathroom," Lisa volunteered.

"I'm on the water and carbs mission then." Jake agreed. "We've got you, Pres."

"I'm helping!" Bailey scrambled off the couch to follow Jake. Presley tried to scratch Baron's head when he rested it next to her, she could feel him wiggling his body with an excited tail wag.

Lisa was the first to come back. "Uhm, excuse me," she scooted on the couch next to Presley. "Why do I see a set of men's clothes on the floor in your bathroom? Pres," she smiled and leaned closer to Presley. "Did you take a shower with Trent fucking Hayes?"

Presley laughed and then held her head at the movement. "No," she answered. "I mean, technically we both did shower in there this morning, just not together."

"Why the *hell* not?!" Lisa laughed.

Presley giggled. "Have you failed to notice my condition?"

"All that liquid courage and you didn't hop in the shower with him? I have to say, I'm a little disappointed in you, Pres," Lisa concluded. "If nothing else, I was looking for a sexy story at the very least!"

Presley slid her sunglasses down just enough to make eyes with Lisa. "I did get an invite." She smiled widely.

Lisa didn't care what her head felt like, she reached down and shook Presley.

They were both giggling, and Presley was begging for Lisa to quit shaking her when Jake and Bailey walked back in.

"Oh hell." He shook his head. "I don't even want to know, you two." He held out a glass of water for Presley. "I'll go fill one of your water bottles too, but this is for the aspirin, and then I found an Uncrustable in the freezer." He handed her the unwrapped treat. "We'll stop off and get you a couple scones before we hit the market today." Jake promised.

Presley slowly lifted herself up enough to take the water from him. "You guys are the best."

Twenty-Six

"Hi kids." Mardele waved when she spotted her family at the farmer's market. Everyone took their turns greeting one another.

"Where's Papa?" Lisa asked.

"Oh, he took off to go see if that vendor with the specialty hot sauces is here again." She waved her hand around and then picked Bailey up. "How's Nana's boy?" She pecked his cheek.

"Good." He smiled and then rested his head on her shoulder.

"Oh my gosh." Presley spotted the Grundley's cart. "Corn Dogs." She turned to the group. "I'm going to go get one, anyone else?"

Everyone shook their heads and watched Presley make her way towards a corn dog.

"Is she okay?" Mardele asked.

Jake and Lisa laughed. "Well," Lisa started. "Not sure if she's still drunk, or if she's hit the hangover stage yet."

Mardele smiled. "I guess as long as she had fun."

"Yep." Ron caught up with the group. "Got about a month's supply." He proudly held his bag of sauces and rubs.

"Good, maybe your meat won't be so bland now." Jake teased.

"I'll let that slide, so I don't embarrass you in front of your boy." He rolled his eyes.

"Oh, it's the entire Hofner clan!" A woman called out as she approached.

Mardele was the first to speak, she always tried to project

kindness, especially in situations where she wasn't sure what may come out of her husband or son's mouths. "Oh, hi Phyliss, so good to see you."

Phyliss stood in front of the group and reached out for Bailey. "My, he's getting so big! What a handsome little fella." She commented while giving him loving leg pinches.

"Can you tell Mrs. Bando thank you?" Lisa rubbed her son's shoulder. Bailey just hid his face.

"Michael told me he saw him yesterday, said he's just cute as a button! He wasn't lying." She smiled.

"He did." Lisa knew full well her husband would end up saying something snide, so she tried to take a page out of Mardele's book. "Bay, honey, remember your donut yesterday from Mike? This is Mike's mommy; can you say hi to her?"

Bailey finally lifted his head from Mardele's shoulder. "I like donuts." He smiled at her.

Phyliss smiled. "Well, then you've got great taste." She noticed Ron had made himself scarce and Jake had checked behind them a few times since she had been standing there. "So, did you kids have a good time last night? I heard a lot of the team made it out to the bar."

Jake hated Mike, but his mom was really nice, so he decided he should play nice as well. "We did, it was a really good time, actually."

"I'm pretty sure Mike was still there when we left, is he around today?" Lisa asked, wanting to be sure he wasn't going to be popping up while Presley was off getting her corn dog alone.

Phyliss laughed. "Oh, no." She shook her head. "I'm not sure when Mike actually got home, I found him on the front porch this morning around five." She waved her hand. "He apparently walked home from the bar and couldn't remember which key was for the front door." She laughed. "I don't ever see him like that, but I'm glad he was able to enjoy the evening with all the old pals."

"Yeah." Jake nodded his head. "He was knocking them back pretty good all night."

"Oh my gosh." Presley was walking up behind Mardele and Bailey.

"This corn dog is life right now." She claimed while taking another bite, she slowed when she saw who they were talking to.

"Oh, Presley, dear!" Phyliss walked over and hugged her. "I haven't seen you in a while, so good to see you honey."

Presley returned the hug. "Hi Phyliss, good to see you out and about, how've you been?"

"Still kickin'!" She replied. "Mike said you and him had dinner last night, I was really sad that you guys didn't come by the house first."

Presley's eyebrows furrowed. "Oh, no, we had all just met up and had drinks at the bar last night." She tried to politely correct her. "I had Mardele's famous meatballs over at the Hofner's last night for dinner."

Jake and Lisa were exchanging looks.

"Huh? That's odd, I could've sworn he said that was last night." She shrugged. "I forget the days of the week from time to time, so who knows?"

"It's okay." Presley assured her, knowing full well that was exactly what Mike had likely told his mom. Presley did remember when Mike had recently forced dinner with her after Baron's injury, but Mike had probably been very honest about having dinner at the cottage alone with her.

"So, how have things been going at the house, with the movie?" She asked.

Presley bobbed her head up and down as she swallowed another bite before responding. "Really good actually, I've enjoyed having them there."

"Mike sure has been worried about you." Phyliss looked around the group. "He said he's been doing extra patrols because there is someone on set that's a little over the top with you right now."

Presley caught the facial expressions Jake was making, and it didn't seem like it would end well if he opened his mouth, she was beyond grateful when Mardele hopped in.

"Over the top? More like sweeping the sweet girl right off her feet." She smiled and rubbed Presley's shoulders.

Phyliss looked genuinely confused as she watched Presley blush.

"Yeah, are you talking about Trent Hayes?" Lisa chimed in.

"Well," Phyliss continued to watch Presley's expression. "Yes." She looked at Lisa again. "Mike tells me he has been hanging around a lot. And I mean, I do pick up all of those God-awful gossip magazines at the grocery store, so I've seen quite a few stories and understand his concern."

Jake grabbed Presley around her shoulders. "I would *never* let anyone creepy or unworthy around my girl here." He smiled at Phyllis. "I put Trent in the hot seat last night and I have to say, he seems like a great guy."

"I'm sorry." Phyliss looked at Presley again. "I must have misunderstood, Mike was sure you were feeling uncomfortable, dear."

Presley shook her head. "Trent doesn't make me uncomfortable at all." She was sure to make it clear. "That is kind of Mike to be concerned but Jake's right, Trent is a really wonderful man."

"And so handsome." Phyliss added.

Presley chuckled and nodded her head in agreement when her phone started ringing. She smiled when she saw the screen, it was Trent.

"Speak of the devil." Jake rubbed Presley's shoulders.

"Excuse me." Presley smiled at the group before she took her phone call away from them.

Phyliss smiled as Presley walked away. "Well, that sure is a big smile. I didn't realize things were like that for Presley." She admitted. "Is Trent Hayes her boyfriend?"

Lisa smiled. "I'm not sure the official boyfriend bomb has been dropped, but it's something."

"Talking?" Jake suggested.

"Yeah." Lisa rolled her head. "Talking, dating… certainly seeing each other regularly." She looked at Phyliss.

Phyliss put her hand to her chest. "She is such a lovely girl, I'm glad she's finding happiness. You know," she giggled. "I'll admit, I have always secretly hoped she and Mike would find their way together."

Jake made a throw up motion behind Phyliss's back and Lisa quickly shot him a glare. Phyliss seemed completely oblivious to how obsessive her son was and there was no reason to take it out on her.

"Based on what I've seen, this may be end game." Lisa shrugged. "I couldn't be happier for her, Trent is so perfect for Pres, he does treat her really well."

"I'd second that after the conversation I had with him last night." Jake offered.

Lisa gave him a look; he hadn't shared any of this with her.

"Mrs. Bando, you may need to let Mike know Pres is the center of Trent's universe and he doesn't seem like a guy who shares." Jake held his hands out for Bailey when he reached for him from his Nana's arms. "The Trent Hayes shit list isn't something I'd want to be on." Jake looked at Phyliss with a flat smile and heightened brows.

Phyliss laughed. "He isn't feeling too well today, I'll hold off. Plus, that's just a mother's dream, not sure if it was Mike's dream too. I mean, he has obviously commented on her beauty in the past, but he has never said anything to me about any kind of long-term interest."

Jake and Lisa held their tongues.

It was Mardele who offered her opinion. "Trent certainly seems to be Presley's dream come true."

Presley joined the group again, her corn dog devoured and her phone back in her pocket.

"How's Trent?" Jake gleaned and then smacked his lips a few times.

Presley playfully rolled her eyes from under her oversized sunglasses. "He's good, they were just on a quick break. And actually, he also called to let me know some of the crew is headed out this way, they want some random scenery shots for the movie, so basically if we want to be extras in the movie, we're in the right spot."

"That's actually pretty fuckin dope." Jake admitted. "You know I'm always camera ready." He made a motion to slick his hair.

"Will the actors be coming out here too?" Phyliss asked.

Presley shook her head. "Not today, they do have a few scenes in town that they still haven't done yet, but the filming out here today is just for like filler or whatever in the movie I guess."

"So," Phyliss directed her attention to Mardele. "How long do you get to have your kiddos in town?"

"Well, Presley, always." Mardele smiled at her. "But the rest of the kids are leaving sometime tomorrow, unfortunately."

"Early." Jake added. "Honestly, probably before breakfast, Mom."

"What?" Mardele was immediately disappointed.

"Yeah, sorry." Lisa scrunched her face.

"Well, then there will be no negotiating, we're all spending the evening together." Mardele demanded before she turned to hold her hands out to Bailey. "Nana wants to snuggle you more, come here, sweet boy."

Bailey happily jumped back into her arms. "And find Papa?"

"Yes, honey, let's go find Papa," she agreed. "It was good to see you, Phyliss."

"Bye." Bailey waved at her as they headed out to find Ron.

Phyliss waved to both of them as they left the group. "You guys sure are lucky, what a wonderful little man you have." Phyliss was smitten by Bailey, really the idea of a grandbaby.

Presley watched Phyliss, she was one of the nicest people Presley had ever met, it was a wonder how she raised such an unstable son. Mike had his dad through high school, his parents were that couple who probably should have just split, but didn't want to get a divorce until Mike had graduated. So, it wasn't as though Mike had grown up without a father figure in the home during his childhood. Phyliss was always on the PTA, she was the unofficial team mom on virtually all of Mike's sports teams growing up, and the few times Mardele or Lisa's mom weren't filling a motherly role for Presley, Phyliss had stepped in. The only thing Presley couldn't seem to love about Phyliss was her son.

"Yeah, we kinda like him." Jake looked back and watched his mom carrying Bailey through the market. "Hell, we may even keep him."

Phyliss laughed. "I can't wait for grandbabies; oh my heart is just going to explode."

"Well, is Mike seeing anyone?" Lisa asked, definitely wanting anything and everything she could get on him.

Phyliss shook her head. "Oh, he doesn't talk to his mom about stuff like that." She waved her hand around. "Although, I imagine he does have lady friends over from time to time, he keeps his room and basement area all locked up. I can't blame him, probably not the most inviting thing to have your mom around when you're trying to date."

"Mike could live on his own though." Jake shrugged.

Phyliss bumped Jake's arm. "Don't tell him that." She laughed. "I love having him at home."

"He's about to be swimming in all the ladies when he wins the Sheriff election." Jake suggested.

Phyliss smiled wider. "I do hope he wins; he would be such a great Sheriff, he is so good at what he does already, it would just really be a fine fit. I should actually call him about the filming this afternoon, I'm sure he would love to be an extra, maybe I'll run home and get my campaign tee shirt on." She laughed.

"Hopefully he's recovered enough from sleeping on the porch to be able to make an appearance." Lisa laughed.

Phyliss returned the laughter. "Dear, don't go getting me in trouble for sharing his secrets; it was quite a sight though."

"My lips are sealed." Lisa promised, knowing full well the only people she'd tell and laugh about it with were standing right next to them.

"Well," Presley walked over and leaned into hug Phyliss. "It was so good to see you, Phyliss."

"Oh, you too, honey." Phyliss gave her back a few quick rubs. "So good to see you happy and enjoying life, honey."

Jake and Lisa waved as Phyliss left them.

"Mike *had* to have been adopted." Jake shook his head. "Or she's really good at pretending she doesn't know what a little fuckhead he is."

"Love, be nice." Lisa warned. "Phyliss has always been really good to all of us."

Jake rolled his head, reluctantly agreeing with his wife.

"Honestly, she's a saint." Presley shook her head. "I do love her, but I can imagine Mike probably isn't all that honest with her, unfortunately. So, I do feel really bad for her too."

As they all went to look for Bailey and his grandparents, it was Lisa who responded. "Do you think Mike brings girls home? His mom said he keeps his room and basement locked, that seems odd, right?"

"Fuck no," Jake immediately responded. "No shot he is with any other girl when he is still hung up on Pres. Plus, when would he have time for another girl since he's always showing up at her place?" Jake gestured his thumb towards Presley.

Lisa knew Presley probably still had the night before fresh in her mind when Mike had her trapped. She definitely didn't want to bring that up with her husband now, but also didn't want him to continue talking about how obsessed Mike is. "He is honestly probably hiding all his sex toys from her, no way in hell I'd want my mom finding stuff like that! And we all know Phyliss is probably still doing his laundry for him." Lisa laughed.

"The basement is kinda weird though, you think he's just got his little playroom down there or something?" Jake continued.

"Well," it was Presley this time. "Phyliss probably shouldn't be going up and down those stairs, and we all know how much she likes to do for Mike, so maybe he does that so she doesn't get down there while he's at work and wouldn't be able to help her right away if she fell?"

"Solid point," Jake agreed.

"He does also work in law enforcement, maybe it's like work stuff." Lisa added.

"Okay," Jake waved his hands around. "You two are too rational, we can't just make fun of the guy instead?!"

Lisa and Presley laughed but it was Lisa who responded. "How about we don't talk about that guy at all?"

"Fair enough." Jake's head bounced around. "Hey, Bay isn't with us, let's go do a tasting at that little winery tent over there."

Presley immediately felt a gag reflex. "I will join you guys for the cheese and whatever other snacks they may be providing, but I may have to bail if I even smell alcohol of any kind."

Jake laughed at her and grabbed both of them around their shoulders to walk them towards the wine.

Twenty-Seven

Ron wanted to show off his fancy new market finds, so he invited all of them over for dinner that night. After Presley caught a power nap, she waited for Trent to be done with work so he could join them all. Bailey had also requested an outdoor movie on the Hofner's back patio that really was like an additional living room, so the final night with the Hofners for the weekend was all planned out.

✦

"Doesn't it just make your ovaries scream with utter desire to watch that?" Lisa whispered into Presley's ear as they were sitting on the back deck watching Trent and Jake teaching Bailey how to play wiffle ball. Jake was doing an overly exaggerated warm up for his pitch while Trent was on his knees behind Bailey helping him hold the bat. Not too far from home plate Baron was gnawing on the bone Ron had given him from dinner.

Presley giggled but never took her eyes off them—she couldn't deny how amazing Trent was. And he fit so seamlessly into her little chosen family, it certainly made her heart happy. She wasn't sure her ovaries were exactly ready to be begging Trent for kids though. Lisa was a few steps ahead of her in that department.

"Because mine are literally being terrorized right now. Honest to God, I can feel them screaming for Jake." Lisa came around from behind the patio couch Presley was on and sat down next to her. "Not sure how we're not pregnant yet." She laughed. "No IUD for two full months now and we've definitely been trying more nights than not."

"Oh Lis." Presley patted her leg and then leaned onto her best friend's shoulder. "It'll happen soon enough."

"Trent is great with him." Lisa took a sip of her wine and watched her son laughing at Trent who helped him tip Jake's pitch just off the edge of the bat.

"Trent," Bailey giggled. "You missed!"

"*I* missed, bro?!" Trent pretended to be shocked. "You're the batter… and we didn't miss, that's called a foul ball." Trent went through the routine of where Bailey's hands needed to be again before he held the bat with him, and they waited for the next pitch.

"He is." Presley agreed with a smile on her face. "Generally, it's a really good sign when children and animals gravitate towards you and both Bay and Bare can't seem to get their fill of him."

"And just when are you going to get your fill of Mr. Hayes?" Lisa prodded. "You cannot possibly be thinking about holding out on him still? I'm ready to jump the poor guy's bones for fuck's sake!"

Presley laughed. "You are such a perv sometimes, it's definitely time for Jake to knock you up, the crazy hormones are starting to show face again."

"You bitch." Lisa nudged into Presley. "Going to deflect and hold out on me like that then, huh?"

"You'll want to remember that you held out on me for *months*." Presley looked up and narrowed her eyes at her best friend. "Jake told me way before you did."

"First of all, that was way different because we were all basically kids and that was my actual virginity I had just given up." Lisa laughed. "And that better not mean you plan on notifying Jake first."

Presley laughed. "I didn't know I needed to send out a memo if that happens."

"*When*," Lisa stressed. "*When* that happens, Pres."

Presley smiled, she knew Lisa was right, it was definitely a when issue versus an if issue. Everything was in Presley's court, and she knew that. Trent promised her they'd move at her comfort level, and he had done nothing but make her comfortable since they met. If she was being honest with herself, she was ready to fully be with Trent, all she had standing in her way was that smidge of fear that lived in her mind. And even at that, she had already expressed those fears to Trent, and he shut down her doubts and only offered her assurances. She knew this would be their next step… And soon.

Ron and Mardele had taken themselves to bed earlier in the evening, and Bailey didn't last too much longer after that. The rest of them enjoyed their last few hours together of this visit before they decided to call it a night.

"Trent, it was so good to meet you." Lisa allowed Trent to fully engulf her. "Truly, you've been a pleasure to hang with."

"Same, Lis, I really hope I get to see a lot more of you guys." He squeezed her shoulders. "And Bay too, he's my guy."

"Oh, he for sure loves you." She laughed. "You've got a new little best friend."

Lisa looked over and saw Presley and her husband giggling away like they always did. "Trent, I also wanted to thank you for being so good to Pres. After the fire and everything else this week, I really thought we were going to come out and have to do some emotional restoration." She checked to be sure Presley and Jake were still chatting on their own. "But I see that you've had her all along, and I couldn't be more grateful."

"Lis, of course." Trent hugged her again. "I promise, she's safe with me—her heart is safe with me." He backed up slightly so he could see Lisa's face. "I want nothing more than to take care of Pres and make her happy."

Lisa nodded her head and offered him a smile.

"Come here, girlfriend." Jake gave Presley a bear hug. "Loved seeing you so damn happy this weekend." He pecked the side of her head.

"Thank you." She squeezed her best friend. "Despite all the bullshit going on, I am really happy, Jake."

"Trent's a great guy, Pres." Jake looked at her. "And you know I don't just accept everyone, *especially* when it comes to my girl."

Presley smiled. "Oh, I know."

"And the bullshit is on its way out the door. We're going to kick that bitch's ass this week and as far as Officer Dickbag is concerned, I think Trent can handle my light work."

Presley laughed. "Thank you… for all of it, Jake." She hugged him again and before separating she tried to whisper to keep her next comment very private. "And I want a niece next, Missionary seems to be the suggested position for that if you could please."

Jake laughed out loud and picked his best friend up. "No promises." He stated and then leaned into whisper to her. "Your bestie over there is a fucking freak."

"Aghhhh, eww." Presley laughed and tried to push away from him.

Presley finally won the battle and Jake set her back down, she looked over at Trent and Lisa who seemed to be saying their final goodbye. Lisa had just nodded her head at Trent and then he turned to find Presley's eyes.

"Ready, babe?" Trent asked.

They walked towards each other and their hands intertwined, they waved up at the Hofners before heading out to the truck.

Twenty-Eight

It was another late night for them and Presley felt the munchies take over when they got back to the cottage from the Hofner's. Trent had assured her he was fine; despite the lack of sleep he'd managed to get the last couple of days. Presley was ready to get out of her sundress, so she slipped into pajamas before suggesting they go raid the pantry for some snacks. She came back down from the loft to see Trent had made it into comfier clothing as well. He was more than happy to snack with her.

"I thought you were worried about us getting in trouble for being on set?" Trent teased Presley as they walked up the lawn towards the main house.

Presley giggled. "Okay, so I may have overreacted a teeny bit after our little bourbon bender," she admitted. "But I can't stop thinking about those chips and the pantry is where I keep the stockpile."

Trent laughed. "I'm so glad you have a stockpile that you're willing to share. Those are my favorite chips and the only grocery store in this town doesn't carry them."

Presley opened the back doors. "I know." She rolled her eyes. "I have to buy them in bulk when I go to Seattle. I've asked a few times about them and I guess other people in town just don't have an advanced pallet like ours." She laughed. "So, I'm absolutely more than happy to share with a fellow superfan."

They collected a few items from the pantry and then stopped at the back door, on their way to the cottage, when they realized it had started to rain.

"In the middle of the summer?" Trent watched as it was coming down pretty good.

Presley rolled her head from side to side. "Sometimes. This is pretty heavy for this time of year though, we should wait it out, so we don't have to run with all this." She smiled up at him. "These little summer storms don't usually last too long."

"Let's give that comfy couch another go then." He suggested and led them towards their new snacking spot.

Presley turned the sound system on in the house as they set down their snack spread.

"You like Country, huh?" Trent was familiar with the song.

Presley smiled. "I'd say my music taste has a pretty wide range, but Country is top tier for sure."

"I happen to enjoy Country too." Trent confirmed and took a drink of the iced tea he had grabbed from the kitchen. "George Strait is my guy—he's always been one of my favorites."

"Oh yeah?" Presley was intrigued. "He's a classic, solid pick for sure." She agreed and then handed her iPad to Trent. "Here, why don't you play your best George Strait jam so I can see if you're a true fan."

Trent immediately found the song. "Okay," he looked at her, "to clarify, this isn't my favorite, but it is what you would call top tier *and* it fits the moment." He hit play.

The second the first tunes projected from the speakers Presley's smile spread across her face.

Trent set the iPad down and stood up in front of her with his hand out. "Let's go, sweetheart."

Presley accepted his hand.

He moved them into a more open area of the living room, as he twirled her he joined George Strait at the start of the song, "*I don't want to be the kind to hesitate, Be too shy, Wait too late, I don't care what they say other lovers do, I just want to dance with you, I gotta feeling that you have a heart like mine, So let it show, Let it shine…*"

Presley giggled, interrupting his serenade. "Okay, Trent Hayes, you are *very* impressive. Singing *and* a little country spinning two-step too, huh?"

"You didn't think I'd pick this song and not know how to swing you around the dancefloor, did you?" He twirled her again and then pulled her in to peck her lips.

As the song came to an end Trent gave her one final spin and then held her hand to go back to the couch. He immediately stopped them when a slower ballad came on next. "Nope." He turned to face her as he put one arm securely around her waist and the other gently holding her hand. "It's a rule, we don't leave the dancefloor on a slow song." He pecked her.

Presley rested her head on Trent's shoulder and allowed him to lead them, swaying to the slower song now. Halfway through the song, Trent released Presley's hand and put both of his along her waistline as he rocked her to the beat. He kissed her forehead and contemplated how he would approach offering her the 'special little something' he promised her the night before.

He made a few assumptions based on what her intoxicated mouth was spewing about her 'bedtime friends' and things feeling like the first time. The conclusions he settled on were that she was actually telling him either it had been a long time, her little friends hadn't truly provided her much pleasure so she felt somehow inadequate, or the last and hopefully least likely scenario, she thought Trent was going to be some kind of kinky freak that would demand things even the Kama Sutra would blush at.

Whatever it was, he wanted to make sure she was going to be more than taken care of with him. He needed to put any doubts or fears in her mind to rest for good. Given what he had learned about her these past couple of weeks, she definitely wasn't the type who was just out there offering herself to anyone, so he wanted to respect the trust she would be giving him in this next step. Initially, he was willing to wait and give her the time she needed to feel comfortable enough to sleep with him, and he would still honor that, technically. He wanted to pleasure Presley in an infinite number of ways to give her release and make her senses explode from the inside out before he made any kind of penetrative move with his strapping manhood.

His mind drifted back to the night before when she told him just massaging her breasts made her eyes roll back; he could only imagine the things he could do that would… *Ah fuck*, he thought, *Grandmas and outhouses, my mom's bridge club, that dead carcass I saw on the road earlier…* Trent tried to think of a million different things to clear his mind as he felt the front of his pants moving. He knew they didn't have the coverage of jeans this time. They were basically rubbing on each other as they swayed to the music and he had on a pair of basketball shorts while Presley was in tiny little, thin pajama shorts that were just barely covering the bottoms of her cheeks, exposing her gorgeous sun kissed legs… *shit shit shit grandmas and outhouses grandmas and outhouses*, he chanted in his head and put his hands a little higher on her back. If she noticed anything going on below his waistline, Presley was decent enough not to make a big deal out of it, her head simply stayed comfortably planted on his chest.

As the final tunes slowly played the outro, Presley looked up at Trent, he couldn't resist reaching for her face and leaning down to kiss her. This kiss was filled with passion, and it was coming from both sides, they were active with their tongues until it wasn't enough. Trent reached down to her cheeks and lifted her off the ground, she wrapped her legs around his waist, and they continued, Presley now holding on to Trent's face. He more or less blindly walked them back to the couch, carefully placing Presley down first and lying beside her, their lips barely disconnecting. Trent massaged her hip bone before his hand started to venture up to her breasts, he rubbed her a few times over her bra, just as he had the night before and then made his first move for a little more.

He reached around between Presley and the couch cushion to try to make it to the clasp on her bra, he was struggling with having enough room between the two to be successful when he felt Presley turn further onto her side to expose her back. He took that as a very good sign and swiftly made her bra disappear. Trent could feel the goosebumps on Presley's ribs as he slowly made his way up to her now exposed breast.

There were no more chants for grandmas and outhouses because the second he made contact with her nipples that had hardened under his touch, he heard a soft mixture of a whimper and a giggle from Presley and felt himself at full attention. He made long and passionate circular kneading movements with his hands and felt Presley lose a little more control when she sucked on his tongue. It made him smile that she was already unwinding, and he felt like he hadn't even started yet, he paused contact with his hand momentarily so he could lift her shirt. Presley's lips slowed, so Trent followed, and they slowly opened their eyes together, neither said a word as Trent continued to remove her top.

Once her top was off Trent joined her and then he pressed their bare chests together before going back to the familiarity of just gently rubbing her chest. Presley bit her bottom lip and her cheeks transitioned to pink. Trent couldn't take it anymore, she was so fucking pure and perfect, he was 400 steps ahead in his mind but was determined to go back to take the scenic route with her. Trent slowly lowered his gaze to watch his hands as they worked, she was beautiful. He could've stared at her perfect chest all night, memorizing each freckle and committing the color of her nipples to memory, but he decided to lean in to kiss one of them.

The gentle peck transformed into a light suck and felt Presley's grasp around his head tighten in the sexiest kind of way. He moved to the second breast for the same sequence, when his tongue touched her nipple Trent felt a slight arch in her back, and he smiled. He gently pressed her shoulder, so she was lying more on her back than her side now and worked his free hand down to her waistline. He reached back up to kiss her lips and ran his fingers along the inside of her shorts, catching on her thong so he slipped his fingers under that band as well. He didn't go beyond either of the bands yet, just comfortably rubbing her from her hip bone to her navel. He could feel her breathing becoming slightly irregular each time his fingers got closer to her navel. Trent came out from under the thong band and just tugged gently on her shorts, he pulled one side down past her hip bone and reached his hand under her to hold her exposed cheek. He only squeezed it a couple of times before he came back around and suggested the shorts come down more.

"Pres," he separated their lips by less than an inch. "Pres, I want to give you something," he pecked her. "I promise, I'll keep my pants on," he kissed her neck this time. "But baby, I need yours off."

Presley looked him in the eyes when he came back up to meet hers, she rubbed the side of his face and simultaneously lifted her hips so he could keep sliding her shorts off of her. Once they were off Trent continued his game with the band of the thong, gently sliding his fingers from her navel to her hip bone. After the third pass, he rubbed his hand all the way down in between her legs.

Holy. Fucking. Shit. Trent thought. He could feel the moisture that had built up already, he hadn't even done half of what he wanted to her, and she was already so ready for him. He didn't play down there for long before he was tugging on the band of the thong for that to come off as well, Presley took a moment before she allowed it, but nevertheless she lifted her hips again. Trent went back to her breast for a millisecond before his hand found its way to her hip, he slid his other hand completely under her back and in one motion turned her to her side so her back was to his chest. He pulled her hips into him, and she felt the full result of how worked up he was. Trent was true to his word and kept his pants on, but it didn't stop him from readjusting himself so he could lay comfortably between her legs. He felt her immediately press back into him which made him tug her hip to be even closer.

He could feel himself pulsing just outside of her entrance, he started to realize he may very well make a mess of his pants even with them staying on. After he pulled her hips into him a few more times his hand reached in front of Presley and cupped her between her legs, she was even wetter now and his first motion towards her lips was faster than he intended. He heard her let out a slow exhale that could've passed as a mini moan, so he started to massage her, that elicited movement in her hips and it only made his fingers work faster. He kissed her neck and tried to keep his concentration on where his fingers were when she made the most noise. He thought he had it, so he spent a little extra time in one spot and felt her hips jerk slightly and then she was giggling and holding a hand to her face.

"Pres," Trent smiled. "Is this okay?"

"Uh huh." She arched her back and tried to reach his lips. Trent decided to get her turned back around so he could go back to the familiarity of kissing her. Their lips connected and Trent placed her leg over his hip before he went right back down between her legs, each time pressing a little harder to make his way a little further until he finally tried to put two of his fingers inside of her. Presley couldn't maintain their kissing rhythm because she was moaning and whimpering each time Trent went in, her hips had joined the sequence as well and he knew he had to stop if he was planning anything else for her before she lost it. He pulled his fingers back out of her and instead put her on her back again; this time, however, he opened her legs by crawling in between them.

Once he was on top of her, he held himself up with his palms on either side of her face and took her in, she was glowing, she was trying so hard to hide the smile he knew he put on her face. He helped her hide it when he bent down to connect their lips, as he did, he reached for one of her legs and put it around his hip. Trent gave her a few gentle thrusts while he was on top of her, he could feel her holding her breath as he pressed into her and then exhaling in pleasure when he created space. Trent slowed so he could make his way down her body with his lips. He started on her neck, spent a bit of time playing with her chest and massaged her hip bones as he did, and then he made small pecks in a straight line down to her navel. Presley felt Trent crawling his knees away from her and then his lips were well below her waistline.

Presley's eyes got big, and she partially lifted her shoulders off the couch and reached for the sides of his face. "Uhhm, just where exactly are you going, Mr. Trent Hayes?" She giggled.

Trent shot his gaze up to her but stayed put, hovering just above her very low and maintained bikini line. "What do you mean?" He smirked with devilish intent and drew circles on one of her hip bones with his fingertips.

She suggestively tickled the monkey fuzz on the back of his head with her nails, still maintaining her smile. "That's just a new and interesting place your lips are wandering." She managed.

Trent slid one of his hands from her hip bone and worked his way in until he had his thumb resting gently on her clitoris. "I'm just working on giving you that special little something I promised you." He answered.

Presley put her hand on his that was now moving around to sway her mind; she wasn't stopping him; she was just allowing her hand to gently rest on his. "If I'm being honest." She bit her bottom lip because he teased a touch between her lower set of lips. "I'm a little nervous about that detour of the special little something," she admitted.

Trent tried to mask any shock he felt, *there was no way she was actually nervous because no one had ever done this for her?! Who the hell had deprived this woman and themselves from this? In all the contemplation he'd been doing about what they would explore when Presley was good and ready, this was at the damn near top of his list.*

Trent came back up and laid on his side next to her. "Why are you nervous?" He reached down and held her hand.

Presley, of course, started to fidget, she looked up at the ceiling. "I just…," her rosy cheeks were getting a shade darker. "Like is that something you even want to do? You don't have to do that, that's not," she stumbled, "I didn't insist on us waiting until you…"

He cut her off before she continued rambling. "What?!" Trent tried not to make it seem like he was laughing at her, but he couldn't hold back laughter completely. "Pres, I promise you I absolutely, without a shadow of a fucking doubt, would love nothing more than to do this."

He choked out a laugh, his fingers slid along her lips and circled her clitoris again and then he whispered in her ear. "If you let me, I want to put my face in between your legs until your eyes are permanently stuck in the back of your head, baby."

Her giggle was immediately halted when she whimpered from him sticking his fingers in her again, they slid in so easily with the continued fountain he was creating with each and every touch. "Pres," he kissed her neck and then looked into her eyes. "I promise, I will stop the second you don't feel comfortable, or you don't like it."

She looked into his comforting eyes and knew she could take any leap with him; she trusted him with her entire heart. So, she connected their lips for a brief moment and when she pulled away, Presley gave Trent an approving nod.

Presley was immediately blasted into another galaxy the second Trent's mouth met her skin. He had slid his tongue from her opening to her clitorus and that was where he was currently performing a series of tongue exercises. She felt her entire body tingling as he worked, she struggled to make a sound at all because she kept sucking in breaths until he plunged his tongue into her. She felt the most harmonious call of pleasure coming from her mouth and her back arched.

Trent's mind went rabid when he heard her crying out his name and felt her body squirming in pleasure. He couldn't touch enough of her; his face was buried while one hand worked to keep Presley's shaking legs open and the other reached up to massage her breasts. She was grasping for his head, frustrated that his hair was so short she could barely grab any of it; so, she rubbed his ear and continued to allow the force of Trent's face to give her a slight bounce that she managed to match every once in a while.

She barely registered the noises Baron was making from the other side of the coffee table wondering if he needed to come save her when Trent sucked her clitoris while plunging into her with his fingers—that was it. She couldn't hold anything inside of her any longer; she felt her hips buck again while one of her legs tightened towards Trent's head. She felt her soul leave her body right out of the same area Trent was tending to. Her heart was pounding, and she felt paralyzed in a way that she could certainly live with.

Presley was still floating out of her body when she felt Trent lifting her on top of him. He was now laying on his back and he draped her right over his torso, making sure she had a leg on either side of his hips. He grabbed a small throw blanket from the arm of the couch over his head and put it over Presley, so she wasn't completely exposed. His hands immediately went under the blanket to hold her cheeks and he just rubbed them in a circular pattern, feeling satisfied for a job well-done.

Presley felt another peck to the top of her head when she finally attempted to use her voice again. "Baby, don't ever let me be nervous about you again."

Trent laughed and squeezed her, his hands started rubbing her back and he kissed the top of her head again. "Careful, babe, I'll fuckin hold you to that."

"I hope you do." She replied.

✦

After Trent had provided rounds two and three of his gift giving, Presley reluctantly admitted she was tapped out. They exchanged a semi-awkward conversation, moreso for Presley than Trent, about how much she would love for him to scrub his face and mouth before the lips on their faces met again. Trent agreed under a dramatic and playful protest, he also convinced himself it was a good thing because it gave him a quick little getaway to take care of himself to avoid a case of blue balls. He had allowed Presley to hold him and rub all over the front of his shorts in any way that seemed to please her, but he was insistent that, as promised, his shorts would stay on because he wanted nothing more than to just continue giving all night.

They decided the couch in the main house probably wasn't the best sleeping arrangement for the evening and the fact that neither had much sleep the night before, they should probably get to their own beds before the sun was coming up again. Trent walked Presley and Baron down to the cottage before he left, she wasn't upset that he provided a round four on the porch before she went in. She thought it was just going to be a very juicy, long kiss goodnight, but once Trent's hand found its way down her shorts again, she let him give her one last little something to put her to sleep that night.

✦

Presley had just barely closed the cottage door when her phone went off, she walked over to where she had left it on the kitchen island hours earlier and saw it was Trent.

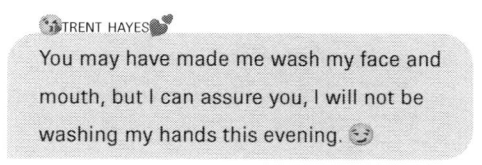

> **TRENT HAYES**
> You may have made me wash my face and mouth, but I can assure you, I will not be washing my hands this evening. 😉

Presley grabbed her forehead; she could feel him all over again.

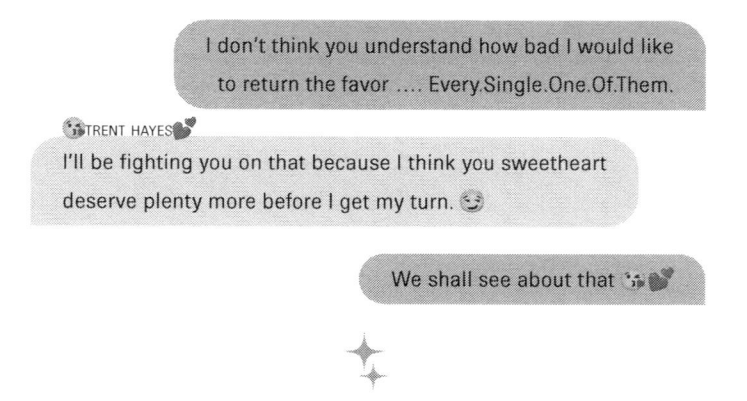

> I don't think you understand how bad I would like to return the favor …. Every.Single.One.Of.Them.

> **TRENT HAYES**
> I'll be fighting you on that because I think you sweetheart deserve plenty more before I get my turn. 😉

> We shall see about that 😉

✦

After a night of drinking, Mike's eyes finally opened, he had a vague recollection of seeing his mom when he got home from the bar but had woken up in his own bed. He looked at the clock and it was already the next day; he had slept until almost 2 o'clock the next morning. There was no clear memory of when he left the bar, the last thing he remembered was chatting with Presley. Not too long after they were gone without notice, and he had picked up another beer and joined Aaron with his new harem of women he had found on the bar's patio. Mike shot up as quickly as possible, given his state, to be sure he didn't drunkenly bring anyone home… He hadn't cleaned up enough to be sharing his space with anyone.

To his relief, he was definitely alone and had even managed to lock himself into his room. He grabbed his phone to see what he missed all day at Presley's and when he did, he noticed he had only just missed the last notification at the cottage. He opened the kitchen camera to find Presley with her phone in her hand smiling at it. He took a screenshot of her, she looked beautiful. She was clearly ready for bed, her pajamas were on, her hair loosely tied up on top of her head, and her face was projecting relaxation and happiness.

Mike continued to watch her and then decided to head to his basement, his mom was still fast asleep down the hall when he left his room. He was anxious to see the day's videos within the privacy of his sanctuary, even before he got himself showered. Once he was in his recliner, he checked the footage from throughout the day, the cottage really didn't have much activity. He thought that was odd, but he was glad to have seen Presley was currently at the cottage alone—no Trent in sight.

He worked his way backwards and pulled up the movement her porch camera had just recorded. He wasn't too pleased to see it was Trent's punk ass. He watched them as they were playfully pawing at each other. He was going to spare himself and shut it off until he watched Trent press Presley into the side of the cottage. It was a consenting move, and her leg came up to his hip the second her back hit the wall. He watched as Presley's hand dove down and presumably grabbed the front of Trent's pants. She was only there for a little because Trent moved his free hand to go right up her shorts. Presley's head fell back against the wall and Trent consumed her neck while he still had his hand in between her legs. Mike hit fast forward to be sure Trent's pants weren't coming down.

Once he watched Presley walk into the cottage, he backed the recording up to when she was first pressed against the wall, he zoomed in so Trent was mostly out of the frame and Presley's face took up most of the screen; Mike was really kicking himself now for not having any audio. He paused just to inspect the look on her face, her eyes were closed, and she had a sexy grin developing as she clung to Trent. Mike started to slide his pants down, followed by his boxers, he hit play and then reached for his lotion.

✦

Presley slept like an absolute log all night the second she hit the pillow.

Twenty-Nine

"I GUESS IF YOU HAVE TO WORK ON A SUNDAY, THIS ISN'T A BAD OFFICE view for the day, huh?" Trent approached the gazebo at the end of Presley's dock.

She smiled when she heard his voice, Baron perked up as well but didn't get up, he simply slapped his tail against the dock in anticipation of Trent's arrival. Trent was sure to pat Baron and give him a proper greeting before moving to Presley. She set her laptop on a side table and waited for him; he wasted no time in joining her on the sunbed.

"The view is much better now." She reached for him and put her arms around his neck.

"Did you get any sleep last night?" Trent asked after kissing her.

Presley kissed him back before replying. "Honestly, I don't think I've slept that good like ever in my whole entire life."

Trent smiled. "Good." He rubbed his hand up and down her side. "I couldn't stop thinking about you all night."

"We should've considered a sleepover." Presley kissed him again. "Because I was certainly dreaming about you all night."

"Would we have had to sleep at this sleepover?" Trent asked as his lips hovered over hers.

Presley giggled and Trent reached his hand behind her ear to hold her head while they kissed. They didn't seem to want to get back to talking so they followed each other's lead and continued to make out and caress each other. Trent got dangerously close to the bottom of the light cotton dress Presley had on, it crept up her leg each time he rubbed her side. She could feel that her dress was now hiked up exposing her panties, she continued to kiss Trent anyway. Their hands got more active on one another, Presley went under Trent's shirt and caressed Trent from his ripped stomach and up his chiseled chest. In one, smooth motion Trent put his hands on Presley's cheeks and pulled her on top of him. She had a leg on either side of Trent and pressed into him as he squeezed her cheeks; she could feel him getting more erect each time their bodies pressed together. Trent softly circled his hands on her exposed butt, he very much appreciated that she was wearing a skimpy, lace cheekster pair of panties. He pulled on the band to try to take them down before she whispered to him.

"Trent." She pulled her lips away for a millisecond before kissing him again. Trent's hands paused but his lips continued moving. Their kissing intensified so Trent attempted to take her panties down again. Presley allowed him to get them down past her cheeks in the back, but the front of them were still holding their position. Presley stopped kissing him this time and she lifted her face away from his, she looked into his eyes and rubbed his chin.

"Pres," he whispered and rubbed his thumbs on her cheeks. "Pres, is this okay?" He pulled on her panties again.

Presley lifted her pelvis and allowed Trent to take them off completely.

"I don't know about all this," she whispered into his neck after she had just sucked on it. "Today is your day, Trent Hayes, I think your pants need to be coming off." Her heart was pounding.

"I never agreed to that plan." He smiled and then turned so they were now laying on their sides facing each other. He pulled her leg on top of his hips and then maintained the comfortability of just rubbing against each other for the time being, in his head he wasn't sure when to make his next move seeing as he didn't have a condom on him. He wanted her, condom or not, but he knew it would make her more comfortable and that was his main priority. "Pres, c'mon, let's go back to the cottage." He kissed her down her neck and lightly squeezed her inner thigh.

"Why?" She whispered and let out a quick sigh when he rubbed his hand between her legs.

Trent ran his hand back down in between her legs because he liked her initial reaction. "Because," he continued to massage her. "I didn't know this is how our morning would go." He smiled shamefully at her. "I don't have a condom."

"Trent." She held his chin, not wanting him to stop, but knowing she couldn't be that irresponsible. "I don't have any at all either."

He wasn't surprised to hear that in the least bit.

"That's okay," he smirked. "You know I'll happily work around that." He began kissing her neck and started to head down to her chest while his hand stayed between her legs.

Presley giggled. "Trent." Her fingertips lightly scratched the back of his head as he continued to explore her body with his lips while his hands wandered below her waist. "Trent, baby, that's not fair." She giggled again.

It seemed like Trent was going to continue offering Presley all the pleasures before he tried to revisit the idea of them taking the next step.

Just as Trent had made it to her hip bone with his lips, they heard a car door shut in the distance, Trent lifted his head and looked towards the main house. "Shit." He rolled his eyes. "Officer Bando."

Presley's eyes went wide. "Trent." She smiled. "Where did you put my panties?"

They both scrambled to find them. Trent didn't mind Mike knowing what they were headed for, but he didn't want Presley to be embarrassed or uncomfortable if Mike came down there and saw her panties lying on the dock. If he was being honest, he didn't want Mike to see any of her undergarments at all. Mike was getting closer, and they still hadn't found where they went.

"Here." Trent pulled on her dress. "Make sure you've got this down at least." He helped her pull it back down to cover her up. Trent looked up again and noticed Mike was walking to the cottage, he hadn't noticed they were on the dock. "He's not coming this way yet." Trent pulled up a couple of the pillows to look under there as well.

Baron barked when he heard the faint sound of the doorbell to the cottage which gave their position away. Trent was standing near the sunbed and looked up towards the cottage when Baron barked. Mike immediately turned his head to the sound and was met with a wave from Trent. He didn't see Presley right away but then noticed her head as she was sitting on the sunbed. Mike headed towards them.

"Well, he's on his way now." Trent lightly scolded Baron while smiling at him. "Good job, loudmouth."

Presley wasn't paying much attention because she was still worried, they hadn't found her panties yet, "Trent." She looked on either side of the sunbed. "Where are they?" She was getting distraught. "I won't even have time to put them on now." She quickly whispered.

Just as Mike got to the dock Trent saw them balled up under the sunbed, he bent over and grabbed them smiling, there was no time to put them on because Mike would surely see so he shoved them into his pocket and then took a seat on the end of the sunbed with his knees up and feet flat to conceal the front of his pants until he could calm himself and relax from what had happened as a result of their little morning exploration.

"Officer Bando." Trent nodded his head once.

"Good morning, Pres." He ignored Trent. "Didn't expect you'd be sitting on the dock this early." His hands went directly to resting on his duty belt.

"Oh, Baron and I did an early walk today, I have lots of work to get done." Presley put her laptop back on her lap trying to be sure she was as covered as much as she possibly could be.

"Huh," he looked pointedly at Trent. "And you guys shoot soon." He turned back to Presley. "So, you'll have the peace and quiet you need here pretty soon."

Presley shrugged. "I don't need complete peace and quiet, I'm just looking through the quarterly reports right now."

"So, you helping her out with those then?" Mike addressed Trent with a sharp tone.

Trent shook his head. "Nah," he smiled. "Just offering a little break to help her get through the day." He rubbed her leg and smiled. Mike couldn't knock the images of Trent and Presley on the cottage porch hours earlier out of his mind. All he could see when looking at him was his playboy ass hands going up Presley's shorts.

Presley blushed at Trent's touch, and she opened her laptop.

"Day's just starting, hopefully you'll be able to get through and enjoy the evening, huh?" Mike adjusted his duty belt and started again. "I was going to see if you wanted to come by the house for dinner tonight? With mom and I, that is." Mike tried to entice her with the promise of his mother's company as well.

"Oh, I did see your mom at the market yesterday, she's always so sweet. It was really nice to see her." Presley genuinely replied, she didn't like the idea of blowing his mom off, so she informed him that she had just visited with her. He didn't seem to react much, so Presley fumbled around with her laptop and continued. "I'm not quite ready to commit to any plans tonight though, I'm not sure how long this'll take me today. But thank you."

"No worries, when I come back for lunch I'll go ahead and see where you're at." Mike looked at Trent.

Presley was distracted by the thought of Trent's hands in between her legs, she could almost feel them still caressing her, she couldn't help but smile and then she tugged on her dress to be sure it was covering her pantiless state.

"What can I bring you for lunch, Pres?" Mike noticed she was off in space.

"Oh," she snapped out of it. "It's okay, you really don't have to do that, I haven't even had breakfast yet, so I don't know when I'll be ready for lunch."

"It's okay, I'm happy to bring you whatever you feel like having." Mike pressed.

There was a short moment of silence as no one knew what to say. Presley stretched her legs out and ended up sliding them right under Trent's which were still bent, hiding the crotch of his pants just before she opened a couple documents on her laptop. Trent reached down to rest his hand on her legs and to ensure her dress stayed down to hide what she wanted to conceal.

"I better head out so I can come back and have lunch with you." Mike smiled at Presley.

Trent narrowed his eyes, but kept a protective hold on Presley's legs, knowing exactly what Mike was doing. He hated the thought that Presley was uncomfortable, but as far as Trent was concerned, he was confident in what was developing with her and he knew Mike was in way over his head.

"Okay," she replied, knowing all she wanted was for Mike to give her and Trent some privacy.

"I'll see you in a couple of hours." He reluctantly walked back up the dock to head out.

Trent waited for Mike to be out of earshot. "He has the *worst fucking* timing imaginable." He slid his hand under her dress and up her leg.

Presley allowed his hand to reach the top of her quad before she reached down and gently caught it, she smiled at him and rubbed the top of his strong hand as it made its way to her inner thigh.

"Well." Trent leaned back next to Presley after Mike was well on his way to his patrol car. "I guess we missed our window this morning, huh?"

Presley looked behind them and saw that two crew member cars were parked at the house already; her lips formed a frown so he reached for them. Trent slid his hand behind her head and grasped her hair while kissing her. Presley leaned into him and was soon placing her leg on top of him. "Okay," he mumbled. "Maybe we didn't miss our window, huh?" He smiled at her.

Presley giggled. "It's just not private enough now for all that." She whispered into his ear.

"You're right." He agreed and dug into his pocket. "Is it private enough for me to help you slip these back on though?"

Presley nodded her head, Trent slid his hand up her inner thigh before sitting up, he gently squeezed before he reached down to help her back into her panties. "Shit." He took a deep breath. "I'm glad we found those but taking them off was better than having to put 'em back on."

Presley turned red and she looked down smiling.

"Look at me, beautiful." Trent held her chin and tried to direct her eyes towards his. "I'm going to let you get back to work." He kissed her neck. "While I go take a cold fuckin shower." He kissed the other side of her neck.

She smiled back at him and bit her bottom lip. "Do you mind wet clothes?"

"What?" He furrowed his brows but smiled, he was intrigued.

"We can jump in the lake real quick before you hit the shower, it's still a bit cold, even at this time of year." She smirked in anticipation of his answer.

"I'll just strip down to my boxers if that's what we're doing." He smiled and quickly took his shirt off.

"Given the size of my panties and the fact that the crew is showing up, I think I'll keep my dress on." She laughed and stood up.

Trent had his shoes and shirt off as he reached for his socks next, followed by his pants. When he removed his jogger sweats, she could tell he wasn't anywhere close to being relaxed from earlier. Presley blushed while she tried not to stare and instead took a couple steps towards the edge of the dock.

She reached her hand back and interlaced her fingers with his to lead him to the edge. "So, we run the last couple steps and then jump, okay?" She glanced over at him.

"While holding hands?"

"Unless you don't want to?"

Trent squeezed her hand. "I was making sure because I don't want to let go."

Presley looked into his eyes for a brief moment and then reached up to give him a soft kiss, she opened her eyes smiling. "Ready?"

They counted to three before they took off towards the end of the dock and flew into the air, hand in hand, splashing together into the lake. Their hands were ripped apart after they hit the water but they both bobbed up and quickly found each other.

"Shit." Trent swam over to a wading Presley. "This water is cold." He got to her and put her legs around him and kept them afloat.

She pecked him before responding. "See, perfect segway because now your shower doesn't have to be cold."

He laughed. "Oh, it'll still need to be cold, that's for sure. Just a millisecond thinking about anything from the last twenty minutes with you and I'll need to throw ice down my pants."

Presley put her arms around Trent's neck to initiate a mini make out session. Trent didn't want to leave but he was losing focus and wasn't doing as well keeping them afloat as he was before. "A prime example of why I still need a cold shower." He smiled.

"We can stop." Presley pulled away, smirking.

Trent followed her to the ladder of the dock, she hung on to it and waited for him to get to her.

"You stayin' in?" He grabbed the ladder.

"No." She playfully shook her head smiling.

"Well, c'mon." He motioned for her to get out first. "Ladies first."

"You first," she quickly suggested. Presley knew her dress would cling to her, and she'd be climbing the ladder with her butt at eye level, she was far too embarrassed for that.

"Alright." He shrugged and climbed up the ladder. "You can check me out this time, next time it's my turn to watch you climb the ladder first though."

Presley laughed while taking full advantage of the view she had. Trent got onto the dock and then turned around and held his hand out to help her up. He scooped her right into his arms and hugged her, he gave her an innocent peck on her head before they walked back to Trent's clothes.

Trent watched out of the corner of his eye as Presley pulled on her sundress and did her best to ring it out to keep it from clinging to her body and showing every curve. He also noticed they didn't have any more towels down at the dock.

"Here, babe." Trent held his shirt out to her. "You can put this on over your dress if you don't want to walk up to the cottage like that."

"Thank you." She graciously took the shirt and slipped it on and then dropped her dress from underneath the cover shirt.

Trent loved the look of Presley in his shirt, it was just long enough on her to cover her, but if she reached her arms up, he would get quite the show. He tried to kick that thought out of his mind for right now because he had to walk up the lawn and report to the set soon. He pulled his joggers on but carried his shoes. "I'll walk you up to the cottage, sweetheart." He winked as he offered his hand to her.

Presley warmly accepted it, and they walked down the dock with smiles on their faces.

"You know." Trent was holding her once they reached the cottage porch. He whispered near her ear, "I can't leave that job undone." He kissed her ear and then pecked her neck a couple of times.

His lips teasing her elicited a giggle. Trent's hand slid down the front of her and then made its way to cupping her cheek that was mostly exposed due to her cheekster style panties.

"We'll have to carve out some private time then." She whispered back and allowed her hands to glide down his back and to his cheeks, matching where his hands still held firmly on her. "You're not the only one wanting to finish a job."

Trent exhaled a laugh. "Holy shit, I wish I had long enough to show you right now." His hands moved to the back of her head as he gripped her wet hair. "You deserve all the time and attention in the world though." He looked into her eyes and lightly pecked her lips before continuing. "So, I'm gonna wait and do this right."

Presley looked back into Trent's blue eyes; she enjoyed the back of his fingers stroking her face. She took the moment for all it was before she responded. "I appreciate you, Trent Hayes."

Trent's hands came up and held the sides of her face, he kissed her lips and softly sucked her bottom lip before backing up. "I appreciate *you*, Presley Williams. And you can expect I'll be showing you sooner than later just how deep that appreciation runs."

Mike was seething at the sight unfolding on Presley's porch. He had barely just hit the highway from Presley's, and they were both soaked, Trent was half dressed, and Presley was only wearing the shirt he remembered Trent being in. He had had enough of watching them play kissy face; when he watched Trent's hands disappear under the back of the shirt Presley had on he reached for his phone and dialed her number. At the very least the sound of her ringing phone would pull them apart. The phone rang multiple times and there was no movement, he realized she may not even have her phone on her. He decided to cut the feed and check in when he had a bathroom notification instead.

✦

"Wasn't that just the most adorable thing I've ever seen?" Michelle called out when a shirtless and shoeless Trent walked into the main house.

He immediately smiled and looked down at the ground until she was done smacking her lips and clapping.

"What?" He shrugged.

"What?!" She laughed. "That's it?! You're sure laying it on thick with this one, it's like I don't even know who you are these days." She maintained her accusatory smile.

"I've been telling you." He tried with all his might to suppress his smile. "She's different, Shell."

"Lookin' that way, got her all wet and left her to take care of that on her own," she teased. "*That's* definitely a new one for you."

Trent just rolled his head back trying not to laugh at Michelle's joke. He headed for the bathroom to get cleaned up.

"Better use cold water, Hayes!" Michelle shouted as Trent walked into the bathroom.

✦

Presley walked into the cottage with a smile on her face, the thought of Trent's hands gliding around her body and the feeling of his lips touching her skin sent butterflies throughout every inch of her. Mike's timing was less than ideal, which was the only reason she wasn't completely in love with the nearly perfect morning she'd had with Trent. She waltzed up the stairs and headed for the shower. She was just getting ready to get in when she heard a ping coming from her phone, she walked over to see who it was—Trent, she smiled and opened his text.

> 🍪TRENT HAYES🍪
> Can I cook you dinner tonight babe?

> Oh you're a chef too huh? I'd love to be your taste tester 😋 😋

> 🍪TRENT HAYES🍪
> I figured it's only fair I cook you a meal tonight since you provided such a delicious spread last night.

> OMG!! 🙈🙈 TRENT HAYES!!!!!!!!!!!!!

Presley couldn't stop laughing, her face was completely flush with color.

> 🍪TRENT HAYES🍪
> 😌😈😌

> What can I pick up so you can dazzle me with this home cooked dinner of yours?

> 🍪TRENT HAYES🍪
> Nothing sweetheart I got it—see you around 7?

> I can't wait 😋 😋 have a good day handsome.

> 🍪TRENT HAYES🍪
> You too gorgeous 😌

Thirty

Presley headed into town while Trent was at work that day. She wanted to grab a coffee and enjoy some time with Baron for a bit before going home to finish work and do some deep cleaning at the cottage. She was walking out of the coffee shop and noticed Mike crossing the street, headed her way. Presley unclipped Baron from the bike rack right outside the door that he was waiting at and pretended she hadn't seen Mike yet. It was one thing to have Trent with her when Mike was around, but her last two solo interactions with Mike were anything but comfortable. He had crossed multiple lines when he groped her on the porch of her cottage and his latest trap and lecture routine at the bar was still sending alarms in her mind.

"Hey, Pres!" Mike called out.

Presley turned around after she had Baron unclipped. "Oh, hi Mike, are you on your lunch break?"

"I can be, do you want to grab a bite?"

"No, I'm not all that hungry right now, just grabbing coffee and taking him for a quick walk." She gestured towards Baron who wasn't the least bit interested in greeting Mike. "Just needed a little work break."

"How's work going lately? I haven't noticed you back at the mill…"

"Yeah." Presley had avoided it as much as possible since the fire, she wasn't ready to look at it yet. "It just doesn't make my heart feel very good to be looking at that right now," she admitted.

"I know." He reached for her shoulder and Baron stood up. "I'm sorry, Pres." Mike took his cue and didn't rub her shoulder for long. "I don't mean to throw salt in the wound, but I do have a few things about the investigation if you have a minute."

"If we can walk and talk, that'll work, I do need to be getting back to finish some things up today." She didn't want him to think she had any availability in her schedule to be anywhere with him besides the public street they were already on. She could have dropped to her knees and hugged Baron for his move to her left side, creating a physical barrier between her and Mike.

"Sure thing." Mike matched her strides and walked down Main Street with her. "So, I did officially clear Trent from the suspect list today."

"Mike," Presley gave him a soft warning. "Really? Just today? I promise you, Trent is not the horrible monster you think he is."

"Pres, we have to be very thorough with these things," he defended himself. "Not to mention, I told you I wanted to keep you safe, I needed to be sure."

"Well, I appreciate you officially clearing him, but honestly, Trent didn't need to be on that list in the first place." Presley took a drink of her coffee.

Mike closely watched her lips around the straw of her iced drink, and it sent a wave of desire down his spine because she gave the straw a tiny bite before removing her lips completely.

They walked a couple of steps before Mike started again. "Pres, why didn't you tell me you're having legal trouble at work?"

"What?" She looked at him.

"I found out Jake's firm has been defending you and the company against Dana Jenkins." Mike didn't remove his stare, he wanted to know Presley's reaction when she heard the name.

"Mike," Presley shook her head. "For as much as I'd love to be able to rid myself of her and the problems she's been creating for me, I truly don't think she's a suspect." She quickly added, "and I don't love having to admit that."

"Well, first off, you know you can ask me for help whenever you need it, Pres. If she's been a problem, you could've come to me."

Presley shrugged. "It's not the kind of problem you can just arrest her for, but I do appreciate that."

"If and when she does cross that line, you know who to call." Mike smiled at her.

Presley nodded her head as she was looking down at the sidewalk.

So," Mike was uncertain about his next question. "Have you spoken to her?"

Presley shook her head. They took a few steps down the street before she said anything. "I will only virtually attend any meeting she's at because I don't actually want to see her." Presley took a few more steps. "And Jake is obviously the best. He doesn't make me talk to her; he always takes care of addressing her specifically whenever I *am* subjected to her."

"So, why don't you think her burning down Pap's shop is a possibility?"

Presley took a deep breath. "Honestly?" She looked at him. "She likely doesn't grasp the concept of love or family or any kind of human emotion or bond. So, I don't think she'd be the type to understand how burning that down would literally shatter me to my core. She wants money and power, not to specifically hurt my feelings—that would just be a bonus for her, I'm sure. She would have threatened to take something like that from me to get what she wants, not just randomly do it and get nothing in return. Whoever did it was either a messed up little kid who got in way over their head while dicking around and trespassing, or it's the worst kind of human that literally wanted to just rip my heart out and stomp all over it. There's no middle ground, in my opinion." Presley shook her head. "Whoever it was, I could never forgive them for what they destroyed."

Mike was initially concerned about her last statement, but then he thought about how grateful Presley would be towards him when she found out he had removed many of the pictures that had been hanging in the shop before he set the fire.

"Pres, I'm sorry about what happened. I'm doing everything I can and chasing every possible lead with the Fire Marshall." He looked down at her. "I will let you know I did officially clear Dana Jenkins today as well though."

"Did you talk to her?" Presley wondered why Mike would even ask if she was already cleared.

"I did." Mike left it at that and didn't let her know for how long he'd been talking to her, or what all they'd talked about.

Presley looked up and saw they were less than half a block from her car. "You know, I actually need to get going, Mike." She pointed towards her G Wagon. "And my car is just up there. I appreciate you updating me on the investigation."

"No problem, Pres. I do still have a bit more to share with you." He didn't disclose that it wasn't about the investigation.

"Can we revisit that later?" Presley asked.

"Sure thing, I'll be in touch." He nodded.

"Thank you." She unlocked her car.

"Hey, Pres, you wanna do dinner tonight?"

Presley had the door open for Baron to hop in, she closed it just before replying. "Oh, thank you, I can't tonight though." She waved. "See you later, Mike." Presley quickly walked around to the driver's side to get in before he could say anything else.

Thirty-One

"Do you have any idea how much I love Pad Thai?" Presley bumped into Trent while they were cutting vegetables.

Trent smiled and snuck a kiss to the side of her head. "Yep, I sure do, and I was happy to know it's something I'm pretty great at cooking."

"Lisa?" Presley laughed.

"Jake," Trent confirmed.

Presley shook her head smiling and continued to slice bell peppers. "So, you can act, sing, dance, *and* cook? Are there any limits to what you're capable of, Trent Hayes?"

"You forgot to mention my professional dart skills." He shrugged. "But basically everything I try out I'm immediately a professional at."

She rolled her eyes, smiling and then noticed Trent drawing her kitchen blinds that looked down to the lake. "Is the view too nice to look at?" She laughed.

"No." He held her around her waist and kissed her neck. "But what if I wanna kiss you and someone is standing out there spying?" He moved to another window to close the covering.

Presley laughed. "There's no one out there, Baron would notice if there was."

"Just covering all my bases." He winked at her and then walked over to turn some music on as well.

Presley appreciated his efforts and thanked him with a small peck before getting back to her chopping duties.

Bunch of fuckin bullshit, Mike had thought when he watched Trent walk into the cottage that night with a bag of groceries like he lived there or something. The way Presley's eyes lit up for him was getting real old, and he was getting tired of her declining dinner with him to spend time with Trent. And fuck Trent for thinking closing the shades would keep his eyes off Presley; he'd continue watching and listening from his own cameras on the inside.

"Okay, well, you're an amazing cook." Presley leaned over and kissed Trent after polishing off her last bite.

Trent put his chopsticks down and held her face while he intensified the kiss.

As their exchange slowed, he peeled back and spoke softly. "I hope you left room for dessert." He smiled. "I thought we could take Baron for a walk and bring dessert on the go."

Presley couldn't help but connect their lips again. "That sounds perfectly delicious." She slid her hand across the top of his leg. Trent exhaled his fondness of her touch and gave her a final kiss before getting up to prepare them for the short walk down to the dock.

Mike watched, as he had been for the last hour, all the touching, flirting, and kissing; he was furious and needed to find an excuse to go over there to break up their evening before it turned into something else. He figured he'd re-assess when they came back from their al fresco dessert, he'd be able to check the mood then. Based on what he watched on the porch the night before he knew Trent was going to be getting all of what he wanted from Presley very soon and Mike couldn't stomach that.

Presley's brows furrowed when they left her porch and walked towards the lake, her dock looked different. There were candles stretching along the dock and it looked like sheer curtains hanging around her gazebo. She looked at Trent who reached for her hand with a smile on his face.

"Trent," she almost whispered.

"I had a little help to set up our dessert venue, I hope it's okay?"

"It's beautiful."

They continued walking, she watched as they passed all the candles lined on either side of her dock and went into the gazebo. It looked like a mattress topper had been set over her sunbed, it was neatly made with white sheets, pillows and a cream-colored light cotton blanket folded and laid across the bottom of the bed. The sheer curtains were on three sides of the gazebo leaving the view to the lake open and there were lanterns with candles in them scattered around the bed. Again, she looked at Trent.

"I told you," he held her face. "I wasn't going to leave that job unfinished."

Presley let Trent take her dessert and set it on a small table near them, they soon had their arms around each other and their tongues dancing in sync with one another. After making out for a few moments Trent stepped his foot in between Presley's legs to walk her backwards and towards the bed, she let him lead them until she felt the bed touch her calf. Trent leaned her back and laid her down gently, she scooted herself up towards the pillows with their lips still connected. Trent laid on his side while Presley was on her back, he wasted no time in caressing her inner thigh. He was grateful she was in a dress again, just like the morning.

His hand massaged her inner thigh and beyond before he slid his thumb under the elastic band of her panties. Presley turned to face Trent, she rubbed his face gently and looked into his eyes. They looked at each other for a moment under the glow of the candles around them,

Presley was the first to lean back in to kiss him. Trent's hand rubbed down her back and cupped her cheek, squeezing it gently several times before he went back for the band. He slowly slid her panties down from the back, Presley assisted him in getting her out of them. Once they were off Presley rubbed her hands up Trent's shirt to get it off of him, he followed her lead and took his shirt off and then pulled their bodies together. Presley's leg found itself on top of Trent's hip as they continued to kiss each other.

Without her panties on, Trent reached back down to massage her, Presley let out a quick exhale when his hand landed on a pleasurable spot. He noticed her demeanor and it excited him, so he continued going back to that spot. Presley bit her bottom lip as she filled with pleasure at every touch, his massaging motion made her want all of him, her hand tugged lightly on the waistband of his pants, Trent didn't make her ask again he pulled his own pants down immediately to be even closer to her. Their pelvises pressed against each other a couple of times before they mutually decided it wasn't enough. Trent grabbed the bottom of Presley's dress and pulled it up, she disconnected their lips to get the dress up over her head. She wanted their chests touching so she reached for the clasp on her bra, Trent stopped her and smiled. "Can I?"

Presley smirked and put her hands around his neck while he reached behind her to take her bra off. They found themselves very nearly naked, Trent's boxers were their only barrier.

"Come here," Trent whispered and pulled Presley on top of him. He took control of her hips, pulling her into him as they continued to kiss. Presley could feel Trent through his boxer briefs, she truly hoped he was more prepared this time than the morning because she was ready for all of him. Trent felt the same about not wanting to stop. He couldn't take the teasing anymore, so he put an arm around her to lay his hand flat on her back and he effortlessly switched Presley places, Trent was now on top of her. He wasted no time in leaning down to continue kissing her while he simultaneously scooped one of her legs around his hip. Presley's hands found Trent's cheeks and squeezed as he thrust towards her.

They found a rhythm between their bodies that had both of their hearts thundering. Presley's hands firmly scanned Trent's back and then landed on his head where she massaged his scalp, gently scratching her fingers through his hair. She lost slight focus as they continued with their synchronized thrusting. After massaging her fingers through his hair a couple of times, she put her hands on the waistband of his boxers and then paused, she wasn't sure if she should take them down quite yet. Trent noticed her hesitation, so he stopped kissing her. He opened his eyes to look into hers, a sly smile formed on his face, he pecked her forehead, and then leaned across the bed for his pants; he came back with protection.

"I came prepared this time." He smirked.

Presley lifted up towards his ear to whisper, "good." She softly pecked his ear. "Because I don't want you to stop, Trent Hayes."

Trent felt a deep booming in his chest, he didn't hesitate on rolling to his side to slide his boxers down. Presley barely let him get them all the way down before she put her arms around his neck and closed the gap between their bodies. She knew they couldn't forgo the condom completely, but she very much wanted a quick moment with nothing between them and Trent didn't deny her of that desire.

Trent welcomed her body against his, he glided his hands down her back and landed on her backside, fully indulging in her cheeks. Presley could feel Trent and his frighteningly large erection as it was folded up and nearly spanning the length of her belly, not exactly where she wanted him to be. As their mouths were dancing along with each other she pushed herself on his shoulders to be just a bit higher, so their pelvises were a little more in line with one another. Her hand delicately slid its way down his side, triggering goosebumps as she worked along his ribcage and beyond. Once she got to his waist, she separated their hips just enough to get her hand around his pulsing erection. She had felt him through his shorts before and had a rough idea of his larger size, but trying to wrap her hand around him and lightly stroke the appendage was a mix of emotions regarding how it was going to fit.

Trent wasn't shy in showing her how much he liked her hands on him, so Presley continued to tease him with her hands. After that maneuver she held onto him again and angled him a bit lower to capture him in between her legs. Trent grabbed her cheeks again with slightly more intensity this time and Presley did everything she could to keep her top leg from completely opening up to him. As they were currently, he wasn't aiming to be inside of her yet, she was able to just slide along the top of him back and forth, allowing the skin to skin contact she wanted before they had to be more responsible.

Trent exhaled a muffled laugh into her hair. "Pres, baby," he sucked her collarbone. "You like playing some dangerous games."

She slowed the motion of her hips so this time when she slid from the tip of him to the base, he felt every millimeter.

He squeezed her. "You're fucking lucky I love it," he whispered in his ear.

"Well," she whispered back into his ear and then sucked on his earlobe. "You didn't let me do any of the work yesterday." She rode down him slow and steady again, feeling herself slide even easier each time. "So, I'm playing catch up." She nearly lost her rhythm because he felt so good gliding between her lips.

Trent must have felt the same because in one motion he had her on her back and he was on his knees in between her legs with the condom in his hand. Presley noticed he was working as fast as he could with the package, but she had time to reach down and cradle his balls while she patiently waited. It may have created a bit of a distraction for him and ultimately a delay in what was coming, but one she was so thankful she got to witness when she saw the pleasure he took in her hands working on him for a change. Once Trent had finished, he leaned down for their chests to meet, he stroked Presley's hair before he thrust forward into her. Just as he was making his way into her, Trent put his lips on hers. "Oh, Pres," he moaned as her wetness welcomed him, he used a little more pressure to continue as he felt how tight her entrance was.

Presley softly held his hips and exhaled into his shoulder but kissed his neck as he continued.

"Pres," he tried to be gentle and decided to pull out slowly. "Are you okay?"

She delicately squeezed one of his hips and her other hand came up to scan his strong chest. She slowly looked for his eyes and when they met, she nodded her head and whispered. "Gentle."

"Of course, babe," he promised her. It would take more concentration on his part, but he wanted it to be perfect for both of them.

Trent couldn't help but pick up speed after a few thrusts, he checked Presley's expression and her eyes were closed as she was arching her back, he felt himself sliding perfectly inside of her now, so he put their chests together again and kissed her. It was like she was waiting all her life for that kiss at that moment, she wrapped her legs around Trent and tried to match his pace. Her arms found themselves around his neck and their lips only separated to exhale expressions of pleasure and each other's names. Presley knew Trent was close when his pace ran away from hers, she didn't care, he felt like nothing she'd ever experienced, and she wanted him to finish in her. Trent did exactly that, he held Presley until he had nothing left; he planted his lips on hers as he slowly pulled out of her.

Presley's body was in a state of euphoria. Trent quickly tossed the condom in a bag set out next to the sunbed and immediately pulled Presley in; he placed her leg on top of one of his and held her against him before he kissed the top of her head. Presley laid snuggly under Trent's arm with her hand resting on his strong chest, he could smell the sweet floral scent of her hair, and he started to gently caress her back. Presley moved her leg up a little higher and across Trent's exposed lap, he caught the bottom of her thigh to keep her close and she could feel his heartbeat trying to slow down from loving on each other. They enjoyed this slow moment together listening to the endless crickets and frogs around them who were crooning to the moonlight. Presley felt Trent kiss her head, so she began to rub his chest just before he took a deep breath.

"Baby, I didn't know if anything could top how sweet you taste but fuck if I don't know which one I enjoy more now."

The comment made her smile, she was definitely still juggling all of the options Trent was capable of—part of her regretting the fact that she held back like she had. Her reservations were completely unnecessary, on every level with Trent, he had been a man of his word. She couldn't think of a single thing that she didn't absolutely swoon over about Trent; he had been the literal definition of perfection since the second she met him. The only thing she'd found to taint that picture she painted was his reputation before he had met Presley, and besides weighing on her mind, Trent's actions with her had never made her feel like that was going to be her experience with him.

He felt the smile on her face as she was lying on his chest. "Do you still want your dessert, sweetheart?"

"Oh," Presley lifted her head and looked at him. "That wasn't dessert?"

Trent laughed and squeezed her before he got up. "You get two desserts tonight I guess."

Presley covered up with the blanket and smiled at Trent's confidence as he walked naked to grab their sweet treat off the table. "You sure have a nice ass, Trent Hayes." She smirked at him just before he turned around to continue the show, she bit her lip and pumped her eyebrows at the front view.

He reached her plate out to her as he came back to the bed. After she took it, he leaned down and kissed her forehead. "You sure have a nice *everything*, Presley Williams."

It made her blush.

They ate the multi-layer dessert bar Trent had made with the light cotton blanket over them and the moonlit lake in front of them.

Thirty-Two

MIKE WAS PACING IN HIS KITCHEN WONDERING WHY THEY WERE taking so long on their walk. It was pitch black out by this hour, there was no way they needed to walk for this long. He began to think about the possibility that they made a detour he wouldn't like when the porch camera alerted their return. He watched them walk back into the cottage holding hands and nothing but smiles on their faces. Baron grabbed one of his toys and brought it straight to Trent when he was setting down the empty dessert plates on the kitchen island. It didn't look like he wanted to play, it was more like an offering. *Even Baron is under this fuckboy's spell.* He was glad he had already gotten dressed, he needed to get over there sooner than later.

"I'll help you clean the kitchen." Trent offered when he saw Presley bringing the dishes to the sink.

Presley disagreed with a shake of her head. "You cooked, I can clean." She smiled.

"If we do it together it'll go quicker though." He hugged her from behind. "Then we can watch a movie or something." He kissed her neck.

Presley giggled and turned around to kiss him.

"Trent Hayes." Presley scooped her arms up around his neck. "You are the Master of the Universe when it comes to date nights."

"Just wait until I unlock even more tidbits about you." Trent pecked her a couple of times. "And have more time on my hands."

"While I'm looking forward to all of that, I'm more than happy lingering on how unbelievably perfect tonight's date has been." Presley initiated more than pecks and Trent was happy to continue along with her and leave the few dishes they were going to do for the moment.

✦

"Should we watch one of *your* movies?" Presley taunted as they both took a spot on the couch once the kitchen was cleaned up.

Trent laughed. "Just can't get enough of me, can you?" He rubbed his hands up and down his chest.

"Oh geez." She rolled her eyes and started flicking through the options. Trent pulled her in between his legs, and she relaxed into his chest like he was a backrest. He began to brush his hands through her hair as she contemplated something to watch. She felt so connected to Trent at that moment, he was everything a man should be and more. She was also still in shock at the fact that he was able to make that entire night so special despite the fact that he had been working all day. He strung together the perfect dinner and an overly romantic lakeside set-up for them to finish what they had started that morning. Time with him made her forget about everything reality had waiting for her, and she wanted to indulge in every last bit of that feeling. Her body was tingling in places as she thought about Trent's touch, she didn't notice that she was so far off into space until Trent reached for the remote.

"Maybe I should pick something." He smiled.

Presley let him have the remote and then looked up at him, returning his smile. She reached up and held his chin, her head lifted off his chest far enough to connect their lips. Soon, Presley was twisting her body in order to better connect with his lips. They found themselves in a steamy make out session that was working towards round two of their love affair for the evening. Their lips and bodies slowed when they heard the doorbell.

"I'll get the door." Trent smirked and lifted himself off of her. "But I'm coming right back, so don't go anywhere." He winked.

"Don't you worry about that." She gently pulled him closer to her by his shirt. "I need you to hurry back though." She kissed his lips.

Trent exhaled heavily and leaned back down to kiss her, he was pulling her leg over his hip when they heard the doorbell again, they smiled at each other and Presley watched him go to the door as she sat up on the couch straining to hear who was there.

"Officer Bando," Trent flatly greeted him. "To what do we owe the pleasure?"

"Huh," Mike huffed. "Figured you'd be back at the motel by now, haven't you been on the set long enough already today?"

Trent laughed. "As you know, this isn't the set. I can certainly point you in the right direction though if that's what you were looking for?"

"Looks to me like the set has been expanding." Mike gestured towards the dock, having no idea what had just happened there. "The crew gonna clean that up, or does Presley have to share her house and provide janitorial duties now for whatever this movie's got going on that's now out of scope of the original agreement?"

The playboy version of Trent would have loved nothing more than to provide Mike with a very detailed play-by-play of every touch, sensation, and sound from Presley's body just an hour earlier on that dock. But out of his genuine feelings for her that were developing, he set aside his hatred of Mike in favor of preserving the privacy of his relationship with Presley.

Trent looked down at the dock. "I don't have a problem cleaning that up for her." He put his hands on his hips. "Anything else?"

Before he could answer, Baron came up behind Trent and a low growl developed before he headed back to the living room only to walk right into Presley who came out to see what was holding Trent up. She wasn't excited to see Mike standing just beyond the doorway.

"Hey, Pres." Mike smiled as he walked through the door, to Trent's disapproval, towards her.

Baron was sure to maintain his stance warning Mike not to get too close to her. Presley looked down at her dog who was visibly uncomfortable by Mike's approach, so she crouched down behind him to rub his chest. "Hi Mike." She offered just before kissing the top of Baron's mammoth head.

"Didn't realize you'd have company. I brought over wine and some dessert, figured you'd like something to unwind from a long, hard day of work." He smiled. "And I know we didn't get to finish our conversation from this afternoon."

"Oh." Presley looked at Trent quickly and then back to Mike. "Yeah, I was really hoping we didn't have to finish the conversation about the mill until there was more information from the investigation." She stood up after another firm pat to Baron's chest. "And thank you, but we just had dessert." She blushed thinking about both courses of dessert Trent provided.

"Yeah." Trent shut the door. "We do have some leftover pad thai though if you're hungry, Officer Bando?" Trent offered him a smug look. "My special recipe."

"I ate, thanks," he sharply returned. "Not dessert though." Mike looked at Presley. "I know you've always got room for dessert, Pres." Mike tried again for her attention.

"Oh." A giddy smile formed across her face. "I was considering more, but I think I'll wait a bit." She blushed towards Trent.

Trent immediately returned her expression knowing full well the type of dessert she was referring to that he would happily provide infinite helpings of the second Mike left.

"So," Trent cleared his throat. "Were you just dropping off, or…?"

"Actually, I was planning to enjoy the wine and cookies I brought with Presley. So, I don't mind just hanging out for a bit." Mike countered.

Presley looked visibly uncomfortable now, a quick change from the eye flirting she had just been projecting Trent's way.

"Well," Trent walked to Presley's side and held her around her shoulders. "We were just going to settle in for a movie, maybe you can work on those treats you brought while we watch a movie, huh?" Trent didn't wait for any kind of response; he walked Presley and Baron back into the living room so they could get settled back onto the couch.

Mike had no other choice but to follow them. He watched as Trent pulled Presley into him and then patted the couch for Baron to come curl up next to them. His feet were propped on the ottoman before looking back over to Mike. "You can take the other sofa over there if you're staying for the movie." Trent offered before pecking the side of Presley's head. *Yeah, go ahead and settle in, you schmuck,* Trent thought, *you seem to enjoy making others uncomfortable. You're about to find out what the definition of uncomfortable is, you fucking prick.*

Mike reluctantly made his way over to the shorter of the two sofas, it didn't have its own ottoman, so he slipped his shoes off to rest his head on one end and his feet up on the arm of the other end to face the television instead of having to continue watching Trent paw all over Presley.

Just as Trent hit play, he spoke to Presley. "You comfortable, babe?"

Mike rolled his eyes and decided he was more than okay not understanding her mumbled reply. He was even less thrilled when he watched the opening credits… *He's playing one of his fucking movies?! Of course it's his goddamn half naked Viking warrior film.*

"I know you wanted to watch one of my movies." He teased Presley and then turned to whisper in her ear, low enough to where Mike wouldn't be able to hear. "Hopefully this one makes Officer Dipshit take a hike." Trent slid his hand up Presley's inner thigh and only stopped when he couldn't go any further. "Because I'm ready to dish out another round of dessert and it's not fucking wine and cookies."

Presley reached back and grabbed a blanket that was draped over the cushion she was leaning on, she flung it out so it covered both she and Trent's laps and then reached her hand to rub the front of his sweats while whispering in his ear. "Let's see how good of an actor you are." She gently rubbed him. "You're gonna have to keep your composure." She slid down and stroked him a couple of times before she laid her hand flat on his belly to go under his waistband.

Trent caught her hand and crossed his legs, smiling at her. "I'm good, but not that damn good, sweetheart." He whispered his reply smiling as he set her hand on his quad and then reached his arm around her shoulder before he kissed the top of her head.

Presley giggled and reluctantly left her hand simply resting on his leg, waiting for them to be alone.

"Officer Bando, have you seen this one?" Trent asked as he was rubbing Presley's shoulder.

Fucking dick, Mike seethed, of course he'd seen it. The entire world had seen this one, but he didn't want to outright have to admit he had watched Trent's godlike physique for two straight hours and actually enjoyed the film before meeting the guy.

"I have," Mike replied. "But my personal favorite has always been MRR Elite." He shrugged. If Trent wanted to play this game, Mike would play, he picked the only movie on Trent's resume where he died.

Trent smiled, *touché Officer Bando.* "That's probably my least known film, thank you for being a fan, Officer Bando."

Smug ass mother fucker. Mike didn't say another word, he had to simply be satisfied with the fact that he'd at least stopped them from progressing their intimacy that night.

✦

The movie ended and Trent looked around to see Mike sleeping; he knew Presley had fallen asleep far before that. He kissed her head and tried to reach for the remote. He was almost shocked that Mike had the balls to not only come over that late at night, but to feel comfortable enough to stay like he had. Trent was literally under both Presley and Baron on the couch. Presley's legs were intertwined with his and she was comfortably clinging on to him in her sleep—yet Mike stayed. Trent laughed at the thought that Mike was trying to be some kind of chaperone, he was too late, and the bond Trent and Presley were forming wasn't something Mike could just shove his way in between. Trent didn't mind staying where he was, he flicked through to find something else to watch. Once the movie started, he slightly repositioned himself and reached down to put his hand under Presley's shirt and hold the soft skin on her back. It didn't take long for Trent to drift off to sleep.

✦

Presley's eyes started to open; her legs were asleep from Baron's top half laying on them. She wasn't sad to see she was still tucked snuggly under Trent's arm; she could feel his hold on her and she loved it. She looked up at him, sound asleep and looking perfect. Presley lightly ran her fingers down Trent's chest and then ruffled the top of Baron's head when she felt him lying around Trent's waist. It made her smile that the three of them so comfortably fell asleep, it gave her desire for him another surge, so she rubbed Trent's chest again. She stopped and her eyes widened when she heard a faint and unfamiliar snore.

At that moment she remembered Mike had come over. She wanted him to go home, while Trent's hold made her feel safe, she just felt uncomfortable with Mike around. She thought about pretending to sneeze just to wake everyone up, she considered whispering to Baron to get him to bark, but she settled on quietly waking Trent up. Presley reached up for his ear and gently kissed it, it was so soft that he didn't react at all. Presley pushed her hand under Baron and found her way to Trent's inner thigh before she reached up to Trent again; this time she started on his neck and worked her way up to his ear while gently squeezing his leg. Trent didn't let her work alone for long, he squeezed her to let her know he was awake too, his head turned towards her, and they locked lips. They kissed quietly for a moment before Presley pulled her lips away and moved towards his ear again. "Trent, do you want to go to bed with me?"

Trent smiled at her and then turned her head so he could whisper back into her ear. "You know I do." He pecked her ear. "At the very least, I need homeboy off my junk because he's being a cock block right now."

They giggled and pressed their lips together while Presley squeezed his inner thigh again.

"You keep teasing me like that and you're gonna have to pay up once I figure out how to get off this couch." Trent spoke softly to her as he rubbed his hand up her back and kissed her forehead.

"A debt I'll happily pay." She gently squeezed his inner thigh, higher this time.

Trent noticed Mike still sleeping on the loveseat, so he rolled his eyes. "You're gonna want to slow down too, we've got company."

Presley bit her bottom lip. "I'm going to try to squeeze out of here, I'll get Bare to follow." She pecked him. "And then we can go to bed."

"What about him?" Trent motioned to Mike.

At first Presley shrugged, then she had a better plan. "Why don't you just *sleep*." She emphasized. "I'll take Bare outside, and he will bark or make some kind of noise that a cop would typically wake up to." She smirked. "But since you're such a heavy sleeper, you just stay here."

Trent caught what she was saying. "I've been told I'm a pretty decent actor, I think I could play that part." He smiled at her.

Presley rolled her eyes smiling. "Not that damn good though, right?"

Trent squeezed her cheeks as she had just about made it over him and she tried not to laugh, she let him pull her back in for a quick peck before she got up. Baron lifted his head once Presley was free, she motioned for him to get up, so he reluctantly got off the couch. Trent winked at her and then closed his eyes.

Presley opened the door and whispered to Baron which prompted him to assume someone was outside, he barked once and ran off the porch chasing what he thought may be a threat prowling around under the cover of nightfall.

Mike immediately opened his eyes to the sound of the familiar bark, when he noticed Trent still lying on the couch, but Presley and Baron gone, he took the opportunity to have Presley alone.

A sudden jolt of fear ran through Presley when she realized she just put herself in an isolated situation with Mike. At least she still had Baron, she thought, and Trent was not only close, but he was awake.

"Can't sleep?" Mike smiled at her.

"Oh," Presley looked out into the darkness, trying to find Baron.

"No, he just needed out, we'll hop back into bed once he takes care of business. Are you heading out?"

Mike stretched, "Eh."

Presley wasn't sure what that meant but she was ready for him to leave. She continued to scan the dark lawn for a sign of Baron. They stood on the porch in silence, Presley crossed her arms and quickly looked back into the cottage.

"So," Mike started.

Presley waited before looking over at him. "So," she repeated.

"Do you need to get to bed?"

"I'll probably head that way when Baron comes back in," she told him.

Mike nodded his head up and down. "Should I grab Trent?"

"Oh," Presley shook her head. "No, he's fine, let him sleep."

"Overnight?"

Presley laughed through her nose. "It's okay."

"I don't think he should," Mike stated very matter of factly.

Presley laughed and shook her head. "Mike, that's not your business at all."

Mike didn't like her response. "Pres, you give him an inch and he'll take a mile, he can't stay here."

"Bare!" Presley was done waiting for him and done with Mike's conversation. She wanted to linger in the feeling of what had developed between her and Trent, not stand there and justify herself to Mike. "Mike, I won't have this conversation with you." She watched as Baron ran towards her. He was breathing heavily when he got to the porch.

"Why not?" He shrugged. "Because you know I'm right?"

Presley turned towards her door. "Goodnight, Mike."

"Pres," he reached for her and held her shoulder. "Pres, please." He looked into her eyes. "Please stay out here with me."

Baron was on the porch, growling now when he saw Mike intruding on Presley's bubble.

"No thank you." She shook her head and continued walking

through the doorway. "Goodnight." With that she shut and locked the cottage door.

✧

It took her a minute to walk back towards the couch, she didn't want her face to give away any indication that she was upset. Letting Mike overshadow her day with Trent was unfair and she wasn't going to allow it. She wanted to finish her day with Trent just as amazing as it had started. Before making it to the couch she stopped and hugged Baron around the neck and patted his side. "You're a good boy, buddy." She pecked the top of his head, and they continued towards the couch where Trent was waiting.

Trent lifted the blanket and smiled at her. "Come back here, gorgeous."

Presley smiled back at him and quickly took him up on his offer. They moved around to get comfortable, and Trent made sure they were completely covered by the blanket before he laid a kiss on her forehead. "Are we alone finally?"

Baron hopped on the couch and stepped across their legs to plop right on top of them.

Presley laughed, "Well, not *alone* alone."

"He's alright." Trent reached for the side of her face and then began kissing her. They were passionate in their kissing but couldn't get close enough to each other with Baron basically in between them. Trent tried to pull Presley closer to him under Baron, but he was like a log. They soon felt Baron right next to their faces as he had his mouth open and was panting his hot, kibble dog breath onto them.

"Dude." Trent lightly pushed him back. "There are times for sharing and this definitely isn't one of 'em."

Presley laughed. "We can always go to bed." She kissed his neck. "I'll tuck him in his bed first."

"And then you'll tuck me in?" Trent smirked.

"Not right away." She bit her bottom lip and started to get up.

Presley reached down to the coffee table for the remote to turn the tv off and then turned back around to find Trent and Baron waiting for her. Trent held his hand out for her with a smile, she accepted it, and Trent led them up the stairs to the bedroom loft.

"What side of the bed should I take?" Trent pulled her hand up and kissed it.

"Whatever side you want." She smirked and then gently let go of his hand. "I'm going to get Baron all tucked in." She walked over to her lovable pit bull's bed and kissed the top of his head. "Love you, bud. Goodnight." She caressed his head as she stood back up.

"Come get comfy, babe." Trent smiled and patted the bed next to him.

Presley crawled into the bed and quickly curled up next to him with her head and a hand on his chest. Trent stroked her hair a few times before planting a kiss to the side of her head.

Oh shit, Mike rolled his eyes. He had made it to his car at the main drive in front of the house and was watching in one of the bedroom cameras. Presley didn't have a television in there, so he was able to hear them clear as day.

"Goodnight." Presley smiled up at Trent.

Trent smirked. "Goodnight, huh? I thought you weren't going to be tucking me in right away." He rubbed his hands up and down her back.

"Well." She tried to hide her smile. "We both have to work in the morning, right?"

"You're right." He shook his head. "Shit, I better set my alarm." Trent rolled his body over Presley to reach his phone on the nightstand. Presley giggled as he was suddenly straddling across her. Trent quickly set his alarm, set his phone back down, and then looked into Presley's eyes as she was lying under him. He held the side of her face and reached his lips down towards hers.

After their lips comfortably slid across one another's for a long minute, Presley broke the silence. "You just have all the smooth moves, huh?"

Trent shrugged. "Thought you wanted a goodnight kiss?" He leaned into her and pushed his tongue past her lips. "Was I wrong?" He asked after separating their lips.

Her fingers pressed into Trent's back before running them up and holding his head. "Not even close." She reached up and continued kissing him. Trent's hand made its way around to her back to find her bra clasp and effortlessly loosened it for her before pulling it out from under her shirt.

Oh, fuck no, Mike watched through his phone as Trent was clearly trying to get her undressed. He wanted to see her body, but not under these circumstances. He severely underestimated where Presley's comfort level was with Trent. Mike watched helplessly as Trent removed Presley's shorts, followed by his shirt. He saw nothing but red when he lost sight of Trent's hand and heard a brief whimper from Presley. Mike turned the siren of his patrol car on and hit the flood light to point it towards the woods.

Presley jumped at the sound of the siren and Trent held her tight.

"What the fuck is that?" Trent looked around.

Baron barked and trotted down the stairs to wait at the door.

Trent got up and looked through a window in the loft, he saw the light of the patrol car shining towards the woods beyond the garage, *what is he doing?*

"Is there someone out there?" Presley clutched the blanket just under her chin.

"I'm pretty sure that's Mike." Trent shook his head. "I don't know what he's doing though."

Presley got out of bed and went to Trent's side to look out the window. They watched as the flood light scanned side to side and Mike honked the horn a couple of times.

"I'll go check it out." Trent walked back towards the bed to put his shirt on.

"No!" Presley reached out for his arm. "There might be a wild animal out there."

Trent laughed. "What like a Mike?"

Presley covered her smile.

"I'll be fine." He shrugged before looking out the window again.

Presley slid her hand up his chest. "You don't have to go out there though." She wrapped her arms around his waist. "I'm sure Mike's just scaring off a coyote or something." She reached up on her tiptoes to kiss him.

Trent didn't take much convincing, he swept her up in his arms and brought her back to the bed where he laid her on her back. He climbed on top of her and their lips connected, they continued to listen to the sirens and the random honking but decided to love on one another anyway. It wasn't long before Trent had his shirt back off and Presley's final piece of clothing was coming off.

Mike didn't want to see anything else; he floored the patrol car and spit up rocks as he headed back down to the cottage. Presley didn't exactly have a driveway that led to the cottage, so he drove across her lawn.

Baron went crazy when he saw the patrol car approaching the cottage. Presley knew her dog didn't bark without cause, so she was distracted to the point of slowing down. "Trent." She rubbed his chest. "Something's wrong."

Trent let out a small exhale and gripped her hair, wishing they could find a quiet moment to explore more of the intimacy that had formed between them earlier that night. Baron's nails scratched against the wood floors as he scrambled to the front door and soon there was a loud pounding.

"I'll see what he wants." Trent reluctantly got up and put his sweats on but didn't bother with his shirt. Presley giggled when Trent tucked himself into the boxers a bit more before he went downstairs. She was appreciative Trent was willing to go get the door because she didn't want to see Mike again that night. He had been plenty pushy with her already, she'd let Trent take this one and clear the rest of their night.

Trent flicked the lights on as he made his way through the living room and towards the front door, he flipped the porch light on as well before unlocking the door.

Mike wasted no time and pushed right in the door, taking Trent by surprise. Baron was lunging on the attack as Mike came in, but Trent grabbed him by the scruff of the neck as he wasn't wearing a collar.

"Oh shit!" Mike jumped to the side as Baron nearly grabbed his leg.

"Yeah, oh shit's right." Trent scolded him. "What the hell are you doing?"

Mike barely heard Trent over Baron's intimidating bark, he glared at Trent anyway.

Trent leaned down and pat Baron's chest, he knew better than to let him go while he was still visibly upset about Mike's presence. It took him a few moments to calm him down, but he decided to look back up at Mike when Baron had settled on just growling. "So, what the hell, man? What's going on?"

"Where's Pres?" Mike looked around, knowing full well she was in bed.

"She's in bed," Trent replied tersely.

"She's got a coug out there, I wanted to warn her to keep Baron in tonight."

"Oh, thank you, I'll let her know." Trent finally released Baron and watched carefully as he approached Mike. Baron was anything but relaxed with his hackles still raised as he got closer to Mike. "You probably would have been safe just texting her, she already let Baron out for the night." Trent gave him an accusatory look.

"Well, I came back down to give you a ride to your car too." Mike looked at him. "You don't want to walk back up that way with a coug prowling around."

"Thanks man, but I'm straight."

"Seriously." Mike had his hands up. "I don't think you understand how dangerous those cats can be. No one should be walking around the grounds until later this morning." Mike waited for a response that didn't seem to be coming any time soon. "And since you're up now I can get you to your car so you don't have to stay over, Presley works in the morning, and you should really be staying at the motel."

Trent laughed and shook his head. "Thanks for the heads up, I'll be alright."

"I insist." Mike lowered his glare.

"Alright." Trent smiled wide. "Let me go grab my keys."

Trent walked up the stairs to grab his shirt and keys. Mike regretted the fact that he couldn't pop into the camera knowing they'd hear it on his phone.

"Mike says there's a cougar up by the house and he's here to give me a ride to my car so I can leave." Trent bent over and dug his keys out of his pocket.

Presley's face immediately showed her disappointment. "Are you leaving?" She watched as he put his shirt on.

"*Fuck* no." Trent laughed sarcastically. "But he's not leaving so I'll play along and just pull my truck down here." He shrugged and then leaned down to kiss her.

Presley smiled at him and held his chin to kiss him once more before he left.

"I'll be right back, babe." He got up but quickly turned back to her. "Don't fall asleep on me." He winked.

"I won't." Presley assured him.

Trent jogged back down the stairs and jingled his keys at Mike. "Pres is going to keep Baron in tonight."

"Okay good, is she alright? I can stay if she needs me to?"

Trent laughed through his nose. "She'll be more than fine."

He leaned down and pat Baron. "Ready?" He looked at Mike.

Mike was surprised he was so agreeable to going with him, he figured they'd get into a verbal altercation at the very least.

"Yeah." Mike nodded and walked towards the door.

The short car ride was silent, neither of the men talked until Mike pulled up next to Trent's car. "She was peering through the woods right over there." He pointed towards the house.

"Huh?" Trent scratched the scruff that was growing on his chin. "Seemed like your lights were shining back that way." He pointed towards the garage.

"That's where I spotted her first." Mike backtracked.

"I'll keep an eye out." Trent unhooked his seatbelt. "And Officer Bando," he stepped out of the car and looked him in the eyes. "Don't ever fucking tell me what to do again." Trent firmly shut the door and got into his truck.

Mother fucker. Mike shook his head, glaring as he watched Trent drive back down to the cottage. He didn't have another reason to go back down there without looking completely obvious; defeated, he decided to head home. Mike didn't get very far down the road when he pulled off to the side. He was pissed that he failed at stopping any kind of intimacy between Presley and Trent for the evening. It was very likely Presley was going to completely give in to him tonight, they were definitely not going to stop at just the kissing he had seen lately. Despite his hatred of Trent, and the inevitable disgust he would feel watching Trent ruin his prized Presley, he had to watch. He wanted to see how her body moved while being loved on, the sounds she made when something felt good; he had to know what she liked, had to know her favorite touches that he would be able to master once she realized they were meant to be. Mike took a deep, irritated breath and selected the bedroom camera that was pointed at the side of Presley's bed. Trent was already back in bed, so Mike backed the video up to watch his approach.

He watched as Presley smiled when Trent was coming back into the bedroom.

"Baby, you're back." She smiled.

Trent took his shirt off and continued to walk to the bed. "I told you I would be, sweetheart." He slid his sweats off and opened the covers. Mike was able to see a glimpse of Presley's bare chest when Trent slid onto the bed and then she was almost completely gone from the screen aside from her arms that were clinging around Trent's neck and back.

"Is everything okay?" Presley asked. Mike could barely hear her now.

He watched as Trent was working on her neck before he answered. "It is now."

Mike angrily shook his leg; they were almost completely under the covers so it was impossible to see what exactly was going on. He just continued to hear random giggles from Presley only broken up by a quick whimper or moan here and there. The only gratitude he found was that he had audio and could close his eyes and imagine Presley with him. He cut the feed and decided to wait until he was in his basement to lay in his recliner listening to Presley.

Thirty-Three

The next week and a half were like a dream for Presley and Trent. They had unlocked a very healthy, physically intimate part of their relationship, their work schedules were aligned, and they were falling into such a domesticated routine that Trent rarely even went to the motel anymore. Nearly all of his belongings were now at the cottage with Presley and Baron; he had a spot in the garage and all the codes to allow him full and unrestricted access to Presley's entire home. Presley was developing a sense for the dramatics when she had to throw tantrums because Baron chose Trent over her a handful of times when they were all getting their spots on the couch. If she was being honest with herself, her heart melted each time she watched them together.

Michelle and Pete were even stepping more into the spotlight with their relationship, so they joined Trent and Presley for a double date night at the romantic Italian restaurant outside of town. Phil didn't necessarily appreciate that date night when he showed up on set the next morning and the four of them were still up playing poker at the main house. On another night Trent and Presley hosted a game night at the main house with members of the crew, Phil was sure to heavily suggest everyone call it an early night after they had played a couple of group games. It wasn't like they were hiding the fact that they were together before, but now that some of the dust was settling from Presley's stressors and her walls had completely dropped with him, she and Trent could just be together and enjoy life. Trent had already provided relief and comfort to Presley, she was now accessing and becoming accustomed to how big Trent's heart truly was. He wasn't only the rock she needed when things were tough, he made life fun and worth living to the fullest. The only thing that scared her about Trent was the fact that the production wouldn't be in town forever.

Thirty-Four

"Officer Bando." Phil and Marco, the head of the security team for the set, greeted Mike as he arrived at Presley's that morning.

"Phil, Marco." He extended his hand to each of them.

"Thank you for coming." Phil started. "We have quite a few updates and changes for the next two weeks." Phil thumbed through a file. "I just didn't realize all these damn people were so off schedule down there." He was rattling along about a scenario neither Mike nor Marco knew anything about. "Ah, here," he pulled a few papers from his bag. "So, there are new times for when we will have people here on set, and then also, we have a few more names who will be joining us. I know as a condition of us shooting here, we are to provide their names and the backgrounds we've already run."

"You ran these?" Mike looked at Marco.

"Yes sir, I did." He stood in a very military style.

Mike examined the pages. "Yeah, nothing out of the ordinary, but I'll take a closer look today."

"Thank you," Phil smiled. "And then the changes to the schedule shouldn't impact you too much, I know you operate on your own times here with the patrol. Our guys have also been a steady presence, and we haven't had any notable concerns."

Mike continued examining the set times. "I've noticed," he nodded his head. "You guys have kept a tight ship here, I like it." He looked at Marco.

"It's our pleasure, sir." Marco gave him a quick, single nod of his head.

"Oh, so changes start tomorrow on the times then, huh?" Mike realized.

"Yes, sorry for the late notice, this was as much time as I had to figure out my ass from my head too." Phil disclosed.

"No problem at all, I just like to give my shop a good idea of what to expect out here." Mike nodded along thinking the schedule changes over the next two weeks could really play in his favor. "Thank you for these." Mike held the stack of papers up and then headed back towards his patrol car.

Mike looked briefly down at the cottage, he saw Trent's Tahoe down there, just as it had been as of late. He considered barging in down there, but he decided to check the cameras first. The movement was happening in both the bedroom and the bathroom, so he checked the bathroom first. *Ah fuck, him again*, Mike thought when he saw Trent in the shower. He didn't spend any time on that camera, instead he flipped to the bedroom one hoping Presley was getting dressed for the day. She wasn't in there anymore when he checked, the only other camera that continued to alert him of movement was the bathroom… *shit*.

"Oh, hey babe, you joining me this morning?" Trent said as she walked towards the shower.

Mike looked around to be sure no one was headed his way as he turned the volume on his phone down.

Presley dropped her robe right before sliding the glass door open. "If that's okay?"

"It will never not be okay." Trent welcomed her with open arms.

Oh God, Mike rolled his eyes, *another fucking shower fuck*. Mike loathed the number of times Trent managed to slide himself into Presley. The showers had been especially hard to swallow because there weren't any blankets to cover any part of Trent. He only found partial gratitude for the last time they were in the shower because Trent pressed her against the glass door where Mike got a full frontal, mainly unobstructed view of her wet body. Mike watched as Trent turned her around, so her back was to his chest. He wasted no time in rubbing soap all over her chest and began massaging her breasts with his mouth on her neck and shoulders. Mike was glad the shower steam was making their figures look hazy, he didn't need the detailed version of where this was headed right then.

"Baby," Presley reached up for the back of his head. "That feels so good."

"I know you appreciate a good boob fondling, sweetheart," Trent replied. "I'll always be happy to oblige."

Mike stomped to his car when he heard Presley giggling, he still had the video on but wasn't looking at it and since turning the volume down he wasn't able to hear them. Once he started his car, he reluctantly looked down at his phone again. *What the fucking fuck?! Goddamn mother fucker!* Mike saw red, his face painted in anger, as he watched Trent's hands pulling what was left of the messy bun Presley walked in there with while Presley was on her knees. Mike had assumed there was a possibility Presley had already performed this on Trent in a place he didn't have cameras, but seeing it now made him blow a gasket. He cut the feed and slammed his phone down on the passenger's seat before hauling ass out of the driveway. It only took him all of ten seconds to pick his phone up again to make a call.

"You better have your fucking shit together. We'll have a window tomorrow night." Then Mike hung up.

Thirty-Five

After filming had wrapped up early for Trent that evening and Presley was able to finalize a few things she had for work, they decided to make a little escape for the night.

"Pres," Trent kissed her head as they were laying under the stars. "You remember the first time you took me out here?"

Presley was cuddled up under his arm just like she was the first time they came out to her stargazing spot after the Jubilee, she pushed up against his chest nodding her head with a smile on her face.

"Me too." He kissed her again. "That was an unforgettable night. I've been thinking about how damn grateful I am that you gave me a shot."

Presley looked up at him, her head still lying on his chest.

"Pres," Trent held her gaze. "I want to bring you to LA." He paused to look at her. "I want you to meet my family."

"Really?" She was optimistically shocked and taken a bit by surprise. "Trent, you don't have to feel obligated to do that if you're not ready…" She looked down, she didn't want him to be guilted into bringing her home to mom because they slept together. "I'm happy with us and I don't want to push anything."

Trent reached for her chin. "Pres," Trent exhaled. "I know why you'd say that, but you don't have to be tough or guarded with me." He rubbed her face. "You know," he tried to explain things the best he could. "My mom's been asking literally for years now when I'm going to settle down." He paused. "I've finally met a girl that I'd be proud to take home to meet her, one that's actually worth being loyal for. Pres, you're the girl I want above anything else in the world. No other girl has been good enough because I was always looking for you."

Presley moved up towards him until their lips connected. Trent reached for her leg and pulled her on top of him, he was consumed by her and wanted her. It scared him that his feelings were this strong, but he couldn't distance himself from her, he continued to want more. He had thought long and hard over the last couple of weeks what he was going to do as their time filming at Presley's dwindled down. Every time he'd play the scenario out, he was only happy if he ensured the bond with Presley was going to stay intact when he left town. No other option was acceptable for him, he concluded he couldn't be happy without her. For a split-second Trent opened his eyes and saw the woman he was developing deeper feelings for loving on him with the light of a million stars above them, nothing else would have made that exact moment better so he shut his eyes and continued to kiss her.

✦

"Can we stay out here tonight, just like this?" Trent rubbed Presley's bare back as they lay intertwined with one another under a blanket, their hearts working on their descent after making love.

Presley was curled up under Trent's arm with her head on his chest staring at the stars. "I've never slept up here, but we certainly can if you want. I'm not sure how long I'll last," she admitted. "It can get quite chilly up here at night."

"Oh," Trent reached down to grope her in the most inviting way. "It would be my fucking honor to accept the job of keeping you warm, baby."

Presley squirmed and giggled before she looked up to give him a peck. They both settled back into looking up at the stars.

"It's like time stops up here with you." He kissed her head.

Presley rubbed Trent's chest softly.

"And," he smirked, "this is hot as shit."

Presley laughed and looked up at him. "You're right," she smiled. "Not much could compare to this."

"I'm going to try to top it. You get cred for this slice of heaven, but Trent Hayes will not be outdone when it comes to romance," he assured her. "I'll be coming up with something that will compete with this moment."

"I'm already looking forward to it." She pecked his cheek.

"There's one more thing I wanted to talk to you about," Trent whispered into her ear.

Presley felt goosebumps shoot down to her ankles when his breath touched her ear. She shivered involuntarily and then looked up at him, she was curious and nervous all at the same time.

"I want to talk about us, Pres." He brushed her hair from her forehead. "Shooting for me is over soon and I've got another set I have to be at not even a week after we wrap up here."

Presley felt her throat tighten—she was afraid of losing Trent. But why would he just ask her to meet his family and then immediately want to have 'a talk'? She took a deep breath and waited for him to continue.

"But I've been thinking a lot." He rubbed her face and took a deep breath. "I want to be sure my intentions are clear and we're on the same page before I have to go." He affectionately put a piece of hair behind her ear. "I still want to see you… and only you, Presley. I don't want anything stopping or changing between us when I leave."

She pressed into him and caressed his chest. "Trent," she looked into his eyes. "I know that's a big step for you."

He held her gaze and finally replied. "It is, but I've never been more confident in a decision all my life."

A smile broke across her face. "I want to be with you too, Trent. I'm in."

"Perfect." He smiled and cupped her butt with one of his hands. "Then I don't want you to just come down to meet my family, I want to introduce you to all of them as my girlfriend."

There was no hesitation, Presley reached her arms around his neck and kissed him. Trent responded by rolling on top of her and finding himself in between her legs which he was working on spreading open for himself.

Presley giggled and whispered to Trent. "Again?"

He smiled and rubbed her from her hip to her breast. "Uh huh, get used to it, girlfriend—I'll always be ready to put more lovin' on you."

Presley followed Trent's direction and comfortably settled into loving him, she had a new sense of confidence flowing through her as Trent had declared her to officially be his girlfriend. She felt like that's what they had developed, but neither of them had outright used any titles or dove into the subject since she told Trent weeks ago, she didn't want to just have a fling. He heard her.

Thirty-Six

The sound of Baron barking woke both Trent and Presley up. Presley held the blanket to her chest and shot up looking for her dog. He didn't sound like he was too far away.

"Bare!" She called out. They could hear him rustling back through the trees and bushes to get to them.

Presley smiled as he approached. "Hey bud." She ruffled the top of his head. "What're you barking at?"

She felt Trent's hands sliding up her back and then his lips started pecking the small of her naked back. He took his time tickling his hands along her body and kissing up her spine; he finally made his way up and was kissing her neck.

"Good morning, babe," he whispered in her ear.

"Good morning," she giggled.

"What time is it?"

"Time for coffee," she laughed. "We can head back into town and get some breakfast?" She turned to him and pecked his lips. "We could even grab it to go and head to the lake?"

"Mmm," he smirked. "Maybe you'll let me get lucky and you'll wear this same outfit to breakfast, huh?" He leaned her back down next to him and wasted no time in making his hands comfortable below her waist.

She laughed as he squeezed her in all the right places. "I'm not picking breakfast up in this outfit." She put her arms around his neck as he leaned over her. "But I'll certainly honor your request once we're home, boyfriend."

"I love the sound of that off your tongue." Trent smiled and simultaneously pressed their chests and lips together. He turned to lay on his back and Presley followed him, partially resting her chest on his with one of her legs in between his.

When their lips separated Trent's fingertips continued to lightly scratch her back, he could feel all the goosebumps forming.

"Pres," he started. "Can I ask you something?"

"Of course," she replied with her face resting on his chest.

"What's the story with your tattoos?" His hands softly scanned both birds on her back.

Presley had wondered if he'd ever ask about them, she was more than positive he'd seen them. "Oh, you noticed my little mini flock?" She smiled.

"I did. I really like them, but I was just wondering why a dove and a raven?"

"Look at you, you even knew it was a raven and not a crow." She rubbed his chest.

"I'll admit, that was purely a guess." He smiled. "I had a 50/50 chance."

She grinned while caressing his dreamy abdominal section before she began. "I've always loved birds, and when Paps passed away, I decided I needed a little permanent reminder of sorts." She lightly shrugged. "Just something I'd always have on my back through all the shit life throws." She was lightly rubbing Trent's brawny chest now. "Obviously lots of people already memorialize the passing of loved ones with a dove, so that's my love and light, peace and hope, basic bitch portion of my tattoo."

"I haven't taken a real close look, babe, but from what I've seen it's anything but basic," he assured her.

She smiled. "I meant it as in like the concept is basic, I would very much agree that the design is far from basic. I wanted both of them to look more realistic versus like cartoons or anything."

Trent gently slid her to the side so he could prop himself up to take a better look. Presley laid flat and rested her head on her hands, she felt Trent outlining the dove with his fingers.

"So, I guess my dove isn't completely a basic bitch design. I do have him on my back right about where my heart would be, and roughly the size of an actual human heart; each of his wings also has my dad and Paps handwriting snuck in there." She smiled and felt Trent's fingers as he gently outlined the dove.

"And then the raven," she started. "I've just always loved those birds, well, crows too. I just think they're so... majestic. So, when I was looking for a compliment for my dove, I started digging into ravens and what they symbolize. There's the obvious gothy-type death symbolism and some people treat them like some kind of omen. But then there are spiritual meanings too, which I didn't realize before. There is one where some people believe they are messengers for loved ones that have passed and others associate ravens with healing—like a good versus evil kinda thing or something."

Presley noticed Trent had stopped tracing her tattoos, his hand was just resting on the small of her back, below the raven, and he hadn't said anything.

She turned her head to face him. "So, I suppose, having them both together, I see it as the love I have for Dad and Paps will always be in my heart, and they've always got my back in a way," she shrugged. "But also recognizing that life isn't always sunshine and rainbows, so embracing the dark to find the light in everything—like always accepting and embracing the healing process so I don't ever give up in life."

Trent laid his hand flat on her back and delicately caressed it. "Sweetheart, I love that." He kissed her on her back. "I don't love that life's been so rough on you, but your birds suit you beautifully." He pulled her top half back onto his chest and pecked her forehead before he continued. "And while they're here to remind you of those things, I'm here so the bad shit doesn't even have a fighting chance with you." He looked deep into her eyes, "Presley Williams, I've got your front, your back, your heart, and everything else in between." He gave her back another firm and comforting rub before he kissed her temple.

Presley smiled, but Trent continued. "I'm glad I waited to ask about them, I didn't want to end up being inadvertently disrespectful the first time I saw your bare back."

Presley chuckled. "Baby, I promise I won't be mad or offended, what were you thinking that was disrespectful?"

Trent just continued to rub her back, pausing before he disclosed his actual thoughts. "Okay, well, I have seen little peeks here and there when you've been in a tank top, or your swimsuit." He admitted before he laid himself down next to her and spoke in her ear. "But the first time I really saw your back completely bare, I had just turned you around in the shower and you had water dripping all over it." Trent lightly slid his fingers along her back and felt all of the goosebumps forming. "When I bent you over, I wanted to tell you your tattoos were sexy as shit."

Presley felt tingling sensations throughout her body.

"But," Trent's hand landed on her cheek to cup it, "my horny ass finally realized that might come across as douchey if they had special meaning. So, here I am disclosing yet another embarrassing fact about myself and hoping you'll still be my girlfriend." He laughed at himself.

Presley giggled and then reached her hand between Trent's legs this time and smiled up at him. "You are not a douche," she confirmed while softly stroking him. "You can think they're sexy," she cradled his balls. "And you're stuck with me now, Trent Hayes," she gently gripped him. "You can't chase me away with any of your embarrassing facts, I love every single one of them." Presley felt Trent at full attention now, so she put one of her legs in between his and reached up to kiss his lips. Trent only allowed for one exchange of their tongues before he was sitting up and pulling her on top of him.

Presley, now on her knees straddling Trent, giggled as he pulled on her hips, their chests touching. "Trent," she managed. "You know my hips can't go down any further right now." She felt their bare skin touching.

"Yes, the fuck they can." He countered and then put his mouth on her chest to distract her while he kept working her hips.

Presley's head rolled back, and she smiled. "You're playing dirty, that's not fair." She felt her knees giving up, so she quickly reached down for the sides of Trent's face to connect their lips again.

Trent smiled, he knew he had been close to her giving in, it gave him a different kind of pleasure to test his limits with her. "That's the only way I know how to play, sweetheart." Trent tried to reach for his pants to get another condom.

Presley felt his hand when it left the back of her body, so she knew what he was doing, if he was going to play dirty, then so could she, and she was in a position to win the contest. "What happens when you find out I'm much better at that game than you are?" She kissed his neck and gently nibbled on his collarbone.

"Babe, you have no idea how much I'd love to see you try." He ripped the package open and that was Presley's cue.

She allowed her legs to open wider to slide him right into her as she opened her eyes to look directly in his. Trent was in a mesmerized state of disbelief, she barely reached the base when she slid herself quickly back up to her original heightened position and then reached for the condom in his hand.

"Oh, hell, no," he gripped it and smiled at her. "*Hell, no* do you get to do all that and expect me to just…" He shook his head all over the place. "…Just put this on right away!"

Presley giggled and kissed his forehead. "Baby, you started it. I was just trying to show you that I could win that game."

"You fuckin won," he assured her. "I'll give you that, but I'm here to claim my consolation prize for not completely losing control when you caught me by surprise like that."

Presley bit her bottom lip. "I'm sorry." She did feel slight regret for not thinking that through. "I didn't think about that."

"Oh, I'm not mad," he assured her.

Presley held onto his shoulders and pressed herself closer to his chest, to whisper to him. "I was only thinking about how good it would feel."

Trent rolled his head back, "Ah, fuck." Trent looked back into her eyes and reached for her face. "You, Presley Williams, are trouble," he planted a kiss on her lips. "And I absolutely love it."

Presley lowered herself again, this time not right on top of him, but a more respectable distance so she could connect their lips again. Trent wasted no time in putting her on her back. Presley wasn't opposed to a quick consolation prize, so when Trent made his request by slowly sliding his tip along her lips, she encouraged it and embraced all of him in her. They almost got too carried away before Presley was finally able to bring herself to put her hand on Trent's hip to slow him down and remind him about the condom they still needed.

Thirty-Seven

Trent and Presley finally managed to agree to get dressed and head back to town. Their evening was capped off with an incredibly slow and sensual morning so neither were in too much of a hurry. They pulled up to Presley's favorite coffee shop later than they had originally planned, but still acceptable for the breakfast hour. Since they were just running in to pick coffee and breakfast sandwiches, they had Baron stay in the car, he wasn't afraid to share his disapproval when he kicked the back door a few times. Trent quickly intertwined his hand with Presley's once he met her on her side of the truck. They hadn't said much since leaving their stargazing spot that morning, both of them were still very much reflecting on everything that happened in the last twelve hours or so. While they didn't say much, their bodies continued to crave each other and there was an invisible tether of desire between them. Trent's hand had just released Presley's so it could venture down to cupping her cheek. Presley couldn't resist, her soaring confidence since establishing titles encouraged her to turn towards him and reach up for his lips. Both of Trent's hands found themselves comfortable on Presley's hindquarters to indulge in the moment. They had just separated and were reaching for each other's hands when they heard a voice behind them.

"Presley!" Mike called out from about a block away.

Trent let out a prolonged exhale as they turned. Mike was still about a half a block away, so they waited for his approach.

Presley responded as he got closer. "Good morning, Mike."

"Hey, I was worried about you, Pres." He jogged to catch up to them. "I went by the house a couple times last night and it didn't look like you were there?"

"Oh, we were safe." She assured him.

"Late night?" Mike pressed. "Where were you hiding?"

Trent had never actually liked Mike, and he definitely didn't like his interest in Presley or the continued stalking and possessive type behavior that he watched. He had already told him as much, so until one day when he got the hint, Trent would continue to keep his body situated in a way that Mike would literally need to go through him to even think about touching his girlfriend. He also didn't miss an opportunity to give Mike a hard time.

"We weren't hiding," Trent laughed. "Just took her away for the night to have some *uninterrupted* alone time."

"Huh," Mike rested his hands on his duty belt. "Didn't see you at the motel either, must've been outta town."

Presley couldn't stop smiling, she just looked down and didn't answer him.

"Well," Trent squeezed Presley around her shoulders. "I'm going to get this sweet thing some coffee." He looked over at Mike. "You following us, or will we just see you around later?"

Mike furrowed his brow.

"Sure," Mike twisted it a bit. "If you're offering, I could use a cup, I'll join you." Mike removed his hands from his duty belt and followed them. He hated watching Trent and Presley interact with each other, he knew something went down the night before and they were still riding the high from it. Neither of them did anything overly obnoxious but he watched as they held hands, gently bumped into each other, and snuck smiles towards one another—he *hated* all of it. His insides were screaming in anticipation for the moment when Presley finally saw Trent for what he was so Mike could move in.

"Officer Bando, you taking yours for here or to go?" Trent asked as he stood at the cashier ready to pay.

Mike knew the 'Officer Bando' routine was more of a condescending insult than anything, and he was getting sick of it. "To go." He shortly replied.

"Good morning." The cashier blushed, trying to suppress her giddiness.

"Hi." Presley and Trent smiled back in unison.

"All together?" She asked.

"Yeah," Trent held Presley around her waist while he had her securely against his hip. "We're together," he smiled before pecking the side of her head. "But I'd also like to go ahead and take care of Officer Bando here too."

Mike adjusted his duty belt and rolled his eyes.

The cashier took payment from Trent and tried to bat her eyes at him.

"You know," Mike narrowed his eyes at Trent as he picked his black coffee up off the counter. "You may think you're safe since we're such a small town, but you'll want to watch the things you say. 'Together' is something the tabloids and gossip sites would run with if they heard it. And that may bring more attention, not to mention negative attention, to Pres that she really doesn't need—it's just not safe to put her in that position." Mike glared. "And you don't strike me as someone who admits to being with anyone." Mike rudely continued, "Let alone claim anyone."

Trent, despite his desire to punch Mike square in his face, smiled back at him instead. "Well, it's not like Pres and I were going to stay a secret for long." He shrugged and looked down at her green eyes that were just begging him for a kiss. He delivered a quick peck before continuing. "So." He looked back at Mike. "While I appreciate the warning, I don't mind if everyone knows Presley's my girlfriend."

"Girlfriend?!" Mike's demeanor immediately changed from irritated to irate.

"That's right." Trent smiled as Presley took a sip of her coffee from the comfort of being under his strong arm. "*Girlfriend*," he repeated with a firm sureness to his tone.

"Presley." Mike started, his full attention on her before his radio interrupted his incoming speech.

"Officer Bando, we have a report of a suspicious vehicle off the 101 right outside of town. Are you able to check it out or should I send someone else?"

Mike was still reeling from the news Trent just dropped on him but answered the call. "Yeah, be there in ten."

Mike gave Presley a very pointed look and then left.

"You really love seeing him squirm." Presley looked up at Trent. "Don't you?" She smirked.

He smiled back at her. "Hey, he started it. I thought he liked making people uncomfortable, I'm just matching that energy until he figures out a way to ease up on my girlfriend."

"Thank you, Trent." She rubbed the arm he had around her. "And I hope you're sure about that whole boyfriend girlfriend thing, because everyone and their mom is about to know," she laughed.

"I wouldn't have it any other way, babe." He leaned down and pressed his lips against hers before they walked out of the coffee shop.

"Well, just to prepare you." She kissed him again, smiling at the warning she'd be delivering. "You are going to have to be the one to answer to the Hofners when they find out you told Mike before them about this news." She giggled.

"Shit." Trent smiled. "I'm sure I can take Jake, but I may need your help with Lisa."

Presley laughed and lightly bumped her head into his shoulder.

Presley intertwined her fingers with Trent's, and they watched Mike race down main street, his quick glare as his patrol car passed them didn't go unnoticed.

Trent watched the car until it was out of sight. "And you'll have to let me know when I'm allowed to kick that guy's fuckin ass." He gestured towards the dust Mike had left when he made his right turn.

Presley sipped her coffee and swung their hands. "I truly do appreciate how you handle Mike. I just don't want things to be even more uncomfortable with him when you're not here every day, so I think what you're doing has been a perfect balance." She smiled up at him. "Plus, he's harmless, he's probably going to pout about the news for a bit and then who knows, maybe he just won't pop up all the time randomly?"

Trent was opening her door for her after shoeing Baron back to his seat when he started again. "Harmless, huh?" He watched her get in and reach for her seatbelt. "I'd hardly consider basically harassing you harmless, Pres. It's not easy to watch."

She clicked her belt. "Okay, well I guess I meant that's just Mike's normal." She rolled her head from side to side.

Trent accepted it for the moment and closed her door to walk around to the driver's seat.

"When you say normal," Trent started the truck. "Has he always been like this when you've had a boyfriend?"

Presley took another drink and stared out the windshield before answering. "Well," she paused again. "I don't know that Mike has ever met anyone I've dated."

"What?!" Trent laughed. "Pres, you cannot be serious! As much as he's around, he's never met anyone you've dated?!"

"Well, like in high school it was just like a prom date and the only time Mike really saw that guy was that whole night because he didn't go to our school." She thought about the next time she had any commitment to a guy. "Then Mike wasn't around at all while I was in college, he joined the military right out of high school, so I didn't physically see him for a few years. He always just kept in touch on like social media," she shrugged.

"Okay, what about the last five years or so? You're telling me he didn't just show up at your house like this with any other guy?"

"You assume a lot, Trent Hayes." Presley laughed. "Mike's never had to see anything like this." She gestured between the two of them. "I don't just invite whoever to my house, you know my dating history isn't *super* extensive. Plus, anytime I like even saw anyone, it was from meeting them through Jake or Lisa really, so I'd just go to Seattle for dinners and dates," she shrugged. "Dating has mostly been a Seattle thing for me. I don't just invite every single guy to this house, I feel like that's how you get ax-murdered when you don't really know someone all that well." She laughed.

"I guess that makes sense, I don't think about things like that because I'm not a female." Trent accepted her explanation.

"Oh, I'm aware." Presley reached over and slid her hand onto his lap.

Trent caught her hand so he could kiss it before he put it back down to where she had it. "I'm just trying to say that he and his behavior are not normal, babe." He looked at her. "You shouldn't have to put up with that, so if you need me to be a little more firm with him, you just let me know." Trent hadn't disclosed the conversation he had with Mike at the bar a couple weeks ago, he didn't think Jake had said anything to her about it either. She had enough on her plate to worry about petty bullshit when Trent was more than capable of just continuing to put Mike in his place.

"Honestly, I'm surprised he still comes around as much as he does, you've made it pretty clear he isn't welcome whenever he shows up." Presley rubbed her dog's face when he poked his head over her seat.

"Yeah, well, I don't like how uneasy you look when he's around, that alone makes me want to rearrange his damn face or throw him off a cliff somewhere." Trent turned onto the highway that led to Presley's. "And secondary to seeing you look uncomfortable; the guy is the biggest fucking cock block I've ever encountered."

Presley rolled her head towards Trent laughing.

✦

Girlfriend, fucking girlfriend, Mike terrorized himself on his way out to the call. He had seen the development of their relationship over the last few weeks but honestly didn't think Trent would actually place a title on them. He assumed this was going to be his normal playboy bullshit where he got what he wanted out of Presley, more times than Mike would like to admit, and he'd just move along in a couple weeks.

The only two reasons he had been able to bear watching them in bed, on the couch, in the shower, that one time on the kitchen island, and Lord knows where else since Mike didn't have 24/7 surveillance on them was, one, he was able to see Presley naked quite frequently; and, two, he needed to study all of her preferences for when he replaced Trent as her lover. None of his previous plans of separating them had worked and now that they'd given their relationship a definitive title, it was going to be even more difficult for him to separate them on his own. This was a much larger job than he had anticipated, and he was so happy to have made an advantageous connection with someone who could help him execute his new strategy. *Things will be very different soon*, he reassured himself.

Thirty-Eight

"You know," Trent started and swung their hands as they walked down the lake trail after breakfast that morning. "I haven't had a girlfriend since I was like fourteen."

"Lies!" Presley playfully accused.

"Pres, babe, I swear." Trent turned to her and motioned across his chest. "Cross my heart, not like an actual girlfriend."

Presley's eyes narrowed as she looked at him and tried to suppress her smile.

"Not that I *actually* want to discuss it... or know details, but it seems to me you've had many girlfriends." She countered.

Trent stopped. "Those were different kinds of..." He tried to remember the term she had used when she was drunk. "...Bedtime friends, no titles or exclusivity." He surely didn't want to dive into any other details about those women either. "I'm talking like an official girlfriend." He pulled her into his chest, "one that I'm grateful to wake up next to each morning." He pecked her chin, "who has me wrapped around her finger." His kiss moved to her cheek, "and who I'm head over heels for, just *begging* her to let me spoil her beyond comprehension." He finished with a juicy kiss on her lips.

Presley giggled, while flattered she couldn't help but be skeptical. "Alright, Trent Hayes, what is it that you'd like?" She cocked her head to the side offering the most flirtatious smile.

Trent bit his bottom lip and reached for her chin. "I want your heart, darlin'." He slowly reached down and met her lips softly.

Presley melted in his arms, she didn't want a soft kiss after that, she wanted passion. Trent picked up on her desire for more and lifted her right off the ground to wrap her legs around his waist. Their tongues danced around between each other's mouths and Trent held Presley firmly. They finally began to slow when Baron came running towards them with another stick he had found. He wasn't patient at all, he barked immediately after setting the stick down.

Presley laughed. "Part of having my heart is accepting my spoiled kid over there and keeping him happy too."

"Please," Trent scoffed. "That job's been in the damn bag." Trent set her down so he could throw the stick for Baron. "He called me Dad the other day." Trent shrugged.

Presley laughed and pushed him playfully.

"So, you sure you're not upset with me bailing on dinner plans tonight?" Trent wrestled Baron for his stick this time since he didn't drop it right away.

"Baby," Presley looked up at him. "I get it when your work schedule changes, of course I want to spend all kinds of time with you, but I'm not mad at you."

Trent hated when they had to cater to changes for nonsense, like people not being ready to do their jobs. Phil had just handed out a schedule change right as they left the set the night before; not exactly how he wanted to celebrate his evening. His girlfriend had surely done her part to take his mind off that though.

Presley reached out for his hand and interlaced their fingers. "I may not be outright mad, but you'll still be getting a spanking when you get home tonight, that's for sure."

Trent turned to her and planted his lips on hers as he dipped her back, he went straight for separating her lips. When he returned her to her upright position he looked her in her eyes. "You know I'm the one who hands out spankings around here," he winked.

"Hey girl!" Lisa answered her phone.

"Hey Lis, what are you doing?" Presley asked.

"Oh," she let out a large exhale. "Just about to leave the school, Jake's working late, Bay's got swim lessons, ya know, the ushe."

"You wanna chat at your bestie for a bit, or do you need to go?"

Lisa laughed. "Oh, you'll be riding home with me of course."

Presley was walking Baron along one of the trails by the lake. "Perfect, I'm commuting home right now too, from the lake." She laughed.

"No Trent?" Lisa asked.

"Nope, he already walked with us this morning, Baron and I just came out for a quick walk before dinner."

"Oh, well that's nice too, how is Trent?" Lisa asked as she was getting into her car.

Presley blushed, amazing, Trent had been amazing. But she knew that's not what her friend meant. "He's good, working pretty late tonight, unfortunately."

"Girl, don't act like you won't be waiting up for him, I sure as shit would be." She laughed.

"I mean, obviously," Presley joined her laughter. "Especially tonight, I think we're celebrating."

Lisa's bluetooth was connecting so she wanted to be sure she heard her correctly. "Wait, did you say celebrating? What did I miss?"

"Uh, ya know, the ushe." Presley's smile projected through her voice. "Just celebrating official titles and him asking me to come down to LA and meet his entire family."

"What?!?!?!" Lisa squealed into the phone. "Presley Marie, are you fucking with me?!"

She shook her head and tossed a stick for Baron. "No ma'am, serious as all get out."

"When did this, well, how did this all go down?!"

"It's very new," she admitted. "We took a quick little trip last night and he talked to me about going down to meet his family, which I obviously was like are you *sure sure* and I think he thought I was crazy for a hot second," Presley laughed.

"He's partially right about the crazy," Lisa teased. "But in the best kind of way, of course."

"Up yours," Presley shot back, chuckling. "After I agreed and was totes on board to go meet the family, he started talking about how he wanted us to stay together and exclusive even after he's done with the shoot here and then told me when I meet his family he wants to introduce me as his girlfriend."

"Aw, Pres, that's so flipping cute! I just love him for you, legit girl."

"I do too, Lis," Presley giggled. "I'm not sure how I'll survive when he's on a different set location, like he's been the surprise of a lifetime, and I cannot believe I'm legitimately his girlfriend." She shook her head smiling. "I sure can't get enough of that man."

"Oh shit, girl," Lisa bounced along. "I know what you can't get enough of! Pres! So many exciting changes!!"

"I don't want to kiss and tell," Presley started.

Lisa immediately cut her off. "You bitch! You'd deny me, your dearest friend, any kind of story?!"

Presley knew Lisa was joking with her, she laughed. "Okay, Lis, I'll give you this… I don't think I ever actually had an orgasm until I met Trent Hayes."

Lisa laughed. "Girl, I hope you're lying! You're almost thirty! I mean, good for you now, but Pres no, girl."

"Have you ever felt like your uterus was going to escape your body to chase down whatever was bumping into it? I should probably also Google if I can spontaneously combust or if it's possible to be sent into a different dimension from too much pleasure all at once." Presley stated. "Lis, I know, on everything, I've *never* experienced anything like this… over and over and over and over again too," she was sure to add.

"Ha ha ha ha ha," Lisa couldn't stop laughing. "Girl, that does sound pretty amazing. Sounds like he's making up for all the times you never got yours."

"Amazing isn't even sufficient for what I've experienced, Lis," Presley confirmed. "Honestly, there probably isn't a word in the actual dictionary for it."

"Am I allowed to tell Jake about the titles, or do you want to?"

Presley smiled. "You can let my boyfriend know he has officially been replaced, but I'll reconsider his status if Trent and I ever advance beyond this stage."

Lisa rolled her eyes. "You know him, he will likely have a counter-offer."

"That's why he gets the big bucks."

"Oh! Can I tell Officer Dickweed? I would give my next ten orgasms to see the look on his face when he finds out." Lisa laughed.

Presley laughed out loud, "Lis!" She tried to stop her giggling so Lisa could understand her when she spoke. "We actually ran into him when we went into town this morning."

"Did you fuckin tell him before me?!"

"Nope," she halted her best friend's assumptions. "We were walking to coffee and Mike saw us, of course he was butting in, so it was Trent who very smugly informed Mike we have titles."

"Shit, what did he say?!" Lisa was giddy.

"He was like mad, it was kind of uncomfortable for a second, I got that whole scolding, 'Presley!' kind of look."

"What did Trent do?"

"He just kept me right under his arm, smiling."

"What a dick," Lisa laughed. "In the best way, I love it."

"And I did give Trent a heads up that he will be answering to the two of you for telling Mike first."

Lisa laughed. "Atta girl, he's definitely getting an earful when I see him next." She continued. "Hopefully Mike starts to really get the hint. I mean, if he didn't have a chance before, he can't be dumb enough to think he could steal you away from Trent O-Machine Hayes."

Presley fell forward laughing. "Oh my gosh, you better *never* repeat that in front of him!"

"Pres, I'm just so happy for you."

"Despite some of the shit going on, I really am happy right now."

"Ride that high, girl… and your boyfriend too."

"I swear, you've been married to Jake too long." She laughed but knew full well she would be taking both pieces of advice for the foreseeable future.

"Oh shit, speaking of, he's calling me right now."

"No worries, girl, I just had to call to let you know."

"Thanks, Pres, we love you and congrats. I'll give you a call a bit later if I can."

"Sounds good, give everyone love from me."

"I will, bye, girl."

"Bye."

Presley continued to follow Baron back to the cottage, it was within sight now. She looked at the trail ahead of her and remembered the first time they had run into Trent down there; gratitude took over and painted a smile on her face thinking about everything that had followed that meeting. Her thoughts were interrupted by a text notification, *Jake*, she smiled.

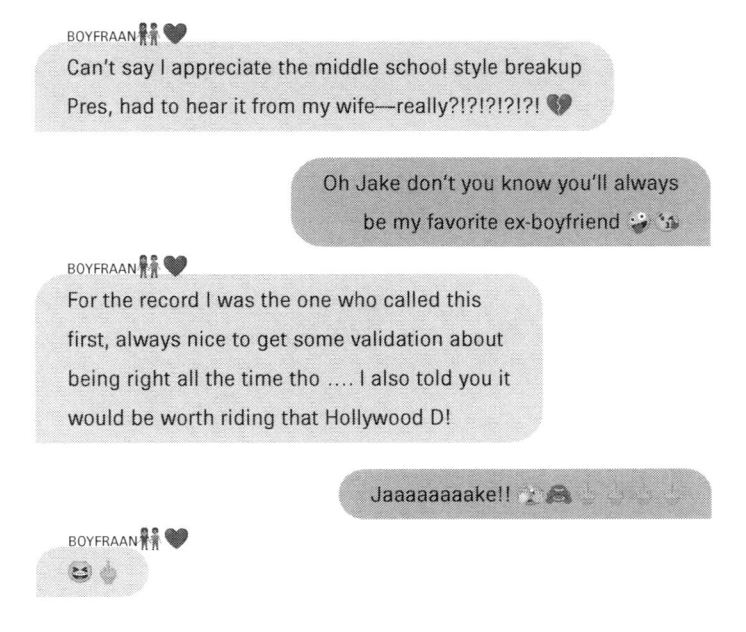

> **BOYFRAAN 👬 💜**
> Can't say I appreciate the middle school style breakup Pres, had to hear it from my wife—really?!?!?!?!?! 💜

>> Oh Jake don't you know you'll always be my favorite ex-boyfriend 🙃

> **BOYFRAAN 👬 💜**
> For the record I was the one who called this first, always nice to get some validation about being right all the time tho …. I also told you it would be worth riding that Hollywood D!

>> Jaaaaaaaake!!

> **BOYFRAAN 👬 💜**
> 😈👆

Presley was looking down, still laughing at Jake and ended up running right into the back of her dog. "Bare," she stumbled around him. "What are you doin', bud?"

Baron's body was completely stiff, and his hackles were up. All of his focus was off to the right of them, opposite of the lake where it was heavily wooded. Presley had never seen him like this on the trail, but they also didn't do a lot of later twilight walks through here. She wondered if there was a predator out looking for a meal, a chill went down her spine at the thought. Baron released a guttural growl that was absolutely lethal. The last thing she wanted was him taking off and ending up nose to nose with a cougar or something, she slowly reached for his collar to gain some kind of control if her voice didn't stop him from taking off.

"Come on, bud." Presley gave his collar a tug and tried to continue walking down the path. Baron didn't move, his focus didn't alter as the growl was becoming more feral. Presley was really starting to worry now; she saw a rock within reach so she picked it up and chucked it towards Baron's gaze. He lunged at the sound the rock made into the bushes and let out the kind of bark she'd never heard from him. It was a threatening one for sure so she held on as tight as she could and again tried pulling him along the final leg of the trail. He was too strong to drag so she paused and let him continue barking into the bushes. She thought for sure an animal would have at least moved at the sound of his barking and the movement of the rock, but nothing. Her heart started pounding a little harder as she mentally begged Baron with each tug that he would finally decide to walk with her. It took her an uncomfortably long time to break his focus, but he finally started trotting alongside her, still watching and growling. Once they were into the lawn Presley put him in a sit and tried to coax him to look at her, he refused, still fixated on the woods near the trail.

"Well, you will be on a leash anytime you need to go out for the rest of the evening, bro." Presley patted him on his chest. "But you're a *very* good boy, always keeping us safe," she praised him.

Presley was finally able to get him into the cottage, but he uncharacteristically skipped his immediate trip to the water bowl and sat by the front door still on alert.

Yikes, whatever it was, I'm glad we're inside now, Presley thought.

Thirty-Nine

"WHAT THE FUCK IS THIS, DANA?!" MIKE RUSHED INTO THE RUN-down, one room cabin. "This wasn't part of the fucking plan!"

Dana's smile was deadly. "Well, it's about time you joined us, Michael, I was just waiting for her to wake up."

Mike roughly ran his fingers through his hair and left his hands clasped on the top of his head, relieved that Dana hadn't outright killed her daughter... Yet.

"You were only supposed to have your men scare her, not take her! How the fuck are we, are *you*, going to explain this?!" Mike's voice was getting louder.

Dana brushed Presley's hair behind her ear as she lay bound and unconscious on the ratted, burnt orange couch. She continued to pet her daughter's face softly. "Michael, Michael, Michael, it does amuse me that you think I didn't realize how deep your unhealthy obsession with my daughter runs." She had a low, evil laugh.

"I could just arrest you right now, how long has she been out?" He made a move towards Presley.

Dana shook her finger at Mike. "Ah uh," she stopped him. "Why don't you listen to a little something I have to say first before you try to act like the hero in this story?"

Mike felt a cold sweat down his back, *what did she do*?

"Your mom sure is a friendly gal." Dana swiped a piece of fuzz off Presley's head. "While we met for tea and caught up like old friends do, do you know what my men were up to?"

Fuck, Mike tried to keep his face from turning white.

"I see why you keep a lock on your bedroom… And your basement." Dana's lethal eyes slowly met Mike's. "I'm not sure what my favorite part was about your… collection." She tapped a finger to her chin. "The live feed of her property in your basement was pretty intriguing, and the fact that you keep some of those tapes like your own vintage video store? Gosh, the time and commitment it must have taken to catalog every event you have." She put a hand over her heart. "I am curious, Michael. How does it feel to watch those steamy clips of Trent Hayes fucking her while she moans his name?"

Mike's face snarled.

"You are either one very confident man, or one of more than adequate size because I watched a few of those." Dana warned. "It seems my daughter has really taken a liking to that huge cock of his." She got closer to Mike and stared down at his zipper. "It also seems like you like to play along while watching those videos." Dana shrugged, thinking about the lotion and tissue that were sitting next to his recliner. Dana didn't stop, she had seen plenty more than his basement stalking headquarters. "I think you know what we found in your bed, Michael." Dana's sultry voice lowered as she was now just inches from Mike's face. Without losing eye contact, she reached for her phone and held a picture up for him. Mike finally let out a breath, it seemed like it had been forever. "This is a true work of art, Michael. Where do you even have something like this made? And you keep her under your bed while you're not home?" Dana finally turned the phone to herself so she could have another look. The picture was of Mike's bed, sprawled out on his comforter was what looked to be a naked Presley. "She must not moan your name though?" Dana guessed knowing full well Mike's dirty little doll wouldn't be talking or moving. "She's got hair like Presley." Dana zoomed in on the picture. "All the important holes you may be exploring, very lifelike breasts I may add—was that a premium add-on?"

Mike didn't say anything, he could feel his stomach trying to escape right through his ass to hit the floor.

"I didn't realize my daughter had any tattoos, but when we turned this pretty girl over…," Dana scrolled to the next photo. "There they were, two birds." Again, she zoomed in on the picture. "A little white Dove and then a black Raven." She shook her head. "I wasn't sure if this was just some kind of kink you had, so of course I had to look at Presley's back this evening." Again, she scrolled for another picture. "And there they are, just as you have them on your own personal little Presley."

"What the *fuck* do you want, Dana?" Mike spoke through his teeth.

"I still want what I wanted before." She turned her back to him and walked to the couch again to assess Presley. "I want her to sign these papers." She pointed at the coffee table. "But to ensure that happens, I need you to keep playing nice, Michael."

Mike continued to glare.

"I actually thought you'd be pleased about this offering." Dana crossed her legs. "In your diary that we found; it seems like you think you just need her to see that she belongs with you? Michael, this is your chance, she can stay here with you and you alone. You'd be able to show her what she means to you." Again Dana was caressing the side of Presley's face. "Imagine how much better the real thing is when all you've known is your doll. And haven't you been trying to separate her from Trent Hayes for a while now? It's done, she's yours, Michael."

Mike considered what Dana was offering. This wasn't exactly the deal they had in mind, Dana was only supposed to show up to town and rattle Presley's cage a bit so she had to come to Mike for help. All he wanted in this deal was for Presley to come running to him, needing him, wanting him. He knew he wouldn't be able to arrest Dana right now and just claim to be the hero when Dana had so much blackmail on him. He had been so careful to keep all of that hidden, and now she could expose him quicker than he could draw his gun. His goal was to get Presley physically away from Trent and this would do it, as Mike pondered, he walked towards the couch. Presley looked so peaceful, aside from the zip ties around her hands and feet. Mike dropped to his knees by the couch and brushed his fingers through her hair. He wanted to lean in and kiss her; her mom knew plenty of his shameful secrets already, what would it matter if he kissed her while she was passed out? Instead, Mike rubbed his hand from Presley's hair all the way down the side of her body, not missing any of the curves. Once he reached her hips, he reached back to feel her backside, it made him lose his breath entirely. Rather than have Dana watch him continue to work himself up with the thought of Presley's body, he gave her cheek one last, soft squeeze and then rubbed his hand back up her body.

Dana watched, smugly knowing full well she would be getting exactly what she came for.

Mike momentarily came out of his trans. "Where's Baron?" He knew Presley would crumble if anything happened to her dog.

"Oh, he's fine," Dana assured him. "He's at the cottage still." She shook her head. "I can't believe she didn't have him outside with her when we picked her up, very unusual but fortunate for us. We figured he'd have to be dealt with, but he wasn't even out there."

"Did you hurt her?" Mike scowled.

Dana didn't seem phased. "I wasn't physically there, but I was told it was quick and painless, just a bit of chloroform and a little hood. She wasn't much of a match for the two hired hands I sent."

"If there is a single scratch or bruise on her body, I'll be coming for them." Mike threatened.

Dana laughed. "Such steep threats, Michael. I'll have to let my men know because I am confident that if anyone would notice any changes to her body, it would be you."

Mike stood up; he leveled his gaze at Dana. "So, what's the next move then? And make it quick because I need to go make an appearance at the set soon. And obviously go get some supplies if we're staying here."

Forty

"Hey, sweetheart." Trent wasn't expecting to hear from Presley since she knew he was on set, especially not a phone call.

"Trent." Presley's voice was weak and trembling, she sounded far away from the phone.

Trent's heart raced when he heard her voice. "Presley? Baby, what's wrong? Are you okay?"

Presley tried to stop crying so she could talk to him. "No," she cried, and her voice cracked. "Trent, I don't know where I'm at… I'm scared."

Michelle had watched Trent answer his phone. She was ready to tease him for his infatuation with his new girlfriend, but instead she watched his face and immediately picked up on his worry.

Trent's words were rushed as he started to panic. "Babe, what happened?" Trent noticed Michelle watching and he put his phone on speaker. "Pres, baby, are you hurt?"

"Trent, I need help, I don't know what happened." She cried into the phone. The crew had taken notice, and they all stopped their chatter and were now listening to Trent's call.

"Pres, I want to help you, can you FaceTime me? Baby, I need to know where you're at." Trent tried to return his tone to a neutral one, but he felt an absolute pit in his throat that was making it extremely difficult. "Pres, what do you see around you?"

"Trent." She sobbed hard enough to make her words difficult to make out. "I don't know, I don't know this place."

"Get security in here *now*." Trent tried to whisper to Phil who nodded and immediately ran to the other room to make the calls.

"Baby, listen to my voice, I'm here Pres." Trent grabbed his forehead and tried to take a deep breath before he continued. "Tell me what you remember, how did you get there?"

"Baron!" Presley wailed into the phone. "Where's Baron? Trent, I don't know where he is." She frantically cried out. "Is he still at the cottage?! Trent, please check." Presley continued to sob.

He didn't give it a second thought before he took off towards the cottage. "Pres, I need you to tell me what happened, baby take some deep breaths." He was in a full sprint headed down to the cottage. The run did the exact opposite of calming him down at all; every one of his nerves was on alert as his concern of where Presley was continued to terrorize him. "I'm running to the cottage to see if Baron's down here. Pres, I need to know where you are, what happened?"

Trent could hear Presley trying to breathe, but she was still sobbing so each of her inhales sounded jagged. He was getting closer to the cottage and heard barking, it didn't quite sound like Baron though. Trent hopped onto the porch and punched in the code. It was Baron barking, but it seemed like he had been barking for hours and as a result, was very hoarse and panting heavily.

"Pres, he's here, Baron's here, I've got him, he's okay." Trent made sure Baron stayed in the cottage and he knelt down to rub his sides to try to calm the distraught pit bull.

Presley cried out. "You promise? He's not hurt, he's home?"

"I promise, I'm looking at him right now, he's upset, but he's here." Trent ruffled Baron's head before the distressed canine went straight to the door, pacing and whining. "Presley, I need you to focus, baby, what happened? I need to come get you, I need to know what happened." He repeated.

"Trent, someone grabbed me." She cried. "I just went outside for a second to put trash out." She wiped her eyes on the couch despite its smell. "I didn't even see or hear anyone and then something was over my face." Her voice trailed off as her cries were taking over again.

Trent felt lightheaded, he had to battle the fear that now lived in him to try and help his girlfriend. "Did you go into a car, babe? Did you hear anyone's voice?"

"I don't know," she cried out. "I don't remember anything else." She fumbled around trying to keep her phone from slipping into the crevasse of the couch. She had used all of her strength to even manage the phone from her pocket.

"What do you see around you right now?" Trent paced with Baron on his heels.

"It's like a cabin… I'm on a couch… baby, I don't want to be here." She blubbered a bit before she could find enough of her voice to continue. "I'm tied up, Trent. I can't even get up or turn over and I don't want to drop my phone again." Her head felt groggy, and her wrists and ankles were already sore from all the pulling and moving she had been doing since waking up. "I'm trying to get out of these but my wrists are just so… they're so… Trent, I just want to be at home with you," she wailed.

Trent hunched over and held his knees, *holy fuck*, he felt tears forming on his face but suppressed the knot in his throat to talk her through. "I want you home and in my arms, baby. I want to come get you. Pres," Trent paused as a few people were coming through the cottage door. It was Michelle and Pete with a few private guards from the production. Somehow Trent was relieved Mike wasn't there, if he was being honest with himself this situation did seem like something Mike was capable of. "Pres, baby, I'm going to find you, I'm going to come get you." He promised.

They could all hear Presley crying. Pete held Michelle tightly while the guards encouraged Trent to set his phone on the kitchen island so they could record and hook up various devices to it.

"Pres." Trent took a deep breath. "Can you remember where you were when they took you?"

One of the guards nodded his head at Trent, encouraging these types of questions.

"Behind the cottage." Her voice was cracking again. "I just stepped outside for a second to put the trash away."

Two of the guards walked through the cottage to investigate the scene.

"That's good, baby." Trent nodded his head. "Pres baby, take a couple breaths with me." Trent needed them just as much as she did.

"Trent!" Presley bawled his name.

He finally broke, he felt helpless, and he couldn't hold back tears anymore. His body bent over, and his arms were on the kitchen island with his head resting on his forearms. He felt Michelle reach out to him and put her hand on his back. "Pres," he choked out and tried to hide his emotions. "Pres, sweetheart, we're going to find you, I promise. Just stay with me on the phone, baby." He stood up straight. "Listen to my voice and breathe with me, okay?" He steadied his own breath.

"Okay." She strained just before terror struck her voice. "Trent, someone's here!" Her breathing was hysterical. "Someone is coming, I have to go." Presley began hyperventilating.

"Pres, no!" Trent desperately shouted. "Don't hang up, baby, stay on the phone with me!" Trent's voice was hurried, and he could feel a frantic shaking shooting throughout his body as they listened to Presley's cries muffle and finally it sounded like the phone fell somewhere. "Pres! Pres, baby!" Trent anxiously tried again. He remembered she said she was on a couch, maybe the phone just slipped. He hit the mute button on his end so none of their conversation could be heard by whoever just entered that room if she did drop the phone.

One of the security guards was the first to speak. "We need to get the location of that phone, keep that line open. Does she share her location with you?"

Trent gravely shook his head as they listened.

Presley was still crying, but they weren't able to hear it as clearly.

"Sounds like someone's up." A voice called out. No one recognized the voice.

It sounded like there was more than one person, but they couldn't clearly make out the voices.

"Trent," Michelle bumped his shoulder. "Maybe Jake and Lisa have her location?"

Trent's face lit up. "Yes." He reached for his phone. "Shit." He couldn't kill the line and even at that, he didn't have their phone numbers.

"I'll go outside and see if I can get a hold of one of them through their social media." Michelle whispered. Trent thanked her and watched as both she and Pete went outside with their phones to try to contact the Hofners.

"Hey there, Sleeping Beauty." The unfamiliar voice was much closer now. "We were wondering when you'd join us."

Presley didn't say a word.

"Even with all that worrying, you're still a looker. Got a fine ass too."

"Hey," a second voice was in the room. "We've got a little time before the others get here, let's clean her face up and have some fun?"

Presley burst into tears.

Trent's heart pounded, he felt an uncontrollable surge of rage brewing as he listened and couldn't do anything. His world was about to shatter, this could *not* be happening, not to his sweet, strong, glowing girlfriend. Presley had been the best thing to ever happen to him. He felt like his insides were ripping away from his body as he listened helplessly.

"You're scaring her." The original voice spoke up again, closer to wherever her phone was. "Sleeping Beauty, don't you worry." He reached down for a piece of Presley's hair. "We've seen your videos, neither of us are packing what your fuckbuddy does, we won't hurt you."

"Please don't touch me." Presley managed, her voice sounded so defeated; it was purely a plea, like a bunny begging a lion for mercy.

Trent's frustrated rage swelled as he heard Presley's broken tone begging to be left alone. The fury escaped his body as he screamed out and threw his fist through the kitchen wall of the cottage.

Michelle came running back inside as Trent was pulling his hand from the drywall. "She's got a lock on her!" Michelle waved frantically with Lisa on speaker.

"Lisa!" Trent's chest felt slight relief. "Where is she? She needs us right *now*!"

There was a lot of scratching and ruffled noises coming from Trent's phone and all they could hear was Presley sobbing and two men laughing.

"She's got a feisty side." One of them laughed. "It's kinda hot."

Michelle's face went white with dread when she realized what they were listening to.

Lisa was frantically screaming into the phone now. "Presley! No, what's going on?! What's happening?!"

"We have to go *right fucking now*!" Trent demanded while kicking in one of the cupboard doors on the island in another surge of unmanageable anger and misery.

A black Suburban pulled up in front of the cottage and the security guards ushered everyone towards the door to go. Trent was sure to bring Baron with them. They all piled in the truck and continued to listen as they raced up the lawn to try to find Presley's location.

✦

"Please, no!" Presley sobbed again.

"Oh, not only is it fine, it's a firm little ass." One of the men was kneeling over Presley as she was pinned face down on the couch, he had both of his hands consuming her backside. "You can wait your fucking turn to feel it." He swatted his partner's hands away. "Why don't you make yourself useful and get the ties off her legs so I can spread them."

Presley heard a belt unclasp and she tried her best to pry herself away from her attacker, her cries were more frantic now. "No, no, please don't!"

Her begging was interrupted by a gunshot, her pleas immediately turned into hysterical screaming, and then, they all heard a second gunshot.

Everyone in the car went silent, Trent grabbed his face and leaned over in his seat, everything was spinning, he couldn't breathe.

Presley started screaming even louder, the panic in the sounds that were coming from her echoed on Lisa's end and Trent wanted to throw up. Suddenly, they heard a familiar voice.

"Pres, calm down."

She was still bawling and shrieking.

"Pres," he tried again. "It's over, they're not going to hurt you. Shhh, shh…"

Officer Bando. Trent knew the voice, clear as day.

✧

"Presley." Mike had shoved the man who landed on the couch with Presley onto the floor and then he sat her up to put her in his arms. "I'm here, you're safe."

She hadn't said a word yet, she was in hysterics.

"Shhh," Mike rocked her. "You're safe."

"Mike?" She finally managed. "How…," she stuttered. "H-how did you find me?" She sobbed, "I don't know what happened, they were…"

He cut her off. "I know, Pres." He petted her hair. "They won't touch you now. I got here just in time."

Presley was shaking uncontrollably. "Can you…," her teeth were chattering wildly. She had to dig deep to get enough of her voice back in between the violent, involuntary spasms thrashing throughout her body. "Mike, can you get me out of these?" She held her hands up. "Please?" She had been struggling so much with the zip ties that her wrists were bleeding. "They're cutting my wrists and they're on my legs too." She cried with an unsteady voice. "They're so tight."

"Pres." Mike put her hands back down into her lap and covered her hands with one of his, he didn't answer her right away.

Presley started to realize Mike wasn't in a hurry to free her. Any relief she found after her assumed captors were taken care of completely fleeted from her body. She watched Mike hold his gun in one hand and the other was now lightly gripping her upper thigh.

"Mike?" Presley's voice shook.

Something was wrong, a pin could've dropped in the Suburban and every single one of them would have heard it. What was going on? Trent looked at Michelle's phone where Lisa was projecting Presley's location, and he just prayed they'd be there in time.

Forty-One

"Mike?" She tried again, her voice still breaking. "Can you take these off my hands, please?"

Mike stood up, he holstered his gun, which did ease Presley slightly. But he didn't answer her, he looked down at the bodies. He warned Dana what would happen if they hurt her, he didn't expect they'd be doing what they were when he showed up at the cabin earlier than expected though. He was still trying to calm his heart rate, if he had been even a minute later than he was, things could have been much worse. The bodies lying on the floor didn't bother him, after the military and working in law enforcement, he had seen his fair share of dead bodies, just not any up close that had ended by his hand. There wasn't even any movement in either of them as he had executed two perfect headshots. He came out of his daze and realized Presley was still crying and asking for the ties to be taken off, but he made no move to do so for her. He stood there watching, waiting.

"How much longer?" Trent demanded.

"ETA is about fifteen minutes." Jones, one of the guards, admitted. "Her exact location may be a little tricky."

"Like hell!" They heard Lisa shouting. "We know the place! We used to party up there in high school. She's at the old McFadden cabin, it's literally where the ping is taking you. It's in the woods, but the tracker will take you right to it!"

"Press on the fucking gas and get her the fuck out of there!" Jake himself was ignoring every traffic signal and speed limit sign as they raced from Seattle.

"She said she doesn't know where she is, are you guys sure?" Trent didn't want to waste time going to the wrong location.

"It's been almost ten years, and it was a dump when we used to go, it may not look the same." Jake reasoned. "But the location pin is exactly where that cabin was. I'm sure of it."

Trent's leg shook uncontrollably, and Baron was nervously pacing in the cargo area of the Suburban.

✦

"What the hell happened here?" A female voice asked, it wasn't Presley, but the voice also didn't seem to be shaken by the scene.

"Your fucking guys!" Mike's voice was loud, and he was moving away from the phone. "I told you, if they fucking hurt her, I'd be coming for them." He pointed his finger right in Dana's face. "I'm only sorry I didn't drag their deaths out, that's what they fucking deserve for what they were planning to do to her."

Dana smiled. "They did always have that proclivity, I guess I should've thought better about bringing them in for this." She continued her way into the cabin and looked to find Presley's eyes. "I owe that much to my precious Presley, right, honey?" She was now in full view of her distressed daughter.

The wind knocked right out of Presley's lungs, "Mom?"

✦

"That fucking bitch!" Jake was going ballistic. "I can't fucking believe this! She's dead, *fucking* dead!" His speed increased even more.

Forty-Two

"Hi Presley, honey." Dana spoke with an unbothered tone; she walked over to Presley and held her chin. "Oh Michael, you're being dramatic, they hardly touched her. These marks on her are self-inflicted." Dana looked down at Presley's wrists.

A steady stream of tears was running down Presley's face.

"This one has his fucking pants down still!" Mike pointed at one of the bodies that now had a very large pool of blood around his head. "So, spare me your bullshit, Dana, they did plenty."

Dana held both sides of Presley's face. "But honey, your pants are still on, so I guess no harm no foul, right?"

Presley couldn't bring herself to look into her mom's eyes, she closed hers hoping when she opened them this would all just be a nightmare that she could wake up from.

Dana stood and rolled the pantless man over with her foot. "And look how tiny that poor man's dick is, Presley, honey." She swatted Presley's shoulder. "You wouldn't have even noticed that little poke." She looked at Mike. "Michael, honestly, you and I both know from your little videos that Trent is at least double, if not triple that size."

✦

Videos? This was the second time videos had come up suggesting intimate footage of Presley and Trent. *When the fuck did anyone get anything like that? And what did it have to do with her mom?* Trent helplessly sat in angst hoping they got to Presley sooner than later. He looked at the clock again knowing they were close, but he wasn't sure what kind of time they had.

✦

Presley wondered about the video comment, *what videos were people talking about?* But she stayed silent, she just needed to buy some time, she knew Trent would be looking for her.

"Dana." Mike warned through clenched teeth.

"Oh, that's right, we're keeping that little secret between us." She took a seat in an old wooden chair next to the couch.

Presley couldn't look at her mom or Mike. Looking down only provided a direct view of the men who were just attacking her, now lifeless and bleeding out—she didn't want to look at them either. She tried to focus on her wrists through her blurred vision, not that the sight of her injured wrists gave her any relief at all. At that point all she could be grateful for was the fact that her black yoga pants were disguising the blood coming from her wrists.

Dana took a deep inhale before she began. "Presley, honey, I truly don't enjoy doing all of this, but you just haven't been listening to reason." She opened the folder that was on the coffee table. "I have been patient, and quite civil, especially given what an arrogant asshole your lawyer is. But you just continue to be, quite frankly, a selfish and entitled bitch, with the family business." Dana checked Presley's expression before continuing. "I have tried to do this through the courts, but at this point, honey, I'm willing to simply make a deal of our own so we can settle everything once and for all."

Presley, through her tears, finally looked at her mother; she didn't meet her eyes for long before she turned her focus to Mike. "You helped her with all of this?" Presley knew if she could break either of them, it would be Mike, her mom was a soulless piece of work.

"Pres." Mike sat next to her and tried to hold her restrained hands. "I promise, it wasn't supposed to be like this, things got fucked." He reached for Presley's hair and tried to offer a comforting sweep of it behind her ear. "I would never hurt you, Presley." Her reflexes jerked her head away the second his hands met her head, and Mike shot an icy glare towards Dana.

Presley struggled to be free of the hold Mike had on her leg and then she tried to scoot away from him on the couch.

Dana laughed. "Oh, Michael, I guess your fantasies of her running straight to you for safety and comfort wouldn't have worked out in your scenario either, now would it? I mean, you said yourself, my guys did plenty, and yet she isn't even showing any gratitude."

"Mike?" Presley couldn't even look at either of them. "Why would you work with her to hurt me like this?"

Mike's leg had been shaking and he finally stood up, his voice booming. "Why?!" He held his arms out. "Why the fuck do you think?! Presley, I have tried so hard to give you *everything*! I've always been there for you! Always fucking watching out for you!" Mike was getting closer to her again, still yelling as saliva flew towards Presley. "I know everything about you and still it's never fucking been enough for you!" He held her shoulders and spoke directly in her face. "I love you, Presley, and would do any goddamn thing to be with you." He stood back up with anger in his eyes. "I've been right here all these years, and you have never given me a single fucking chance." He snarled.

Presley didn't look up, she didn't feel bad about not wanting to be with Mike, but the last thing he needed to hear was her agreeing with him. He did still have a firearm on him after all and she was still bound with no way to escape. The tears she was shedding now were out of fear that she was trapped with two of the most unpredictable enemies. She didn't know what kind of strings her mom was capable of pulling with Mike. It seemed like, despite Mike being armed, her mom had the upper hand. Mike had always made her uneasy, but now, after what she had seen in just the last ten minutes, she honestly didn't know what he could be capable of.

Dana shook her head while flipping through her paperwork, not looking up at either of them as if the whole situation was completely beneath her. "Like I said, selfish and entitled bitch."

Mike's head moved back and forth with his hands on his hips.

"Now," Dana wanted to get down to business. "This is what's going to happen, honey." She gathered each of the pages that required Presley's signature. "All of these pages here need to be signed by you. Now, full disclosure, because I want to be transparent in this deal, I did have a few of the terms changed up a bit since our last offer." She sarcastically laughed at her. "You know, because I've had to wait so long and pay out the ass for attorney's fees thus far; not to mention, I had to come all the way out here. I figured it was only fair to get a little more from you."

Dana slid the papers towards Presley who didn't look at them, she sat in silence until she felt another resurgence of tears. "I don't know why you're doing this." Presley cried. "My Dad *loved* you and you just left, you left me…" She gathered as much of her broken voice as she could and finally looked at her mother with tears streaming down her face. "You didn't want us. Everything that company has become is because of Dad and Paps, you don't deserve any of it. How can you feel right taking any of that from me?"

She smiled and clicked a pen for Presley. "Oh, but I do deserve it, honey. I spent a whole eight years with your father, I put in my time, even gave him a kid that he so desperately wanted, and now I'd like to be paid for that." She reached out and tried to hold Presley's hands.

Presley pulled her hands away from Dana. "You're taking everything I have left of them." Her voice was quiet and heartbroken.

"Oh honey, you've known for a couple years that house would be mine, don't try to play the victim now. And you don't need to worry. You know my husband Toby is in this industry too; we'll take excellent care of the company." She tried to assure her with her tone. "And we have already discussed you staying on. I mean, until the deal completely merging the two companies goes through, it kind of makes sense to have someone with the family name still on the payroll. We'll even provide you with a stipend that we deem appropriate for you." She looked up. "Given you'll be living here now, I don't think you'll need much."

"What?" Presley's heart pounded in fear, and she looked up at Dana.

Dana's mouth formed a wicked smile, and she slowly shifted her gaze to Mike. "Michael, can I tell her?" Dana was thoroughly enjoying herself.

Mike just glared at her, he was still pissed at Presley, but now it would be much easier to keep her here and not feel bad about it. Mike crossed his arms and continued to focus on Dana.

"Well," she tossed her head from side to side. "I may have changed the plan a little, I'll admit that much. Honestly, Michael here isn't much of the masterminding type, he's just for looks, obviously. When he called me about the fire investigation, an idea sparked, no pun intended, honey." Dana walked over to Mike and reached her arm under his to continue. "During the initial phone call, I couldn't help but get the sense that there was something else there between him and my bitch for a daughter." She released Mike's arm. "So, I did some investigating of my own. I even came out here to spend some time with his mom, fine lady, Mrs. Phyliss Bando is." Dana smiled at Mike. "And during our chat, my men," she gestured to the two corpses, "found some very interesting evidence to support my inclination about your relationship."

Presley was confused, *they'd never had a relationship, what evidence of anything between them could she have possibly uncovered?*

Dana continued, "We aren't talking details about that though, are we, Michael?"

Mike didn't budge, he cut through her with his glare and then looked at Presley.

"Honey, it just sounds like you haven't given him the chance he deserves." She rubbed Presley's shoulder which she tried to squirm away from. "So, I elevated the original plan, which was Michael's, and he just wanted us to scare you so you'd need his help in trying to arrest me." Dana laughed. "Can you imagine?"

She looked back and forth between Presley and Mike, no one gave her the satisfaction of a response.

"I just figured if I got you here instead, it would benefit both of us. I can get my well-deserved deal executed, and Michael here can be assured he will get what he's always wanted. Honey, I've seen you with Trent, there was no way Michael here would have been capable of getting between you two all by himself, he needed me. So, as a token of gratitude for this alliance Michael and I have made, I am presenting you to him. The two of you can have some focused time now on one another and really explore all the plans he has for you guys and your future together. It'll align perfectly with us no longer needing you at the company, you'll be able to retire and focus solely on raising babies here with Michael."

Presley's face was horrified, they were just going to lock her up in this abandoned cabin? "I'm not staying here." She cried, her voice was hoarse, "I can't, I don't want to." She shook her head feverishly, and then looked at Dana. "I have people who will look for me—Trent will find me!"

Trent's heart ached as Presley cried, but she was right, he was absolutely coming for her. *Just hang on a little bit longer, sweetheart, I'm coming*, he tried to send her through the universe.

Mike laughed at that. "You think so, huh? You don't think he'll just move along to another set of open legs, we all know that's his fucking specialty. And honestly, you've been a lot of drama lately Presley, in fact, a lot of drama since they started filming. He's not going to keep putting up with that shit, especially when he moves on to his next movie. You'll just be another notch in his fucking belt like he planned. I know you think you mean something to him with all that girlfriend bullshit he's now spinning, but that's all for show so he can keep fucking you. He doesn't love you."

Presley knew in her heart that wasn't true, none of it was true. Trent hadn't told her he loved her, but she felt loved by him. Presley found a calm in her weak voice even while her face was soaked in tears, "You're wrong about him. You've always been wrong about Trent."

Dana laughed, "Oh Michael, you have quite the task ahead erasing him from her memory. I told you she's really fallen for that huge cock of his."

"I'm not worried." Mike challenged. "He would never love her the way I do, she'll see."

Presley knew she had to keep them all talking. Talking meant she wasn't being physically harmed, talking meant she could be buying time for hopefully someone to find her, talking was the only thing she had to help herself right now, no matter how small the impact overall would be. "What about Baron? Mike, you know what he means to me. Where's my dog?"

Mike opened his mouth to say something, but Dana cut in. "Oh honey, that's the other really good news. I'll be taking over ownership of Baron, you'll get weekly pictures of him if Michael here reports good and cooperative behavior from you."

Presley knew Trent already had Baron. She knew he'd never let her take him, but she didn't want to show her hand; they couldn't find out that she had her phone. "No," her face melted into a frown. "I won't agree to that, I'll give you whatever you want, but you're not taking my dog!"

"Honey," Dana leaned in, inches from Presley's face. "We already have him." She lied with a deadly calm to her voice. "You don't think we dealt with him too when we picked you up?" She held out the pen. "So, if you want him to live with me instead of sitting in an urn on my fireplace, I suggest you get to signing."

Mike didn't like this tactic, he knew what Baron meant to Presley, but the sooner these papers were signed, the sooner he could be alone with Presley to sort all of this out.

Presley's eyes watered, but she took the pen, and Dana swiftly pushed her hands away. "Oh, Presley!" Dana looked at her wrists. "Honest to God, I can't have you bleeding all over these documents." She turned to Mike. "Michael, do you have something to cover the bottoms of her wrists so she doesn't get blood everywhere?"

Mike looked around, there wasn't much in the cabin, he reached down to one of the bodies and ripped part of a shirt off of one of them. "Here." He offered it to Dana.

Dana lowered her chin and smiled at Mike from under her brows. "Oh, I wouldn't dare take away the pleasure of touching her from you." Her head flicked towards Presley quickly. "Why don't you hold that around her wrists while she signs?"

Presley's wrists stung the second Mike wrapped them, she sucked in air when he applied pressure, and she really looked into his eyes for the first time that night. She hoped it would change Mike's course seeing the pain in her eyes. For a split second she thought it was working, Mike's eyes softened a bit, but not enough.

"Pres, you have to stop pulling on these, it's only going to make it worse." His voice was much calmer than it had been.

"Mike," she pleaded. "They're too tight."

"I'll fix them later, Pres." Mike rubbed his thumbs on her forearms as he held the shirt around her wrists.

"The quicker you sign, the quicker that can happen." Dana pushed the papers closer to Presley again, "Here, I'll move these around, you just sign."

Presley stayed locked on Mike's eyes a bit longer, still holding a shred of hope that he would change his mind about what he was doing. The longer she watched him the more comfortable he got in caressing her arms with his thumbs. She wanted him off her, so she gave up and looked down at the papers Dana had.

"Just so you know." She signed the first paper. "This contract will never stand, my arrogant asshole lawyer will make sure of it." She continued signing.

"And if he does," Dana got uncomfortably close to Presley's face and threatened her with a smile. "I guess we will be sending you a picture of your dog's ashes."

Forty-Three

"There's a car up ahead," Marco pointed out.

"Let me out!" Trent reached for the door handle.

"No." The guard was firm. "Mr. Hayes, we can't let you do that, there's a hostage in there and at least one firearm."

"I don't give a single fuck." Trent leaned closer to the front of the truck as his voice got louder. "That hostage in there is the love of my life!" He declared. "Like fuck if I'm just gonna sit here while she needs me!"

Michelle and Pete's hands tightened around each other. Lisa and Jake were silent on the line, Presley hadn't mentioned either of them declaring their love for one another.

"Sir," Marco turned around in his seat, and took a deep breath. "Hold tight, we will devise a plan where you can come with us, but we need to be smart about this so everyone can leave that cabin in one piece."

"You have about thirty fucking seconds before I rollout a plan of my own." Trent warned. "Presley is the *only* person in there I care to have come out in one goddamned piece."

They decided to park the Suburban up the road, Michelle and Pete were to stay in the car, with Baron and Jones. The Suburban would be at the end of the road and Jones would stop anyone from fleeing the scene. Trent and two other guards, Marco and Schwartz would go by foot to the cabin.

"We don't have another earpiece, but you're wearing a vest." Schwartz demanded and handed one over to Trent, he quickly put it over his head and fastened the velcro. "And, have you ever used a firearm with live rounds?"

"Yes." Trent confidently nodded his head.

"Glock 17." Schwartz handed the gun over and Trent quickly racked it to be sure there was a bullet in the chamber. "And here's another magazine. Do not fire unless you are willing to kill someone, this isn't a movie." The guard leveled his gaze at Trent. "Are you good, Mr. Hayes?"

"Yes." Trent held his finger on the side of the Glock and pointed it towards the ground as he headed down the dark dirt path towards the cabin. "Let's go."

"Michelle?" Lisa was crying into the phone, "What's happening?"

Trent and the two guards were lost to the darkness.

"Lis," Michelle's voice was shaking. "Trent and two of the guards are going in to get her. Baron is here in the car safe with us."

"Oh, thank God." Lisa let out a large exhale but was still crying.

"I'll keep you as updated as I can, I just can't see anything. We do still have Trent's phone though, she's still in there, they're all still inside."

"Well, see now, honey, wasn't that easy?" Dana verified the signatures and then stacked the papers neatly back into her folder. "This could've been taken care of two years ago, you know."

Presley didn't bother to look her way.

"Michael," Dana stood up and reached her hand out to him. "It was a pleasure working with you, I trust you can take care of this mess you created?" She looked down at her two men, who she clearly had no attachment to. "Don't be sloppy, Michael, we're still partners." She winked indicating she had more than enough to bury him if he tried to make a move against her.

Mike offered a quick nod of his head.

"Good then." She reached up to his shoulder. "Please do send me pictures of my grandkids when they arrive, I know you have your heart set on two."

Presley tugged on the zip ties around her hands and ankles, all she was doing was cutting herself even deeper at this point, but she could not allow herself to simply be left here with Mike, alone.

✦

"Hayes." Marco instructed Trent while they were under the cover of a few bushes across from the entrance of the cabin. "The Mom is coming out. Let her be, Jones will get her before she hits the highway. Not a single sound." He warned.

Trent had a look that could kill smeared on his face, but he shook his head in agreement.

The guards were still able to hear inside the cabin through their earpieces, and like clockwork, the cabin door opened and out stepped Dana. Trent's heart was pounding, she shut the door too quickly to be able to see anything inside, but it didn't stop him from raising his sights to Dana.

"Hayes." Marco harshly hissed.

Trent heard him but kept a steady aim, his finger still on the barrel of the gun and not on the trigger, so Marco watched without additional verbal warnings.

✦

"The female has been detained." Moments later Jones confirmed through the earpiece that Dana had been stopped before she fled.

Marco reached out for Trent's shoulder. "Jones has the mom, we are listening to them for our shot at getting Presley out without incident. You still with us, Hayes?"

"Yes." He said with chilling confidence. Trent wasn't completely confident he'd go along with their entire plan because he didn't know what would go through him when he saw Mike.

Forty-Four

"Presley." Mike locked the door and then walked over to the couch with her.

Her body recoiled from him. "Your mom would be so disappointed in you," she almost whispered.

Mike put his arm around Presley, not caring that she wasn't interested. "My mom adores you, so she's going to understand. And your mom seems to like me."

"That's not something to be proud of," she countered.

Mike looked down at her wrists, they were a mess and part of him did feel bad. "Pres, stop pulling on those, it's making it worse." He gently rubbed her forearms to avoid touching any of her open wounds.

"I want these off," she said softly.

"Pres, you know I can't do that." Mike rubbed her leg. "We just need a few days getting settled into this new lifestyle and then we can talk about taking those off."

Presley just looked down, she didn't know what to do, she was already afraid of being alone with Mike and now they were more alone than two people could ever be. The only person who truly knew the location was her mother, who wouldn't be helping her anytime soon; and for all she knew her phone had either died or hung up on Trent when it fell into the couch cushions.

Mike reached for her face, he stroked it a couple of times and tried to turn her to look at him. "Pres, will you look at me?"

Presley's face was stone, and she didn't budge towards him.

"Won't you just kiss me, just one kiss, Presley." Mike tried. "I have done a lot to get us here, I even *killed* for you, just one kiss, please?" His thumb continued to caress her face, despite the obvious disinterest Presley's body language was projecting. "I know it will feel like magic, you'll see, we've been meant to be for a long time. You just need to give it the chance we deserve, we belong together, love."

The sound of him calling her 'love' made Presley cringe, but she finally gained the energy to speak again, in a very soft tone, still not looking at him. "I've been through a lot tonight, Mike."

"You're right," he kissed her temple. "I'll get these guys outside and then come back in to get you all cleaned up, my love." He kissed the base of her neck which sent bile up Presley's throat. Once Mike had a taste of her neck he continued along until he reached her ear. His final attempt at changing her mind was a quick nibble of her earlobe as he reached up to cup her breast which elicited a new wave of crying from Presley. The realization sunk in deeper now that she was absolutely defenseless against him, all she had were her words and those wouldn't keep Mike at bay for long.

"Mike, please," Presley cried. "Please don't do that to me." She tried to turn her body to get his hand off her chest at the very least.

Mike pulled his face back but kept his hand on her breast, he started to massage it even more now and he felt his pants getting tighter. "Pres, I know you like this. Here, let me rub both of them, lover." He took full advantage of her hands being bound and he placed both of his hands on her breasts now. "You have no idea how long I've waited for you."

Presley sobbed. "Mike, stop, please."

Mike's hands were even more active, and he leaned in to nuzzle close to Presley's neck and hair, she felt him take a deep inhale. Presley felt sick.

Mike removed one of his hands and pulled Presley's hands onto his lap so she could feel how stiff his pants were. Mike's breath shuddered at her forced touch. "Pres," he whispered her name and started to thrust himself towards her bound hands.

She gritted through the pain of her wrists and pulled them away from him while sobbing. She tried to curl her body in another attempt to get his hands off her chest.

Mike allowed her to close in on herself, he rubbed her shoulders as he stood up. "I know, love, this is going to take some time, but you'll see." He leaned down and kissed the top of her head.

✦

"Marco, Schwartz, did you hear that? He's planning to remove the bodies; you should have a window soon." Jones notified them.

"Hayes," Marco gripped his shoulder. "I need you to hold your shit together. Officer Bando is about to come out of that cabin. Hold it the fuck together, do you hear me?"

Trent didn't acknowledge him; his gaze was fixed on the cabin door.

"Hayes, look at me *right now*." He shook his shoulder.

Trent slowly looked at Marco.

"I know what this means for you." Marco tried to level with him. "But Presley needs *you*, do you understand? Do not make a move on Officer Bando. He is going to come out with those bodies and Schwartz and I will detain him. Do you understand? No shots fired unless you are fired upon."

Trent just looked at him and gave a very stern nod.

"We need you to move to that bush over there." He pointed towards the cabin where there was a perfect hiding spot near the entrance. "When he's far enough away from the porch, slide in there and get your girl, we will handle him. Your only job is to get to Presley, do you understand?"

Trent nodded and took off to get closer to the cabin. He tried to suppress his desire to kill Mike the second he saw him; Presley needed him and he wouldn't let anything slow him down from putting her back in his arms. He situated himself against the side of the cabin, hidden from the door by a few shrubs. The broken window he was near allowed him to hear the conversation from inside the cabin clear as day.

"Presley, my love, I know it doesn't seem like it now, but you're gonna thank me one day for everything I've done for us." Mike was tugging on the heavier of the two bodies, he was just about to the door when he stopped to try to look her in her eyes. "We are going to create a very happy life and a beautiful family here, I promise. I'll be right back to give you another chest massage, I know how much you like those; it'll help relax you from such a long day, sweetie."

Trent could have blown a bullet in his head the second he stepped out of the cabin, but he closed his eyes and took a deep breath, picturing Presley in his mind. He had to keep his composure for about thirty more seconds before she was in his arms.

Mike opened the cabin door and made his way down the rickety porch steps, dragging the body with him.

Shit, Trent thought, *he's facing the goddamn door.* He looked up and saw Marco and Schwartz closing in behind Mike with their guns drawn, so he went for it.

"What the fuck are you doing here?!" Mike shouted; he dropped the dead man and reached for his firearm. "I'll kill you, mother fucker!"

"Trent!" Presley wailed as she saw him coming through the front door, he couldn't get to her fast enough. She tried to lift herself off the couch as he ran to her; her eyes blurring and a rush of hope finally surging through her.

Suddenly, a shot was fired and Trent dove over Presley, he had no idea who shot it or where it was headed. He covered her head and consumed her body with his, both lying on the couch now.

"Get down!" Schwartz yelled, as he kicked Mike's gun away from him and Marco wrestled him to the ground. "Stay the fuck down!"

Trent lifted himself up and checked Presley. "Sweetheart, are you okay?"

Presley sobbed in response, she couldn't believe he was there—he came for her, he found her. After everything that happened that night, nothing else mattered because Trent was there.

Trent jumped up with the gun in his hand when he heard someone racing up the steps.

"We're all clear out here," Schwartz confirmed. "How is she?" He walked towards them.

Trent lowered his weapon and instead put Presley back in his arms. "You have something to get these the fuck off of her?"

Schwartz reached into his vest and pulled out a pocket knife, he approached Presley calmly and slowly to release her from her plastic shackles. "Presley, can I?" He had his hand out but asked before he touched her.

Presley nodded and lifted her hands towards him. The second he touched her hands she jumped and jerked them back.

"I'm sorry," she managed.

"Pres, you don't have to be sorry." Trent held her face. "Let's get you out of those. I'm here, you're safe, okay?"

Presley slowly nodded her head and reached her hands out to Schwartz.

Trent held the bottom of her bound hands watching her hesitation again. "I'm right here with you, Pres."

Presley nodded her head again.

Trent touched his forehead to hers. "Sweetheart, just look at me, those will be off before you know it, okay? Just breathe."

"I'm sorry, Presley, I have to pull a little to cut you loose—it's not going to feel great." Schwartz knew with how tight the ties were he'd have to put a little more pressure on them than he'd like.

Trent maintained her eyes until the zip ties were off. The second her hands and legs were unbound Trent fully engulfed his girlfriend.

"Baby." Presley sobbed. "You came for me?" She was gripping his vest and his shirt, pulling him as close to her as she could.

"Of course I did, sweetheart." He kissed the top of her head and finally just picked her right up to be in his lap. "Pres," he exhaled relief. "I've never been so fucking scared in all my life." He squeezed her with the force of the thousands of hugs he'd given her the last few weeks. He wanted her to know he was truly there, and nothing was going to happen to her now, he needed her to feel safe in that moment.

Presley stayed in the comfort of his strong arms and continued to cry.

Trent couldn't help but release tears of his own. He kissed her head again. "You're safe now, Pres, I've got you, baby."

Presley tugged on the collar of his shirt in response, she could feel the velcro of his vest digging into her face but she didn't care, she just needed the comfort of him holding her. Their embrace was cut short when they heard yelling and growling out in front of the cabin. Trent shot up and put Presley behind him to go see what was happening.

"Shit, Baron! Heel!" Pete called but the dog wasn't listening, he had Mike on the ground. Marco finally reached down and grabbed Baron by his collar. The dog lunged again but Marco held firmly on him while Mike tried to catch his breath.

Presley's knees buckled but Trent caught her and slowly lowered them both to the ground. "Bare," she called out weakly.

He immediately ran for her and nearly knocked her over if Trent hadn't been holding her up. The three of them sat in the doorway of the cabin, Baron standing on Presley's thighs and licking her face. She sobbed into his chest and held Trent's hand firmly, it had been a long night.

Schwartz kicked dirt on Mike. "Get up, pussy, it's just a scratch."

Mike was writhing in pain, he had more than a scratch. Baron had lunged up and caught him on the shoulder, he managed to rip part of his ear once he was down and before Marco was able to grab him, Baron had made hamburger meat out of Mike's shoulder trap. He couldn't get up on his own since Marco had zip tied his hands.

"Ah fuck!" Mike yelled and continued to roll around on the ground, grunting out in pain. "Presley! Ah, Pres!"

Presley heard his voice and scrambled into Trent's lap. "He's coming!" Her voice was frantic, and her breathing sped up. "Trent, don't let him take me!" She wailed.

Trent stood up and brought Presley with him, he had her securely against his chest with her legs wrapped around his waist as she continued to cry out.

"Pres, you're safe." Trent backed up enough to shut the door, so Mike was on the other side. "He is *not* going to touch you, I promise you. I won't let you go."

Baron growled at the door as Trent tried to ease Presley.

"He's calling for me." Presley cried, her body shaking uncontrollably. "I don't want to be with him."

"I know, you don't have to. I'll keep you safe, Pres, you don't have to worry about him." Trent held her tight and rubbed her back with one of his hands.

They could still hear yelling outside, so Trent tried to hold Presley's head against his shoulder while covering her other ear and talking to her. "Babe, I've got you, you're safe," he continued to assure her.

Presley didn't ease her grip at all, she was trying to focus on Trent's voice.

Suddenly the door swung open, Trent relaxed when he saw Pete and Michelle.

Michelle had her phone out, "Here, she's here, she's safe!"

They immediately heard Lisa and Jake.

"Pres! Oh my god, Presley, are you okay?!" It was Lisa's voice first and Presley heard the frantic sobbing in her bestfriends tone.

"Pres, we're on our way, we're going to be in town in less than two hours," Jake called out.

"Thank you," Presley sobbed. "I love you guys," she continued to cry.

"Pres, we love you, girl, we're on our way!" Lisa assured her.

"Trent," Jake called out. "You there?"

"I'm here," Trent responded while he was still holding Presley.

"You are the fucking man, thank you."

"Anything for her." Trent pulled Presley even closer to him and kissed the side of her head.

Michelle took the phone off speaker to chat with Lisa privately.

"Pres, are you alright?" Pete asked even though she wasn't facing him, her face was still buried in Trent's neck and shoulder.

Trent offered him a flat smile.

"I'm better now," she sniffled. "Thank you."

"Sorry I let Baron loose." He grinned. "He's just too strong for my grip, I guess."

Trent smirked at his co-star turned friend.

Forty-Five

They got back to Presley's house and noticed the crew had been cleared out for the night. It really didn't make sense to have them there when the three cast members had taken off; Phil was waiting, however.

Pete stopped the Suburban right at the front doors. He had taken Michelle, Baron, Trent and Presley back while the guards waited for the State Police with Mike and Dana in cuffs. The Sheriff's Department were the first on the scene, followed by the ambulance, but Jake encouraged the State Patrol to also assist given Mike's involvement.

"Is everyone alright?" Phil rushed to the truck.

Pete nodded flatly and whispered. "Don't hug her, she doesn't seem like she wants to be touched."

Phil nodded his head to confirm.

"We're staying in the house tonight, okay, sweetheart?" Trent got out of the truck first and then turned back for her. Presley simply nodded her head, she didn't rush to get out, but Baron did, and he was already on patrol, sniffing every inch of the lawn and up the porch.

"Come here, babe." Trent picked her up with her legs wrapped around him and her head tucked on his shoulder, nestled into his neck.

"We put her Master Suite back together, everything in there is hers, and the equipment is gone." Phil gently let Trent know as he passed them. If they had to reshoot anything, they'd cross that bridge when it came. At this point, they had all the scenes in that area wrapped so Phil had the crew get things ready anticipating Presley wouldn't want to stay in the cottage anymore.

Trent thanked Phil with his eyes and walked her up to her bedroom with Baron on his heels.

"I need to take a shower," Presley whimpered.

"Of course," Trent squeezed her and walked into her bathroom. "Do you need me to get anything for you?" He set her down on the vanity bench and squatted in front of her.

Baron posted up on the bathmat, not willing to leave her side; Trent gave him a quick smile.

Presley shook her head. "Please don't go far." She reached out and held his hand.

Trent looked down at her torn-up wrists and his heart ached. "Pres, I won't leave you." He looked into her eyes. "I'm going to lock that door," he pointed towards the one that led to her closet. "And I'll be sitting right outside that one," he gestured towards the door that led to her bedroom. "Bare looks like he's staying." He looked into her eyes. "Babe, I promise I won't go far, just right outside this door, okay?"

"Okay," she confirmed with a soft, broken voice.

Trent started to get up, but Presley reached for him, she had tears in her eyes and held his hand. "Thank you, Trent."

"Sweetheart," Trent held her face in his hands. "You're welcome, I would do *anything* for you, Presley." She didn't shy away from his face being so close so he leaned in to kiss her, Presley accepted his lips with a noticeable sigh of relief as they connected. Trent rubbed the back of her head and kept their lips together until she moved. He wanted so badly to tell her he loved her right then and there, but she had been through a lot that night and he thought he should wait for her to get her bearings before dropping that on her.

✦

Pete, Michelle, and Phil all found Trent leaned up against Presley's bathroom door. They said their goodbyes as Trent thanked each of them.

Phil let them know they were going to be given a week-long break. Given things that had happened, he was willing to cut time somewhere else in the schedule, this incident warranted the break. When they left, Trent looked down at his phone. Presley had been in the bathroom for almost a half hour now and the shower had been on for at least twenty minutes, he didn't feel settled about that.

He knocked on the door and called out for Presley, no answer. He knocked again, but didn't hear anything so he slowly opened the door. Trent's heart broke a little more when he saw her. She was sitting in the middle of her massive shower, under two of the six showerheads, and she had her legs curled up with her arms around them and her forehead resting on her knees. Trent shut the door behind him and quickly walked into the shower; he felt the water to be sure it hadn't gone cold on her.

He squatted down to her. "Pres, sweetheart," he rubbed her shoulders. "Are you done in here?"

She just shook her head that she wasn't. Trent immediately decided to join her, he kicked his shoes off and stripped down. Presley melted into his arms when she felt him scoot in behind her. He had a leg on either side of her and she twisted to sob into his chest with her still folded legs resting on his left thigh.

"Baby," Trent kissed her head, "I am *so* sorry." He let out a large exhale as he felt a bulge in his throat. "Shit, Pres, I don't ever want to let you go."

"Trent," she cried out. "I was so scared."

"I know, Pres, I know." He rocked her in his arms. He didn't even want to think about a scenario where they'd been smart enough to realize she had her phone on her, or one in which she wasn't sharing locations with the Hofners, or one where she had to endure more than she had that night. Just the thought of anyone forcing themselves on her made him sick to his stomach and boiled his blood with pure rage. He would have killed someone that night if that had happened, there would have been no restraining him from Mike.

"Sweetheart, you were so strong, and you did so good," he kissed her forehead. "But I'm here now, you're safe, and you don't have to be strong right now."

Presley slowly lifted her head to look at him. "I know," her trusting eyes responded.

Trent didn't think twice this time. "Presley," he held her chin and looked into her eyes, "I love you."

She held his gaze and felt her heart swell at the words that just came out of his mouth. "I love you too, Trent." Presley reached up to connect their lips.

Trent held her face during the short but sincere peck.

Lisa and Jake didn't wait when they pulled up to Presley's, they had the code and let themselves in. They hadn't heard back from Trent and according to Michelle, they all had left the house almost an hour ago and Presley was in the shower. They headed towards Presley's room and heard the shower but didn't see Trent. Jake checked the bedroom and the closet but didn't see anyone, Lisa decided she would slowly open the bathroom door. Baron lifted his head when he saw the door move and got up to check it out, Lisa put her hand down to him letting him know it was just her. He didn't seem to mind and headed back for his bathmat so Lisa poked her head around the door.

Tears filled her eyes as she saw Trent holding her best friend on the floor of her shower. Presley was only partially visible because Trent had her completely consumed. Presley was in between his extended legs with her back to the door Lisa was at, she only saw the back of Trent's head because it had Presley's securely resting on his chest and his arms were firmly wrapped around her. They simply sat with the water falling on them. She decided to give them the privacy they needed, at least her friend was home, and she was safe.

"She in there?" Jake asked.

Lisa put her hand on her husband's chest. "They need a minute," Lisa's eyes were watering. Jake reached to her and held his wife, relieved that things were going to be okay.

Jake's phone was going off just moments later, he gave Lisa one last squeeze and then went down the hall to take it. Lisa headed to Presley's closet to get some cozy clothes ready for her once she got out of the shower. She set them on the bed and made her way to find Jake.

Forty-Six

THE GIRLS AND BARON WERE IN PRESLEY'S BATHROOM WHILE LISA tended to the wrist and ankle injuries that Presley refused to allow the paramedics to treat. While she had allowed and welcomed Trent's embrace, she was visibly upset at even the thought of anyone else touching her. Even as Lisa and Jake had approached her initially, she felt tense until their familiar bodies were embracing their best friend. Trent kept a watchful eye on Lisa working on Presley's injuries and only made his way downstairs to find Jake when he felt she was relaxed with Lisa's touch.

"Keep her bitch ass in her cell until someone from my firm is there." Jake's tone was anything but friendly. "I don't give a fuck what you have to do, she has absolutely no fucking rights tonight." There was a pause when Jake removed the phone from his ear and looked at the screen. "My guy will be there in ten minutes, his name is Hawthorne, be sure whatever piece of shit representation she has connects with my associate… Yes. Thank you." Jake hung the phone up and slammed it repeatedly on the bar top out on the back patio, and then quickly planted his face in his hands.

"You good, man?" Trent asked in an exhausted voice.

Jake lifted his head and looked at Trent, "Fuck!" He shook his head. "Shit's absolutely fucked."

"What do you mean? What's going on?" Trent's tone was wide awake now. He didn't understand how this wasn't just going to be open and shut, they had all been caught red handed.

"Some of this isn't exactly my swimlane." Jake admitted and took a firm wipe of his face from his forehead to his chin. "Obviously the contract that stupid cunt, Dana, made her sign is worth less than fucking toilet paper, but there's some other shit." Jake took a deep breath before he hesitantly looked up at Trent. "I've got one of the partners just about to be at the jail for the other piece because he knows a hell of a lot more than I do with these types of cases." He took another, heavier breath this time. "Fuck, man, I'd prefer you hear all of this from me, privately, before anything else." He shook his head. "And I'm really not sure how to tell Pres, but you guys need to know."

Trent immediately projected primal rage. "Mike's not fucking out, is he?"

"Fuck no," Jake clarified. "That sick fuck is still in the hospital, apparently his little pussy ass needs quite a few stitches. But he is under police, *state police*, custody." He clarified since none of them had full faith in the Sheriff's Office at the moment. "And I've got an undercover that we use at the firm from time to time just to be sure we track all of that piece of shit's movements. That mother fucker won't even have a bail option once Hawthorne has his say with the judge." Jake confidently predicted. "But I pulled Hawthorne in because Dana tried to dangle some bargaining chip bullshit with stuff she had on Mike. Obviously, we're not negotiating any fucking deals with that dumb cunt, and after what Mike did, we didn't need much to search his house." Jake paused and shook his head, "Trent." Jake stood up straight and looked him in his eyes. "That man is a *sick fuck*." He put his hands on his hips. "I know we never liked how he was with Pres, but...," he paused, trying to find the appropriate words. "It wasn't just some harmless crush." Jake's face moved on its own, he could feel his upper lip stiffen and there was a quiver in his cheek bone. "Trent, I can't even fucking stomach the fucked up shit I'm finding out."

Trent felt his own stomach churning and he could only imagine what his face was projecting. He wasn't able to form any words, so he looked at Jake for him to continue as he felt the speed of his breathing slowly climbing.

"His basement is a fucking shrine or some kinda shit of Presley. I'm talking pictures, *thousands* of them, most of which it doesn't look like she has any idea she's in a picture. Other pictures I know damn well were taken from my own social media, and I know I'm not the only account he took from. He has a box of fucking trinkets, including several pairs of underwear and swimming suits, which they'd obviously need to either test or outright ask Pres if they're hers to verify, but the obvious and unfortunate assumption is they all belonged to her. Partially used chapsticks, hair ties, a traveling size container of the perfume she wears—basically a bunch of shit that she'd easily overlook or assume she had misplaced. He even has empty coffee cups with her name on them like he's been digging through her fuckin trash or something just to have anything she's ever touched."

Trent was shaking with fury and rage, he felt his skyrocketing blood pressure pounding in his chest for an escape, and his hands started to tingle because he was clenching his fists so hard.

"Just all kinds of creepy fucking shit. Mike has also been watching you guys for weeks, he has this goddamn sadistic little video collection. The videos are very private and quite… Detailed from what I've gathered. He has cameras set up all over her place feeding right into his little dungeon of horrors. Complete with a fucking television and a masturbation station for all of those videos too." Jake didn't dive into more details right away, he wanted to see how Trent took this first wave.

Trent saw red, the clench he had on his jaw felt like he was capable of breaking every last one of his molars. He knew very well what Mike could have captured on his cameras over the last couple of weeks. Those moments were extremely private, and it was nothing to be shared.

"Jake." Trent's tone was ice cold. "Where are the cameras?"

"Honestly, I don't know where all of them are located. A team is coming out here to look for all of them, but they're gathering as much as they can from his house first. I do know there are cameras in the bedroom and the bathroom down at the cottage." He shook his head. "There is an obscene number of photos that look like screenshots of her in the cottage bathroom and there was bedroom footage on his basement television when they executed the search warrant." Jake paused for a split second. "Both of you are in that one…"

Trent wasn't concerned about himself, but he knew Presley had already been self-conscious when it was just her and Trent in bed, she had been steadily coming out of her shell with him. She would never want anyone beyond the two of them being privy to any of that intimacy. How was she going to react knowing Mike, and now possibly countless others, watched them? "What about her main house?" Trent gestured towards the second level. "They're in the fucking bathroom right now."

"I don't know, bro, I've been trying to get all the information I can. I've requested that they limit the number of people investigating the basement—it seems like that's where all the videos and pictures have been stored." Jake looked into Trent's eyes. "I know Pres, I know she's already been violated and tormented enough as it is, this is going to fucking send her, man."

"I can get over people seeing me, I don't give a shit about that." Trent's face was feral. "But not while I'm with her." He declared with a possessive tone in his voice. "I know Pres has some very vulnerable moments on that footage, I sure as shit don't want anyone, law enforcement included, seeing any of that! And in her fucking bathroom?! I can only imagine what kind of pictures and videos he has."

Jake shook his head. "I get it, honestly." He held his hands up. "I swear to you we're doing everything we can to minimize what gets leaked. I don't know who all Dana sent some of this to though. Her lawyer has already disclosed she had quite a few photos and videos on her cell. Look, I don't do girl talk with Pres, and my wife keeps that shit on lock, but I'm going to assume some of those videos aren't just of you two sleeping. I have some serious concerns on who Dana could've shared those with mainly because you're in them."

Trent didn't say anything, he was leaning on the railing of the back patio. He had done absolutely everything in his power to make Presley feel confident and comfortable with him. Despite all he'd done to try to be better for her, and protect Presley, it was his fame that may be partially responsible for her undoing.

Jake continued. "Look, I'm sorry to be such a dick with the what ifs, but if you've got some pull with your people to help us keep that shit the fuck out of the media's hands…," he got cut off by Trent.

"Absofuckingloutely," his head shook with surety. "I have contacts and resources to get in on that immediately. Whatever we can do to put a lid on things and minimize exposure." He didn't look up at Jake. "I remember you telling me how strong Pres is, hell, I know she's strong," he paused. "But I don't see her just bossing up on this topic." Trent finally looked at Jake. "We need to just bury all those videos because I do know exactly what's on them." Trent didn't want to draw it out for Jake, he was smart enough to know exactly what Trent was saying. "She's already been through an emotional living nightmare, has been physically violated, and she's barely goddamn hanging on as it is—people seeing those videos will fucking shatter her."

Jake knew Trent was spot on, he let that sit for only a brief moment before he continued reporting what had been found. "They also…," Jake felt guilty continuing, but had to fully disclose everything. "Uh," he let out a defeated breath and spit the rest of it out. "They found this goddamn life size sex doll that looks exactly like Pres." He shook his head and squinted his eyes. "Down to the goddamn freckles near her collarbone and the fucking tattoos on her back. If I didn't know any better, when they sent those pictures, I would have sincerely thought it *was* Presley."

Trent didn't want to think about the doll, he was obviously disgusted beyond comprehension, but his main concern was stopping the spread of any of the videos or pictures. Trent held his hands on his head and took a few small laps, trying to work out exactly how they were going to tell Presley this news.

"Jake," Trent looked him dead in the eyes. "I am going to kill that mother fucker."

Jake had seen Trent deliver threatening lines in movies, but seeing him right then, given the context, he truly wasn't sure how valid the threat was.

Forty-Seven

"Have them sweep the vehicles for any kind of tracking devices," Jake instructed someone from the private security company his firm had obtained for this case. Lisa was helping Presley pack a bag while Trent was getting Baron's things together and running interference with Jake as people were coming in and out of the house now. Morning light had hit about an hour earlier, so at least they had that on their side.

"I don't like leaving her house just open to whoever like this," Trent tried to lower his voice to Jake.

"I get it bro, but I have three guys here right now on our payroll. They know not to let shady shit fly. We have to get her out of here for a while."

"I know," Trent reluctantly agreed. "She doesn't need to see all this."

Presley and Lisa walked down the staircase with a couple of bags and Baron not far behind. Trent watched Presley's face as she scanned the foyer and watched all of the strangers buzzing around her house; she was visibly agitated.

"Here, babe." Trent reached for the bag she was carrying and replaced it with his hand.

"What's going on?" Presley worried.

Trent looked at Jake, they hadn't given Presley the full rundown of what was going on yet, just that they needed to head to the city for a couple of days to reset.

Jake shook it off. "Pres, we're just trying to be thorough, I want us to have everything possible to bury everyone involved." Not exactly a lie, but not the full truth either. Trent and Jake exchanged a look, they could live with that for now. Lisa noticed their exchange and shot her husband a look, he gave her a silent signal to discuss it later.

Presley just nodded and held on to Trent's hand even tighter while they walked out to the Hofner's Wagoneer. Trent loaded the last of the bags into the back and then slapped the tailgate for Baron to make his way up there.

Presley looked up at him, he could tell she was missing the glow in her eyes, and it killed him. Trent reached for her face and put it in his hands. Presley returned his gesture by putting her hands on his chest. They looked into each other's eyes for a long moment, it was Presley who made the first move and Trent welcomed it. They locked lips and both of their hearts finally found some serenity for the first time since everything happened. Trent massaged the back of Presley's head and reached for one of her hands to interlace their fingers, he felt Presley squeeze, so he rubbed her hand with his thumb.

"Baby," Presley looked up at him after their lips separated. "Are you sure you can come with me? I'll just stay at the motel with you if you can't leave work."

Trent let out a large breath, of course she was worried about someone besides herself. "Pres, sweetheart," he rubbed the side of her face. "Even if Phil didn't shut things down for the week, there's absolutely nothing out there that would keep me from you." His lips connected with her forehead for a long moment before he looked into her eyes. "I love you, Presley Williams," he held her face again. "I am *in love* with you, I have been for a while, and my place will always be with you, no matter what."

Presley's eyes watered. "Trent Hayes, I love you with my whole heart."

Trent engulfed her in his arms. "A love I will forever cherish."

"Is she asleep back there?" Lisa asked.

Trent petted Presley's hair again and looked at her face which had been lying in his lap since they hit I-5. This was the first time he noticed her eyes closed. "Yeah, she's out," he rubbed her shoulder. "For now, anyway."

"So, you boys want to fill me in on what else is going on?" She looked pointedly at her husband behind the wheel just as he was sneaking a glance at Trent through the rearview mirror.

Jake provided a full overview of what he and Trent talked about, in addition to other information he had picked up since they left the house. He also had a better direction for tackling the task of shutting down the distribution of the items found at Mike's, with Trent's manager and publicist also wanting to contain the story for him. They seemed to have a good handle on it. After Jake had finished Lisa sat silent, holding her mouth and looking out the passenger window. Trent continued to play with Presley's hair and scratch Baron's head since he had popped it over the seat and rested it on Trent's shoulder.

Jake's phone rang, which was connected to the bluetooth, Trent looked down and Presley's eyes had popped open.

"Hawthorne, one sec." Jake disabled the bluetooth and put the phone to his ear. "What's the latest?"

Trent continued to rub Presley's hair and shoulder, grateful Jake had at least made the conversation a little more private, but knew Presley was still going to be hanging on to every word coming from Jake's mouth.

"Yeah, no, you're spot fucking on, I'm good with that." Another pause. "Yeah, why don't you give me a call after that, and we'll touch base then… Yes, thank you, man, I owe you big… For sure, yep, bye." Jake put his phone in one of the cupholders.

"Honey," Lisa reached across the console. "Let's head home first, everyone needs something to eat, I'll make brunch."

Jake checked the rearview mirror at Trent who wasn't objecting. When he looked at his wife, he saw tears in her eyes so he picked her hand up to kiss it before he put their hands in his lap and stroked them with his thumb.

"Bare!" Bailey screeched as he ran down the hall towards his favorite canine who took full advantage of cleaning the leftover syrup from his face.

"Gah! That child." Becky, Bailey's babysitter, laughed as she made her way from the kitchen with a wet washcloth in her hands. "Bay, you definitely just lost the stay put game. Becks gets to pick our morning cartoon now, not Bay."

Lisa laughed at them. "Bay, honey, are you not listening to Becks?"

"He's actually been an angel all morning, up since five." She smiled at Lisa and caught up to the toddler to give his face a real wipe down. "Hey Bare," she scratched the top of the pit bull's head.

"Oh joy." Lisa rolled her eyes thinking about what a treat a sleep deprived Bailey was going to be after their sleepless night.

They lost Jake to the front yard when he took another phone call upon their arrival, but Trent and Presley were the next to walk through the mudroom and into the house where they were immediately greeted.

"Trent and Auntie PP?!" Bailey pushed off Baron and ran directly for them, he attached himself to Trent's leg.

Trent leaned down to pick him up and then put his other arm around Presley. "Hey, bro, missed you." Trent squeezed his little leg.

"Missed you." He hugged Trent around his neck and then looked at Presley. He extended his arms and did a trust fall into her. She caught him and Trent carefully held the rest of the toddler, so Presley didn't have to feel the weight of him on her already injured wrists.

Presley hugged Bailey as he sang, "and missed Auntie PP." He had her around her neck and played with her hair.

Presley's eyes watered and she squeezed him before he started pushing back to look her in the face. He sat upright, still in Trent's arms and staring at Presley with a worried look on his face.

"Auntie PP, is crying?" His brows furrowed. "And you're got ouchies?" He had noticed the bandages on her wrists.

Presley tried to clear her throat. "Auntie PP is okay." She fibbed and felt Trent's hand on her back.

Bailey gave Trent a look before he turned to Presley again, Lisa didn't let him inspect her any longer. "Hey Bay, baby, you want to show mom what you had for breakfast?" She held her arms out to him.

He took them but then squirmed until she set him on the ground, he took off towards the kitchen.

"Hi Pres," Becky gently greeted her. She knew there was an emergency Jake and Lisa had to take off for, but she didn't know any of the details.

"Hi Becks," Presley tried to smile but knew her face was a dead giveaway. Presley tried to avoid any more attention, she put her arm around Trent and looked up at him. "Trent, this is Becks."

He reached his hand to her. "Nice to meet you, Becks, I'm Trent, Presley's boyfriend."

It was the first time Trent introduced himself as such, Presley leaned her head onto his chest at the sound of it.

Becks smiled in return, but Presley was so off from her normal personality, she knew whatever happened must have been pretty major.

✦

"It's actually pretty fucking basic so just fucking get it done! I'm tired of being the damn hall monitor because people can't do their fucking jobs! If Hawthorne said to add it to the charges, then fucking add it to the charges!" Jake yelled as he walked through the garage door, even with the mudroom door closed they heard his anger. "I've fuckin got a lot going on too, join the goddamn club." By the time he came out of the mudroom and made it to everyone his face was clear of any frustration, and he wasn't on a phone call anymore.

"Daddy!" Bailey came running in, his hands were full of flowers he had clearly just plucked from Lisa's beautifully maintained pots on her back deck.

"Hey, buddy!" Jake swept him up and blew fart noises into his neck as he kicked and laughed.

"No monster kisses!" Bailey finally freed himself and went stomping over to Presley. "These are for you." He held up two Zinnias that still had their roots attached and dirt falling from them. "Auntie PP is all better now." He was so proud of himself.

"Bay, these are so beautiful, thank you." Presley held it together long enough for Bailey to squirrel away to find Baron again. She turned to run in the small bathroom right off the kitchen as she didn't want anyone watching her cry anymore. They all heard the sink turn on immediately and knew Presley just needed a moment alone.

"So," Becks was pretty great at reading the room. "I was hoping to take Bailey to the zoo today if you guys are okay with that?"

Relief blew over Lisa for this gesture. "That sounds so helpful actually, we would really appreciate that. Here," Lisa motioned for them to go to the kitchen. "I'll help put some snacks and lunch together for you guys."

"Well," Jake lowered his voice and gestured for he and Trent to take themselves out of earshot from the bathroom Presley was in. "Got something else that will just fucking make your skin crawl."

Trent wiped his face and then took a glance towards the bathroom door that was still shut.

"Honestly, this might be good fucking news at this point, I don't fucking know." Jake harshly rubbed his hair. "They were sending pictures over of some of the evidence and I noticed a particular photo that I remember seeing in Pap's shop."

Trent immediately knew where this was going.

"So, I had them FaceTime me to look around that box and there are multiple photos that I would bet my last fucking dollar were in that shop. I think that sick fuck took them down before he burned the goddamn place."

Trent took a deep breath. "You know what, at least she'll have those back. That is so fucking fucked, but I will take literally anything that will make her feel better no matter how big or small it is right now. I can't fucking wrap my head around how sadistic and perverted that guy is, but if we can get Pres those pictures back, even if it's only some of them, that will give her something."

"I agree, I asked them to just photograph everything and if there's any way they can release the actual pictures to us, I want to know immediately." Jake put his hands on his hips, "I asked Hawthorne about just piling on arson charges too, he's going to roll with it. I say everything including the fucking kitchen sink at this point. Hawthorne is a cutthroat son of a bitch and I guarantee you he will have charges nearing triple digits on both of them."

"Good," Trent agreed. "And we need to tell her all of this… Soon."

"I know."

"I already feel like we've been lying to her, I think it's best to let it all out now."

"You're right," Jake agreed. "Lis and I will be here too; we can all talk to her together once Bay is out of the house."

They both turned when the bathroom door opened.

"Hey sweetheart," Trent walked to her and gave her a hug.

Forty-Eight

The Hofners invited Trent and Presley to stay with them after they had done their best to gently inform Presley of everything that was discovered at Mike's house. Jake and Lisa completely understood when Trent delicately told them it was best that they left before Bailey got home from his day at the zoo with Becks. His energy and likely the questions he would have about Presley weren't something Trent felt comfortable having her navigate full-time. They all knew she loved him, but she needed a place to be able to work through her emotions as they came and not have to worry about holding anything in or hiding how she felt. Trent hoped that staying at the penthouse would also allow them to just be alone and feel as though they were getting a little bit of their privacy back. He knew this situation was far from over and it would be a long road to any kind of emotional recovery.

"Pres, are you still awake?" Trent couldn't see her face, but she had been pretty still for a bit.

She nodded her head.

"Babe," he stroked her hair. "You need some sleep."

"I know," she agreed. "I can't relax my mind."

"Come here." He turned her over and pulled her on top of him, so her top half was draped on his chest with her head right under his chin. "Just close your eyes." He began massaging her back. "Pres, you don't have to worry about anything at all right now," he assured her and moved to the base of her neck where he found a comfortable rhythm with one of his hands.

Her fingers clung to his shirt at his gentle touch, his hands were basically playing a lullaby on her body, and she closed her eyes. Just as soon as she closed her eyes her body jerked her awake again.

"Pres, I'm right here, you're safe," Trent whispered. "Are you okay?" He continued to rub his hands along her back and neck.

"Sorry, I'm so exhausted but I just can't settle enough."

"You don't need to be sorry," he assured her. "Do you want to talk? We haven't really talked—you've done a lot of listening."

Presley was quiet, she didn't even know where to start.

Trent's familiar and reassuring hands never stopped their rhythm. "It's too much, sweetheart, I know it is, you can talk to me."

She took a breath. "I just keep falling back to that couch whenever I close my eyes. I can smell that place, still feel those ties on me… I feel them touching me… and watching those dead bodies," she paused and her face quivered against Trent's chest. "I can't stop thinking about what would've happened if you didn't come save me." Her voice had broken, and he could tell she was crying again.

Trent's jaw tightened; he too had considered how much worse things would have been if they didn't get to her as quickly as they did. It had been bad enough as it was.

"I didn't realize they were capable of something so heinous. And I've been sick to my stomach since those men touched me."

Trent kissed the top of her head and gave her a firm, loving squeeze. "Pres, I am so sorry you had to endure all of that, you didn't deserve any of it. No one should ever touch you like that."

"I feel stupid because I always just thought Mike was harmless." She gripped his shoulder. "Trent, he was going to keep me there forever and make me have his kids."

"I would have moved ten thousand mountains to get you out of there, baby. It took me everything not to put a bullet in his fucking head. The only thing that stopped me was my love for you is so much stronger than my hate for anyone, even that psychotic fuck." He rubbed the back of her head. "And you don't have to feel stupid, no one knew just how fucking sick he is."

They were quiet for a long moment; Trent still hadn't come close to getting over the guilt of not getting a better handle on Mike from the start. Sure, he had a few pointed conversations with him and always made sure Presley was safe when he was around. But he couldn't shake the feeling that he should have been more of a threatening presence instead of trying to be civil with Mike knowing he was still always going to live in the same small town as Presley. He would never be able to forgive himself that his compromise to keep everything amicable ended up hurting Presley more than anything.

Presley's soft voice started again. "And when you grabbed me from there, I thought it was over, I thought I was safe… But all that stuff he has at his house?" She readjusted herself slightly before continuing. "Trent, those moments were ours," her voice broke, he felt her swallow hard before she started again. "I'm so ashamed that he saw all of that, he stole from our love story."

Trent closed his eyes, letting out a heartbreaking exhale, and held her tight. "He had no fucking right, Pres." He kissed the top of her head. "I'm so sorry he got to see those parts of you. I know how much trust you gave me for us to start our love story, no one should have been able to invade our privacy like that."

Neither of them spoke right away, Trent continued to rub her back until he decided to start again. "I know we can't take back what's been done, but Jake and I are doing everything we can to minimize anyone else seeing what he had. I love you, Presley, and I will do anything you need to help you heal."

Presley looked up at him and then scooted herself up to share his pillow, she reached for his face and held her hand to his cheek. "I could never properly thank you for everything you've done for me and given me, Trent."

Trent smiled. "You don't ever have to thank me for loving you." He kissed her lips this time. "But, if you do insist on trying to thank me, you can close those gorgeous green eyes of yours and try to get yourself some sleep."

Presley nodded her head. "As long as you promise to hold me, so I know where I'm at."

"Sweetheart, I don't ever plan to let you go." Trent promised her and then leaned in to kiss her goodnight. In that moment, Presley felt Trent putting her in his arms for the first time again, their first kiss, the first time he made love to her, she even felt him pulling her off that couch and in that moment, she felt like they were alone and this was just theirs. She opened her eyes for a split second to confirm what her heart already felt and then closed her eyes to fully indulge in her boyfriend's familiar and comforting kiss. Trent took his time in escalating their tongues, he wanted to be completely in tune to her body language and cater to what she needed—he wasn't sure if she would suddenly require a hard stop if something triggered being back at that cabin. There was a natural separation of their lips before they looked into each other's eyes.

"I love you, Pres." Trent pecked her forehead this time and encouraged her to rest her head on him so he could have a secure hold on her.

Presley's head found a comfortable spot just under Trent's chin with her cheek against his strong chest.

"I love you too, Trent." She closed her eyes to deeply engulf her senses in Trent's comforting scent and the feeling of his devoted and powerfully protective arms surrounding her. Presley tried to slow her breathing to relax completely into his loving embrace. With each breath she inhaled her boyfriend and exhaled the trauma that she had gone through. Another breath, inhaling Trent's cedarwood aroma and exhaling thoughts of Mike's unsettling collection. Her eyes opened momentarily, and she took another inhale of Trent's presence and shortly after closed her eyes to exhale the feeling of what could have been if Mike hadn't arrived at the cabin when he did. She felt her breath jump this time as she sucked air in through her nose, she soon exhaled thoughts of the lengths her mother had taken to get what she wanted from Presley. Her eyes began to get very heavy. Presley knew the road ahead was terrifyingly steep. She knew there would be many sleepless nights, she would have to battle through yet another healing journey, and likely be subjected to multiple trials facing the depraved individuals who had caused all of this pain and suffering. The one thing that kept shoving those thoughts to the back of her head and allowing her body to fall deeper into the sleep she so desperately needed was Trent. Trent wasn't going to just be with her while she healed herself, Trent was going to be the force in front of her that was fearlessly clearing the path ahead of them while simultaneously acting as a shield and gently holding her hand and her heart. She finally let sleep take her over when her heart convinced her mind they were safe tonight and would wake up tomorrow to face the next chapter under the protection of her faithful and loving boyfriend.

Trent was caressing Presley's back with both of his hands when he noticed her fingers that had been gently tickling his chest slowly come to a stop. He assumed she had fallen asleep, so he gave her a few more strokes from the small of her back to her shoulders before he gently pecked the top of her head. Presley didn't move.

Trent attempted a very deep, yet controlled, breath. Barely twenty-four hours ago he didn't know if he'd ever be able to hold his girlfriend again and in this moment, he couldn't have been more grateful to have her in his arms. He leaned closer to the top of her head to take in the sweet and familiar scent of her hair. While he was overcome with gratitude that she was safe, his heart ached for the journey ahead that would terrorize Presley for the foreseeable future. He was determined to take on anything and everything his girlfriend needed; there was no cost too high or sacrifice too great to give her the peace, safety, and happiness she had once known. He loved Presley more than anything he had ever loved, himself included. There was nothing more important to him than protecting her through what was to come. "I love you, Presley Williams," Trent whispered as he held her a little tighter before closing his eyes.

Acknowledgments

NEVER TRULY THOUGHT THIS CONCEPT WOULD EVER LEAVE MY PHONE. It was really just a way of escaping reality from time to time and a distracting creative outlet. I started jotting scenes and ideas down (only using my phone) in my little google docs app and suddenly I'm publishing an entire story… well, mini series as it turns out!! Thank you so very much for sharing some of your precious time by reading my book—it really does mean a lot. 🖤🖤

I'd like to give a very special thank you from my whole entire heart to my fearless group of beta readers—y'all are truly the best!! Thank you for being brave enough to dive into this one. When I say I was shaking in my dang space boots with a brown paper bag over my head during the beta read—I am NOT joking in the least bit. 😂🤣 But each of you ladies gave amazingly supportive and constructive feedback which I am forever grateful for. I even feel like you guys love my characters and this world just as much as I do. Thank you for supporting me along my little Starstruck journey!! It's basically our journey now. 🖤🖤

- 🖤 My sister, Jordyn, who literally probably thinks I could build a rocket ship and fly to another galaxy completely—she always has so much dang faith in me. Anytime I have an idea she is the first to put her hand up and say let's do it—my forever biggest cheerleader. May I never fail her!!

- 🖤 My near and dear long time friend, Kay, who many moons ago was ready to read my crazy content. One day (years later, lol) I randomly hit her with an entirely different book than I had originally told her about and she was ON BOARD!! It's been very special finally getting to share this with her before it was official.

- 💕Publisher, editor, biz partner in crime, long-time friend, Niss—I 1000% would not be where I'm at with my books if not for her professional eye and forever judgment-free work-zone mentality when I send her content. Always a fan and a voice of encouragement that I'll be forever grateful for.

- 💕Shelby aka the OG BADDIE of all things booksta, business, and being a girl's girlie!! I haven't known her for a zillion years (yet), but instant friends for sure. [Thanks Tanner!!] Also, the best social media coach (who I DEFINITELY need to listen to much better) and promoter/hype-girlie on the planet.

And of course, just another very special thank you to my family. While I sincerely hope they support me from afar, as in NEVER reading an unredacted copy of this book 🙈🙊, their love and support is absolutely unmatched. I have an infinite amount of gratitude to call each of them family. I definitely owe my parents a huge shoutout for arming me with quick wit and a smart mouth, without which I wouldn't be able to write such fun banter between my characters. I'm ashamed to admit I kept this book VERY quiet from my mom—even though she's an avid reader and obviously a huge cheerleader of mine. I only let the cat out of the bag just weeks before I planned to release it. Honestly, my 'rents know I'm an anxious little worry-wart and a square bear, so while I know they're so proud, I will NEVER be ready to discuss the entirety of this book with them. 🙈🐻 And thank you to Tanner, who I know will have my back by not reading this and instead tease me about it like a good brother would. So, thank you to my family who never lets me fail and will forever continue to lift me up… while dishing out a healthy dose of friendly bullying, it is our love language after all.

Whether your family is biological, found, chosen, or otherwise—always love them big!! I know I will.

Stay Connected

I would love for you to stay connected!!
Here are a few ways:

AMAZON AUTHOR PAGE

It's free to follow and you'll be updated
when I have new content available.

INSTAGRAM @BALEY.NOAL

Let's follow each other on Insta!! You'll get real time
updates and see what other content I'm working on.

SPOTIFY

I've created a playlist that is FULL of *Starstruck*
vibes. If you'd like to know what I was listening
to, or felt inspired by for a few scenes, check out
the playlist by using one of the codes below.

Made in the USA
Columbia, SC
11 October 2024

ca2fe218-ed8b-45b9-bf0a-13d5e4e55d77R01